D0350536

THE BURNING GIRL

BOOKS BY HOLLY PHILLIPS

THE BURNING GIRL

IN THE PALACE OF REPOSE

THE BURNING GIRL

HOLLY PHILLIPS

PRIME BOOKS

THE BURNING GIRL

Prime Books
www.prime-books.com

This book is dedicated to

STEVEN MILLS

who has read far too many of those million words of crap, and commented insightfully on most of them,

and especially to

LYNNE and MICHAEL PHILLIPS

who have provided more education, emotional support, rent, rides, tolerance, avowals of confidence and enthusiasm, and dinners, than should be reasonably expected of any two parents.

Thanks, you guys.

one

So, Ryder Coleman thought, this is freedom.

Rooflines and telephone wires cut the gray spring clouds into slices and rhomboids of sky, a mosaic of rain. The same rain had wept down the wire-scarred window of Rye's hospital room, the quarantine room with the locked door and the walls dark with the shadows of her delirium. A whole season of rain had slipped across that window, wet lines like cracks in the ice, raindrops like the drumming of restless fingers. Tap. Hello? Tap. Let me in. While Rye had asked, pleaded, begged, *let me out.*

And now they had. The fine rain hissed against Rye's bare head, trickled down her forehead, her temples, the back of her skull, chill and painless as razorblades across the sensitive tracery of her lesion scars. The not-quite-pain brought a flood of saliva into her mouth and a shudder that rippled down her spine. The social worker, that plump brown man with his willing blindness and his professional kindness, had given her clothing, jeans and sweater and jacket, thrift store clothes that rubbed like sand against her skin. He had given her a check from his department's emergency funds, her own ID that he had rescued from her missing person's file, and an apology for all her belongings that had gone more permanently missing than she, but he had not thought to give her a hat. The muscles in her scalp twitched and writhed under the pink-scarred skin, trying to shake off the cold fly-crawling rain.

The quarantine is lifted, the social worker had said. You're free to go! He had smiled with pleasure, but when Rye, in the buoyant confusion of release, had made an instinctive move to embrace him, to press herself into those plump, tweed-covered arms, he had made an equally instinctive move away, just as his eyes had flinched away from her face the whole time he was in the room.

Freedom. She had lost seven weeks of her life to the hospital and six years to the fever that should have killed her and only burned a hole in her past. Sometimes Rye imagined her brain etched with a lace-pattern of scorched tissue, a black shadow of the pink-shiny scar-pattern on her skin. Like feathers, a nurse had said, her eyes trying to be kind above the edge of her doubled mask. Like feathers or scales. Rye had privately agreed that the comparison should not be a human one. In her eyes the scars were like a million pinworms frozen mid-writhe across her skin. The fever lesions had opened in delicate crescents all over her body, like tiny eyes or smiling mouths that wept or drooled lymph and blood, everywhere. The scars made a worm-mask on her face, most densely clustered on her forehead and cheeks, less so across her features, as they were scarce under her arms, across her breasts and her loins. They had shaved her scalp, her hair had been impossibly clotted and scabbed, and the scar-worms crawled through the new black stubble there, down her neck and back, across her shoulders, arms, buttocks, legs hands feet *everywhere*, sensitive and ugly as sin.

The spring rain was cold outside the hospital doors. The morning traffic was steady. Cars, their candy colors spangled by rain, prowled by, low and purring like great predatory cats. They were so colorful and so quick, so varied in their shapes and so steady in their motion, that they absorbed Rye's attention. She felt like a time traveler, an alien, they seemed so strange. The growl of engines and the hiss of tires on wet pavement seemed unconnected to the movement of the auto-beasts, a background as constant and natural as the thrum of a river between its banks. Rye probably did not stand transfixed for long; the traffic light at the corner changed, chirping to alert the blind, and the car-stream eased itself to a halt. Her gaze, released, drifted up and she saw a woman in a pale raincoat standing on the trash-blown meridian, waiting to cross the street. A woman who stood and stared across the glossy cars at Rye.

Freedom.

Rye pulled the collar of her charity jacket up to her chin and walked away.

Fever dreams slip in to fill her memory gaps, just as the gray thing slips dense as fog between alley walls. A memory of Rye's delirium, prompted by the rain. The gray thing's motion is panther-like, insect-like, and so smooth it could almost be un-alive, like oil-sheathed pistons or the unfolding of a sheet blown free from the line. It is hard to tell how many legs it has, whether it goes mostly upright or otherwise, where it carries its head. Sliding, folding, wafting angles of gray. Starved for memory, Rye also recalls a rotten-fruit alley-stink, the dull flicker of dying streetlights, the chill of damp feet, the slipperiness of armpits under shirt, hoodie, leather coat. The iron taste of fear and running, the cold dilution of sweat in the rain, the echo of footsteps, the look on his face—someone's face—whose face? The feel of him bulking at her shoulder, the glimpse of a gun. Fever dreams as real as the real world, the real world as strange as the dreams.

The social worker had also given Rye the address of a boarding house not far from the hospital.

It was a big old frame house with a leaning porch and a rough lawn starred with dandelions and soaked with rain. Its gray paint was peeling, its high façade marred by the sketch of homemade fire escapes and too many telephone lines drooping from the pole. Rye stood on the sidewalk with the social worker's paper in her hand, comparing the rusty house number with the numbers he had written down. His handwriting was perfectly clear until the rain began to blur the ink into black smears. Rye knew that she knew someone with eyes that color of black, the deep liquid black of wet ink, but did not know who that someone was. Six years gone. She found herself saying the house numbers aloud: not that she could not read them, but that she felt as though it had been six years since the last time she had read anything at all.

Six years ago she had been sixteen, newly emancipated from her mother's house and perfectly literate.

I'm sorry, the social worker had said. Your mother moved several years ago and no one seems to know where she is.

Rye folded the piece of paper, tucked it in her pocket, and walked up the cracked and grassy walk, up the wooden stairs and across the hollow porch, to knock on the door.

"What can I do for you?"

The person who answered the door was skinny, with peroxide-orange hair and a gravelly smoker's voice, and so ambiguous of gender that Rye lost her untried grasp on the social world.

"I," she said. "I—"

The person seemed to take her confusion, and her scars, in stride. "You looking for a room?"

"I," Rye said, as the word *yes* slipped like a sliver of wet soap out of reach.

"Are you okay?" the person said.

Rye, who had not been asked that simple question in seven weeks or six years, whichever was longer, burst into tears.

"Hey," the person said. "The world's not wet enough already?"

Rye nodded, trying to laugh as she cried. Her tears were as yellow-white as a field of daisies in her mouth, salt bright as sunlight in the fever-wrought synesthesia the neurologist could not explain, tears bright and bitter as freedom. Rye nodded, and wiped her cheeks and, surreptitiously, her nose on the edge of her hand, and said, "Sorry. Yes. I was told you might have a room to rent."

"Come on in." The person stepped away from the door. "I'll show you around."

The person's name was Glenn. Glenn's skinny butt preceding Rye up the stairs was as ambiguous as Glenn's name, and as ambiguous as the expression in Glenn's eyes, which might have been acceptance, or only indifference to Rye's conduct, Rye's emotions, Rye's scars. Rye's hunger for kindness, that had tried to hug the social worker and cried at Glenn's offhand question, threatened to turn into something darker, offense or anger or, worse yet, a sullen, whining insistence that the world pay attention to her. Let it go, Rye advised this sixteen-year-old ghost. The now-Rye, the Rye with a burnt out brain, had gotten good at letting go. She could let go of the fever, let go of the nightmares, let go of the missing past. She could even let go of the hatred and terror of confinement that grew so huge sometimes it had thrown her like a trapped bird against the walls of the quarantine room, against the steel door and the unbreakable wired window, until the lesions started to bleed again and they strapped her down for her own safety and she screamed and screamed.

"It's not pretty," Glenn said, "but I guarantee you it's clean."

A bare bones room with scuffed-up hardwood floor, patch-mottled plaster, one tall sash window overlooking the street. There was a battered dresser, a closet with wire hangers and no door, a twin bed with a metal frame so old that black iron was showing through the white enamel. The room was as small as the quarantine room, and Rye might have fled except she knew that even with the social worker's start-up money she could not afford anything better. She might have fled anyway if not for the un-antiseptic wooden floor and the window that she could wrestle up to admit the smell of rain and the hissing growl of a passing car.

Glenn named a price and Rye said okay. Glenn said there were sheets and blankets Rye could borrow until she got her own things, and Rye said okay to that too. Glenn told her where the bathroom was, where the supermarket was, gave her a greasy old brass key for the door, and Rye said thanks. Glenn went away, closing the door on the way out. Rye stood by the window for a while, breathing in the smell of rain, of diluted exhaust, of wet spring grass and the flowers in the chestnut tree across the street. She watched the passing of cars and pedestrians, the guilty sidle of an escaped golden retriever and the plodding tread of a woman in a long pale raincoat, a stocky blonde who for one glancing moment teased Rye's mind with a phantom familiarity. A lie, like all the other fever lies. Rye turned away from the window, and then she went to the door to the hall and opened it, just to prove to herself that she could.

Fever dreams. She slips like fog between the alley walls, her mouth wet with the sour-metal taste of electricity, her skin wet with shameful sweat, with worse than sweat on her thighs. She is naked, in flight, seeking shadows in this bland gray alley-world, knowing and, in the way of dreams, not knowing that the shadows she seeks contain far worse than the brightness she is running from. Flashlights spark at the crossings of the maze, the alleys get darker and darker at every turn, she is always conscious of her humiliation and shame. She runs, chased by flashlights, by sparks and beams and circles of light that dance and skip in rhythm with her pursuers' steps, that seek to draw her out and hem her in with revealing, shameful light, and as the alleys get darker and darker she gets more and more afraid, until blackness hides the lights and she does not know where her pursuers are, they could be right here, right here, near enough to touch.

She woke, hot and restless in the cool of her room. The window was open, the borrowed blankets cast aside. The taste of the dream filled her mouth even while the details drained away. She let them go without a struggle. Just another dream. The room was under-populated by them, as though her fever ghosts had not been able to follow her to her new abode. Her mind touched on them lightly, careful not to reach out to those monsters and those ordinary people who had wandered in and out of her quarantine room. Those antiseptic tiled walls were crowded with them, but here, there was only featureless plaster, the dresser, the empty closet, the open window, the bed where she lay, all of it strangely and delicately precise in the aftermath of the dream's confusion. Rye felt the rain-cool air on her over-heated skin, drafts like innocent fingers teasing the fever that had never quite died.

That had never been cured, any more than its cause had been found, although the quarantine had lingered long past the time the specialists had thrown up their hands. But finally, finally, finally, she was free.

And thirsty.

And she had to pee.

So she got up, sleepy and feeling happily normal, and padded to the bathroom. She used the toilet, rinsed her hands, padded down the stairs toward the kitchen, and for some reason, she never knew exactly why, she realized that she had not yet opened her eyes.

She was walking around blind, her hand going unerringly to door-knobs, light switches, the bathroom tap, as comfortable as if she had lived in this house for a hundred years. The realization startled her eyes open, and she suffered a moment's disorientation, brief but profound. *Silver lines on black (architect's sketch) bitter as dandelions (glassy as ice and cool as fog) light from the moon (down below).* Rye threw out her hands, banged the left one hard on the wall, brushed the banister on the right. Her toes groped for the edge of the step. The disorientation passed and she knew, as if someone had just turned off the light a moment before, where she stood on the stairs, though it was very dark, the door to the front hall closed at the bottom.

Had she just woken up? Sleepwalking, or nearly so—there was a dream—but it was already gone. She was still calm, still sleepy, but with more things welling up through the clarity. Puzzlement. A temptation to laugh in surprise. Experimentally, she closed her eyes.

The stairs, there. The door below, there. The banister, there. She could picture it all in her mind, but she was not seeing any of it. And then, moved by an instinct that belong to the fever dreams, she pulled off the T-shirt she had been sleeping in and stood naked on the stairs. She closed her eyes, and it was all still there, sketched against her scars. The stairs, the walls, the door down below. Perfectly, utterly, incontrovertibly *there.*

Hallucination, delirium, fever dream. The normal Rye, the Rye who wanted desperately to be normal again, found the known quantities of her raddled brain less frightening than the possibility—the impossibility—that the lesions scars could see. She pulled on her shirt and groped her way, open-eyed and blind, back to her room.

two

She found a job, a crazy job for her considering her condition, but it was what she could get: sticking advertising pamphlets under car windshields, in mailboxes, under doors. It meant being out where people could see her, where people could stare, all day every day, but at least she wouldn't have to talk to anyone. (Thought Rye, trying to have, as Glenn would say, a positive attitude.)

There was a supervisor who drove around town to make sure that her minimum wage employees weren't just dumping the leaflets in the river and smoking dope or working another job. This did not worry Rye. She did the work, riding an ancient bike bought with the tail end of the social worker's check. It was an old road bike with curled handlebars and a tiny, crippling saddle, and it weighed a ton, and its tires were worn almost to cloth and needed to be pumped every morning, deadly when it rained. But it got her across town, and she learned not to lean it against a Dumpster while she made her rounds after one morning when it was nearly collected with the rest of the trash.

The company's office was a warren of small basement rooms made even smaller by the boxes and bundles and loose sheaves of printed matter that lined the walls. On her first day, Rye propped her bike against the alley wall, descended the steps, and groped her way past the printer's boxes in the acidic gloom of one too many burned out fluorescent tubes.

The early hour and bad light was not kind to the deliverers. Seeing the soon-to-be-familiar faces, lined or pimpled, sunburned or waxy or pale, Rye could easily imagine every one backed by a story of bad health and rattled mind. Kindred spirits, maybe, but there were no offers of kinship here, not at six in the morning. Just bad coffee and surly tempers. Lana the supervisor, brawny and black and suffering permanent exasperation with the world, handed out counted bundles and badly photocopied maps, signed the time sheets, and sent them on their way.

On that first day, an anemic boy with dyed hair and too much steel in his face said to Rye, "That's cool. What is that?"

"What?" She felt shy, nervous with the first-day jitters. She wanted these people to like her.

"With your face." He said it, this studded boy, as if challenge was the only way he could relate to the rest of the human race. "Is that like a tattoo, or just bad-ass acne, or what?"

She had not expected this, though maybe she should have. She had no answer, but the sixteen-year-old Rye who lived too close to the surface these days blurted, "Screw you."

"Hey, bitch, I said it was cool. But whatever you like." He clutched his crotch, two fingers pointed in the devil sign.

Rye, jagged with adrenaline, turned to collect her papers from Lana. She shoved them into the old paper-carrier's bag Lana was loaning her (emphasis on "loan") and Lana, yellowed eyes on Rye's shaking hands, said testily, "Don't crumple them like that. Client's not paying you for crumpling."

She got them in the bag somehow, got the strap over her head, got herself out of the office into the alley. Anxiety, fury, misery mingled in a black-and-neon starburst under her skin so fiery she could hardly see her bike, just taste the sweet-metal tang of blood in her mouth. The alley was clean and bright with rain. It was the first day of June.

Not, please God, the first day of the rest of her life.

Fever dreams.

She's in a cage. No bars or wire mesh, but that's the feeling, at once contained and exposed. The floor is gritty under her feet, a vivid sensation, like tracked-in dirt. Her toes curl away from it. There is a connotation of sewage, of filth. Maybe it's the smell, intense but without identity, that fills, not just her nose, but her mouth, a smell like tallow, waxy and greasy, that has her drooling rather than swallow. This also is intense, the warm slippery feel of the drool on her chin and her arm, the shame of it, like she's pissed herself. And there is something she has to do, something she *is* doing, her hands occupied on the minutiae of this task. It's like a camera lens coming into focus, first doing, then seeing, and then understanding, that this chore she has to perform, that she is performing, is the killing of

it's already injured, is this a merciful? necessary?

a black and burnt and bleeding cat.

Only, when she wakes, as she will, aching with sweat and horror and shame, she will know, whatever the dream said, it was not a cat. Not a cat.

But it was just a dream.

After the rainy spring, June was gorgeous. The sun was hot and yellow in a blue sky made bluer by the occasional fair-weather cloud, the breeze off the river was cool and still pleasantly humid, and the whole city was burgeoning. Trees that had been graceless as lamp-posts all winter were suddenly full of sunlight and shade, greenness and wind. Flower boxes appeared on sidewalks, in café windows; the parks were riotous with peonies and roses, a profusion of scent and color as lush as velvet to Rye's cock-eyed senses. She rode her rattling beast of a bike through the parks whenever she could for the pleasure of it, a sweet, safe, impersonal kind of pleasure, innocent, even, though the word rang strangely in her mind. Innocent. Innocence. Why not? But she wore long sleeves and long pants and a baseball cap, because the distractions offered by her sensitive skin sometimes threatened to overwhelm her.

Once she was confronted by a drugstore display of products for the care of "sensitive skin" and she had a genuinely crazy moment. Torn between hysterical laughter and the desire to spend the month's rent on creams and foams and scrubs and gels, she stood there with tears in her eyes, fixating on labels until she was distracted by a blond woman staring at her from the hair products aisle. No one she knew, but the woman looked at her as if she knew Rye—except that when Rye met her eyes, she turned away. Feeling hunted, feeling lonely, feeling the scars down her back pinch and writhe, Rye ducked her head and moved on.

The first week of work was so hard she wasn't sure she could stick it out. Not just the inimical hour and the inimical people, though the prospect of the second day tied her stomach in knots. But the work reminded her that whatever changes the fever had wrought in her system, she was also suffering the results of several weeks spent in bed. She had to ride the Beast to her first section, park it, walk, carrying the heavy bag of papers, stuffing windscreen wipers and mail slots, go back to the bike, ride it, park, do the next section. Exhaustion killed her appetite, wreaked havoc on the tattered remnants of her sleep patterns. The first time she climbed off the Beast and felt her legs threatening to collapse came as such a shock, such a betrayal, that Rye decided she must have been a fit person before the fever got her. The shock was repeated daily for a week, but after the first day off, she found it was not quite so bad. And then a bit better, and then quite a bit better, which confirmed, she thought, her prior fitness. Good. So she knew something about herself, the self from Before. A triumph, like the feel of muscle working in her legs. Good.

And she wore her turtlenecks and the second-hand chinos and the cap pulled down to the bridge of her nose, which was not hiding—wasn't she out here in the world, doing what she had to? Not hiding, no, just avoiding distraction. Protecting herself from the weirdness of her skin.

If only she could protect herself from the weirdness of her mind.

Rye is riding through Steamwheeler Park. It's late morning on a weekday, but there are people out in the sunshine, riding, walking, sitting on the benches that look across the river to downtown. Rye is on her lunch break, looking for a seat where she can eat her sandwich. There is a free bench coming up, one of a cluster in front of the bandstand lawn, but just as she takes her feet off the peddles and begins to coast, a pregnant woman sits down, puts her bag down beside her, and starts rummaging for her lunch. Rye feels a momentary irritation, so mild it's hardly that, and puts her feet back on the peddles. She is passing the bench now, and from the corner of her eye she sees the pregnant woman—very pregnant, her child-belly stretching out the knit top she wears—sit back on the bench, one hand resting on the upper curve—

And she is stricken, Rye is, with this huge leaping ambush of horror, of revulsion, for *what's inside.*

So intense she nearly loses her balance and sends the Beast reeling into the path of a strolling blond woman. Rye reaches for the pavement, rights herself, peddles hard to get away. As if women weren't having babies every day. As if she hasn't seen pregnant women every day since she left the hospital, so commonplace as to be invisible. As if she hasn't seen that same goddamn blonde every day. Which of course she has not. Except it feels like she has. When she looks back, risking collision, there is no blond head in sight, not the whole way down the esplanade.

Crazy.

And it's not just a dream.

All the way through June she quartered the city, plaguing car owners and householders with the proliferation of throw-away advertising. Band-Anna's, the hottest newest club, free beers to the first 100 customers! Lose pounds now! Revival tent meeting, old-style religion, coming soon! Cheapest dry-cleaning in town!

Exclamation points at warehouse prices! Rye thought on a rare lighthearted day. Hottest deal in town!!!

And sometimes the city was just the city, the place she had lived half her life, known a little more intimately every working day, and sometimes it warped, bent through the lurking fever like light through a lens, twisted into something strange. Some places were worse than others. One block in the riverside district haunted her, a commercial block built in the 1920s out of the grim local brick, rust-red darkened by decades of soot, with 1940s signage: clothing stores, appliance stores, antique stores. Nothing weird, a block like dozens in the city, but some days the buildings cloaked themselves in shadow. Some days—she teased herself by going back, even when the street wasn't on her route—some days, the signs were hard to read, as if English were a foreign tongue, the alphabet a secret code, and the shop windows hid deep dark mysteries behind their reflections.

Rye-reflections, the lesions mellowed from pink to old-scar silver, the shaved hair growing back in a plush cap like a black cat's fur, the thin, over-dressed figure bent over the ugly bike's handlebars. People stared a little less, or maybe she was just getting callused, but sometimes, not only on her haunted block, a woman catching a bus, buying a paper, waiting on the cross-walk signal—sometimes a man, but mostly it was a woman—would look up at Rye, her stare catching in the corner of Rye's eye, catching like a spider-thread in the thorns of Rye's scars. The stare was always the same, compassionless and inquisitive, and perhaps that was why it always seemed to be the same woman, a woman who, if she knew Rye, had some reason not to approach her, introduce herself, renew some lost acquaintanceship. Unless that reason was simply that she was not real, but only a ghost conjured by Rye's loneliness, the newest member of the host of fever dreams.

Can one resign oneself to being a little bit—just a little bit—insane?

She remembers. Walking down a sidewalk, stuffing pink notices under wipers (Perfect skin in 20 days!), she passes an old-fashioned butcher shop, its chilled window hung with chickens, sausages, a leg of lamb. And she remembers *truncated limbs seething skin hot blood* hot *on her hands taste in her mouth black-silver eyes watching her eyes*—

Fever dreams, she says to herself with every footfall. Fever dreams, fever dreams, sweat like a sickness on her skin. It takes her a block to notice that the pink papers under the windscreen wipers bear a hand-print of red. The scars on her palms have feathered open and are seeping rust.

Never happened, never happened, never happened.

" ..—my God, oh my God, somebody wake up, is anybody awake? Oh my God . . . "

Not me, was Rye's first thought, her mouth gummed shut by a deep, slow-in-coming sleep. *Not my fear.* Then she realized where she was, in bed, and where the voice was, a fearful half-whisper outside her door.

" . . . is anybody else awake but me?"

"Yeah." Rye croaked, coughed, worked her tongue. "Yes. Hang on."

She got a shirt over her head, pants on. Made sure her eyes were open: yes, the streetlight made a black-and-silver pattern out of her red-and-cream curtain. She padded to the door, knowing it was maybe not wise to get involved with her housemates' crooked lives, but probably, in this instance, a good thing to do. She felt virtuous, opening the door.

Outside was Kelly, a thin, faded woman with the hunted look of a persecuted wife.

"You okay?" Rye asked.

"Sorry," Kelly whispered. "I shouldn't have, I'm really sorry."

"Are you okay?"

"Yes. No. Yes. I just . . . " With the wide-eyed look of need. "Please come and tell me you see this."

She grabbed Rye's wrist in a cold, strong grip and pulled at her to come, down the hall to Kelly's room that overlooked the back. Rye went, so startled by the touch—nobody outside of the hospital had touched her—that she was slow in thinking that she wasn't really the best person to ask to differentiate between reality and the alternative. She really was not. She shook loose, or maybe Kelly let her go. They were at Kelly's door now and the older woman needed two hands to ease it open without making a sound.

"Outside," she whispered, clinging to the door. "On the lawn." Showing no intention of going to the window herself, she stared at it, the yellowed gray of a city night behind glass.

Rye knew she should go back to bed. She could feel a wrongness in the situation, a danger to her psyche lurking in this question of real/not real. Although she did not believe there was anything bad out there, unease rippled under her skin, as if such an intimate, inward threat spurred the fever-shadow, fever-beast, rousing it from sleep. Colorless phosphorescence oozed between her eyes and the dark room, a fluid grid that seemed to leak through the walls ceiling floor. Vertigo tilted through Rye, gravity slipping away like water off a sheet of melting ice, then back, slip and slide, not overwhelming, but distracting. Instead of leaving poor Kelly to whatever nightmare had followed her out of sleep, Rye went to the window, quiet in her bare feet, and looked down at the lawn.

Darkness on darkness, shaggy-grass dark meeting up with crooked-fence dark. The building across the alley, a huge old frame house caged within a permanent scaffolding of fire-escape ladders and outside stairs, showed up gray in the diffuse light. One window was lit, a yellow square made dim by blinds. Nothing else.

Relief and unmoored gravity tilted Rye against the window glass. She could feel the almost-cool against her forehead, quickly warmed by the waking fever. She was loose inside her skin, soft, verging on molten, and then her skin loosened too, a painless—it was the only word—*loosening*, like the fabric of a cloth bag giving way under the weight of water it carries. Sweat poured off her, sudden as a tap turned full on. She hoped it was sweat.

"Is it there?" Kelly whispered.

Rye closed her eyes and ran her tongue across her upper lip. Fearing blood, she tasted sweat-salt bright as daisies. She grew buoyant with relief, or maybe it was only gravity slip-sliding again. When she opened her eyes, the house around her was a liquid shell, floor ceiling staircases walls, and so was the house across the street, hollow as an architect's drawing basted with black light, and something hot, something black and brilliant with heat was sliding stilting boneless down the alley suddenly gone.

"There isn't anything there, is there?" Kelly said, quiet but no longer whispering.

Nausea churned in Rye's gut, abrupt and demanding.

"No. Maybe a dog in the alley? Sorry. Don't feel so good." As she stumbled by on her way to the john. It was too dark with all her clothes on to run.

That really happened, though it seemed unlikely when she woke again in the morning, more unlikely than many of her fever dreams. Rye might for once have written it off entirely as imagination, dream, except for the thread-fine smears of blood on her damp summer sheets. And except for the sight of Kelly sitting in the kitchen with Glenn, both of them curved silent over their morning cups. It was late, the day already hot, but the burner was on under the old-fashioned percolator pot on the stove.

"Coffee," Glenn said. "On me."

"Thanks," Rye said, because it would have been churlish to make her own, though she was the only one in the house who used fresh-ground beans. Doubly churlish with Kelly sitting there, bent over like a woman in pain.

Welcome to my world, Rye thought, but she felt bad for that. She poured herself a gritty cup and sat down with the other two.

"Bad night," she said.

"I gathered," Glenn said, dry and concerned.

Kelly said nothing.

"You were there?" Glenn said, looking at Rye.

Rye shrugged. "I was up."

"Kelly said there was something on the lawn."

"Gone by the time I looked out." Rye drank, subdued her grimace for politeness' sake. "A dog, I guess."

"No," Kelly said. A small silence fell, during which Kelly seemed to hear something, or decide something. She straightened, shook her head, smiled wanly at Glenn. "I guess I had a bad dream, and then I got up and needed some air, it's pretty hot in my room, but the dream was still in my head I guess. Saw a dog and couldn't make sense out of it, 'cause of the dream I guess. That's probably all it was." She added, with perfect sincerity, "Scared the piss out of me, though."

"Hot nights," Glenn said, "mess up everybody's sleep. I won't tell you the dream *I* had last night." Making it sound salacious enough that both Rye and Kelly forced a smile.

But Kelly didn't look at Rye, and Rye kept her gaze on her cup.

three

She should have called in sick. Unable to stay in the house with Glenn and Kelly and the residue of last night's not-a-dream, she went to work.

The fever seemed to spiral as the heat of summer grew. It was nearly July now, and the fair weather meant heat-glare off the streets, sun-glare off the cars, gritty river-damp in the air. Rye rode the Beast with her bag of flyers dragging at her shoulder while last night's hallucination threatened from every shadowed alleyway (and the shadows were all too dark today, blinding as the whip of sunlight off a windshield), as if black heat could fold itself into a long-legged, insect-panther glide. The fog-creatures of her nightmares reincarnated in the summer night.

Just the fever, Rye thought in despair. She should have gone to her follow-up appointments. She should go now to the hospital, let the specialists start all over again. She did not. Her terror of confinement beat in her chest like a trapped bird. She rode her bike, her clothes chafing unbearably against her raddled skin, until the damp cotton rubbed up a taste in her mouth, prickly as hemp, bitter and thick as linseed oil, the color of ripe red pears. She couldn't ride like this. Could hardly make enough sense of the traffic to get across the street, down a side street, into a black-shadowed parking bay. Still on the bike, she propped herself against the wall, and tasted the sour bricks against her cheek.

Oh help, Rye thought—not to God, she didn't believe in God. *Help me, Mama.* But her mother was long gone, as glad when Rye had moved out as Rye had been to go. Tears pricked. She refused to cry them. They ran down inside her nose, into her mouth, where the salt touched brightly on her tongue.

The parking bay was hardly private. A woman shouted, some word cried out above the noise of the street. Rye looked up, numb with sensation, stupid with fever, and saw a woman—store owner? delivery person?—standing on the sidewalk in the mouth of the bay. Some woman, the light behind her, making her seem bigger than she probably was. She loomed, her hair silvery gold and her face a shadowy blank, like the woman from Rye's paranoid dreams. The same woman, the fever insisted. Rye stared, her mouth full of yellow and white, tears like petals on her tongue. The woman raised one arm from her side, her loose sleeve making a graceful arc of the gesture, her palm cupping sunlight, as if she offered the street to Rye. *Here,* the gesture said. *This way.*

Rye shook her head. Was she being told to leave?

No. The gesture wasn't for her. A man appeared at the woman's side, as stocky and as blond as she, and as faceless, so he might have been the woman's twin. Rye knew that there were pedestrians on the sidewalk behind them, cars and trucks on the street beyond that, but the whole city had become as unconvincing as a stage set, a flimsy background to those two dark figures with their blond halos of sunlight. The fever's deception, Rye knew, but that knowledge was likewise only a tissue-paper scrim between her and the huge, glorious, and terrible significance of this man and this woman standing like angels against the sun.

So it came as the stupidest kind of music-hall surprise when a large, dark, bear-like figure blundered into the man and shoved him aside, swung the woman around and hit her so hard in the face that she fell, and shouted at Rye in a deep, rough, coarsely human voice, "Run, you stupid girl, there are more on their way!"

"What are you doing?" she asked him, shocked and testy with surprise.

"Saving your fucking life! For Christ's sake, Rye, will you move?"

The sound of her name struck Rye like a brick to the back of her head. "You you you," she said.

The blond man had scrambled up from between two parked cars and flung himself at the dark man's midsection. Rye felt her mouth and eyes go round when she saw, moving fast but perfectly discernable, the twisted fury on the blond man's face and the sunlight sparking on the blade of the knife he held. The dark man turned like a toreador without moving his feet, snatched at the shirt between the blond man's shoulder blades and threw him head first into the parking bay wall. The impact made an ugly sound. The blond man collapsed, and his knife made a sharp little clink as it fell out of his hand.

Snapshot: woman on the sidewalk leaning into a run, her mouth opening for a scream.

"Move!" yelled the dark man.

"You you you," said Rye.

He lunged at her.

She threw herself back and fell, tangled with the Beast and her courier's bag.

He bent over her, big hands reaching, and even as she tried to scramble away, even as she tried to fend him off, she was struck by a sudden shock of recognition. She knew him. Did she know him?

"You!" she whispered.

One big hand clenched around her upper arm, the other gripping her under her armpit, the dark man dragged her to her feet, hauled her painfully free from the Beast, and gave her a shove toward the street.

"Run," he said.

She took one shaky step, and almost tripped over the blond man's feet. Another step took her past the blond woman, who was trying to stand up. A third step took her into the sunlight. She turned, blind, to look into the parking bay.

Passers-by stared. A siren spun out above the traffic noise.

"How do you know my name?" Rye said.

"Run!" he bellowed, and came at her like a charging bear.

She ran.

She ran until she had the wit to look behind her, and did not see the bear on her trail.

Then she turned around and ran back the way she had come.

Every blond head caught her eye, every tall dark shape brought that burst of adrenaline to her gut. Not him, not him, not him—and then a tall, black-haired man glanced back as he turned a corner, his dark face cut by shadow and sunlight. She did know him. Recognition flashed all through her, as physical as a laugh or a sneeze. She knew him. Not his name, or where they had met, or what their relationship had been, but *him*. He turned onto the cross street and out of sight. A siren gave one last angry whoop somewhere close. Rye, too, glanced back at the corner and saw blue and red lights dulled to nothing by the sun. She turned the corner. Never mind what was behind her.

Where was *he*?

She lost him, found him again, his height putting his head above the general level of the pedestrian crowd. Not a real crowd on these lesser streets, just people doing their business, getting from here to there. He wore a gray T-shirt, tight across his shoulders, and jeans that must have been hot to walk in. Rye was hot, damp and quivering like a kettle about to boil, but she felt strong, as if the fever powered her stride. He turned another corner, glanced back: another glimpse of his face, not enough to describe, but enough to recognize. Again, that primitive *yes* in her gut. She followed him, saw him cross the street against the light, saw him run to catch a bus—

—that drove off, leaving her hot and panting and wild in the colorless heat-mirage of its exhaust.

Rye didn't give up, although the strain of her paranoia grew with the heat of the day. Following the bus wasn't impossible at first, though she could not catch it. It had traffic to contend with, red lights, passengers who wanted on or off, and Rye was fit enough to run every time it pulled away from the curb. But she lost ground at every green light, and eventually the bus pulled too far ahead: out of sight: gone.

Her knees were grazed and bloody under her torn pants, her arm bruised where he had grabbed her, her brain seething within the black burnt lines of the fever's web, but she did not give up. *Therefore* she did not give up, even then. It seemed to Rye she could follow the bus's trail by the smell of the exhaust, by the look of people on the sidewalk, ex-passengers who were still just hitting their stride. More sensibly, she could also spot the tin flags of the bus-stops and the rare paint-peeling bench, but her hunt had nothing to do with sense. It had to do with the fever and the vivid meaningfulness it lent to inconsequential events; it had to do with the holes the fever had burned in her memory and her sanity; it had to do with the desperate, soul-killing loneliness she had suffered since leaving the hospital; it had to do with the sound of her name in another person's voice; it had to do with the touch of another person's hands. Rye ran until she tasted blood, and walked until she could run again, and her need only grew more intense the more hopeless the chase became. Like a crazy woman—yes, she knew this perfectly well—like a crazy woman she ran and walked and ran again, guided by nothing but the smell of diesel exhaust, the flare of sunlight off of bus-stop signs, and eventually, by nothing at all. She ran, and walked, and ran again through a city that lurched around her like a primitive cartoon, that jerked her through too-black shadows and too-bright sunlight, across streets that squealed like burning tires, down alleys that flooded the mouth with disgust for the smell of rotting garbage, and onto the bottom step of an outside flight of metal stairs.

What?

Here.

What?

Rye caught her balance against a filthy brick wall. Sunlight cut down at her through several layers of painted steel grills. Shade stamped into checkerboards, the sun like a pat of butter in her eye. She looked down, panting, dizzy, sick from the long run. Behind her lay a black street deserted at lunchtime, fresh tarmac like a lava flow rippling under heat-waves. Some air-born illusion seemed to arch the street upwards like a petted cat. Window boxes drooped like sleeping mouths. Awnings slumped under the heat. The brick wall above Rye's head sported the ghost of a word, *livery* just visible under the newer warehouse sign someone had tried and failed to scrub away. The metal stairs climbed up in zigzagged ranks, their only railing a swag of rusting chain.

Here.

Rye felt the same pounce of recognition. Here what? Here where? Here who? Crazy. Heat made her tremble so hard that the chain railing quivered without her even touching it. Crazy. She climbed the stairs in a *world gone mercury mirror slide (gray ice black glass) gravity in a sudden wet tilt and glide* so she had to catch her balance on the green painted-steel door at the top of the stairs.

The alley was silent with a silence cocooned within the restless city's buzz. Huge and reckless with her lunatic fever, Rye made a fist and knocked.

And waited.

And—

"Who's there?"

A man's voice, deep and anonymous behind the door.

Rye skittered back, losing her conviction, and felt the chain touch her thigh and open space touch her heel. Stairs, alley, landing, door.

"Who's there?"

What was she doing? She could not go forward or back. She heard the sound of chains falling, bolts sliding, the single clunk of a lock. She put her hands like a guilty schoolgirl over her mouth.

As the door swung open and there he was.

Yes.

Rye laughed. She couldn't help herself. The world was just as crazy as she was.

Recognition moved behind his dark eyes, mirror-image of that *yes.*

"You do know me!" she said. "Do you know me?"

At that, something else moved in his eyes. He raised his hand and pointed the gun he held in her face.

four

"Hum," she said, a sweet little noise of surprise. The gun barrel was only a foot away from her face. He was very tall, his arm very long.

"What do you want?"

"Don't you know me?" Fever shiver knocked her voice from whisper to sound. "Didn't you help me?"

"You tell me."

Sunlight painted his expression in black and gold. Another laugh shook itself out of her mouth.

"You're the one with the gun."

"What do you want?"

"You helped me." If help was the right word. "Were we . . . did we used to be . . . friends?"

"If you don't know—" His hand shifted around the gun butt. The barrel did not move. "—then you aren't the Rye I knew."

I'm not! I am! Which would get her killed?

"But! Wait! It's this fever! I forgot so much and I don't even know how I found you but I remember your face and I must have remembered your address without even knowing and I don't even know what else I know or how much is real but it's just this fucking *fever*!" She snatched a breath. Not dead yet. "Please, just, if you're going to shoot me, please, maybe even you have a reason, but will you just tell me first? Who are you and how do I know you and why are you going to kill me?"

He was silent, the gun like a balance point between them. Then he said, "You have never been here before."

Her turn for a long pause, heat on a rampage among her bones. "I don't know, then. I guess I just don't know." She started to cry.

"Jesus Christ!" The first emotion she had heard in his voice: anger. "Is that the best you can—" He cut himself off.

Rye tried to do the same, gulping and wiping her face with her palms. "Sorry," she said, "it's been a bad couple of days." And then she was laughing and crying at once, so she turned away, as if her shoulder would be less provocative than her face.

"Don't." He grabbed her bare arm. And let her go. "You're burning up."

The touch sobered her. She could taste it, salt copper soap. "Sorry."

"Fuck," he said. "*Rye.*"

"Yeah," she whispered.

"Come on," he said, sounding weary now. "Come inside."

The hand with the gun was hanging at his side. She sidled past him through the door, inside darker than the noon-bright alley, but that was all right, everything, like the air on her face, was *there.*

It was a loft, big and bare, warehouse space made marginally livable. Dirt-blackened planks for a floor, steel posts instead of interior walls, few windows, a lot of room. Rye sat where he pointed her with his empty hand, on a couch where some furniture made an island in the gloom. She watched him cross the blind-shaded darkness. He opened a refrigerator door, the bulb coming on to light the kitchen. It was just an alcove between two outside walls and a short interior one: bathroom, Rye guessed, the only real room. The coarse fabric of the couch burned mustard yellow against her bare skin, although the cloth was blue in the light streaking through the window at her back. The fridge door clunked shut and a moment later she felt through her sweat-damp clothes the chill of refrigerated air passed along by the electric fan humming on the floor. Her skin itched, twitched, writhed, like it wanted to get up and crawl away. She wished it would, thought how cool and peaceful her naked flesh would be, and then shuddered, wet with blood in her mind.

The man came back with the gun out of sight and a jug and two glasses in hand. He set them on a small table between the couch and a chair, knelt down to pour.

"Here." He handed her a glass.

"Thanks." She sipped, thirsty and shivering.

"You want some aspirin or something?"

She looked at him, blank.

"For the fever."

Like putting a couple of tablets in the way of a speeding freight train. But she was absurdly moved by the kindness of the offer. "No—"

He moved so suddenly she spilled water down her arm. But he only hooked a knuckle under her chin and tilted her face into the sunlight. His eyes were narrow, black even in the light.

"Jesus, Rye, what the hell did they do to you?"

"Who?"

His eyes went blank. He took his hand away, the copper spark of his touch cooling as the instant sweat on her chin dried. The shock of being touched lingered longer. He stood over her a moment, then moved to the chair, sat, picked up his glass. His black gaze clung to her scarred face, so that she looked away. The silence went on so long the water on her arm dried, and she began to take in a few details. The smell of dust, cooked meat, a ghost of machine oil. The sweat stains on the man's gray shirt. The ache in her overused feet. She toed off her sneakers and bent her legs beneath her, lesions threatening to open across her battered knees.

"Amnesia." His voice, his face, were unreadable.

Familiarity nudged her, recognition, here and gone. Stranger or friend? Or enemy?

"Not everything, just six years, about. Since I left home."

"Ran away."

He knew her. He did. She drank some water, tasted brass roses blood. Water. She held the glass to her face against the stifling heat.

"Tell me," he said.

"Tell me your name," she said. "Please."

He said nothing, staring her with a hard, intrusive stare. His hair was almost as black as hers, with maybe more of a red tone, and eyes far darker, like strong coffee, bitter chocolate. His skin was darker than hers, though the long bones of his face were caucasian, and etched with deep lines at mouth and eyes. He was probably older than thirty, probably younger than sixty. Rye realized she was staring, glanced aside, looked back in defiance.

"If I used to know you, it's not exactly a secret, is it?"

"How far are you going to take this?"

"Why would I *lie*?" Her voice spiraled up. She reined it in.

He rubbed his thumb across his lower lip. "Dan Bardo," he said finally. "I guess you know who you are."

Daniel Bardo. Like an echo, she heard another voice, a woman's voice with a musical lilt, speaking a name that chased light like sparklers down her spine. "Daniel Bardo," she said, trying it out in her own voice. Yes, yes, *yes*! She wanted to punch the air with triumph.

"Tell me," he said, his voice, if anything, flatter than before. Enemy or friend?

Rye sipped her water, trying to put herself in order. "They found me by the river, covered in blood. I had these lesions . . . "

"And a fever."

"It should have killed me. It just scrambled my brains."

"What—"

"Don't know. Nobody knows. They did a million tests, but . . . " She shrugged.

"Are you contagious?" He sounded reluctant to ask.

"No. Probably not. They let me go, but nobody knows what it is, so how can they know?"

"They."

"The hospital. I was in quarantine for, I forget, seven weeks." She looked at him, cheek tilted against her glass. "When I was lucid they asked where I lived, and I thought I had just left home. I thought I was still sixteen. They went to this squat where I was staying that first winter and the building wasn't even there anymore. I don't know."

"But you recognized me in the alley. You tried to follow me."

"Your face. I remember a few faces, places, things happening, but it's all a jumble. And . . . "

"And."

"And I was delirious, crazy with fever dreams, and now sometimes I can't tell what was dream and what was real." She swallowed, but held his gaze. "What is real."

His eyes flicked away as if something hurt. "You haven't said how you found me. I know I lost you."

"I was really never here?"

He shook his head.

"Well. I don't know. I thought I was crazy, only then I found you, and I shouldn't have, so I don't know."

Her voice climbed a scale, smaller and smaller as it rose toward tears. Too tired to cry any more, she stopped to swallow the daisy-field color of salt. Daniel Bardo didn't move, leaning on his elbow, his hand over his eyes. The hum of the fan swelled to fit the silence.

Finally Rye said, voice back to normal, "Who were you talking about?"

"Who?" Bardo shifted to look at her, still propped on his fist, as if he were too tired to move.

"You said, 'What did they do to you?' Who is 'they'?"

So he told her, though it was such a long, strange tale she had almost forgotten her question by the time it was answered. His voice was so deep she felt him as much as she heard him in her bones.

five

There were four of them: Cleände, Marky, Bardo, and Rye. Or rather, said Bardo, three of them to begin with, for he was the last to join.

"Most of this I learned from you, the three of you," he said, and his gaze pinned her in a suspicious frame while he talked.

Really it was Cleände that knew, Cleände, whose name conjured a camera-shutter glimpse of a face, a voice, a laugh, in Rye's mind.

Cleände, who claimed to be from another world.

That made Rye laugh. Her nerves were too raw for her to let it slide.

"Aliens," she said with mocking wonder. It wasn't Bardo's look that stopped her, though, it was the memory of the hot stilting glide of *something* outside Kelly's window.

"No," Bardo said. "Cleände was human enough."

The lines in his face bit so deeply that Rye longed to ask, Enough for what?

There is Earth, he said. The sun and planets, stars, galaxies, the whole universe as vast and as real as human science could comprehend. And it was all . . . a world, hung like a peach on a peach tree, with another world beside it, and another beside that one, an infinite branch on a tree with an infinite number of branches.

"Human worlds," Bardo said, "and others," his voice so flat Rye could not tell if he believed it, or was only tired of puzzling over the question, was it real, or not. She could relate to that.

Cleände was from one of these worlds, a neighbor on the world-tree, and the first part of the story Bardo told was hers.

Universe-as-fruit was not Cleände's metaphor. She spoke of worlds, universes, as if they floated within some mythical, mystical sea, an ocean moved by currents and tides that swept worlds together, drifted them apart, to some pattern incomprehensible to the human mind. Dreams, Cleände said, within the skull of God. Sometimes the drifting worlds met. Sometimes they collided, violently; sometimes they drifted together for a time, and parted; sometimes they joined. Her world had drifted for a time within the influence of another—for a long time, Bardo said. Long enough for the powerful of one world to find away to make the crossing to the other, to Cleände's, where they could do all the things humans might do on a world not their own. There were wars, Cleände had told them. There was conquest.

"And Earth is the other world?" guessed Rye, dubious.

Bardo looked disturbed, as if she'd said something crazy. As if she should have known better. She could see, before he replied, how the realization moved again across his face—amnesia—and then the suspicion.

"No," he said. "Earth is the third world, the new world."

The third world that drifted, God knew how or why, close enough to disturb the hostile balance between the other two. So there were the conquerors, who saw a new world to conquer, and there were the conquered, Cleände's people, who saw . . . what? A place to run to? A place to hide?

Rye began to realize that not all Bardo's suspicion was for her.

"She *said* she came as a refugee. One of the few who learned from their enemies how to make the crossing, and came to hide."

"But?" Belief and disbelief were both suspended. Who was she to quibble over the impossible?

Bardo ignored the prompt. If refugees came, so did those they tried to escape. To find the escapees, to discover what Earth had to offer, to judge what resistance would have to be overcome. Cleände was clear on that point: the conquerors of her world meant to be the conquerors of Earth. And she, Cleände the refugee, needed help. Just to survive at first, Earth was inimical to her as any place must be to an illegal alien, penniless and alone, and she had enemies on her trail. But survival came to have another meaning for her, as friends from her homeland were tracked down and taken, or killed. She began to think about the survival of her homeland, and then, as she lived here, as she saw native humans also taken, or killed, she began to think about Earth's survival as well. She began to think about freedom. She began to think about war.

"And so she started to recruit. You first, then Marky."

Rye, like a child suddenly included in a bedtime story, blinked. "Me," she said blankly. "Then you?"

Bardo held his glass by its rim, tipping it back and forth, watching the last inch of water catch the light. "You don't remember any of this."

"No. Cleände, Marky . . . " She tasted the names, saw a face, round and sweet and lit up with excitement; heard a boy's hoarse voice. "Faces, maybe. Marky . . . " Like a cherub on speed, someone had said. Rye had said. She twitched at the memory. "I remember fighting, I think. I remember you and that gun." And the gray thing? The foggy panther-machine that the gun had been aimed at in her dream? She fumbled for a way to ask the question. Bardo interrupted her attempt.

"I was a detective."

Rye wanted to laugh, as she had over *alien*, for more than just surprise. Bardo, his eyes still on his empty glass, did not seem to notice.

"Major Crimes had all these cases, these homicide victims we couldn't identify." Bardo grunted, his face ironic, bitter. "'All these cases.' Three of them. That's a lot in a town this size. And there were other cases, disappearances, deaths due to animal attack that the animal control people kept trying to put off on us. Everyone was pulling overtime. I was new on the squad, but my partner was a senior detective, so we had the homicides."

Two victims had died of knife wounds, the third from a beating. They had all put up a fight, and at least one of them, by the forensic evidence, had drawn blood from his attackers, so Bardo and his partner speculated that they were looking at gang violence. The pathologist's report showed that all the victims had suffered past injuries; more significantly, the report also stated that all the victims were members of an "anomalous" blood group: no known type.

The pathologist was excited. She sent blood and tissue samples to a national laboratory, spent too much of her budget on genetic mapping, started working on an article. She also explained to the detectives how unprecedented a discovery this was, and how important it was that the victims' genetic community be identified. Bardo's partner, John Marducci, was not much interested in the science, but he was very interested in the hypothesis that the three victims were related, or at least members of an isolated group. He developed his own hypothesis: that the deaths were the result, not merely of gang rivalry, but of ethnic violence. He, too, thought it crucial that the victims' community be identified.

"So we started looking for immigrants, probably illegals." Bardo propped his elbows on his knees and painfully laughed. "John had no idea how right he was."

John would never know. When he and Bardo followed a lead that brought them too close to Cleände's war, John Marducci was killed.

"And I knew—" Bardo stopped. After a long silence, he whispered to the floor, "I knew." He straightened abruptly, startling Rye. "He was killed by something like nothing on Earth, but I had no goddamn evidence. So I started looking all over again. On my own time. And I found the three of you. And then it was the four of us, fighting the good fight," his mouth twisted, his voice louder and harder with every word, "until Cleände sold us up the fucking river, and Marky was dead, and you—" He stopped himself again.

"I *what*?"

Muscles in his face knotted as Bardo bit down on something too hard to swallow. "I don't know. I thought you were captured, tortured, dead. Or worse." He closed his eyes, as if to blind himself to her scars. "They can do things, those people. Things I can't even begin to understand."

"That doesn't help!" Rye cried. She felt betrayed, tears bright in her mouth.

"I know."

"How did I get away? What did they do?"

"That is the question, isn't it?"

"It's not a joke!"

He opened his eyes, met her panicked look with a cold, narrow stare. "I know it's not a fucking joke. What did you think the gun was for?"

"I—"

"Can you tell me I shouldn't have shot you? All sentiment aside, Rye. Can you tell me why I shouldn't have shot you?"

She tried desperately to think of an answer, a reason that would make him trust her, make him ask her to stay. She could not come up with one. It was his sincerity, his real, urgent sincerity, that silenced her. They stared at each other, while the fan whirred, and the refrigerator rattled into life, and the last of the summer dusk slipped, the color of dying embers, through the open windows.

Bardo wiped his hand across his face. "You can sleep on the couch. But in the morning I think you'd better go."

six

hot tar and gravel (meat smell and sex) sunlight ripped on chemical air (acid choir laughing, laughing) lover waiting, waiting (some prisons better than others)

Rye woke, more surprised by the sleep than by the nightmare that was already slipping away. The morning stuffed yellow sunlight like pillars of visible heat through the back windows, and Bardo was rattling in the kitchen. Rye sat up in her nest of sheets, glad to be ignored. She felt terrible, still feverish, the last of the nightmare lingering like a smear of tar across her tongue. Sweat-itchy in her clothes, she got up, dizzy and creaking, and shuffled to the bathroom that sat like an afterthought between the kitchen alcove and Bardo's unmade bed. The room was unfinished; although the floor and shower stall were tiled, the walls showed bare studs and the inside of the drywall cladding. It didn't even have a ceiling. Rye peed with her knees pressed together, flushed, leaned against the pedestal sink. She felt resentful and bereft. How could he just abandon her?

Why shouldn't he? Stranger, enemy, friend.

She turned the tap, watched the water swirl down the drain before putting her hands under the stream. The water was so cold it hurt, then hot, then cold. Not the water, her, feeling worse the longer she was up. She clutched the sides of the basin as the shaking started, violent hyperthermic shivers, rattling hard, and harder, wet hands slipping, dropping her to her knees. Harder still, convulsively hard.

Clutching the rim of the sink, refusing to give in, blood-taste from a bitten cheek.

Then it was over, the shaking letting her go as suddenly as a terrier drops a rat with a broken neck.

Rye leaned her forehead against the sink's porcelain cool and listened to the water gurgle down the drain. From the other side of the bathroom partition Bardo called, "There's food if you want it."

She pulled herself up, rinsed her mouth—spat pink into the basin, but at least the tar-taste was gone—turned off the tap, dried her hands, and somehow managed to leave the room without once catching her reflection's eye.

If she was surprised to have slept, she was astonished at her appetite. Weeks of hunger ambushed her, invaded her the way the fever did, not a damn thing she could do. Bardo gave her fried eggs, sausages, tomatoes out of the same pan, stacks of toast with peanut butter and jam, peaches going brown with heat. He fed her as if in apology, but there was no softening of the lines around his eyes. The lines were sharper in daylight, the shadows around his eyes more visible, but Rye still could not guess his age.

When Rye was wiping her plate with the last scrap of toast, Bardo said abruptly, "You can take a shower before you go."

She ate the toast and licked her fingers. "Why, do I stink?"

"Well. That sounded like you."

As if she would know. Stung, Rye glared at him. "Where am I supposed to go? I don't mean—I have somewhere to stay. But who am I supposed to ask, if you won't tell me anything? Cleände? I don't even know how to find her. The people who did this to me? I don't even know how to find *them*! So where do I go, Daniel? And oh, yeah, thanks for breakfast, okay? Really. Thanks."

"What do you want me to say? *I* don't know what they did to you."

"Would she?"

"Cleände?" Bardo scrubbed his fingers through his hair, his gaze on something past Rye's shoulder. "Probably."

"So how do I find her?"

"I don't know."

"You found her before." Half challenging, half cajoling.

"For all I know she's on a whole other fucking planet. Did you hear anything I said? Maybe she's with her people. Maybe she's with the other side. I don't know, and I don't have any way to find out. You think I can travel between the worlds?"

"What do you mean 'with the other side'? You mean she was captured too?"

Bardo glared at her. "I mean maybe she's *with* the other side. Or maybe there is no other side. I told you, she set us up. She could have been stringing us all along."

"You didn't tell me. You didn't *tell* me anything."

"She—" Bardo shifted in his chair, as if he wanted to get up and walk away. "We were supposed to be ambushing them. Cleände had some way of knowing when someone was coming through. We were supposed to meet them, get them before they scattered into the city, turn them over to Cleände's people if we could. But they got there first. They ambushed us. Marky was killed, they ran you down, Cleände . . . " Bardo shrugged. " . . . disappeared."

"So she might have been taken prisoner. Same as me?"

He turned his black gaze on Rye's face. "She was stringing us. I knew it, couldn't prove it."

"So she might—"

"Damn it, Rye, I've been on the job almost twenty years, you think I don't know when someone is lying to me? You think I can't figure it out eventually? Cleände was playing us all for suckers. Shit!" This time he did get up, pacing to the nearest window and back. "She played us all. I wanted proof that I wasn't . . . that I had seen what I had seen. I wanted to stop whatever had killed my partner and two other cops, and isn't that exactly what she promised? 'Your enemies are my enemies, Bardo.' And you and Marky—Hell. You two were easy. A couple of bored kids who'd rather play video games than get yourselves real lives. She just offered you a life-sized game with all the effects." He leaned over the back of his chair to add, soft and mean, "She just picked you up the way a bad cop picks up a loose weapon, in case it might come in handy some day."

That hurt. Rye leaned her mouth against her clasped hands until she was sure her voice would come out steady. "Okay. You'd know, I guess. But is this the real world? Is this a real life?" She was thinking about the boarding house, her fever, her job, but some instinct prompted her to add, "Hiding up here with your gun?"

Bardo shoved off from the chair back. He looked for an instant like he meant to throw something, but he checked whatever violence moved through him. He turned to the window. Hot sunlight showed the red in his hair.

"Look." Rye lost the thread as the heat of the argument, or the food, turned sluggish and uneasy through her blood. "Look," she tried again, "this *is* my life. Something is happening to me. Do you understand that? You don't have to care. I can see why you couldn't trust me. But I have to know. And I don't know where else to start, except with you. Do you see?"

He didn't turn, didn't move. The fever stirred again, loosening Rye's skin. Not now, she thought, as sweat flooded her pores.

"Can't you at least," she pleaded, sounding shamefully young, "can't you at least give me a hint?"

Bardo bowed his head. His shoulders shifted in a sigh. Then he turned around, saying, "The problem is that everything I know . . . " He trailed off, mouth open with horror. "Rye. Jesus."

As the sweat ran down her face scalp arms back legs hands feet and she realized it was not sweat but blood.

It seemed like a very long time that she sat there listening to her blood patter on the floor.

Rye closed her eyes because the blood stung like sweat, and because she did not want to have to see the expression on Bardo's face. She expected the pain to start every second. It never did. She wondered, a part of her mind detached from the fear, if it was finding Bardo that had triggered this, or the big meal, or if it was just another stage in the fever's evolution. She wondered, not quite so detached, if she was about to bleed to death. The death of a thousand cuts. Wasn't that a Chinese thing? Or maybe it was Japanese. She wondered if she had a thousand lesions. More, probably. She wondered if any of the nurses had been detailed to count them all. Thoughts stumbling through a bloody eternity.

She was distracted by the furry buzz of a fly. She was already frightened, but the sound spurred in her a horror equivalent to Bardo's. A noise escaped her.

"Rye," Bardo said. "Tell me what I can do."

"The fly," she whispered. "Don't let it . . . "

"I've got it," he said, and she could hear his pity. "I've got it."

She heard him moving around, heard the swish of something, a towel maybe, near her ear. Swish, snap.

"Okay. I got it." A pause. Then, reluctantly: "Listen, Rye. I've got to call an ambulance."

"No!" The word came out distorted. Her face was stiff with clotting blood.

He hesitated, long enough for her to hear the silence.

She said, "I think it's stopping."

"Rye—"

"What do you think they can do? They had their chance. They had seven weeks of chances." The blood-mask cracked, already drying in the fan-blown air. Rye opened her eyes. "Anyway, it's over."

Still he hesitated. It occurred to her to wonder, in that same detached corner of her mind, if there was something odd about a cop who didn't want to call 911. It was obvious to her that his reluctance had nothing to do with her own. But it didn't matter. She peeled herself off the chair, saying, "I guess I'll take you up on that shower," and promptly keeled over, drowned in a sudden black wave.

Swimming underwater, the ocean green with sunshine. Rays of light dwindle into the deep dark below her. Bubbles like false pearls spill up to the limpid surface and the refracted silhouette of the waiting boat above. The waiting dark below. Perfect suspension, no need to breathe.

She surfaced for a blink. Soft pain of water, the rubbery feel of a body half numb, wholly out of her control. Hiss of shower, taste of blood, hands peeling at her sodden shirt. Sitting on the floor of the shower stall, propped against the tile

wall fades from beneath her leaning arm, stone melting like a skim of ice on warming water, letting her sink into luminous fog, no up nor down save for the phosphorous lines that mark the alley walls, she runs swims falls

onto a bed, dumped like bundle of damp laundry on rumpled sheets. The soft impact jarred her eyelids open. She caught a glimpse of a man's bare chest and arms, tan skin streaked and smeared with

rust taste (brighter than tar) nest rest (softer than gravel) sex (no sex) waiting (waiting) sun a holler (high at noon)

seven

Rye woke to disorientation, flung out hands and feet—sheet pulled awry—she must be in a bed—that spun, swayed, settled into horizontal. Bed. Daniel Bardo's bed. She groped for the sheet, and only when she was covered again did she open her eyes. And close them.

God damn it.

She pressed the heels of her palms against her eyes, then stared at her hands. Clean, except for the nails. Bardo was thumping around nearby. She sat up, careful with the sheet. He wasn't in sight, but—thump—she could hear him in the bathroom, so after a moment she hauled herself to her feet, wrapped the sheet toga-style, and shuffled to the open door. He was shirtless and barefoot, on his knees with a bucket and sponge, cleaning up her blood. His hair was damp, his broad back showing the bones.

Rye propped herself against the doorjamb, although she did not feel weak—better, in fact, than she had on her first awakening. The curve of his spine was obscurely disturbing to her, as was the prosaic, domestic nature of the chore.

"Shouldn't you be wearing gloves?"

He dropped the sponge in the bucket, wiped his face on his arm. "I thought you said you weren't contagious."

"I don't know what I am."

He glanced over his shoulder. Not a warm look, but, like the recognition he had met her with, it struck a chord inside her. Not a stranger.

"You need to use the john?"

And not a friend.

"No."

"I'll be done in a minute."

"Okay." Rye lingered in the doorway, still stupidly, stubbornly hoping for more.

Bardo fished out the sponge, fisted it to squeeze out pink water and a disinfectant smell. "Something else?"

"My clothes?" she said in a small voice.

"Trashed." He started to scrub the lip of the shower stall. "I'll find you something when I'm done."

Rye pushed off from the jamb and shuffled meekly away.

Bardo had already cleaned up the area by the table. She went to the kitchen sink to rinse the blood from under her nails and found it piled with dishes. Moved by some mother-taught guest-impulse, she stacked the dishes on the counter, filled the sink with soapy water, hitched her sheet toga more securely around her, and started to wash. Doing the dishes was as good a way as any of cleaning her nails.

She was nearly done when Bardo came out, empty bucket in hand.

"What are you doing?" he said testily.

Surely it was self-evident. She didn't answer. Egg yolk was always hard to get off a fork.

Bardo didn't say anything either, but she could feel him seething behind her. She thought if she closed her eyes she would see him, lively as a child's sparkler. He clattered the bucket into a cupboard and thumped off to the bed alcove, where she could hear him getting dressed.

Then he said, over the sound of water gurgling down the drain: "What size are you?"

"Skinny."

He growled, stomped to the door, undid the locks and chains, and slammed himself out.

In spite of everything, the corners of her mouth twitched, more up than down.

He came back with sweat pants that were too big, a T-shirt that was too small, and a man's shirt that was enormous. Rye went into the bathroom-box to dress. When she came out Bardo was sitting on the end of the couch where he could glower at the bathroom door. She padded over to kneel by his feet.

"What are you doing?" he demanded, as if this was one thing too many.

"Shoes." She fished her sneakers from under the couch and sat on the edge of a chair to put them on.

Bardo was silent while she tied her laces, though he caught his breath a time or two, as if he thought better of what he meant to say. Finally, as she finished the second knot, he said, "What are you going to do?"

She glanced up. He was wearing his poker face—his cop face, she guessed—his thoughts hidden behind black eyes. She gave up looking for a hint of warmth.

"I don't know," she said tiredly. "Look for Cleände, I guess."

"How?" Another demand.

"Well." Rye straightened to look at him. "I found you . . . somehow."

"And look what—"

—*happened*, she finished mentally when he broke off. She shrugged, looked back down at her feet.

"You do understand she might be—probably is—on another world? A whole other universe?"

"Well. But so was I. Right? When I was captured? And I guess I got away . . . somehow."

"Or they let you go."

She drew breath, let it go with another shrug. "I know it's impossible, but so is everything else, and, I don't know, she might be in the city. You don't know that she isn't, right?"

He didn't answer until she looked up at him, and then it was grudging.

"I don't know for sure."

"So." She stood, reluctantly, unhappiness pulling at her mouth. "I guess it's . . . Thanks."

"Sit down," he said, derisive and harsh.

Rye stared at him.

"Sit down. Sit!" Impatient now, and Rye realized his derision had been aimed at himself. "I'll help you find her, but we have to think it through."

Slowly, she sat.

Leaning back with his long denim-clad legs stretched out and his hands locked behind his head, Bardo laid the problem out for Rye as an exercise in logic.

"Forget what Cleände ever told us," he said. "What do we know?"

"This is real," Rye said, holding her scar-feathered hands out to him.

Impatience chased across his face. "Start at the beginning."

"This is my beginning," she said.

Bardo sighed. The beginning, he explained, was two men and one woman dead by homicide, never identified, members of a blood group no one could type.

"For you, maybe," Rye muttered.

"Well, hell, Rye, until you get your damn memory back, it's all we've got. All right? Can I get on with this?"

She slumped in her chair and chewed on a cuticle.

They had three people from an isolated population that no one could identify. A point in favor of the other-worlds hypothesis, though not definitive. They had three *dead* people from an isolated population that no one could identify, a fact which lent itself to the ethnic-violence hypothesis; and Cleände's description of her people's subjugation and resistance certainly fit under the same heading. The hypothesis was not proved, but it was holding up: there was a war on. Cleände had a side. And she was recruiting.

"And then," Bardo said, "there are the gray beasts."

Rye prickled, startled out of her sulk. "Gray beasts," she echoed, while a fog-colored panther-machine glided through her mind. "They're real."

"Real," he confirmed. "And killing people."

Including Bardo's partner and one of two patrolmen who had backed the detectives up as they followed a lead in the unsolved homicides. Bardo had seen the gray beasts, had hunted them under Cleände's leadership, and had accepted her claim that they were hunters themselves, conjured by her enemies like hounds whistled up out of the nowhere between the worlds. Setting her claim aside as unproven, the beasts were still unearthly, inimical, and indiscriminant in their slaughter. Remember the deaths put down to animal attack, Bardo said. Remember the disappearances no one could solve.

"So it *is* true," Rye said, still prickling.

Bardo rubbed his linked hands over his hair, then stretched his arms across the back of the couch. "That much of it is. So where does that leave us?"

"Well . . . it's *true*. The other worlds, and the . . . "

"And?" He lifted a sardonic brow. When Rye only bit the offending cuticle again, Bardo pushed himself up with sudden energy. "You want some lunch?"

Remembering the results of her last meal, Rye shuddered and said an emphatic, "No." But she trailed him into the kitchen.

The loft was stifling in the afternoon heat. Bardo nudged the fan toward the kitchen as he passed.

He talked while he rummaged in the refrigerator.

"Accept for the moment that other universes exist, that there are people who live in them, that they can cross over from world to world. Accept that there might be war between them. Why not? Human beings are human beings. It might even spill over onto Earth. Why not?" He piled sandwich makings on the counter and closed the fridge door with his heel. "So in one respect at least, Cleände is probably telling the truth."

"Why not in every respect?"

"You need a reason besides Marky's death, or what happened to you?"

"I don't know how Marky died."

"I do." Bardo's mouth tightened. "Call it instinct."

"Is that," Rye said carefully, "is that good enough?"

Bardo dipped a knife in a jar, spread mustard, neat and even, on a slice of bread. "Not if you were going to court."

"Daniel—"

"Jesus! Why do you—" He loosened his grip on the knife, and reached for the mayonnaise. "Nobody calls me that. It's either Bardo or Dan."

"Sorry."

"And when the hell did you get so meek?"

She hiccuped a laugh, incredulous.

He sighed. "Sorry." And spread the mayonnaise.

"So if Cleände led you—us—into a trap . . . Well. Why would she? Why have anything to do with us at all?"

Bardo peeled cold cuts out of a deli bag, arranged them on the bread. "Because she needed us."

"For what?"

"I told you. Recruits. Look," he said, rinsing a tomato under the tap. "She *says* she's a refugee. Does she hide? Does she even try to join up with other refugees? No, she latches onto a couple of café groupies and an ex-cop who came a little too close to finding out what the hell was going on, and she sends them out after the creatures she says are the enemies'. Fine." He cut the tomato into emphatic slices. "Probably they are. Why would she want to take out her own side? But there is a hell of a lot more to what's going on here than a few loose dogs," he jabbed the knife in the air for emphasis, "and when she sees that her recruits are starting to figure that out, she sets them up and gets the hell out of Dodge."

"Were we figuring it out?" Rye nibbled a scrap of ham and guessed, "You were."

Bardo shrugged, still mad, and went back to building his sandwich.

"So what else was going on?"

"I don't know," Bardo said. "But here's a question for you. Even if everything she said was true, which is more plausible: that her people are looking for a place to escape to, a place where they know the enemy already has a foothold? Or that they're looking for a place to fight their war on an equal footing? Or," he cut his sandwich from corner to corner with one neat slice, "*or* that they're looking to do unto others what the hell has been done unto them?"

Rye used his knife to cut herself a piece of cheese and trailed him to the table.

"I don't know," she said. "Which *is* more plausible?"

Bardo bit, chewed, and swallowed before he answered. "I don't know either. She ditched us before I could figure it out. Damn." He got up. "You want a beer?"

She said, "No, thanks," but he set a bottle down at her elbow and went back to his lunch. She cupped her hands around the bottle, cold and damp with condensation, shimmering creamy-blue against her palms.

"Okay," she said. "I hear what you're saying."

He slanted her a skeptical look, tilting his bottle for a long swallow. "But?"

"Just one thing. Well. No. Two things. Number one: even if Cleände's people aren't the good guys, it doesn't necessarily mean that she set us up, and even if she did, it doesn't necessarily mean she wasn't killed or taken prisoner too. Right?"

Bardo looked at the last bit of sandwich in his hand, then set it back on his plate. "Number two?"

Rye concentrated on peeling the label off her beer bottle. "Number two: as far as I'm concerned it doesn't really matter."

"What doesn't?"

"Any of it."

"Meaning." His voice flat.

Did she want to say it? Would it make him back off again? The label made a papery sound as it peeled loose from the softened gum. "Meaning, if I want to find out what the hell is happening to me, I either ask the people who did it, or I ask Cleände. I know they're not the good guys. I don't know she isn't." Rye hesitated, but she couldn't think of anything to add. She drank, and discovered something new about herself: she really did not like the taste of beer.

"And what do you do," Bardo softly replied, "if you find out that those people and her people are on the same goddamn side?"

Rye tugged at the half-detached label. "That wouldn't mean they wouldn't know what the hell is going on."

"And no doubt they'll just tell you—"

"Well, hell, Dan! Who else am I supposed to ask? Do you have any better ideas? Do you have any fucking answers?" She glared at him, more surprised, apparently, by her shouting than he was.

He put the last bite of sandwich in his mouth. "Settle down, kid, I told you I was going to help. I just wanted you to know what you were getting yourself into."

"Oh, like you know!" She was loud with exaggerated scorn, goofy with relief.

Bardo didn't smile, but his eyes gleamed, she would have sworn with satisfaction, as he drank the last of his beer.

eight

Police procedure for finding someone began with an obvious first step: try the last known address. Rye was doubtful, but she did not argue as she followed Bardo out the door. She stood on the grill-floored landing while he locked up, choking a little on the smell of sun-heated tar from the re-finished roof next door. Hot as it had been in Bardo's apartment, it was hotter outside. As they descended the steep, rusty stairs and stepped out into the street, she saw the thunderheads piling up into the sky south of the city. Or maybe she felt them, an electrical weight against her face. She kept the long-sleeved shirt on despite the heat.

Rye supposed she had lost the right to find anything odd, but there was something strange about crossing the city with Bardo. Perhaps it was being in someone's, anyone's, company, having to adapt her stride to his; perhaps it was the way the sheer size of him cleared them both a path through the end-of-work-day crowds. Bardo, well over six feet tall, wide-shouldered and dark, loomed. But Rye, sticking close as a bicyclist riding a truck's slipstream, thought it was more than that.

For one thing, they walked past three or four bus stops before Bardo, apparently on the spur of the moment, boarded a bus. *Apparently* spur of the moment, because he had change for both of them ready in his hand. The bus took them across the river, a mobile oven packed elbow to elbow with people, and disgorged them on the northern end of Steamwheeler Park.

Whereupon Bardo, who had been walking fast enough to tax

even Rye's strong legs, strolled past the cedar grove, through the blowsy rose garden, and down to the paved walk above the river, where he stopped at a concession wagon to buy Rye a bottle of water and ask her, as if it had just occurred to him, "How are you holding up?"

"Fine." She smiled at him, broke the seal on the cap and drank.

"Just one of those things," Bardo said skeptically.

"One of what?" She squinted up at him, wishing she had her ball cap. She had lost it somewhere, like the bike. "What?"

"Your little episode this morning? Blood from every pore?"

"Oh . . . " *Oh that.* She doubted that response would go over well. But then she had to shrug. "I don't know. Maybe it is, maybe it isn't. Isn't that the point?"

He caught his breath. Let it go. "Right." He started walking again. "So where exactly did they find you?"

She trailed after him in mild bewilderment. "I don't know. By the water. I never asked."

He crossed the walkway in the wake of a rollerblader and propped his arms and one foot on the iron railings above the river. Rye joined him, copying his pose. The river's smell wafted up in an almost-cool almost-breeze, ozone-rich air anticipating the storm. Sun cast a sheen across the water, silver scales outlining the eddies that spun out of the deep, green, silent current.

"By the water," Bardo said, cocking his head to study the muddy bank.

Rye emptied the bottle, capped it. One of her too-long sleeves had come unrolled and she turned the cuff back up. The storm clouds had almost reached the sun and the murky light glanced strangely across her skin. She looked closer, thought she made out a dark tracery centering the thread-thin scars on her wrist. She ran her thumb across the scars, thinking dried blood, thinking scabs. The dark traces vanished as she moved, reappeared, teasing her vision. Scar-silver, scab-dark, there, not there.

Just one of those things.

Bardo turned. Rye clasped her hands around the empty bottle and looked at the river. Swallows wove their daredevil patterns above the surface, chasing midges too small to see. Bardo leaned with his back to the railing, long enough for Rye to register the tension beneath the casual pose, then he said, as if the stop had been her idea, "Come on. It's not going to get any safer."

Rye, trailing him again, realized that he had being making sure that they were not being followed.

Remembering the two blond fever angels silhouetted against yesterday's sunlit street, she wondered if she should be disappointed or relieved.

The storm clouds did not lessen the heat, but only increased the humidity and cast a heavy electrical gloom. The park was emptying, and the sidewalks of the riverside district to the south were already almost deserted. Some people, Rye thought as thunder rumbled, have enough sense to go in out of the rain.

Bardo led her to a furniture factory at the south end of riverside, a red brick monstrosity blackened by a century of pollution. Windows were boarded up, dandelions grew in cracks at the base of the wall. The rain was heavy now, running unimpeded through Rye's too-short hair, soaking cold through her clothes. The chill was welcome; the suffocating feel of wet cotton was not. She was still debating whether to strip down to her T-shirt, the rain on her face tasting like electric blue wine, when Bardo stopped at a corner made by a jog in the factory wall.

He put his shoulder to the wall and peered around like someone in a movie. Rye didn't snort, but she felt the impulse. Unlike someone in a movie, Bardo stayed that way, watching, for a long time. Rye propped herself against the wall beside him, dark brick still warm from the day's sun, and licked rain off her lips. On her tongue it tasted like water, but it was still good. Good to be cool. Good to have Bardo beside her.

And to be unafraid? Good, she decided, but probably not wise.

He turned back to her eventually, and surprised her again by not telling her to wait here. "Come on," he said, and put a surreptitious hand to the small of his back, beneath his rain-blackened blazer.

The gun, Rye thought with an internal wince. She didn't like his gun any better than she had liked his beer. But when he went, she followed.

There was a two-story frame house with gables and a porch set in a small garden bordered on three sides by factory walls. The manager's house, Rye guessed, way back when. It was white, with a green tin roof on the porch that rattled under the rain. Curtains showed in the dark windows. The narrow front lawn was shaggy; lilies lay on the ground, broken by the porch-shed rain. The house looked, and felt, empty.

Did she know this place, or didn't she?

"Well," Bardo said grimly, "let's see if anyone's home."

The porch floor was hollow under their feet. The door sounded just as hollow under Bardo's knock. He had a policeman's knock, full-fisted and loud. There was no traffic on this back street. The only noise was rain on tin. Bardo knocked again, waited again. Tried the doorknob. Locked.

"Wait here." He disappeared around the corner of the porch.

Rye clicked her tongue, a little exasperated, a little amused. Emotional eddies cast up by a deep current of... anticipation? Of... *what am I doing here?* There were footsteps behind the door, the clunk of a deadbolt being turned. Rye took half a step back, stopped. Started to yell for Bardo, stopped. The door swung open, and it was only him.

"Nobody home," he said, and stepped aside to let her in.

Did she know this place?

Standing in the dim hallway—Bardo gone again, she could hear the floorboards complain as he moved around—Rye peeled off her overshirt, shivering a little as the dry air touched her arms. The house was stuffy, warm, smelling of dust. Silent, except for the rain and the creaking of old wood. Stairs bent around two walls on her left; on her right a wide arch opened onto a living room. Sparse furnishings, a few cushions, a lot of battered wood. The curtains, half drawn, were damask. Rye closed her eyes and in that instant, in the fall of her lids, she felt a visceral stab of recognition, gone as soon as she concentrated on it, like a faint star that can only be seen in the corner of the eye.

With her eyes closed, it was only dark. Feeling chilled for the first time, she hung the wet shirt on the back of a chair and gingerly rubbed her arms. Bardo creaked down the stairs and came in at her back.

"It doesn't look like anyone's been here since." Not a complete sentence, but he ended it as if it was. Since. The way Rye thought of Before.

She tried a lamp. Nothing. She clicked the switch off again, as if it mattered, and said, "Now what?"

Bardo sat on a Morris chair that groaned under his weight. "Wait for the rain to stop."

"And then?"

He just leaned his head back and stretched out a foot, settling in for a rest. He looked tired, Rye thought, as if he had missed more than one night of sleep. While he rested, she wandered around the room looking at things. Not that there was much to look at, no pictures on the walls, no ornaments anywhere, not even a rug on the dusty floor. There was a stereo stacked in a corner, though, which struck Rye as incongruous as the beautiful curtains. Maybe Bardo's talk of other worlds had her expecting sci-fi tech or fairyland magic. Singing crystals, not—she slid a CD out of the rack—Björk.

Another memory flicker, music, people, lamplight. Blink and you'll miss it. She blinked.

She tried the stereo's power button, but of course it was dead as well. She put the CD back, wandered to the window. Rain ran like a bead curtain off the porch roof, silver against green against gray, the lawn and the street. The building across the way was a commercial property. There was no one in sight, not even a car. Rye turned and propped her butt on the low windowsill.

Bardo had his eyes closed. Rye studied his face, the long severe lines of it, the creases around mouth and eyes that did not, somehow, make him look old. She wondered why he had changed his mind, why he hadn't turned her out in the street. The more she thought about it—Bardo holding a gun in her face, Bardo kneeling to clean up her blood—the less she understood it. Instinct, or some buried memory, told her he wasn't likely to tell her if she simply asked. So she puzzled in silence, until she realized that the answer she was building was really just the answer she wished for: that he helped her because he liked her. Because he cared.

She swallowed against a lump in her throat, leaned her head back against the glass and closed her eyes.

Rain galloped on the porch roof, driven by gusts of wind. Thunder rumbled distantly, then cracked loud, one breathless instant after lightning flared, hot electric web, across the bare skin of Rye's face neck arms. As if the lightning had awakened something inside her, the room came into ghostly focus, at first just a blind sense of proportion, of space, but then, like a quick twist of a lens, the furniture was *there*, the walls, the archway . . . Bardo, like a sullen fire throwing heat against her cheek . . . Rye looked. He was there, frowning, his eyes still closed. Lightning flashed, a pattern across the sky, across her skin.

The fever woke, black and sudden, running like a tiger through the jungle of her veins.

Rye said, her mouth gone dry as brick dust, "Can we go now?"

Bardo opened his eyes, still frowning. "It's pissing down."

"I don't mind."

"I do."

"I don't feel well. Please. I want to go home."

He said with more impatience than compassion, "Lie down, then. When it lets up I'll—"

"No." Rye stood, urgency like a pressure in her throat.

"—find a phone booth and call a cab."

"Now."

"Fine," he said, just as stubborn. "See you later."

Rye glared at him, her mouth sullen with incipient tears. He gave her a lizard's blink and looked away. She snatched her damp shirt off the back of the chair and pulled it on, unable to explain her urgency even to herself. It was as sourceless and invasive as the fever, and left her as little choice. Without looking at Bardo again, she went into the hall, opened the door, stepped out into the rain wind electric weight heavy as a sea—

And froze when a knife blade licked sweet as honey across her throat.

Two knives, one at her throat, the other hovering by her temple. Two people, hot and vivid with anxiety, on either side of the door. More people stepped softly around the corner of the porch, long coats pale even under the shadow of the rain. The touch of the knife-tip in her hair made Rye's hand twitch, as if she could just reach up and brush it away.

"Call him out," one of them said. An accent changed the words, but they were still comprehensible.

Rye couldn't speak. Behind her she heard Bardo say, "If you're going, close the goddamn door."

"Call him," the same man said.

Adrenaline detached Rye from the scene, as if she watched from somewhere else, the top of the factory wall, say, a foreshortened view blurry and blue with rain. The knife at her throat was still impossibly sweet, flooding her dry mouth with saliva. She swallowed, shook her head.

Not that it mattered. She heard Bardo get up from the noisy chair, step into the hall behind her. Stop.

The knife at Rye's throat shifted. A hand closed around her arm.

"Tell him to leave the weapon," the same man said. He stood in front of Rye, his gaze fixed beyond her shoulder. Not a tall man, eyes shadowed by a heavy brow, blond hair wet and gray-brown with rain. "Tell him to leave it! Or we cut the throat."

Rye thought of Bardo holding the gun on her—probably he had it out now, aimed at her back—and said, "You tell him."

The hand around her arm tightened, pinching muscle and nerve against bone. She didn't move. The man who spoke . . . smiled.

"I tell him. Leave it, down on the floor. Yes."

Rye heard nothing behind her, and jumped badly when Bardo put his hand on her shoulder. The knife reacted to the jump. Blood ran. The cut stung, surprising her.

"You can let her go," Bardo said, so close to Rye she could feel his voice buzz in her chest. "We came here to talk."

"With me?" The man lifted his brow, but the smile faded. "I think not so. Not if you are friend of the house."

"The house is empty," Bardo said, the words so uninflected he might only have meant it literally. Or not.

The spokesman frowned. One of the others—there were three, besides the two flanking the door—stepped behind his shoulder and spoke in his ear. A woman, though the bones of her face were as blunt and heavy as the man's. Rye's blonde, her jaw dark and her mouth swollen from Bardo's punch. She kept her eyes fixed on Rye as she spoke. The spokesman's frown deepened, then lifted, until his face was quite blank. His eyes, like the woman's, were locked on Rye.

Bardo's hand tightened on her shoulder.

"You," the spokesman said, and then he said something else, a quick burst of language as sharp as flint. The knifeman's hand on Rye's arm pulled her away from Bardo. After a step, rather than engage in a tug-of-war, Bardo let her go. This frightened her, the first fear to break through the shock. Careless of the knives, she half-turned and reached out her hand. Bardo, his face a bone-colored mask, caught her fingers in a cold grip, came with her as the knifeman pulled her another step forward.

The spokesman seemed oblivious of this, staring at Rye, the woman still at his shoulder. "This," he said, and traced one finger across his own face. "What is this?"

Rye said nothing. Bardo said, risking, it seemed to her, rather a lot, "If you need to ask, you don't need to know."

The spokesman's hand curled into a fist before his mouth. The woman behind him spat something in her own language, then said in English, "We know you." She pointed an accusing finger at Rye. "We know you."

The spokesman turned his head slightly without taking his gaze from Rye and Bardo and said a few words. His people all stared at him. The knife twitched against Rye's bloody throat. The woman reacted most of all. Her face worked and she put a hand up to cover her swollen mouth. The spokesman spoke again, short and sharp, and after a moment she nodded. There was a kind of bright desperation on her face, an edgy electric tension amongst all the strangers.

"Listen," Bardo said, his deep voice belatedly soothing. "We have a lot to talk about with you people. Whatever you think there is between us, why don't we just put it aside for a minute—"

"We talk, yes," the spokesman said. "We talk soon, and we put no thing aside. But now . . . " He stepped forward and touched Rye's throat, making her shiver and clutch Bardo's hand. The spokesman's fingers came away daubed with red; he rubbed them against his thumb. "Now we have some place to go."

The rain rattled down, sweet and loud, a silvery curtain between the porch and the street, as the men with knives herded Rye and Bardo back inside the deserted house.

Bardo

He would never have believed it would be so simple. The normality, the reality of the place stupefied him. The gravel beneath his feet, the shadowless light of an overcast day, the plain stone walls surrounding the yard, the fresh, dry air, crisp and aromatic with distant smoke. The crossing had been as simple as walking through a door. For him, for those others, not for the girl, who hung, dead weight, against his shoulder. They ringed them round, *they*, the aliens (he used the word with deliberate, self-directed sarcasm): a circle of hostile faces, the dull glint of steel still visible in more than one fist. He backed into the corner made by two stone walls, staring back at them, silently daring them to take the girl away from him. Not from instinct, although later he would recognize how crucial it was that he not be separated from her. Crucial, at least, for him. But in this shifting crowd of hostile strangers, in the dog-pack stink of incipient violence, in the strange daylight, in the strange world, the girl was his anchor. Heavy as iron against his shoulder, hot as black iron left too long in the sun, he held her up, and she held him here. Rooted to the ground, even if the ground was strange. Beyond strange.

Another world.

Despite the danger, despite the bewilderment, despite the shock, he felt a burst of exhilaration, of relief so sweet he could taste it. Because he was here, and not there. Because he had, against all odds, escaped from Earth.

The taste was deceptively, dangerously, seductively, like freedom, even as the stone walls pressed hard against his back.

Rye

Running, running, alley walls rearing up like waves to chase her here, herd her there, hemmed in by water mercury smoke, threatened by drowning, haunted by shadows, hunted by lights, up down over *through*

to squat with the others with her back against the wall. Sunlight on a cold day, bright and thin, the color of frost. Breath smokes in the shade, feet burn on dirty stone. Smock loose over flat belly. Pull the collar up to hide the wound, huddle close, no one complains of a hot neighbor. No one complains. Hunker down, shift with the sun, pray for time not to pass. Pray for time not to pass. Pray for time.

Bite down on a scream

It tastes like blood. Tears are sweeter. Swallow them too. Keep it all inside, don't give them the satisfaction.

Fucking sadists!

Standing overhead while the iron cuffs lock like jaws, while the iron frame bites into shoulders back buttocks thighs.

This is freedom? This is your fucking idea of freedom?

No. Stop. Before the panic comes snarling out of the belly-pit and rampages free. Keep it inside.

While the experts peer down through the iron grill, the specialists in their masks and gowns, eyes earnest and alive in their hidden faces. Watching always, making their rounds, taking their notes. Taking the girl away screaming while her vast belly ruptures spewing blood pus stench don't look don't look don't look *it can't happen to me.*

Quarantined, isolate, alone, not one of the women lining the hospital walls, not one of the women with the swollen bellies and pus-streaked thighs. Not squatting against the wall, feet cold, nose running, trying to drink thick gruel from a wooden bowl, no spoons, no knives, but a woman strangled herself this morning with her smock, tied it tight around her neck and, naked, died. Unless someone did it for her. It was all anyone could do.

Oh mama, how did your daughter come to be here?

Bardo

The servant came in without knocking, set the tray on the floor, went out, bare feet whispering on the cold tiles, and shut and locked the door. The same boy as last time, stocky, sullen, smelling of sweat in his oversized shirt and rumpled pants. Bardo waited a minute before he moved. He had to quell the adrenaline that twitched in his gut when he heard the door being unlocked, and he had to subdue the rage that came after. Only the boy again. Only food.

Only Bardo to cope with the girl.

He got up from the low chair and went to fetch the tray.

The room was large for a prison cell, if that was what it was. One long wall was cut by a dozen windows, floor to ceiling, too narrow even for someone as skinny as Rye to slip through. They looked out on another wall of the same dull, ruddy stone. The floor was gray tiles; the interior walls were dark wood sanded smooth as silk; the ceiling was planks of the same wood laid over thick, cedar-red beams. The scant furniture—low bed, legless chairs, coffee table—gave the room a Japanese feel, but there was something of the southwest to it as well. On Earth, Bardo would have thought it the product of some designer, and tried to decide whether he liked it. He might have, but for the lock on the outside of the door.

On Earth.

He set the tray on the low table, then went over to where the girl lay. The water in the basin by the bed was still cold. He soaked a rag, and only then looked at her. Poor kid. The response was instinctive, and the reason why he only looked at her when he had to. She was flushed with heat, which only made the lesion scars vivid with contrast. Thin and seeming even thinner, though they had only been here two days. Only. That was a long time to be unconscious. She dreamed, Bardo thought, seeing her eyes flicker and slide behind her lids.

Poor kid.

He pulled the sheet back, wiped her down, trying to ignore the heat that radiated off her body, trying to ignore the way the water evaporated in the thin light, trying to ignore the pink tinge that darkened in the bowl as he dunked the cloth.

Trying to think, instead, of what he would say to the Nohan lordling, their captor, Tehega Cirrohn, when he came back to resume the conversation they had begun the day before.

Keep her alive, Tehega had said. If she lives . . .

Then we can deal with one another, you and I.

Rye

Running on the edge of a winter dawn, two of them, running hard. Footsteps echoing in deserted streets, muffled in the trash-padded alleyways. Two of them, running to meet the other two, neither pair knowing now which is the bait and which the ambush. Nothing new.

We are what they hunt, she says, her beautiful face shadows and ivory under the hanging lamp. The bulb is dim, secretive light. *Our advantage is that we know when they come and where they come through.*

So we can throw ourselves in their path, he says. His face is sardonic in its bones, sometimes hard to read any other way.

She smiles, an intimate look just for him. *So we can be sure we are hunted, and not some other unfortunate soul.*

And then we bag the hunter. The boy grins, bright with teeth, excitement, conspiracy. *Just tell us where to go.*

And what we do, the girl says, *what we do when we get there.*

Run hot with sweat in the gray air, take this corner, and that one, this way and that, gray air, gray walls, heart slamming fire through the veins, embers in the lungs, slipping through gray alleys, a quicksilver sea of brightshadow lines, this way, swimming alone/not alone, drawn as gently as a fish with a hook in her mouth, or her heart, or her eye, this way, stone walls melted to silk, cage bars frayed to snapped threads, gone, and the boy runs into a knife and the hot blood burns her hands, and still she runs

through winter rain on shrinking snow, river black obsidian marred by light, bridge crossing over to

Is she alive? No, dead. Tied her shift around her neck and died, unless someone helped her do it. There will be trouble because of this.

hot summer street, new pavement black and stinking with tar, leading to

You are our keys to freedom. You are the treasures of our world.

black tunnel mouth, hot subway wind, oil and meat and sex and death, and something coming to

Listen. I'll make a deal with you. Can you understand me? Please help me. Listen.

blood heat terror pain, the only entrance to

I'll make a deal.

the other side.

Bardo

"Will she live?"

"You'd know better than I would."

"I?"

"Aren't you the people who did this to her?"

"I?" The lordling's amusement was the icy surface of a deep anger. "If you know some thing is done to her, you know more than I."

"I don't understand."

"No?"

"Maybe you should explain it to me. If we're to make some kind of a deal."

"I give you life. Do I need to offer more?"

"If you want me to give you the girl."

"But I have the girl." Delicate confusion, the anger hidden again.

"Do you?"

No smile, but a mocking gesture at the walls, the curtained bed, the bodyguard at the door.

"Then why am I still alive?"

"A useful question. Can you give me an answer?"

Bardo stretched his legs out, almost lying against the cushioned back of the squat chair. He was too tall for the furniture, but if the lordling mistook it for confidence, he was welcome. Bardo needed all the advantages he could get.

"In fact it is a good question, because you know damn well I've been fighting your creatures and your soldiers for more than a year. You know because you, or some of your people, ambushed us. The boy was killed. At least one of us was taken prisoner. And even if I wasn't made then, I damn sure was when we came out of the rebel's house."

"'Made'?"

"Observed, identified, marked down as an enemy target. Yes?"

Faint smile. "Yes."

"But you took me alive when you could have killed me. You brought me here when you could have left me on Earth. And you did that, as far as I can tell, simply because R—because the girl was holding my hand. What was it? Sentiment?"

"I do not know the word." With every evidence of sincerity.

Bardo grunted, conscious of the irony, and made a deliberately rough segue. "You want to know something strange? It took me a while to notice, but not long after Marky was killed and the girl and the rebel disappeared, all the killings, the disappearances, stopped."

"Strange." The lordling's smile was back. The lordling's eyes had never been anything but watchful.

"In fact, from what I gathered, the last attack by one of your creatures happened about two days before Rye was found back on Earth." With bleeding skin and a fever no one could account for. Should he get into that now? Bardo decided not.

"Rye is the girl," the lordling said.

"Rye is the girl."

"The girl you say I do not have."

Tehega was probing, Bardo thought. Drawing Bardo out to see how much he knew, or guessed. Again, the question arose: what to hold back? Maybe nothing. Maybe the more Bardo knew, the more he would be dealt with as an equal. Or at least, as a man playing with better than a tissue-paper hand. All of this a flicker in the back of his mind. He went on without a discernible pause.

"I'm a long way from making a case, but I have these three facts. Coincidences, maybe, but I don't think so. One: Rye is taken prisoner. Rye *disappears*, like more than a dozen others that we know about. Two: Rye *reappears*, which none of the others ever has. And three: at the same time as her reappearance on Earth, all the disappearances, all the attacks by the gray beasts, stop. The rebels have gone into hiding. Your people are keeping their heads down. Nothing at all happens for more than three months." Bardo marked his pause with a thin smile. "Until you follow us to the rebel's house, and your witch does whatever she does, and here we are."

"Also disappeared."

Bardo gave a slow shake of the head. "I don't think so. *Rye got away.* She got away *changed*. And I will bet my life that it's no coincidence that when she came back to Earth, travel between Earth and this world stopped. Because it did stop, didn't it? And I think it stopped because she got away. She did something, or something happened so that she could, I'm not guessing either way, but she got away and you were stuck on Earth. Until your witch got her hands on her." He was sweating now, betting everything on the bluff, the guess: "I think you need her to travel between worlds. Whatever has changed here, you need her. Because that's where your power is. Travel between worlds."

Though Tehega was still expressionless, his sallow skin was white with tension around his mouth. "You conclude I need her. Did I pretend it was not so? You were to tell me why I need you."

Bardo, having brought the conversation to this point, could not feign relaxation anymore. He climbed to his feet, paced to the nearest window slit where he could stand with his face in shadow.

"You don't. You don't need me, as long as your witch can drag Rye around like she has no say in the matter. But I think—I think *you* are damn sure—that that won't be the case forever. Maybe not even for long. Because if not, why aren't I dead? Why isn't Rye locked away in a dungeon somewhere? What I think," forbearing to wipe his sweaty hands on his jeans, "what I think is that someday soon you are going to need her willing cooperation. And that," he had to suck in a breath, "*that* is why I'm still alive."

"So." The lordling, as if he had picked up on Bardo's need, was rubbing his palms on his knees. "So then." He smiled again, a smile tight and thin as a knife blade. "Then I suggest you keep the girl alive, if that is what you think. Keep her alive. If she lives . . . " He rose, graceful with a lifetime of sitting close to the floor, and walked to the door the bodyguard had already opened. "Then we can deal with one another, you and I."

He left, leaving Dan Bardo alone with his guilt, and the girl.

nine

What bed was she in? Which way was she lying? Where was the wall, the window, the door? *Where was she?* Not as awake as she thought, Rye was slow to open her eyes, and slow to make sense of what she saw. Pale gray rectangles bent and slanted above her, painted on black. Shining through black? Floating? Sinking? Although the bed must be beneath her, she had no true grasp on vertical or horizontal; depth and distance escaped her; it was all planes and angles of black and gray. Still too logy with sleep to panic, she blinked, trying to force her eyes to focus, trying to guess . . .

Streetlight through windows?

Moonlight on curtains?

The world shifted, or she finally woke up, and she saw the wall of narrow windows, the gauzy curtains around the bed, the shadowy boundaries of the long, low-ceilinged room. Rye still did not know where she was, but the fact of *room* was reassuring. She became aware of thirst and a full bladder, of a heavy sheet against tender bare skin, of a warm, breathing weight pressing down the mattress beside her. Bardo, she knew without either logic or surprise, and by some emotional alchemy, the knowledge she was not alone transmuted into such a childish, unreasoning loneliness that she eased herself closer to his warmth, his solidity, his human smell. A secret comfort was all she wanted, but her fingers brushed his arm, and he woke, saying loudly, "What?"

"All you all right?"

"Sure."

"Don't give me 'sure'. Do you know how long you've been under?"

"Under what?"

"Unconscious. Catatonic. Jesus Christ."

"Sorry."

"Are you *laughing*?"

"No."

" . . . Damn it. Rye—"

"I'm okay."

"Rye."

"I'm okay. I have to pee."

"Yeah. Right. Of course you do. Can you walk?"

"Yes."

"Come on, the toilet's just at the other end. Here. God forbid they should give us any lights."

"It's okay. I can see."

"If you can call it a toilet, it's more like a closet with—Ouch! God *damn* this *fuck*ing *furniture*!"

"Dan. Please let go. I can see fine."

"Sure you can."

"I *can*."

"Fine. Let me know if you need any help."

"I will."

"Fine."

Someone came in with a tray—an orderly, was how she thought of him—he even stared at her the way some of the orderlies had. Rye, sitting on the bed with the sheet wound around her like a shroud, stared back, sullen at this invasion, until Bardo took the tray and maneuvered the young man out the door. Rye heard the slick thump of a bolt sliding home on the other side, and felt the old hospital panic that had nothing to do with fear and everything to do with confinement quiver beneath her skin. She looked at Bardo, resentful of his calm, and realized he was nearly as tense as she.

He set the tray on the mattress and sat down with her, making dishes slide and clunk together. A covered bowl, a covered plate, a jug and cups, red earthenware with a dull green glaze.

"It's edible." Bardo lifted the covers, set them on the floor. The bowl held something cooked in sauce over some kind of grain, the plate was unmistakably flatbread. The food smelled hot and better than edible.

Rye swallowed and said, "I'm not hungry."

"You have to do it Indian-style." Bardo tore a flatbread and held out one half. "We aren't trusted with silverware."

salty gruel from a wooden bowl

Rye pressed the back of a hand to her mouth. The other hand she put behind her, as if the bread might end up in it by accident. "I'm not hungry."

"Don't be an ass. You haven't eaten for three days. Here." He pushed the bread at her.

"No!"

"What the hell is the matter with you?"

That might have been funny, and the sound she made might have been a laugh.

Bardo hung his head a moment, and then slowly laid the two pieces of bread back on the plate. Then he set the tray on the floor and shifted over until he could put an arm around her shoulder. He was so large that, although she had never thought of herself as small, he could tuck her like a chick against his side.

"You can't starve yourself."

Rye was ravished by his warmth, the friendly touch. "I'm not. I just . . . "

"Don't want to eat."

"Don't want to bleed."

She felt his stillness, and a moment later, when he bent to lay his cheek against her hair, she thought she felt the thoughts turning over in his head: this, then this, or maybe that. Though what those thoughts were, she couldn't guess.

After a bit, he said, "That doesn't happen every time you eat."

"No, but . . . "

"But?"

"It keeps changing."

"It."

"The fever. The . . . Me."

He held her a while, his hand rubbing absently up and down her arm. At first she only felt the warmth, but gradually, like a static charge being rubbed up on a piece of silk, copper roses began to bloom among the thorny lesion scars. She shifted within his grasp and he let her go, leaving her relieved and bereft.

"Try a little," he said, retrieving the tray. "You shouldn't have much after a fast anyway. Just try a few bites and see how that goes."

She sighed, and took a piece of bread from the plate. "You have no idea what it's like," she said, more sad than acrimonious.

"No. But I know starvation will kill you, and the bleeding didn't."

"You want to be cleaning up after me the rest of my life?"

"We'll hire a maid."

Rye smiled a very small smile, and ate a bite of bread.

No one came for the tray. Bardo paced, his long legs making the room seem smaller than it was. It was like being shut up with an electrical storm. Rye sat on the side of the bed by the windows, her own self-restraint eroded by Bardo's restlessness. She stared out at gray gravel, ruddy wall, white hem of sky. Nothing to distract her while Bardo tried to explain their situation, and nothing to engage her. As long as she kept her back turned, Bardo could be talking about someone else.

"But if I'm not their escaped experiment, then whose am I? Cleände's people?"

"No."

"So these are Cleände's—"

"*No.*"

"So—"

"Don't you know anything about politics? You're someone's . . . " an uneasy pause which produced nothing better than: " . . . project. Someone on this world. Someone among Cleände's enemies. You escape. Someone *else* from this world finds you, and now *he* wants to use you—"

"Tehega."

"Yes. Tehega. *Tehega* wants to use you to do whatever those other people wanted you for."

"But how do you know?"

"Rye. Concentrate. This is important. Are you listening?"

She took her eyes off the window long enough to glare.

"Thank you." The sarcasm did not lessen his intensity. "Will you just get it through your skull that this is a whole world? There are groups. There are factions. There are probably fucking nations. Somebody here is performing experiments on prisoners. This is very bad. I'm sorry it happened to you. Somebody else—Tehega—who is *not* experimenting with prisoners, wants to gain an advantage over the people who are. He wants to use you to gain that advantage."

"How?"

"I don't fucking know!" Bardo thrust both hands through his hair, as though he could physically contain his frustration. After a couple of audible breaths, he pushed his hands into the pockets of his jeans and said, "I don't know what he wants. I don't know what he thinks you can do. I just know that we wouldn't be here if he didn't want it, or need it, pretty badly. I also know . . . Rye, will you please look at me? This is important."

As if she needed to be told. She looked at him, a sarcastic twist to her own mouth.

"Thank you," he said again, but this time quite soberly. "I also know that if Tehega ever thinks you can't—or won't—do whatever it is, we will have a fart in a wind-storm's chance of making it out of here alive."

"But I can't! I don't even know!"

"I know." He looked at her, his dark face somber, his black eyes unusually kind. "I know. But consider this: if Tehega thinks you can't, or won't, perform, then the only value you have for him is whatever they'll pay him to get you back."

"They." Rye could not be as matter-of-fact as Bardo. Not in the face of his compassion. She turned back to the window, blind. "The experimenters."

She was not so blind that she did not hear the irony in Bardo's voice when he said, "The bad guys."

ten

Bardo paced. Rye tried to find a better way of turning a sheet into clothing.

"Why did you let them take my clothes?" she demanded, and did not know whether to be aggrieved or relieved when he shrugged, as if he had never noticed her nudity until now. But he gave her his blazer, which she was wearing over an inexpert sari when the bolt rasped and the door swung open.

Faces woke Rye's sluggish memory: the rain, the porch, the knife at her throat. Her fingers found a thin line of scab, and she realized for the first time that she did not know what had happened afterwards. After the porch, before the . . . the dreams.

She recognized the spokesman, though his blond hair was smoothly trimmed, his bony face arrogant and unrevealing above the collar of a long, narrow brown coat. Tehega, she supposed. There were others filing into the room, men and women similarly dressed. Their faces bore the inevitable differences of personality, genes, and age, but the stamp of racial identity seemed stronger, creating the illusion that they all looked alike: blunt, exaggerated bones, tawny-sallow skin, fine, limp, light-colored hair. Or maybe the illusion of sameness was founded in the way they all stared at Rye. She stared back at them until the alike/not alike faces began to look like latex masks (*aliens!* her own voice said in sarcastic wonder) and she looked at Bardo, who stood, arms folded, before one of the windows. She could not read his expression against the light, but his gaze was fixed on Tehega. A mutual gaze, she discovered, turning that way herself, but Tehega quickly looked at her.

"So." His accent was strong, but his words were fluent enough. "You live."

She felt no compulsion to answer the obvious.

"It seemed the passage might kill you."

"Why should it?"

"I am pleased that it did not."

"Why should it have?"

Tehega turned his head a little, as if he wanted to see her from another angle. "A useful question. I cannot answer it. Do you know what was done to you?"

"No." Her voice shaken by her heartbeat. "Do you?"

"Perhaps we discover this together."

Rye knew damn well he could have told her more. She glared. Tehega smiled thinly, a kind of acknowledgement, then turned his head and spoke to the staring frieze behind him. A woman detached herself, the blond woman, familiar as a dream.

"Amaran will search . . . ah . . . will investigate. Yes?"

"No."

Bardo said it, not Rye.

"Yes?" Tehega repeated, an edge to his voice.

"No. Someone else. Not her."

The woman, Amaran, enough like Tehega to be an older sister and not angelic at all, flicked a glance at Bardo. "I am all," she said. "I am the one."

"Amaran-tahi," Tehega said, "is the one of us has the knowledge. She will search the answers. Amaran and" as if he tasted the name "Rye. Yes?"

Bardo, balked as easily as Rye had been, said nothing. Tehega turned back to Rye.

"Yes?"

She looked at the woman who looked back at her. *Just a specialist,* Rye told herself. *Just like one of the doctors at the hospital, except she probably knows more of what I need to know.* It didn't seem to help. Rye dragged her gaze back to Tehega, worked her tongue in a mouth gone dry, and said yes.

"I start with blood," she said: Amaran, the fever's angel, the woman Bardo called Tehega's witch.

Rye, standing just inside the door of Amaran's room in her latest outfit of borrowed clothes, let a small silence bloom before she said, "Hi, my name's Ryder Coleman, great to meet you, nice weather we're having, how 'bout them Yankees."

Amaran looked just as disconcerted as Rye could have hoped. Rye took her first deep breath in hours and decided that Bardo was good for her.

Amaran, her hands clasped tightly before the buttons of her frock coat, looked from the floor to Rye's face to the door. "Yes," she said. "I am tahinit for the house. Amaran-tahi." She bowed, a stiff little bob of the head. "We have tea for begin."

Tea first, Rye thought. *Then* the blood. She swallowed a nervous snicker as she followed Amaran's gesture into the room.

Bare tile and bare wood, a workspace with cupboards and tables and chairs, a pair of the low couches Bardo loathed. Narrow windows looked out on the wooden posts of a cloister, with an atrium beyond: a tile floor, plants in pots, a geometrical pond. Wood, tile, and stone were all dark, the pond reflected the overcast sky, and by contrast the foliage of the plants was an intense hallucinatory green. Rye, sitting with a cup of musty tea in her hands, found the garden attractively secretive and gloomy. Maybe it was only that she would rather have been out there. She drank her tea and gazed out the window rather than meet Amaran-tahi's staring eyes.

When the cup was empty, she set it on the floor, for lack of a table, and looked at Amaran. Her mouth was dry again despite the tea. "Why were you following me?"

"We are look for Tahid."

"Who?"

Amaran did not answer. She fidgeted with the cup between her hands.

"Who?"

"You," Amaran said. "You are at Meheg-menoht?"

"I don't know. You mean that's where we are now?"

Amaran's mouth tightened. Irritation? Frustration? "You was. Were."

"You were. I was."

"Yes?"

"I don't know."

"You were."

"If you say so."

Amaran made a soft sound, a puff of air between her lips, a gesture that lifted a shoulder and shook her head. Just a little expression of frustration with the language, nothing friendly about it, but it was human, and Rye's tension eased by a fraction.

She found herself confessing, "I don't know where I was. I don't know what happened, what was done to me. I don't know what is—" *still happening.* But she thought, be a little sensible, Rye, and cut it off. "You must know more than me."

Amaran frowned at her. "I know the tahirr. I do not know—" The witch cut herself off as Rye had done. But then she continued thoughtfully, "I do not know what you are. You are not within the tahirr. Are you?"

Her tone was almost wistful. Rye shrugged.

"I don't know. What's the tahirr?"

"Tahirr is . . . " Amaran used her hands to define a vague space between them. "Tahirr is the house of power. Is the house we live in. The house made of our blood."

The word *blood* roused a queasy shift under Rye's skin. She said, "Do you bleed?" and heard an echo of Amaran's tone.

Amaran ignored the question. "We are of the house, within the house. You are outside, but you . . . you have . . . " She trailed off, frustrated by the lack of words perhaps. Her expression was strange. "I show. I show you the walls. You show me the door."

Rye did not like the sound of this. Show what? She was here to be shown, not to show. Amaran put her hands out, a bent-wristed gesture that showed her palms, and closed her eyes. Witch Summons Her Spirits, Rye thought in Bardo's tone, but what the gesture summoned was cold sweat and nausea and the sparkling black coil of the fever waking under her skin.

"No," Rye said, for no good reason.

"Do you see?" Amaran murmured, her eyes still closed. "The walls of the house of Nohai."

Mercury threads welled like poison from the joins of walls and floor, a tracery poorly aligned, as if there were indeed another house here, superimposed upon the real one. Lightning sparks bit, marked the lines of a cage's bars—*bars drawing closer, closer, electric cold biting the shadow heat—*

Rye bent over her folded arms, sick with a sudden aversion. Never mind what Bardo said, never mind what she herself wanted, needed, to know. She did not want to be here. Even her borrowed clothes, soft and loose as they were, had become a suffocating confinement. Dark fever-stars, denied release through her skin, rose and burst in her eyes, blinding migraine aura that threatened to take on shape, movement, touch. The shape of prison bars. The shape of a woman. Woman standing, woman kneeling. Touch of cloth on cheek and brow, cool as water, rough as stone.

The witch stands at a table across the room. What is that, a microscope? Rye presses her sleeve against her eyes, looks down to see raspberry cloth marked in a bramble pattern. Bleeding again. Time to go. She stands, gravity side-slips, water under ice, floor wall ceiling door, don't fall through. Floor wall ceiling. Door.

Hand on her arm. Even through the sleeve it's fear roiling gut seething need fear possession control and hot grit of embers between the teeth

cool outside (walls shining clear as water) outside the shirt (scar-feathers ruffled) cool breath (hot as fear) one touch (spear to the heart) outside

electric singing buried deep (blue river thin as thread) web of stone (dancing, dancing) spider shadows (dancing, dancing) welcome lover (hunting flies) dancing, dancing

eleven

"How's it going?"

Rye was startled by Bardo's voice, startled again when he sat down beside her on the atrium floor and put his arm around her shoulders. She shrugged under the weight of his embrace, but didn't shrug it off. She kept her eyes on the surface of the pond.

"I've been better."

"You've looked better." He tugged a short strand of her hair, brought his fingers away dusted with dried blood. "Bad?"

"The bleeding? No." But she shuddered, which of course he felt. He touched his fingers to her cheek.

"Fever's up."

"Yep." She shivered again, oppressed by the Bardo-ness of the touch. This time she moved out of his reach, pulled her knees up under her chin. "Sorry."

He let her go. The little pond had little fish in it. They floated up to nose the surface, making little rings. The windows, shadowed by the cloister, were blank and black as Bardo's eyes.

"I take it you and the witch didn't hit it off."

Rye made a sound in her throat. "If she ever offers you a cup of tea, just say no."

"Gotcha." Bardo lifted a knee to prop his elbow on, ran his hand through his hair. "Damn, Rye. What can I say?"

"Not your fault."

"Hell, I feel so much better."

"It wasn't so bad. It's just, you know, doctors. They poke and they prod and they don't tell you a damn thing."

No platitudes from Bardo. A virtue on his part? Rye couldn't decide. His silence made her look at him. He was frowning at the fish, the grim lines of his face a match for their gloomy surroundings. So Rye thought, and then realized that he was also wearing borrowed clothes, a long soft shirt and pants like hers, only brown and black instead of raspberry and brown. His T-shirt and jeans had been overdue for a change, but she didn't like the Nohan clothes on him. Didn't like the way they made him fit in.

He looked up and caught her staring. "Maybe next time you shouldn't drink the tea."

"Gee," she said, "d'ya think?"

His grin astonished her, his teeth whiter than the sky. She had to smile back.

"Come on." He got to his feet, offered her a hand.

She let him pull her up, but slipped her hand out of his grasp as quickly as she could. "Come where?"

"I'm going to find Tehega and tell him to rein in his witch, or the deal's off."

"Sure. And while we're at it we can tell him to tell her to send us back to Earth."

He just looked at her, and then turned his back and walked away, leaving her to trail along behind him.

Sometimes she did not understand Dan Bardo at all.

They found Tehega at his prayers.

The room was full of lights. Dim, soft lights, but there were dozens, thin lines recessed into the ceiling, tiny lamps set in niches and on shelves, more scattered on the shallow steps that footed the walls. The room was many-sided, giving an effect of almost-round, but the angles were distinct, a folded hemisphere, for the ceiling lifted into a wooden dome. Every surface was polished wood, there were colored ropes strung across the ceiling and hanging down the walls, thick as silken bell-ropes, and small, rich carpets like prayer-rugs on the floor.

Or rather, not *like* prayer rugs, for there was Tehega, kneeling on one with his ankles crossed and his back beautifully erect, looking harassed even before he noticed Bardo and Rye. Amaran, there before them, was hunkered down on one knee to speak with her lord. She looked up as Tehega did, her face stiffening into defensive lines.

"So." Tehega drummed his fingers on his thigh.

"We seem to have a slight problem," Bardo said in his deep voice. "I suppose you've heard."

Tehega made a noise in his throat, a genteel grunt. He had to tip his head back to meet Bardo's gaze, and after another moment lifted his fingers in a minimal gesture at the rug-strewn floor. Rye waited until Bardo had sat, folding his long limbs, before she picked a rug at his side.

Blue and rose and gold. The nap was dense and smooth, like silk blended with wool, and the stylized floral pattern so familiar Rye felt a knot form in her gut. The rug could have come from Earth: Morocco, Turkey, somewhere. Maybe it had. She didn't know why the thought should disturb her, but it did.

Amaran said something testy to Tehega in their language.

Tehega's mouth quirked. "She says she is tahinit. Even if Rye is not, Amaran-tahi has only a tahinit way to learn what Rye is."

"And the tahinit way is to use drugs and intimidation," Bardo said.

Tehega's expression did not change. "Yes, that is the tahinit way."

Amaran made a noise, a stifled protest.

Tehega sighed. "We all need to learn, yes? We all need to know what Rye-tahi is."

"*Not* tahi," Amaran said. "Not tahinit, not within the tahirr."

Tehega drummed his fingers again on his thigh, and then stilled his hands, smiling as if a decision had been made. "I cannot tell you," he said softly, "how this word makes me glad."

Amaran stared at him as if he had lost his mind, then surged to her feet. She strode away until she was brought up by a light-strewn step. She stood with her back to them, her arms folded, apparently staring at the wall.

"Go on." Bardo's voice startled Rye. She could imagine him using that confiding tone to put suspects at their ease, and did not much like the picture that made.

"Long before," Tehega, like a storyteller, began, "this place was the heart of my house. Long and long before. It is here all Tehega peoples met, it is here the songs are made and the stories, it is here the human stands to touch upon God. Long before, every house has this place, and they are all one place, for the people to touch upon God. You have this, places like this, on your Earth."

"Sure," Bardo said agreeably.

"Long before, the light was given person to person—"

"Shared," Bardo offered.

"—shared," Tehega went on with a nod, "from the ones like Amaran-tahi to all of us else, light like a gift of family, a gift of God. Rye knows this light, I think?" Tehega glanced at Amaran's back, but Amaran was resolute in her study of the wall. Tehega sighed. "This all long before the light became power. Now the ones with power say, there is only one place, Meheg-menoht, the heart of the world. One place to touch on God, one people to touch, the tahinit, who do not give, who do not share."

Amaran, stung by this, snapped something at him over her shoulder. Tehega's mouth tightened on the pretext of a smile.

"Amaran-tahi says, the tahinit gather at Meheg-menoht to share power, to build the tahirr . . . as if this is a good thing."

Amaran turned fully around, her arms folded, her expression cynical. "You do not be glad to have a door to Scalléa, a door to Earth? You do not think Andit Teheg is more than it was in your long before?"

"And how much more if the tahirr did not wall us around?"

Amaran spread her arms in a graceful gesture. "Am I not here, Tehega-rohn?"

They locked gazes for a moment of complicated silence. Tehega lowered his eyes in a minimal nod.

"So," Bardo said, still agreeable, "what you're saying is that the power that used to be scattered throughout this world was concentrated in one place—"

"Meheg-menoht," Rye murmured, "the heart of the world."

"—and used to open the gate between worlds." Bardo gave Rye a distracted glance. "And you've profited from the gate, but you don't like the tahirr."

"When the power is shared," Tehega said, serene as a priest, "the people rule. Now, within the tahirr, only the tahinit rule. And they are not kind," he added with a level glance at Rye.

Meheg-menoht, she thought with the fever beating like another heart inside her. She dreaded the sound of the words. She was fascinated by that dread. The heart of the world.

"So what did they want with Rye?" Bardo said.

"Do I know?" Tehega turned his look of false innocence on Amaran.

"Do I know?" she echoed pointedly back. "I am as far from the heart as you, rohn."

"As far as that?"

Amaran turned to pace the angles of the wall.

Tehega, his eyes touching on his witch's restless form, said, "I can tell you a guess."

"Tell away," Bardo said.

"The tahinit say they are closer to God than we else. They say it is certain, for do they not open the gate between worlds? But they are not perfect all the same. They work hard to open even to Scalléa, our neighbor, and it is long years before they open to Earth. Do they seek to be perfect? Do they wish to perfect God's will, and open to all the worlds?"

"Then why don't they do it?" Rye blurted. "Why don't they do it to themselves instead of doing it to me and—"

Swollen bellies and pus-streaked thighs.

"Ah." Tehega smiled, a complicated expression Rye could not decode. "Are they afraid? Do they act God's will, or act against it? This is great courage, and great risk. Yes?"

"Courage," Rye echoed, breathless.

Bardo put his hand on her arm. Comfort? Restraint? The fever roused and bit at his palm. Rye moved out from under his touch. Tehega watched with naked interest.

"You suffer," he said softly. "I see this, if Amaran-tahi does not. But I see also what she does see, which is power. Power outside the tahirr. Power that escaped those walls. What did you take away from the heart of the world? Does that heart beat in you now? Does God's will beat in you?"

Rye stared at him, her heart—*her* heart—beating quick and hard. "Bullshit," she said.

Tehega looked at Bardo. "This word?"

Bardo waved it aside. "Let's get back to the point. Metaphysics aside, what do you want Rye to do?"

Tehega, his face settling into a mask, his eyes dark with his thoughts, looked at Bardo—looked at Amaran, who had gone quite still—looked, finally, at Rye.

"It is not clear?" he said to her. "I want Rye to make me free of the tahirr."

Amaran started as if she had taken a spur to her flank. She gave Tehega a look of outrage and disgust, and strode furiously from the room.

"It is not," Tehega told them, "that she does not agree. It is only that she thinks I am not wise to tell you. It is," he added gently, "the question of trust."

twelve

"What complete and utter bullshit!"

"Fine. Let's talk about this somewhere a little more private, shall we?"

Rye glanced down the long corridor. No one in sight, but she respected Bardo's paranoia: he had pointed out to her all the ways they were watched and unobtrusively contained. So she followed him, the fever chiming like chromium bells under her skin, to a door that opened onto the gravel path outside their room. The path led to a garden, but Rye stopped as soon as they were under the sky. Bardo closed the door and walked around her, gravel crunching under his feet, to prop himself against the redstone wall.

"You can't seriously believe any of that crap," she said, as if they had been arguing all the way here. "'God's will.' Jesus Christ!"

Bardo put his hands in his pockets. "You never know what's been lost in translation."

"Come *on*!" Intended as scorn, it came out like a cry of pain. Rye folded her arms around herself and tipped her head back toward the sky. There was a sun up there behind the cloud. Its light sang against her face.

"What exactly do you not believe?" Bardo said in a patient voice.

"All of it?" she suggested to the sky.

"I grant you, he may have left out a few things."

"Gee," she said, "really? Like what?"

"Like how the witch needed you to do her thing when they brought us across. At least, that was my impression."

Rye's head snapped down. The fever sketched him as an ember skeleton clothed in folds of ash. She blinked him into reality. "You got that impression."

"That was the impression that I got."

She shook her head, swallowed, looked away. It was just one more thing to be confused about, confused being a better word than afraid.

"Rye, forget the God stuff. That's just a language issue. Think about what the man actually said. His whole society revolves around the ability to cross between worlds. You might have the power to do that better and farther than anyone else in three worlds."

Rye stared at Bardo. "He said that?"

"Come on, kid, use your brain. I grant you, the whole freedom-for-the-people crap probably is just a line he's trying to feed us, get us on his side, distract us from the rest. But what did he say about what the tahinit were trying to do with you? It's about *power.* And what power do these people care about—what power is this whole society built on—besides the power to travel between worlds?"

Rye loosened her self-embrace enough to lean back against the doorjamb. "Okay. So what am I supposed to do? Overthrow the government? Open the way for him to conquer whole new worlds?"

Bardo shrugged. "Ultimately, if you're as powerful as he seems to think, I doubt it matters what he wants."

"Have you noticed where we are? *I* don't know how to get home. I'd say it matters a fuck of a lot what he wants."

"Until you *learn*—" Bardo broke off to master his frustration. "Look, Rye, take what the man is offering. Learn what they can teach you. Where are you going to go for a better deal? The folks who did this to you?"

Rye flinched, tucked her arms around herself again. "You really think Amaran is going to teach me how to walk out of here. Out of their control."

"I think Tehega is willing to take a gamble on your friendship."

"Friendship."

"If you are what he seems to think, he can hardly make an enemy out of you, can he?"

"He could cut my throat."

"So maybe he's too nice."

She laughed, humorless and short. "You don't really believe I am what he thinks I am, do you?"

"The way I see it," Bardo said, sounding almost lazy, "the man is gambling for high stakes. What did he say? He is far from the heart of the world? But as long as he's got you, he is *at* the heart. He's at the fucking center of power."

"But I'm not—"

Bardo still ignored her. "It's worth the risk."

"*What* risk?"

"Of being caught by the people who made you, and then lost you." Bardo smiled a thin, black-eyed smile. "Of not having you on his side when they find out what he's done, and what he wants to do."

"Dan." She stared at him.

"And before you get all scornful about the notion of friendship with the man, maybe you should consider the value of having an ally of your own when those people find out that you're here."

Hospital. Her eyes are gummed with blood. There are people here, she is watched and she cannot see. Illness shackles her, or she is tied to the bed. The mattress is obscenely soft, forever yielding as she flounders like a beetle turned on its back. She is drowning in weakness when, sudden and strong, there is a touch at the base of her neck, a cold lick of alcohol and the punch of a needle through skin and muscle and arterial wall.

Rye.

And then someone has sorted out the yielding chaos of the bed, pulling sheets taut (shackles gone) which is such a relief that she stretches pleasurable as a cat though she can feel the scabs catch on the sheets (not alone) who is this? someone with a hand on her ribs, big and hot, breath on her ear (arousing, shameful) she's still sticky with sweat and ugly with scabs, her mouth gummed with something venomous, her breath like a subway wind (piss and death and hot oil) she turns her head away and sees a shadow on the wall cast by bright daylight, a tiger's shadow (are tigers that shape?) she feels claws clasp her ribcage (still aroused) a mouth open on the base of her throat

Ryder. Rye.

and she yields to it (sex on her belly) hot and smooth as a piston shaft (mouth on her throat) and the bite (sting) penetration—

"Ryder!"

"Get off me! Get off!"

"I'm not—!"

Thump.

"Jesus, kid. You okay?"

On the floor. Tile cold through the shroud of torn bed-curtains. Light showed in the windows, thin and gray as dawn, and Bardo was propped on one elbow staring over the edge of the bed.

"Bad dream?"

Rye got herself sorted, at least enough to prop her head on her knees. Adrenaline made a jangled mess of her nerves, her heartbeat, her memory. The nightmare fell into pieces, a few sense-memories that lingered all too vividly. She worked a hand inside her shirt, ran a thumb along the hollow of her collarbone until she felt the hidden artery's hammer-pulse.

Bardo sighed. She heard him tug the sheets into order and lie down. "Should have asked for separate rooms."

"Sorry."

He grunted.

Rye pulled on the mattress until she was kneeling. "You aren't—Are you going to?"

"What?"

"Ask for separate rooms."

Bardo lay with his hands behind his head. He opened his eyes and slanted a look at her down his nose. "You don't want a little privacy?"

"Yes," she said with a tension in her gut that was already old. "But I don't really want to be alone."

He closed his eyes again. "Okay."

"Sorry if I woke you up," she offered, her voice gentle with relief.

"Uh-huh."

The light was stronger now, casting him in tan and ivory instead of shades of gray.

"Are you going back to sleep?"

"Mm-hmm."

The tiles hurt her knees. She stood up, feeling the new bruise on her hip, and walked to the window at the foot of the bed. She undid a button on the shirt and pulled the collar down, but even by giving herself a crick in the neck, she couldn't see the base of her own throat.

"Dan."

He sighed—or anyway, exhaled a little more loudly.

Rye crawled up the bed until she was kneeling at his side. "Dan, do I have a scar or something here?"

"Do you *what*?" His voice cracked. He hauled himself up on his elbows.

"Forget it." She scrambled off the bed in a wounded retreat.

"Rye—"

"Forget it!"

With a growl of extreme annoyance, he dropped back onto his back. "What part of 'sleep' do you not understand?"

Rye crossed to the short couch, sat down, pulled her shirt tail over her knees. "I've got the going-to-sleep part, it's just the staying-asleep part . . . "

Bardo snorted, and sighed, and hauled himself upright. "Give me a minute," he said, and he went into the toilet-closet, scratching the hair on his chest.

Either a piss improved his mood or he had resolved to be nice about it. When he came out again he sat down beside her and said, in a friendly tone, for Bardo: "Okay, what am I supposed to be looking at?"

She undid another button and pulled the collar wide. "Here."

He took her shoulders and turned her into the light. "Nothing personal, kid, but you've got a million scars. What exactly am I looking for?"

"I don't know. A bite mark?"

Rye had her head tipped back and her eyes on the ceiling, but she felt him rear back and give her look.

"Well, gosh, Rye," he said, "if I'd known ve vere playing vampires I vould haff brought my bat."

"It's not funny!"

"Okay, sorry, fine."

"Just, will you look?"

"I'm looking."

He was. She could feel his breath on her skin, the warmth of his large hands. He touched a finger to the base of her throat and rose-colored streamers flashed up her nerves, the scent of clean straw blossomed in her skull, a kitten rolled over behind her heart and clasped her spine in its needle-fine claws.

"Ouch," she said, for lack of a better word.

"Sorry." He took his finger away. "Doesn't look like a bite mark, though."

"What, then?"

He let her go and propped himself against the back of the couch so he could see her face. "Some kind of puncture wound, maybe."

Rye did up her shirt, still tasting the summer grass smell. "A needle."

"Too big. I'd almost say a twenty-two."

"A twenty-two? You mean a gun."

"Yes, Rye. I mean a gun."

"No." She shook her head, rubbed the cloth over the scar.

"Well, it's not a bite mark."

"Maybe I was stung?"

"That's one hell of a big wasp." He studied her, scratching his incipient beard. "Maybe it was just one hell of a big needle. You think that was how they did whatever they did to you?"

"I don't know." But then a shudder overtook her, a convulsive shiver arising from the same dark place inside her that said, *no, whatever they did to you was alive.*

thirteen

"What do you do when I'm with Amaran?"

"You just do the witch stuff. Leave the rest to me."

Witch stuff.

"If I'm supposed to be your way to get out of the tahirr, then why do you keep trying to get me in it?"

Amaran, when asked this reasonable question, threw her notebook on the floor. Pages burst from the binding and scattered hissing across the tiles.

Rye had already offended Amaran by refusing a cup of tea. Now she sat, heart in her throat, while the other woman stormed off, skidding a little on a loose page, and disappeared around the corner of the L-shaped room.

After a bit, Rye put her elbows on her knees and leaned her chin in her hands. The atrium, murky as a dirty aquarium beneath the perennial overcast, held her fascination. Like the whole house it was somewhat strange, but not quite otherworldly. Whatever otherworldly was supposed to be like. Shouldn't there be some atavistic response to leaving Earth? Some primitive instinct that rebelled, some profound dislocation at being Away From Home?

Rye decided that she would have to ask Bardo. She herself suffered some profound dislocation almost every time she woke up.

Amaran came back looking almost constipated with restraint, and spoke as if she despised the words coming out of her own mouth.

"I do not teach you tahirr. I am not free to teach you tahirr. I am not free. *You* are outside. What you are, you teach to me."

Rye cupped her palms over her knees, imposing her own self-restraint. "But I don't know what I am."

"I *learn*," Amaran said. And then, as if it cost her more than she could afford, "We learn."

Rye looked at the backs of her hands. The scars caught the bad light with a metallic sheen, white-silver-black. She started to pull the cuffs of her shirt down to hide them, folded her arms across her chest instead.

"That's not good enough. You know—"

Amaran made a violent gesture and turned away. Rye continued doggedly.

"You know why Tehega kidnapped us. You know what he wants me to do. You know where I was taken before, you know what your people did to me, and I am not going to let you do a goddamn thing to me until you tell me what you know!"

Amaran said nothing, made no move.

Rye stood up, feeling a prickle of horror/guilt/fear. She hadn't meant to shout. Hadn't meant to lay down an ultimatum. Had *not* meant to make their situation any more precarious than it already was. Dear lord, what would Bardo say?

"Look," she said, and then stopped. Because she'd be damned if she would take any of it back. "Look. I admit my ignorance. I admit that I need your—someone's—help. Christ, it's why we ever went to that house to begin with! But if all you want is an experiment, I *did* that, I *escaped*, and I'm *not* going to volunteer for another one. So if Tehega wants me for more than just to exercise his curiosity, then he—or you—*one* of you has to offer me a d-deal . . . off-offer me . . ." She lost track of what she was saying, raised a hand to wipe sweat off her upper lip.

Amaran, still without turning around, said, "I. Am. Not. Free."

"Well, what the hell am I?" Rye yelled.

"Free!"

Silence settled. Emotion had prodded the fever awake. Rye felt the subtle threat of unreality under her feet, the sense that when she blinked, she saw the room with a different vision. She took in a few slow breaths, trying for calm.

And then was knocked off balance when Amaran said, "Do you want to be join in the tahirr?"

Rye stared at the other woman's back, losing her grasp on the conversation, losing her grasp on her physical state. "What?" she said. Feeling as if the walls had gone to mist around her. Feeling as if other walls, bitter-iron lightning walls, were approaching through the fog. "What?"

Amaran repeated, "Do you want to be one of us? *One* of us? Two of us? How many are you?"

"What?" Feeling the floor and ceiling gone to smoke, iron pain biting close.

"Or is this some other thing *I* am telling to *you*?"

Rye said to Bardo later, "I think I'm allergic to her," meaning the way Amaran seemed to provoke the fever. But Bardo had gone silent and grim at Rye's report of the last session, and he didn't respond.

It was hard, lying beside Bardo in the dark, to equate the fever with power. The fever was something that happened to her, something that inhabited her, not something she did. It was not in her control. It was a disease. At best, it was . . .

. . . a cause. She had known she was changing from that moment in the boarding house when she closed her eyes and saw.

(Slipping through her, shadow under skin, pacing the maze of her veins.)

Logic said: the fever was the means, the power was the end.

(Slip sideways, hot summer day, Rye's fever finding Bardo's apartment where Rye had never been.)

Instinct said: the fever *was.* Power and means, cause and end. She carried it or—and—it carried her.

(Riding the tiger, don't fall off, fangs in your throat.)

And what about that? Puncture wound, one scar lost among a hundred. She touched a hand to the base of her throat, found her pulse, felt an echo of the synesthetic shock (neon on water, oily silk, smell of fish) nothing like as strong as when Bardo had touched her there. Bardo breathing all but silent beside her, neither of them short enough to sleep on the couch, and was he really sleeping?

(Tiger behind bars, turn and pace, fluid and black as coals.)

Her fingers pressed down, constricting the artery (faint dizzy swell) triggering (slow-motion fireworks dark chocolate sand-paper grit). Bardo sighed. Rye lifted her hand, laid it carefully on the sheet beside her, obscurely ashamed.

"Dan?" she whispered. He didn't respond.

Power, she thought. Did she believe in power? She believed in the fever. And the fever found Bardo. She wanted to find Bardo, and the fever did. So?

"I want to go home."

(Girl knocks her ruby heels together. Tiger lifts its head.)

The fever was not an elusive thing. It was huge, crowding her body even when it slept, snarling her senses the way a kitten snarls a ball of yarn. (Gutting her memory the way a cat guts its prey.) She could feel it now, prowling through her, slipping color (redstone brown) into her sweating hands, sound (gravel crunch) across her tongue.

Home, she whispered, or thought, and saw, or dreamt

nighttime alley (flooded with stars) paved with ice (walled in fog) warm as (mercury) blood

Tehega at a window, late, chin on his fist, staring at nothing, staring at the dark, teeth in his lip, lip ragged with blood.

warm oil maze (slip over ice) slide through the walls (quicksilver rat) tiger at play

Amaran alone in the bent-corner room, books all around her, staring at wall, lips moving in thought, lips moving in prayer.

How many are you? (and the answer comes) *two.*

Dan? Rye whispers. Dan?

But she's asleep, and he does not respond.

Another session. Jittery with reluctance and nerves, Rye took herself to Amaran's room and found Amaran waiting for her with white showing around her brown irises and her skin stretched to ivory over the prominent bones. She did not look angry. She looked terrified.

Rye froze with her hand on the door latch, caught in an eye-blink of disorientation, and turned her head for a quick, instinctive glance into the hall. Nothing there. Of course there was nothing there, but fear is contagious and Rye had not been sanguine to begin with. She eased the door shut and stood with her shoulders bumping the wood.

Amaran pulled in an audible breath, her hands clasped white-knuckled at her waist. "Today," she said, "today I begin . . ." She stopped, eyelids quivering as if she did not dare even blink, and Rye felt something turn over inside her at the thought of being the cause of this fear. She rejected the thought as soon as it surfaced. *Tehega.* Tehega must have threatened his witch.

Amaran collected herself. "We have tea before we begin. Yes?"

"No." Not even for pity's sake.

Amaran breathed a stiff and careful sigh. "Only tea. We begin again. We . . . I . . . Please." She unlocked her hands to gesture at the couches. "Begin again."

Rye nodded, but the other woman's tension twitched and sparkled under her own skin. The fever was restless after a restless night, teasing her with sensory ghosts. An invisible shark swam in the atrium-aquarium, and for an instant she saw the room through its cold, black eye, a camera shot through a window, a single frame: Rye lowering herself to the cushions, Amaran mid-step to the bend in the room (Amaran at a table, books all around). Then Rye blinked, or the fever-shark did, and Amaran passed around the corner. Rye sat and, despite herself, looked over her shoulder. The worktables were all clear, the cupboards closed. Not a book in sight. Her scar-feathers fluttered to the sounds Amaran made out of sight.

Amaran came back with a glass tray bearing a squat pot black as stone and two small cups. She set the tray on the floor between the couches, sat, handed Rye a cup. The tea had a clean, half-pleasant scent like charred wood, and the warming cup woke sleepy butterflies inside Rye's palms. Amaran sipped. Rye pretended to, not being an utter fool.

"I live in secrets," Amaran said. It sounded like a confession, honest and calming. "You will learn this."

Rye figured a nod would not commit her to anything.

"Your diyash." Amaran shook her head, troubled by something. The language? What she meant to say? "This man, this Bardo, this is outside the secrets. I say this so you understand: Tehega-rohn is also outside the secrets. We are inside. We live inside. This is the first thing true, and the last thing true." She paused, came up with the word: "Always. This is always true. We are inside. Only we. Yes?"

Rye nodded again, touched the tea to her lips. Butterflies of heat brushed their wings against her mouth, colorful and distracting.

"We say: it is the blood that makes the tahirr, it is the understanding that makes us tahinit. We say . . . " Emotion stirred again behind Amaran's teaching calm, tension around the eyes and mouth that might have been sorrow. That was how Rye read it, the charred-wood smell slipping through the cracks of her skin. Amaran looked at the cup in her hands.

"We say: the ones outside of tahirr, the heart of the body moves their blood; the ones inside tahirr, their blood is moved by the heart of the world. You . . . " She did not look up. Her voice fell to a whisper, as if the words came out despite all the strength she put against them. "Did you steal it? Did you kill it? Did—" She wrestled herself silent.

While Rye sat, wings beating in her wrists and throat and breast. Butterfly wings torn in the shark-teeth of memory-dream *truncated limbs seething skin hot blood* hot *on her hands taste in her mouth black-silver eyes watching her eyes*—She flinched, set the hot cup on the floor. Stared at her hands as if they would bleed with a stigmata of guilt. But the scar-mouths were silent, silvery-cool.

"But this is only the tahirr," Amaran said, her voice loud after the silence. "It is the old ways, the ways outside of tahirr, you must learn. You learn, and you teach them to me. So. To begin: the heart. Listen." She put her fingers to the hinge of her jaw. "Do this! Listen. So."

Rye, humoring a woman who seemed closer to the edge even than she was, found the pulse point below her jaw. Just her heartbeat bumping away as the carotid fed blood into her brain. So much simpler than the sensory tangle of the hidden pulse beneath the puncture scar.

"Listen," Amaran said.

Rye listened, her fingertips echoing every beat of her heart.

The lesson seemed like simple meditation at first. Rye did as Amaran said, breathing and moving in repetitive patterns. She was too keyed up to find it either relaxing or silly, but she did find, as Amaran achieved some measure of calm, that her focus shifted from the other woman to herself. After a while the fever began to—it was the only way she could express it to herself—began to follow along. That hot, prowling beast within her breathed when she breathed, moved when she moved, its senses, for once, no longer at cross-purposes with her own, so that she saw felt heard tasted Amaran's room with intense, immediate, sparkling clarity: the tiles (cold rippled glaze grouted edge) beneath her bare feet, the windows (pure glass licked by dust) shedding light (cool overcast building shadowed) into the room (book dust tea steam person smell). That was the fever, following along like a circus tiger following its trainer's baton—no, more like a shark swimming within a current—no. It was as if the fever, that had always had its own shape, was transmogrified into a Rye-shape, perfectly fitted to her permeable skin.

"Listen," Amaran said.

And she, too, came into focus, as if the fever observed, and Rye took note of what it saw heard tasted felt. Amaran the physical being, the breathing sweating digesting mass of her, the shampoo/oil/cloudy day smell of her hair, the clammy determination of her skin over the warm slide of her circulating blood. Amaran spoke, Amaran moved, and the fever recognized an echoing spark that jumped and brightened every time her heart clenched and relaxed, weak and yearning as a firefly calling for its mate on a warm summer's eve.

Calling to Rye's fever, as if a firefly could mate with a summer storm.

"Listen," Amaran said, voice sensuous with trance, hardly her own.

Firefly calling, blink and tremble, need, desire, fear.

"Listen."

And the fever, Rye-shaped, heard. Lightning pounced, one flash raw and hot as teeth in flesh, and then the storm tore itself in two

black tiger (atrium windows) silver ghost

Rye frozen (breath locked) hands open

and Amaran screamed.

fourteen

The silence was stifling, like deafness. Rye thought, with the surface mind that seemed to cling to the back of her eyes, that they must look like mirror images, gaping, wounded, appalled. The rest of her, her psyche, her soul, was groping, childlike, after . . . what? What had just torn? The strands binding her to reality, the mooring lines that kept the her that was *her*, Rye's Rye-ness, from slipping from shape to shape as the fever did, tiger to Rye to storm to—

Amaran moaned, her hands clenched tight on her sleeves. Something in her own language, and then in her rebellious English: "Out. Go out. Go."

Language helped. Rye, mirror-like still, hugged herself, and that helped, too. She was a thinking being, a physical being. Human. Sick with the same revulsion that darkened Amaran's eyes, as if they had together performed some half-willing perversion, she stumbled back a step. To turn towards the door she would have to face the windows, or put her back to them. Don't, instinct said. *Don't.* But she had to, the way the soon-to-be victim in the horror show has to open the door. She had to look.

And where there should have been something black and slavering, something so huge it filled the atrium and cracked the windows with its bulk, something with blood in its eyes and lightning in its jaws, there was

nothing

except the too-green plants, the small pond ringed as if with rain by the noses of the little fish, the cool light of the ever-cloudy day.

"Go," pleaded Amaran.

Nothing. But it was there, *it was there, IT WAS THERE.*

Rye clenched her fists, as if she could physically hang on to the shreds of her sanity, and the scars over her knuckles opened, soft and painless as cheesecloth parting under too much weight. Bright at first, as if they really were eyes that could open up and see, bright as sunshine across Rye's tongue, and then came the serum and the blood.

Amaran made an ugly sound and pressed her hands over her mouth.

Rye tucked her hands under her arms and walked (careful, careful, the soft wet loosening of her skin already begun) to the door.

In some lost classroom long ago on another world, Rye had learned that the word *panic* was named for the Greek god Pan, who drove his victims through the woods until they died.

That was where Rye's mind was, bramble-whipped and lost, while her body was locked, scabbed and stinking of blood, on the floor of the toilet of their prison room.

Bardo was sitting on the other side of the door. She had heard him slide down and lean his weight against it—her ears had heard him, her mind was still listening to Amaran scream—after he had given up demanding she unlock the door, come out, let him in. He was talking, presumably to himself, his deep voice sounding subterranean through the thick wood.

"I saw a lot of blood on the job. You know what I learned? There's this sexist thing that says women are supposed to be more squeamish than men, but they aren't. Most of them take it in stride better than we do. What bothers them—not all the women I worked with, but most of them—is empathy. I think there's this response that happens so deep that most people don't even know it's there. Men look at someone who's hurt, or dead, and this voice says, thank God that's not me. Or maybe, that should be me, or even, I could have done that. It's a guilt thing. Women see someone hurt and the response is, deep inside, I should do something about that. Or maybe not. I don't know." Bardo's weight shifted against the door, a brush of cloth, a creak of wood.

"Maybe everyone's first response is the same—thank God it's not me—and it's just that women know that doing something about it is the best way to deal with the guilt. I don't think women feel guilt the way men do. Women think they can do something to make it better. Men just learn to live with it. Women say, this is something that happened to me. Men say, this is what I did. This is what I am. *This is what I am.*"

Blood was clotting on Rye's skin with a smell like raw steak and a tightening itch. She blinked and her gummy lashes tore apart with a small pain that stimulated the tear ducts. Clean salt water ran over the hardening mask on her cheek and touched her lip.

"So maybe you can tell me what I should do," Bardo said through the door. "I should never have taken you to Cleände's house. No, forget that. The first time I met you, I knew you were too young for what was going on. You and Marky. I don't know which of you was worse: Marky treating it like a life-sized video game, or you taking it all so damn seriously. You'd have thought the sun shone out of Cleände's ass, the way you were. And I knew—I mean, I *knew*—damn it, what did she need a couple of kids for? I could have scared you off. Hell, I could have had you arrested if I had to. But no. No." Another soft thump, his head dropped back against the door.

"So what do I do, Rye? I'm just a man, just a fucked-up ex-cop with a bad conscience. I don't know what to do to make it better. So you have to tell me. What do I do?"

Blood just tasted like blood. Tears were like daisies in the sun. Rye, hampered by her stiffening clothes, got herself to her knees and unbolted the door. Bardo shifted as well, and the door opened a crack.

"Ah, Rye." Pity wore Bardo's voice down to nothing. "Rye."

She said, her face stiff, her voice strangely clear, "She didn't want us for nothing. Cleände. She wanted us for our blood."

And in her mind's eye, in the fever's eye, a firefly flickered its pattern of desire, its rhythm of need.

There was no shower in the closet bathroom, just a tap that ran not-quite-cold. Bardo sponged her off with her bloody shirt, rinsed her with his hands, absolutely indifferent to the pink-red-rust-colored water that ran in eddies around his feet. Indifferent, too, to her naked skin, the roundness of her breasts buttocks thighs, though Rye, perversely, was not. She should have felt terrible, sick with horror and confusion, at the very least weak with the loss of blood, but no. As if the bleeding had cleansed her, she felt . . . light. A little dizzy, a little thirsty, but mostly just . . . light. Bardo's hands were big and gentle, and her skin, as the clotted blood softened and rinsed away, was as sensitive as silk, as moth-wings, as summer dew. Tender as a father, indifferent as a saint, Bardo knelt in the pink-rust pool around the drain and ran his hands down her wet legs, and she wanted to bury her fingers in his red-black hair, lay her palm on the back of his long, lean, powerful neck. She could feel his breath on her hip. She stretched her arms out to press her hands against either wall, keeping them out of trouble, and felt like Christ as he washed her feet.

"I don't think I can bear any more," she said at last.

He looked up at her, and maybe he wasn't so indifferent after all, or maybe he just read her mind. "Fine," he said, getting to his feet. And, as he left her, "Don't lock the door again. Please."

His *please* softened her irrational hurt. Irrational. She stifled a laugh with her hands.

Fresh clothes soft as old cotton but obviously new. Bardo was in a clean shirt as well, black as his eyes. Nothing but the best for the favored guests. The bed, Bardo aside, was too tempting to ignore. She crawled across the tidy covers and sprawled out, belly down, feeling like a spider on the ceiling for the moment it took for her equilibrium to settle. Bardo came and sat on the edge.

"Can you tell me what happened?"

"I doubt it," she said into the blanket, then turned her head to say into her sleeve, "I wouldn't know how to start."

"Try." Bardo's patience evaporated like rain on a hot day.

Sleep like a river in flood. "She did something. I did something. The fever did." *black tiger (atrium window) silver ghost* Her body twitched on the crumbling edge of the riverbank.

"Rye." He put his hand on her back, warm weight in the hollow of her waist. "Does Tehega know what happened?"

Riverbank giving way, water silent as night. Wasn't there something . . . his touch a reminder . . . oh yes. On a sigh: "Thanks."

Hands on her waist, dragging her. Floor cold beneath her feet.

"Wake her!"

"I'll carry her if I have to."

"Come, then. Be fast!"

Bardo, his long arm hard around her. "Come on, Rye. Give me some help here."

"'M awake."

"I've met dead men more lively. Can you walk?"

"'Course."

"You don't even have your eyes open."

Tiles underfoot, cold, always cold here, where did summer go? "Are we going home?"

"Shh."

Bodies all around, walls slipping past. She pried her eyes open, saw dark silhouettes, flashlights that lit up a sleeve, a leg, a sliding patch of wall. The corridor whipped away at a run, spilling them into a courtyard. Flash-lit gravel bit her tender feet.

"Ouch!"

"Will you shut up!"

Darkness and cold. Ah. Nighttime. She felt wise. But what was that noise? Big but tenuous, she could almost see it like a web arching over the house. A lot of heavy engines, vehicles somewhere not too near. Near enough, she supposed, feeling wise again. Engines brought something bad, sending everyone scurrying. They fled with their small lights down a passageway, to a door, but—

Urgent voices, a press of confusion, everyone turned around and scurried back again.

"Where are we going?" Rye hissed, testy after someone stepped on her bare foot.

"Prison," Bardo said in a very strange voice.

"Are you laughing?"

"No."

Back up the passage, a different tack across the graveled court. Ouch, ouch, ouch. She managed to keep quiet. Given the space, everyone was running, flashlights bobbing: gravel, sleeve, leg, face. Tehega was there, another man she recognized from the encounter at Cleände's house. I wonder how they knew we were there?

Tehega stopped abruptly. Some stopped with him, including Bardo and Rye. Others ran on, abandoning him or oblivious. Faces looked stark, cut out of the darkness by electric light. More runners came towards them from another corner of the yard. Tehega said something as short and as violent as a no. No one else spoke, or moved. The second group was shouting, spearing them with too-bright lights. Tehega's group began to raise their hands in greeting.

Bardo swore and grabbed Rye's arm.

"What's going on?" Rye asked.

"Do not run," Tehega said to Bardo. "I should have put you in chains. It would have been a kindness."

"You're just going to stand there and take it?" Bardo demanded.

"Let our enemy take us into their house," Tehega said. "We can make them wish they had not."

"Fuck you," Bardo said. "Come on, Rye."

"There is nowhere to go," Tehega said.

The people around them were not waving hello. They were putting their arms in the air to show their empty hands. Flashlights dropped to the ground, scattering cones of light across the gravel. The running group surrounded them. A few pushed through their ranks. One snatched at Bardo's arm. The lights were bright in their faces. Bardo released Rye to grab the man's coat and strike him hard on the side of the neck. The man fell to the gravel. Other men reached for Bardo, who drew them into a scrabbling vortex of violence. Rye, knocked aside, fetched up against Tehega's steadying arm.

"What's going on?" she asked him.

"We are betrayed," Tehega said.

"Oh."

Bardo was down. He kicked someone's knee. Someone gave a horrible yell. The vortex became a pile.

"This is the word?" Tehega asked. "Betrayed?"

"Probably," Rye said. Then: "Where's Amaran?"

Tehega laughed. "Yes, this is the word."

There was a smell in the cold air, a vague light behind the roof of the house's wing. "Is something burning?"

"I hope it is."

The pile was sorting itself out with Bardo on the bottom.
"Please don't let them hurt him," Rye said.
"There is nothing I can do."

Bardo

Their weapons were no longer visible, but the four men on the train with him and the lordling had the stiff, hostile look of armed guards everywhere: you don't make friends with men you might have to kill. But they made no attempt to lay hands on Bardo again, which allowed him to keep his temper in check. Barely. Anger fueled by panic still knotted the muscles in his back, clenched his jaw so tight his teeth creaked. On the platform, when the girl had been maneuvered from his side, he had shouted to make her look at him, make her stop, make her *think*. Her brown eyes had been heavy with sleep or fever or blood loss and she had not heard. For an instant, looking around him at the crowd of small people, the tallest of them shorter than Bardo by a head, he had felt the towering strength of pure rage, the kind of fury that speaks, compels. *Take them. Take them all. Take them now.* Suicide, of course.

And would that, a different voice suggested, be worse than arrest?

His anger cracked, threatening to let the panic through, as if arrest here meant what it would mean on Earth. He stood up, bracing himself with a hand on the ceiling against the gentle movement of the train, though the move hurt bruised ribs. Three of the four guards looked up at him, but they said nothing, made no move. Tehega looked up as well, his face lined and gray. Bardo had always supposed the lordling was younger than he was; now he looked old with fear. But then, maybe Bardo looked old, too.

He walked to the front end of the compartment, careful to keep one hand on the ceiling and the other visible at his side. The wood paneling was velvety-smooth, a bizarre accouterment for a train. The door at the end of the car was more in keeping with the technological implication of the smooth, near-silent ride. Apparently some kind of blackened steel, it had no handle, no way through. He was all but certain that Rye was on the other side of that door.

The hand that brushed the ceiling still tingled with a phantom warmth. Bardo's hand, with its dirt, its new scabs and old scars, haunted by the ghost of Rye's wet skin.

Bardo, resisting the temptation to pound against the steel, turned around and propped his shoulders against the door. Only one of the guards was watching him now. Tehega had fixed his eyes on his reflection in the night-black window. Bardo dropped his gaze to his feet and tried to think.

But fear broke up his thoughts as it broke up his anger, and his mind kept circling back to the scrotum-tightening, bowel-softening horror of the girl's bleeding skin. Horror compounded by pity for the look in her eyes—her eyes the sweet golden-brown of buckwheat honey held up to the sun—human and afraid in that mask of blood. Horror complicated by his secret fear of the tainted fluids washing down the drain. Horror twisted and changed by the lust that emerged with her young, scarred, silken skin. It had been a long time since he had had sex, and he knew, in the black, conscienceless depths of him, just how vulnerable she was.

But if he were conscienceless, then where did this self-disgust come from? It rose like a sickness into his mouth until he wanted to spit, or vomit, or shout, until he wanted to pound his battered fists into unyielding steel as if that would exorcise the devil that was in him. Which it would not. It could not, because the devil was not in him. The devil *was* him.

A devil with a conscience. He could not but be bleakly amused. It must be as scarred and bloody as the girl, his conscience, and far less valuable. He shifted his position against the door, crossed his ankles. Tried, again, to set his emotions aside and think.

Rye

Not long ago, Rye had wondered if she should be feeling some instinctive response to being on another world. Some animalistic revulsion to the wrong ground, the wrong sun, the wrong air. She felt it now on this smooth humming train: wrong, and wrong, and wrong.

She sat on the bench, alone, she had the whole car to herself. The seat was soft as cushioned suede, the hidden lights drowsy yellow, dim enough for sleeping. The floor was tiled in the same coffee-cream color as the benches, the walls and ceiling paneled in wood, a pleasant room humming through the night. Glass windows showed nothing but her face and the dark.

She had missed the moment when she was herded onto the train, confused by everyone else's fear, and could only take it on faith, now, that Bardo was on the train, making the same journey.

The thought released her hold on herself. The fever stood up inside her, walked her to the back end of the car, pressed her hands against the black metal door. Her hands, her body, her face. Yearning for whatever the fever knew they were being parted from.

Bardo

He stayed where he was, leaning on Rye's door, though he ached with the depressed fatigue of the post-adrenaline crash. The train swayed so softly that even on his feet he nearly dozed. He jerked his eyes open, rocked his head on his neck. Wondered how stupid he was being, not sleeping while he had the chance. Was he on duty or off? The notion was so alien to him he felt an internal slip, a moment of panic that had nothing to do with circumstance. He had told Rye he was an ex-cop, blurring the truth, shading the holes in his story, and had forgotten it was not a lie. How far had he strayed? Not from the training, or the long-abandoned code, but from the mindset, that certain way of thinking that imposed order on the world.

Movement startled him: Tehega standing up to stretch. The guards watched, no doubt seeing as Bardo did the self-consciousness of the lordling's motion. Tehega stood a moment, staring out the window at black nothing, and then walked down the car to Bardo's end. The guards, all four of them, watched, but they did nothing to interfere.

"They will report we talk, of course," Tehega murmured.

"Are they listening?"

"With a device? It is not likely, not the tahinit." Tehega hesitated. "I think not, but what good is my thinking? I did not think

Amaran-tahi would betray me, and see . . . " He put out a hand, the weary resignation of the gesture no more convincing than his stretch. Bardo had seen the look the lordling gave his witch on the platform.

And he had seen the look the witch gave Rye.

"Something happened between Amaran and the girl," Bardo said, his voice hardly louder than the train's hum. "Something that terrified her."

"The girl?" The lordling's eyes were on the floor, but his attention was palpable.

"The witch."

Tehega flicked Bardo a look. "What?"

"I don't know. The girl . . . " How to say this? " . . . collapsed when she got back to the room." Tehega studied the floor. Bardo stared at him a moment before he added, "Your guess is better than mine. What do you think happened?"

"What good is what I think?" The lordling raised his eyebrows, but not his eyes.

Bardo still stared. He towered over the other man, but give Tehega credit, he was not intimidated. Probably he had bigger things to worry about than Bardo. Bardo could almost be amused at the thought.

"Sorry," he said. "Just making conversation. Unless there was something you wanted to talk about?"

Tehega smiled, almost a pleasant expression with his usual arrogance tempered by fear and fatigue. "Always so direct. I will follow you. How strong is your influence with the girl? I ask for truth, not" the smile tightened "not just for conversation."

Bardo did not respond.

Tehega looked up, frowning, earnest. "You need allies. A patron. You know nothing of the . . . of the . . . "

"Politics?"

"The work of power, the balance between the tahinit and we others. Your girl will turn over all of those, and how will you know where to stand on solid ground?"

Tehega's English was still knotty, but Bardo got the drift. He lifted his chin in a gesture at the guards. "Except I guess I don't have to ask you what your influence with your people is."

"You should ask. Matters change, yes, but I am far from powerless. What did you ever have but the influence over the girl?"

"And what do you have now," Bardo softly countered, "besides your influence over me?"

"Knowledge. Allies. My hands are still full."

Bardo considered him, scratching at his prickling jaw. "I need you, and you need me. Is that how it works now?"

"That and more than that." Tehega nodded, as Bardo had done, at the guards, and by implication the rest of the train. "They need her."

Bardo rubbed his eyes. This late in the night, the self-disgust felt like just another layer of fatigue. "And they have her. So?"

"I have friends," Tehega murmured. "Friends who will take us all out of our enemy's hand, if they think we are worth the risk."

"If they think you have me, and I have her."

Tehega shifted to look out the night-black window, and glanced back at Bardo with a gambler's manic gleam in his eye. "Come and see my friends," he whispered.

Bardo moved to prop a knee on the bench. The guards had also moved. All six of them peered out the line of windows to see the false electric dawn raised by Tehega's friends.

"Give them Rye," the lordling murmured, "and they will have power enough to pull the tahinit, and the tahirr itself, down into ruin."

Rye

Daylight slipped so gently up to the windows that it was a long time before it caught her attention. She sat up, feeling an almost pleasurable languor from her feverish night, and looked out, her chin propped on the back of the bench.

Subdued excitement jumped behind her heart at this first real glimpse of Nohai, though the view was not spectacular. Like a wealthy suburban neighborhood, the landscape was parceled out into lots, walled compounds with sprawling houses and gardens and too few lanes between. Something about the tile roofs and the sparsity of green gave it a desert flavor; something about the natural materials and the absence of electrical lines gave it an aura of wealth and age; something about the narrow lanes and absence of automobiles made it seem constricted, enclosed. Compound locked into compound like puzzle pieces locked shape to shape, wall to wall, secretive and confining.

She would have been chilled if she hadn't been floating above and by it all. She stood up, swaying against the motion of the train, and stretched, and happened to glance out the windows across the aisle.

A road ran there beside the train. Not a broad road, and so the huge vehicles that lumbered in the same direction as the train (though more slowly, so they slid back and back) had to travel in single file. But there were other roads, tracks and alleys that cut between compounds and gardens and groves of pale driftwood trees, and they were also trafficked—clotted, Rye thought—with drab steel beasts, elephants and rhinoceri shuffling nose to tail. Tanks, lorries, guns, alien because they were so nearly recognizable, so like and unlike those on the television news at home. They slipped back and back, the dull, clumsy circus parade of war machines, back and back because of the light, effortless speed of the train, but there were always more up ahead. An army, almost thrilling for the fear it evoked.

And then full daylight broke into a cutting edge of sunlight so thin and white it hurt the eyes. Deep below Rye's conscious mind, memories woke. Somewhere inside her, a beaten animal cowered. Rye did not move, she made no sound. Her eyes were fixed wide open, blind with the remembered light.

The train began to slow.

Bardo

He looked for the girl the instant he was off the train. The door to her car was open. The platform was crowded. A dozen men and women in white cassocks, brilliant in the sun, waited by the door to Rye's car, and Bardo knew that he had to get to her first. Moving fast enough to disconcert his guards, he strode forward—

And was stopped, not by the fist in his sleeve, but by the sound of his name.

Daniel Bardo.

Because only one woman in three worlds said his name with exactly that lilt, that rhythm and tone.

He looked down, and saw that it was not in fact Cleände who held his arm. It hardly mattered. He knew—pure instinct, but he *knew*—that she was here. Somewhere. His name in that accent was a message, as telling as the look, cynical and knowing, in the messenger's eyes. Cleände.

Rye stepped out of the train. The sunlight was cruel to the scars that masked her face, giving them the dead sheen of tarnished silver. She looked past the waiting arc of silent white cassocks, caught Bardo's eye above the heads of the crowd.

And frowned at him as if she were trying to remember who he was.

fifteen

Welcome, they said. Welcome home.

Her feet were still bare. Bruised by Tehega's gravel, they were exquisitely sensitive to the floors of Meheg-menoht. The smoothness of glazed tiles, yes, and the grit of dust in abraded lesions. The triangular stamp of a broken tile's corner. A crack like a tear across her sole. The cold.

Once this place was a wilderness, and we lived like mountain primitives who do not know what great land lies across the desert plain. Meheg-menoht is like the first house ever built, the first house ever to have a door, and so our builders made these archways in the old royal style, as you can see here . . .

White sunlight broke through a window. It struck sparks off the mica in the gray stone wall, lay an indigo sheen across the black floor, illuminated nothing of the long hallway beyond. The people ahead of her passed through the light, caught as if in a shutter's blink against the dark. A white cassock sliced by shadows into a sculptural relief of renaissance folds. The tail of a coat, brown embroidery on brown cloth that loosed a thread to drift with the dust motes in the white sun glare. Bardo's red-black hair, the curl of it on his neck, the bony set of his shoulders, the dusty tear in the seam of his shirt. Someone's sidelong, liquid eye. It was her turn. Her own eye, struck by light, wept, and she saw, in the long stretch of the hallway beyond, faces in the walls. Faces captured in the lens of her light-struck tears. The only faces she could see in the walking dark. They spoke to her, but no one wanted to meet her eyes.

. . . the work of a whole people, a work of giving, not taking, so you will not see the small luxuries of Andit Teheg, though of course we make you comfort here. More comfort than the Tehega made you, yes? I think you were not a willing guest, though perhaps we are mistake . . .

Stairs. A broad shallow curve of them, like the curve of an arm. The host that surrounds her descends them. She places her feet with care. Is she walking up or down? The stairs end. She skates across the space, the polished floor sliding like ice dark with the deep water beneath, thin ice slick and cold beneath her feet. She feels hot enough to melt through the surface, cold enough to feel as if she already had. White sunlight slants through high windows above the gray-shadowed space, illuminating only the surface, the top of the opposite wall. A carpet interposes itself between her feet and the icy floor. She stops. There is a cup in her hand. Voices in her ears. Soft laughter. A party. They are throwing her a party in the heart of the world. Bardo stands like a primitive totem above the fair heads, his dark face line-carved, beard- and bruise-shadowed, a thin scab crossing his lower lip. She touches her own lip with her tongue, feels the sweet-metal nerve-pulse of the lesion scar there. She glances up: slant of sunlight, dust-hung, barred with shade, and above that, the ceiling. (Above that, human shapes foreshortened, human feet pressed to a metal grid. Down here, the bite of iron, of heat, stink, and fear.) She drops her cup. Someone apologizes to her. Someone gives her another cup. Someone murmurs, warm breath in her ear.

. . . always suffer the isolation, and the difficult two loyalties of tahinit and lord. If the Tehega has fall in the old heresy—yes? perhaps you know what this means?—perhaps you know if Amaran-tahi has also fall? Perhaps, outside the tahirr, she has teach you also outside?

"Has fallen. Has taught."

"Yes?"

Rye twitched, shivered, spilled a thin dribble from the cup to the rug. Her own voice startled her out of the dream she had been dreaming, except the dream woke with her: the tall room, the clustered people, the pleasant sound of party chat. The woman, with her coarse smock, her huge belly, her hollowed eyes, glimpsed between coat-sleeves, squatting against the wall. Rye dropped her cup again. Nothing there but the wall.

But the wall was only the surface of a seething mercury fever-sea, swimming with ghosts who pressed their faces, bellies, hands against the mirror-ice.

"I don't feel well," she said. "My feet are cold."

Bardo looked over, frowning at the sound of her voice.

They showed her to a room (Bardo: I'm right next door. Rye. Do you hear me?) and left her alone and she tried to lie down and rest (spider on the ceiling, spinning in the boat) but the fever was prowling again (pad of heart pad of paws) until the walls ran shining gray fluid ice (slip and slide) and the weave of the blankets, the threads of her clothes pried at her loosening skin. She crawled off the bed, stripped off her shirt and pants, let the fever her pace her across the quicksilver floor.

Faces shone within the walls, drowned ice-mirror women, no, real women sitting against a gray stone wall, winter cold stealing steam from their mouths, from their naked feet and hands. Women, hollow-eyed with pain, faces masked by despair. One catches her eye, lifts her smock to expose the swollen belly streaked with deadly infection, black and red, the bloody pus, silver-pink, on her thighs. A warning, a welcome, or maybe she only wanted to cool the fever.

Cold air on her skin.

You are the treasures of our world.

And it wasn't the specialists in their green scrubs and doubled masks, it was the tahinit lords in their antiseptic white who stood over the pit, the iron grate biting into the soles of their feet as the iron frame below bit into her flesh. Why do it that way? Why not at least aspire to the subtle degradation of scrubbed tile, padded stirrups, paper sheets?

Because—

(Fever paces the cage, tiger's fur brushes the bars, electric lines like threads of fire within the gray stone gray smoke quickslidingsilver walls.)

Because the pit isn't for her, for them, for the women. The pit and the iron grill and the stinking tunnel and the fear. All that, no, it isn't for the women

You are our keys to freedom.

it's for

mercury skin in a quicksilver slide *(electric river, lightning road)* black-iron shadows, black-iron bones *(white sun chiming, chiming on the track)* the clasp of hands or are they claws *(coming lover)* fever-hot *(slipping silent, moving fast)* and

Rye, riding the tiger, fell, and instead of fangs in her throat, she felt fur soft as velvet (cold tiles, hard floor, dust) and a purr (hyperthermic shivers) that rattled in her bones (the bars of the cage) until she slept.

(coming, lover, coming)

Except that when she woke up, Bardo wasn't there.

sixteen

Her name was Mostahr: Mostahr-tahi, a soft-breasted, broad-hipped woman turned into a grandmotherly caricature by the total indifference in her brown eyes. She had the Nohan look, heavily curved bones at eyebrow, nose-bridge, and chin, that was handsome in some, slightly animalistic in others. In Mostahr those heavy bones looked like stone lodged beneath her softly crumpled skin.

She invited Rye in as if there were no guard standing at attention in the hall.

"Come, sit down, be comfortable here. We are too pleased to have you return to us last day, we made poor hosts. I do apologize. Of course you were much tired, and perhaps surprised to be saved from the heretic?"

Rye sat where she was directed and tucked her scarred hands inside her sleeves. Mostahr's room was high, its wide window set up near the ceiling to show nothing but the cloud-wisped indigo sky. In other respects, the room was much like Amaran's. Different dimensions, different furnishings—there was a picture on the plastered wall of a rough stone arch, isolated from its building, clad in vines—but the room was clearly a workroom, with long tables, cupboards, a stacked set of wire racks full of paper by the door. The chair Rye sat in was low, the blue cushion smooth as fake suede.

Mostahr sat close by Rye's elbow. "And now I see what I feared is true: you do not remember me."

Was this a test? Shocked by Bardo's absence, Rye did not feel equal to tests. She said flatly, "No."

"Amaran-tahi tells us you have forgot. Poor fool she, but perhaps she is not wrong in this?"

"The fever burned it out," Rye said with the sincerity of a wish. A blank would be better than the nightmarish fragments she had. "I lost it all."

"Oh, the fever," Mostahr said with sympathy and regret. "Oh, if you had stayed, much would be different. So much you have lost!"

The woman's warmth was palpable as body heat, an emanation of sincerity and caring. Rye did not dare lean away. She sat in a sullen lump, frightened to her bones.

"Where . . . do you know . . . where Bar—where Dan Bardo is? He said, last night, he would be right next door, but there was no one there."

Mostahr shifted very slightly in her chair. "Daniel Bardo. Yes. He answers questions. You understand—but perhaps you do not?—the Tehega committed a crime when he took and kept you. He and, I am sad, Amaran-tahi, who is like a child of my house. I think you are innocent, but they pull you into their heresy, and this is the crime. You see? So Daniel Bardo answers questions so we know all the crime that they commit. I ask you questions also, but you do not remember so much, so Daniel Bardo is better to answer. And he is against crime in his own place, yes? So he will help us with our crimes."

Bardo or Dan, he said in Rye's memory. Nobody called him Daniel. He hated that. And were they just *asking* questions, or . . . ?

"Oh," Rye said.

"You know this about him?" Mostahr pressed—oh, very gentle and concerned. "You know this much?"

"That he was a cop? Sure."

"And a friend—I think more than a friend—to a certain Scallese rebel. They did not hide this from you? Or you remember it? The Scallité and their bad work on Earth."

Oh shit, oh damn. What was she supposed to say? "I don't remember for myself. I don't remember much since I was a kid. But from what Bardo says, okay, yes, he knew them—her—but he didn't like them. Or trust them. I mean, he knew they, she, were using people. He wasn't . . . " What? Rye shut her mouth and shrugged, knowing she sounded like a dumb, sullen kid, taking refuge in the fact. *I don't know jack-shit, lady.*

"Ah," said Mostahr, as if Rye had been more coherent. "Good. He will help us. I am glad. Oh, and you worry! No, no." She made a move as if to touch Rye's arm, but did not quite. "He is safe. You are safe. The Tehega has lost his try. He will learn so very soon. And you also have so much to learn."

"Like how you know me?" Rye said, mouth gone dry with risk. "Like what happened to me when I was here before?"

And oh, but wasn't Mostahr just bursting to tell her all about it? How Rye was rescued from the reckless Scallese rebels, who had tried to induct her into their warped version of the tahirr. How Rye, once on Nohai, had been dazzled by the one true tahirr, by the priests and scholars at Meheg-menoht who wanted nothing more than to use her Earthly talents, to help *her* use her Earthly blood to build a whole new wing of the holy structure that was the tahirr, to make Meheg-menoht the heart of more worlds than Nohai, the heart of all the worlds that would be Rye's when the tahinit helped her come into her power.

"I think Amaran-who-was-tahi has teach you lies, the stupid superstitious lies of the old religion, the religion of the wilderness. She tells you other lies too, I think, like the Scallité. And now you fear that I also tell you lies. Oh Ryder, child of my house." Mostahr laughed, a warm, rueful chuckle. "Of course you do. Of course you are so wise. But you will learn. You will learn the tahirr. You will learn what it is to live in a house that contains all the worlds, the house where God dwells. This is your house now, and so I say to you again: welcome home."

Your house, your home, with the stinging lightning-flicker bars buried in all the walls.

How stupid did they think she was?

Rye was in her room staring at nothing when Bardo pounded on the door. He always made it sound like an emergency, but when she opened the door he just stood there, arms at his sides.

"Where have you been?" she cried.

Still, he just stood there, glaring.

"What?" she said, automatically defensive, before she realized the glare was not one of anger. She stepped aside and Bardo walked stiffly into the room. She asked him if he was all right. He stared out the window by her bed, silent, and in the last cold light of day his face was pale, the creases around his eyes and mouth scored as deep as scars.

"Dan," she said, "this is a very scary place where terrible things happened to me, so please, will you tell me if you're hurt or—"

"What kind of things?" Bardo turned his back to the window, so big he blocked the light. "Last I heard, you'd lost your memory."

Rye floundered in a conversational back-eddy. She was still wondering where he'd been, what had happened to him, whether he was all right. "I . . . uh . . . it's coming back. Sort of. Maybe."

"So you remember, sort of, maybe, what?"

"Nightmares," she said, aggrieved, back in sullen mode. "Nothing I want to know."

"All *I* know is that you have a fever, and sometimes you bleed. You say you lost your memory. Everyone else wants a piece of you. But I don't really know a damn thing, do I?"

"Well, what . . . " Rye's mouth had gone dry. "What do you want to know?"

Bardo didn't say. She sat down in the room's only chair, and then wished she hadn't, Bardo was so tall, and the chair so low.

"Did they do something to you?" she asked him from the level of his knees.

"They talked." He laughed, a soft, savage laugh. "I talked. Too bad I couldn't tell them anything they need to know."

"Dan," she whispered, appalled.

He moved abruptly, some unfinished gesture. "I'm all right."

"No, you're not."

"No, I'm not." He laughed again, a sound of pain.

It frightened her to see him like this. She got to her feet, hesitantly approached him. "Are you hurt?" She pulled on a fold of his shirt, not quite daring to touch him. "Is there something I can do?"

"Oh, Ryder, you're so naïve." He clasped her face in his hands. "What do you think they did, stuck lit matches between my toes?"

"Maybe you're the naïve one," Rye said. "I know what they did to me."

"And what was that, exactly?"

His touch, bare skin to bare skin, was copper-green brambles, lightning-thorn fishes, electric-rose wine. She pulled loose, backed away into the room.

"Can't tell me?" Bardo said, harsh and almost jeering. "Can't remember? Or maybe you just don't want me to know."

"Just give me a chance!" Her voice was ragged. She wanted to wipe her sleeve across her cheeks, as if she could brush his touch away like tears, but with him in this mood she didn't dare offend him. "I'll tell you. God. Just give me a chance."

He was quiet while she struggled for a steady breath. Then, "Rye—"

"No. I'll tell you. It's just hard to put into words." She folded her arms around herself. "There were these women. Other prisoners. And they were . . . they . . . "

"Don't. Rye." Bardo moved, suddenly enough to make her jump, and hugged her hard against his chest. "I'm sorry. You don't have to tell me anything."

She longed for his embrace, and could not bear it. She touched her hands to his back in brief apology before she worked her way out of his arms.

"Sorry," he said again, more coldly.

"It hurts, okay? When the fever's up, my skin gets so sensitive, it's like being hugged by rose bush. Don't take everything so personally."

He laughed, a flash of real humor and white teeth. "I've never been compared to a rose bush. Should I be flattered?"

She smiled, but her mouth twitched to the tug of tears. "Sure."

"I'm sorry, kid. I didn't know."

"I know."

They regarded each other in silence.

Then Rye said, "If you shut up for long enough, I'll tell you."

And she tried to, while he paced the small room and she folded herself up on the bed. But for memory all she had was a few nightmare images, and even fewer sensations—*quicksilver blackiron glide (smooth sex) tooth or sting (blackfever blood)*—that she could not bear to articulate. And as for the fever . . . what could she say?

"It's like I have this, this thing inside me." She was sitting on the end of her bed, chin on her knees, watching long-legged Bardo prowl the too-small space. "It's like a tiger inside me."

He frowned at her. "A tiger."

"Inside me. I don't know how else to explain it." She bit her lip. The sole lesion scar that crossed the corner of her mouth jumped like a kernel of corn popping under her skin. "Do you know what synesthesia is?"

"No."

"Well, it's like all my senses are cross-wired, so sometimes I see sounds, or taste colors. Things like that." Like your emotions, Dan, she did not say. Like the panic-rage that keeps you bouncing off the walls. "And I hallucinate all the time."

"All the time?"

"Too often. Like the walls go all transparent and . . . " There just weren't any words for it.

Bardo snorted. "X-ray vision."

"No." She said it flatly, wearily. "Just hallucinations. Just like a crazy person."

"You aren't crazy." He strode over to her and glared down. "*You aren't crazy.*"

Rye craned her neck to look up at him, no closer to understanding him than she had ever been. "Thanks."

"What else?"

She put her chin back on her knees and closed her eyes. "Nothing. It's just a disease."

He was quiet a moment. She could feel his gaze on her face. Then he sat down beside her on the bed and said, "You're such a terrible liar. I hope to hell you haven't tried to pull any big ones on the tahinit."

She looked at him, one blushing cheek resting on her knee. "I don't have the words to tell you, Dan. It's like carrying a lightning storm around inside me."

"A lightning storm."

"Will you stop repeating everything I say? A lightning storm, a tiger. I don't have the damn words!"

"Sorry."

"Anyway, whatever it is, I can't control it. It's its own thing. It just happens to live inside my skin."

"That's not what they think."

"Yeah? Well, what do they know?"

He grinned that startling, beautiful grin, and touched one warm fingertip to her cheek. "What does that taste like?"

"Hot copper."

His eyes narrowed. His mouth twitched. He snickered. Then he fell back on his elbows and roared with laughter.

"What?" Rye sat up straight and rubbed her cuff over her cheek. "What the hell's so funny?"

"Copper?" He could hardly speak for laughing. "Cop-per? You hallucinate in *puns*?"

She could not laugh with him, her skin was still full of his taste, bitter and electric, elemental as earth. After a bit she put her chin back on her knees.

Bardo caught his breath, tugged on the back of her shirt. "Sorry."

"I doubt it."

He gave her shirt a harder pull. She turned to look at him. Laughter had left his face undefended, and she was reminded, seeing the deep, sober black of his eyes, of the state he had been in.

"What did they do to you?" she asked him softly.

Bardo lay back on her bed, one fist still full of her shirt. "Nothing."

"Dan."

"Really, nothing. They did nothing." His voice oddly light. "Now ask me what they said."

Rye did not like this at all. "What did they say?"

Bardo smiled, the line by his mouth like a wound. "They have Cleände."

The fever stirred, or maybe that was goosebumps, pricking like claws beneath her skin. Was that what had him in this state? Was that *who* had him in this state?

"Cleände." It was a whisper. "You mean, a prisoner?"

He said nothing, watching her.

"So she wasn't . . . She didn't . . . " Obviously not. And just as obvious was Bardo's distress. *So I lied to Mostahr about that, too.* Rye shifted until she was kneeling beside him. "Dan, I'm so sorry. What do we do?"

His gaze shifted to the ceiling, but his fist was still clenched in her shirt. "God knows. Can you walk through walls?"

"I don't—" Her voice jumped in her throat. "I don't know."

Bardo smiled bleakly. He looked very tired. "I would like to hold you for a while," he said formally. "If you don't think it would hurt too much."

Something loosened inside her, the way the fever sometimes loosened her skin. She lay down within the curve of his arm. "It's not exactly pain."

"Good." His dark voice tangible in his embrace. "Because I don't exactly want to hurt you."

"I'm really sorry," Rye whispered. "I know it's my fault you're here."

"Don't." He rolled on his side, clamped one hand across her mouth. "Don't for God's sake apologize."

Skin to skin, copper roses and electric wine. His leg heavy across hers. His eyes black and hot and too close. She touched the back of his hand, and he drew it away, and kissed her.

seventeen

The span of his long fingers across her ribs, the perfect shape of his hand, drowned her in sweet and bitter new-penny wine. Just a touch, drowning her. His fingers splayed across her ribs, his hands on her hips, drawing her trousers down. His mouth, tasting her, so that she learned her flavors from his tongue, cinnamon and ocean weed, daisies under the moon.

She tried to be a good lover, to give as well as receive, to spill a little of the flood into the channels of his veins. She never knew if she succeeded, hands tongue volition lost in the Bardo-storm. His large hands. His skin, cool and shockingly smooth against her fever-scarred hide. His soft mouth and liquid tongue. His legs, hard with muscle, parting her own. All of him, his size and his darkness and his strength, moving inside her, holding her, wrapping her round. So large and dark he engulfed her, encompassed her, hot as deserts, as midnight in the tropics, as monsoon rains. Bardo.

He inhabited her like the fever.

Does it hurt? Don't let me hurt you.

He moved above her, within her, slower than ocean waves (his throat under her mouth, his breath) slow as the earth (his back under her hands, oiled muscular slide over bone) and she strained to meet him, arched up against him, clinging to him, as if he were far away, as if she could pull him closer, even closer, rising up against him while the beat of her heart stretched into one long pendulum swing streaming banners of rose gold sultry blue across her eyes under her skin streaming

Ah, Christ!

flames from a falling torch (the exquisite, clenching fear of falling) scales breathing darkness (night wings spilling air)

Rye. Oh, God. Ryder. What did I do?

lightning cage (black bone bars) stone trap (electric web) black cat stalking (sliding the surface) dipping under (whispering)

What did I do?

here, lover, here

He carried her, his arms like smoke and black iron, through a gap in the ice-lighted walls. She saw tasted heard with aching clarity the singing blue electrical lines within the insubstantial stone, the hollow shapes of the next room, the room beyond that, the currents of night all around, the copper-green rose-thorn bite of fear, the wild frost-colored fireworks of water sluicing down her watchful skin. Blinded by the cold, she opened her eyes. Bardo knelt with her under the tap, naked, red with blood, his arms streaked with the water he poured over her from his cupped palms.

"Oh," she said wisely. "I'm bleeding again."

Bardo caught his breath, turned his face away. "I thought I'd killed you."

Rye didn't know what to say to that. With the bathroom cubicle slip-sliding around her, she put her head under the tap, twisted to let the water stream down her back. Pink-red-clear swirled around their knees, feathering down the drain. The lesion scars in her skin were still open, a myriad black-lipped mouths, paper cuts, scales, seeping a fine scarlet wash. Nearly done. She filled her hands with water, emptied them down Bardo's chest. He didn't move.

"For a second I thought it was your blood," she said.

"I wish it was."

"You don't really."

He didn't respond. She went on rinsing him off. She marveled at the long heavy bones under lean muscle and tawny skin, the fine pattern of black hair on his chest and belly like a feathered arrow pointing to his loins. She marveled, too, that she could touch him like this, intimate as lovers. Without her fever to warm him he shivered under the cold water, his chin tucked against his shoulder. She slipped a loose-skinned palm under his cheek, turned him to face her. Her blood marred his cheekbone, his forehead, his hair. She smoothed it away with wet hands.

"Poor Dan."

He closed his eyes. "I'm sorry."

"I'm not."

He flinched. She slid her arms around his neck, and he flinched again.

"You're so cold," she told him.

He made some sound, one she felt more than heard, and put his arms around her, drawing her heat as close as he could, as if she could warm his bones.

When did the ordinary things happen?

A bowl of porridge: sweet chewy yellow grain with salty, crunchy bits added in. The earthenware bowl steamed half-visible wisps into the cool dry air of their common room, where she ate her breakfast alone.

A change of clothes: sleeveless white bodysuit, legs to the knees, ribbon between the breasts; brown trousers, heavy cloth with subtle wales; creamy shirt with two fussy cords to tie at each wrist; a long fawn coat, stylistically confused between a frock coat and a Nehru jacket; boots fastened with a complicated arrangement of buckles and ties. Nice clothes? Rye had no mirror but Bardo's eyes, and he wouldn't look at her anymore.

Sleeping: she's in the hospital again, and blind again, though the dreaming Rye can see what the dream-Rye cannot. Tapioca walls, mint-candy floors, carts of melt-bubbled plastic with gummy rubber wheels: a sticky hospital night, quiet, gluey, cloying. No one around, but the rooms are all occupied, restless, there are voices just too low to hear. She walks on gooey feet, knowing the goo is clotted blood. Her scars are open. The hospital is fetid, unwashed, unclean. She gropes, blind, on her wet-sticky feet, and a curtain hiding a doorway slides aside at her touch. Dreaming, she can see the mildewed plastic cloth. In the dream, she feels the tacky curtain clinging to her skin. She pulls free, tearing the soft new scabs of her lesions. The room is dark even to dreaming Rye. She gropes, flinching from the sticky iron bed, the crusted sheets, the oozing flesh of the person in the bed. Overthrown by horror, she tries to tear herself away, but only loses her balance. She falls onto the bed, into the bed, hot oozing flesh beneath her hands. Someone is suffering. She is sick with horror, with fear, with the terrible certainty that this is *all her fault*. Her hands tighten on the ruined flesh, the drool of imminent sickness spills out of her mouth, sweat or blood spills out of her skin. She tightens her hands on the ruined flesh, this is all her fault and *she has to finish this*—

So much for sleeping.

Her room was as small as the quarantine room in the hospital. The walls were smooth stone, seamlessly fitted without mortar, the floors glossy blue-black tile. The windows, narrow and un-wired, looked down on a paved alley, a bench flanked by potted plants, an outside wall that showed nothing but light or dark. No views anywhere, except from the train, which perhaps was why that one long back-sliding glimpse of the Nohan army stayed with her so vividly. It was her one look Outside—and what did that say about these people? These people who wanted to open an infinity of doors onto an infinity of worlds, yet who did not even want to look at their own?

"Bardo-rohn. They ready now. You come, please."

"Come where? Where are you going?"

"Just more questions. Relax."

" . . . Excuse me?"

"It's what it was before, Rye: you do the witch stuff and leave the rest to me."

Mostahr said, "Your power is the half of a whole that bridges worlds."

Rye was dull with fatigue and for an instant this made perfect sense to her, that she could be half a person, the other half being . . . what? Bardo, the fever, her missing years. But Mostahr was not talking about Rye. Mostahr never talked about Rye, she only talked about Rye's power.

"You understand this?" she said, perhaps noticing Rye's bemusement. "The bridge? It is a center of tahinit teaching."

"I know what a bridge is," Rye mumbled.

"The ones outside of tahirr speak of gates and keys. This is old language, from the old religion, before God opened the world. God gave us the bridge, and we built the tahirr for its foundations so we could stand secure on two shores. Alone on one shore, one cannot make the bridge. The bridge stands between two foundings. Power is, must be, two." Mostahr paused, wrinkles deepening as she pursed her mouth. "There is a word for this, I think. A word for two born together?"

"Twins."

"Twins." Mostahr tasted the word, found it to her liking. "Your power is twins. You are the bridge's foot on this shore, the twin who stands behind the glass. But you have another, the power that moves, that stands on the other shore. Your twin."

Rye was quiet, thinking not of twins, but of cages. Lightning spark, black bone bars *(gray stone electric wire web)* around a tiger *(swelling clouds lightning-shot)* fever without form. Gathering herself from the fringes of the growing storm, she said, "Why am I the one to stay? Why am I behind" bars "glass?"

"Because you are here," Mostahr said smoothly. "Where is your other half?"

"I don't know," Rye stammered, "I don't know what you're talking about." And added, edging closer to desperation, "Where's your twin?"

"Ah, but I am only tahinit. We are only travelers, only builders of simple walls. It is for the bridge to be two."

"Well, I'm not," Rye said. "There's only me."

"No," Mostahr said, sweetly implacable. "Two."

Me and the fever, Rye thought. Restless with it, as it swelled to meet some threat she could not understand—*the clasp of hands or are they claws*—she stood up and paced to the high window. Blue sky, a thin smear of cloud. If she stood on tiptoe she could see the edge of a roof down below.

"It is near." By the sound of her voice, Mostahr had followed her across the room. "We all feel it, the return to life in the heart of the world. I feel it now. It has come for you. Where is it?"

The fever? Huge inside her, lightning teeth bared, black eyes mirroring *mercury skin in a quicksilver slide.* Rye closed her eyes, but it was still there, the white sun's black shadow come alive. She could feel Mostahr's urgent, impersonal greed on the back of her neck.

She said, weak and sick with surrender, "What is it?"

"The bridge-builder. The arcwright. God's black left hand."

Arcwright. That one word caught in her mind, echoed through her as if it reflected off a hundred mirror shards in her broken memory, but it bound nothing together, summoned nothing but a black fever surge, a sour-wet taste of *(warning)*, an undertow of some *(ferocious)* emotion she could not name.

Someone knocked on the door. Mostahr ignored it.

"You are bound. You are made again. You are twinned, and you will bring your other home."

black bone cage (lover) twisted ruin (mercury burn)

"*No.*"

Rye whispered it to that other, the fever's twin, the storm creature invisible beyond the glass, but it was Mostahr who answered.

"You will," she said. "It is the only way you can be cured."

The knock came again, polite but in earnest, and Mostahr went to open the door.

A quick walk down the corridor, an anxious escort of strangers, a hard bite of time.

"Your Daniel Bardo is make a mistake, Ryder-tahi," someone said. A man: Mostahr had let her go. "We have only some questions, but he chooses to answer badly. Is he friend to this Tehega and this Amaran?"

"Friend?" Rye stumbled over a dream-jump of logic: Mostahr-arcwright-Bardo-what? "What? No. They kidnapped us!"

Her escort was walking fast enough to make her stretch her legs. She kept her eyes away from the mirror-gray walls.

"But your Bardo saw the Andit Teheg shrine," the man said, insistent. "You saw this shrine, yes?"

"Yes."

A tight stairwell going down, a window like a slash of white paint, a stripe of sunlight. White glare across the cornea, black well below. Rye had to trust her feet to find the next stair. Hadn't she just been talking to Mostahr? Hadn't she just—

You can be cured.

"Then why does your Bardo say he did not see this thing?"

"He's not 'my' Bardo. He's not anyone's Bardo."

"Not the Tehega's Bardo?"

"No."

"Then why does he lie?"

Oh, for Christ's sake, Rye, what if Bardo has a reason? "Maybe he . . . Maybe he doesn't know what you mean by shrine. We saw a room . . . "

The stairwell spilled them out through a heavy door held by a gray-coated guard. The corridor here was much wider and higher, sections marked off by heavy arches. Heat bloomed under Rye's skin. Her scars feathered open—please, not now—making the warm clothes suddenly stifling.

You can be cured.

"The room the Tehega burned."

Her questioner stopped her with a hand on her arm. She flinched from the touch, and like a cat with a bit of yarn, he reflexively tightened his grip before he let her go. He was taller than she, his gray-fair hair cropped almost as short as her own, his pale eyes wrinkled all around like a tortoise's. Rye realized that if he had disappeared a second before, she would never have been able to say what he looked like. Only what his voice was like: hard, ironic, doling out the English words as if he would have spilled ten times as many if she could only have understood the Nohan tongue.

"Ryder-tahi," said this man, while his attendants hovered around them. "Tehega-rohn and Amaran-tahi did a crime to you. Yes?"

Oh, fuck, Bardo, what the hell are you doing?

"They take you from your world. They keep you in Andit Teheg. They teach you heresy. All of this we know. Yes?"

Leave the rest to me, Bardo said.

"Yes?"

And Mostahr: *You can be cured.*

Rye caught her breath. Half of her was still upstairs, looking for the stairs. "Yes."

"Yes. So you say before the people this is so. Yes?"

"What people?"

"This is truth, Ryder-tahi. You say this truth."

Even her dreams made more sense than this.

"You say this truth, or your Daniel Bardo shares Tehega-rohn's crimes. And if share the crimes, share the cost. You understand?"

"But I—" I can't call Bardo a liar!

He understood her. (What was he? Prosecutor? Policeman? He had a look Bardo had sometimes, as if he understood everything, and had compassion for none of it.)

"We do not ask you, what does Daniel Bardo see? We ask you only, what do you, Ryder-tahi, see? Daniel Bardo is not always with you. Daniel Bardo does not always see what Ryder-tahi sees. Ryder-tahi can say, I saw this room, I was teach this prayer. Ryder-tahi can say the truth, only the truth, about the crimes of the bad people who took her from her place. The bad people who make the crimes pay the cost. Daniel Bardo, who did not see, who did not hear, does not."

"What cost?" she said.

You can be cured.

eighteen

Rye hated the doors in this place. Every door opened on a black and stinking pit. Every door opened on a sunlit courtyard full of dying women. The more doors that opened, the more certain it became that the next one would take her into the real Meheg-menoht, the Meheg-menoht of her dreams. If not this door, then the next.

This one opened onto an amphitheater's upper tier. An oval stage was surrounded by ranks of benches, the whole brilliantly lit by the sun staring down through the glass roof. The white sunlight washed out even vivid colors, and the tahinit lords in their white cassocks looked grossly overexposed. They made a blank white frieze around the walls, interrupted here and there by small groups of men and women in dark civilian clothes. There were a few people standing on the stage, but nothing much seemed to be happening. As the people seated on the upper benches began to turn around to watch Rye enter with her escort, she realized this was because the proceedings had been put on hold until her arrival. Whispers ruffled the air, like a flurry of wings in the acoustical space, but Rye had exhausted her reservoirs of fear. Perhaps Bardo's danger had over-ridden more personal concerns. Or perhaps it was the fever, roused and blackly singing in her ears. She looked for Bardo as her escort ushered her onto the floor, but all she saw were Tehega and Amaran standing in ominous isolation at one curved end of the stage.

Don't look at them, instinct said. You owe them nothing. Remember Tehega, smirking while his men held a knife to your throat. Remember Amaran, summoning the fever-beast (the arcwright (real *(here, lover, here)*—

Not now! She felt transparent to the sunlight, glassy with heat. *Please, not now.*

A woman's voice lifted with startling clarity into the heights of the room. Rye's prosecutor/policeman, standing at her shoulder, murmured, "I speak the voddrohn's words for you, and I speak your words for the people."

Where was she supposed to stand? They left her hovering at the foot of the stairs. Amaran and Tehega, together but separate, were on her left, other people on her right. Weren't they going to offer her an oath? But why bother: if none of the audience spoke English, then her "translator" could put any words he wanted into her mouth . . .

"You meet the Tehega on this other place, Earth. Yes or no?"

Rye touched her upper lip with her tongue, knowing with sudden, utter finality that she should not be here. But it was too late.

Where the hell was Bardo?

Too late.

"Yes."

"Tell the people this meeting."

"We . . . " No. Leave Bardo out of it, Cleände, the fever, everything she possibly could. Just the very basic facts. "I went to a house in my city where I thought I might learn something about . . . about the other worlds . . . "

When her translator spoke, the odd, rolling cadences of the Nohan tongue might have meant anything. But when he was done, an older man seated on the lowest rank of benches stood and asked a question in heavily accented English.

"It is the tahinit Amaran that see you is in the tahirr?"

That afternoon in the rain: Amaran with recognition in her eyes; Amaran leaning against Tehega's shoulder to speak in his ear. If that was what the old man meant: "Yes?"

"It is the tahinit Amaran that . . . that . . . " The old man, stiff and lean in a long gray coat, finished the question in Nohan.

"It is Amaran-tahi that force you to bring the Teheg-fedran to Nohai against the tahinit . . . " The prosecutor/policeman had to grope as well. " . . . against the tahinit ruling of no opening the gate from the worlds?"

For God's sake, Rye thought, giddy with fever and adrenaline, Mostahr spoke better English. Hell, *Tehega* spoke better English. She swallowed the impulse to correct her translator, and said simply, "Yes."

The old man nodded and resumed his seat. Murmurs fluttered up to the brilliant ceiling. The actual prosecutor (unless she was a judge?) bowed at him and continued.

"Tell the people about the time you spend in Andit Teheg."

She told. It made a strange story without Bardo. What would she have been doing there if she had been alone? It felt dangerous, editing him out. Where the hell was he *now*?

The prosecutor/policeman spoke for quite a while after she was done. Explaining? Embellishing? Telling the court she was a double-breasted liar? The prosecutor/judge spoke as well. Someone in the second rank across the way stood up and droned on, detailing points of law, Rye guessed from the fussy way he pressed a fingertip against his palm. She snuck a glance at Amaran and Tehega, and wished she had not. Whether or not she owed them anything, she knew them, and could not help the shame that crawled beneath her skin. Bardo, she thought. Dan, you conniving son of a bitch, *where the hell are you?*

When the fussy legal expert sat down—the prosecutor/policeman let out a quiet sigh in Rye's ear—the tall old man stood for the second time. He did not attempt his English again. It was the policeman/prosecutor who said for him, "This shrine you see in Andit Teheg. You see no rituals in there?"

"No."

"Tehega-rohn speaks at no time about religion or the tahirr?"

"He spoke about the history of it, about the history of the tahirr." The old man frowned at her: a formidable person. "It is Tehega-rohn who speaks of the tahirr?"

"Yes."

"And Amaran-tahi. She teaches you the tahirr, Rye-tahi?"

"No."

"Amaran-tahi teaches you other things, Rye-tahi?"

Rye hesitated. But why? She had already stepped off this cliff. "Yes."

The old man bowed and sat down. The prosecutor/judge spoke again. Rye's translator did not bother to translate. It was hard not to look to her left, at Amaran and Tehega. She glanced up, past the benches and the rows of watching faces, to the glaring rim of the ceiling. Panes of glass had been set into a pale metal framework, and their edges seemed to be beveled, for prisms danced in the corners of Rye's eyes. The prosecutor/judge stopped talking. A profound silence fell. Rye, dazzled, brought her gaze back down to the audience as people began to stand. Mostly in white cassocks, they silently stood, looking down at the figures on the stage.

Voting, Rye guessed. Whatever side the standing people were on seemed to have lost, though Rye did not quite dare to turn and count rows behind her. The prosecutor/judge spoke again, and this time Rye caught Amaran's name in the sonorous flood of Nohan. A very few of the people standing, sat. Many more of the sitting people stood. Amaran is guilty? Amaran is innocent? Rye could not bear to look at the tahinit woman, but her eyes drifted that way in spite of herself. The moving sun had cast that end of the oval stage in shadow. Amaran's face was the same gray-white as her cassock, her dark eyes locked on the floor. Had she already made her own count? Surely she knew which way the vote had gone. Rye found she could not tell from the woman's expression.

No one spoke again. The count was silent. After a long, churchly silence, people began to file out of the amphitheater. Most of them wore dark clothes, civilian clothes. The lean old man in the gray coat passed near Rye, heading for the stairs behind her. He glanced at her, his eyes dark with a brooding intelligence that made her wonder, with a sudden jolt of unease, if he was from the world outside Meheg-menoht. What was happening out there? What did people outside the tahirr think about all this? She remembered the army they had seen on their arrival—and was distracted when Tehega approached the old man, who had his foot on the bottom stair. Tehega said something. The old man shook his head and started the climb. Tehega looked sick. Jostled aside by more people seeking the stairs he stepped back into a guard's waiting hands. He looked once at Rye as he was led away. Guilt-sickness swept over her, though Tehega's look had been empty of accusation, blank as if she had meant nothing to him. She was afraid, now, to look for Dan Bardo in the diminishing crowd.

Shade was moving steadily across the stage as the sun slipped beyond the glass roof. The light, colorless though it was, seemed to be taking away all the color in the vast room as it fled. The last of the civilians were eddying by the exits far above. The remaining tahinit, and there were many, descended to fill the tiers just above the stage. Their bleached cassocks formed a ring that blazed white in the sun, stark white-gray in the shade. Rye realized, far too late, that the prosecutor/judge and the prosecutor/policeman were both gone. She was the only person not in white left in the court, and the only person besides Amaran on the stage.

Guilt bled into panic. Rye turned toward the nearest stairs, but even there the tahinit stood, shoulder to shoulder, rank upon rank. It was the pit, the courtyard and the pit, too deep, too bright, no way out.

here, lover, here

She stood between an arc of sunlight and an arc of shade. The fever clambered hugely through her, until she felt like a cage of bones with a black-burning tiger inside. The fever beast was here, here. It was here, though Rye could not see it. Here, between the sunlight and the shade creeping toward her feet. Supplicant shadow, cowering as the fever raged against the sudden spark and press of the tahirr's lightning bars.

Rye saw the ranks of white-clad priests, the abandoned figure of Amaran, the slow movement of darkness across the oval floor. The fever saw the sparks of the tahinit's power pulse and merge from a hundred lightning bugs into a single strobe.

Lightning bars leapt out of the floor, the standing human ranks, the stone tiers and glassy roof. Rye screamed—no—Amaran screamed. The sound shocked through Rye, a seething jolt of heat/color/bile, as if she could vomit the other woman's fear. She did not, locked in place while the fever snarled defiance and the cage closed in. Closed in, leaving Rye outside. Amaran crouched down, shrinking from the lightning bars. They pressed closer, closer, closer still. Caught,

Amaran could not fall, but crouched still, impossibly balanced, while the tahirr bent her into a cubist's monstrosity. Her neck was wrenched impossibly back, her skull broken into a box-cornered angle, her face, angled, bent. One starting eyeball wept scarlet tears in the gray-white shade. Jack-in-the-box. Woman-in-the-box. Still recognizably Amaran, and unmistakably dead.

The tahirr-cage loosened, finally letting her collapse into a bundle of broken bones. Lightning bars frayed into sparks, darkness, nothing at all. The crowd loosened its ranks, sighing with breath, with the touch of cloth on cloth. A hand touched Rye's shoulder.

"So," a voice said. "That is done: the better half. You have our thanks."

nineteen

The walls were inhabited by women forced to carry their own deaths to term; by medical specialists in their green scrubs, plastic visors, doubled masks; by long-legged mantis-beasts gray and fluid as the stone. The fever's shadow, the arcwright, hid in Rye's shadow. It pooled and rippled as she walked down the lighted corridors with her guard. She could not escape it any more than she could escape the ghosts, or the walls.

She understood the tahirr now. God's house a prison cage.

I am not free!

Amaran's death hit Rye like a club, stopping her breath. She braced her hands on her knees, desperate not to fall into her shadow. Caught between two incandescent bulbs, it was doubled, twinned. Fever, arcwright, her mind could not distinguish between them. She believed Mostahr, knew Mostahr was lying. *You can be cured.*

The guard was hovering. The ghosts threatened to shatter the delicate tension at the surface of the stone. Rye sipped air, stumbled forward. Remembered that walking meant falling a little with every step.

Their common room was really the dead end of the hall between their bedrooms. The single window laid a burning brand across the polished table, the floor, the blue cushion of a chair. Bardo sat with the sunbeam like a bar between him and the door.

"Congratulations," he said.

Rye, sick with heat, struggled to undo the buttons of her coat.

Bardo stood, a towering shadow behind the light. "Just out of curiosity, what the hell did you think you were doing?"

Her hands were shaking, her fingertips slick with blood. She could not grapple even with the buttons. Sheer frustration shook hot tears onto her hands.

"I mean," said Bardo, "what the fuck were you doing?"

"Tuh-tuh-telling the truth?" Rye peered down at herself, but she could not even see the damn things. The sunlight was like a white blindfold across her eyes.

"Oh, the *truth*," said Bardo, awed by the revelation. "And the good news is, Tehega isn't even dead! Too bad about the army, of course. But hell. At least you told the truth."

Her hands fluttered like moth wings. She blotted her seeping palms on her coat—cave-painter's signature, ocher red on pale brown—and tried again.

Bardo was shouting at her: "I want a fucking answer, Rye!"

"Amaran's duh-duh-dead." Rye abandoned the buttons to wipe the back of her hand across her cheeks. Was she bleeding everywhere? Sweating? Crying? She blinked and saw the ghosts in the walls. Upturned faces and swollen bellies made stepping stones for the gray beasts. They were in constant motion. Rye pushed her shaking, bloody hands at them, willing them to be still. Shh. Shh. Shh.

Bardo kicked the table. It smashed spectacularly against the wall, spitting fragments of wood across the room. Rye froze, startled rabbit, shoulders high.

"All we needed to do," Bardo said reasonably, "was to let Tehega's allies think we were on his side. No promises. No guarantees. Just let them think we were in Tehega's pocket. Just give them a fucking reason to *hope*, and that army we saw would be tearing this fucking place *down* instead of waiting for the tahinit to send it to fucking *Earth*!"

Rye's hands were still out—shh, shh—dripping scarlet paint on the floor.

"That's it, Rye. That's all we had to do. Tell a couple of little white lies, give the lordlings some reason to think they had a chance at some real power, and we'd be fucking *out of here*."

He kicked a chair. Heavier than the table, it only grated across the floor.

"I didn't know," Rye whispered.

"You weren't even supposed to fucking testify. So what the hell were you doing, Rye?"

"I didn't know," she said. And then: "*How the fuck was I supposed to know?* Did you tell me? Did you ever tell me a fucking thing? 'I'll take care of it, Rye. Leave it to me, Rye.' Well fuck you, Dan! The first I heard about it was them telling me you were committing fucking perjury for fucking enemies of the state, and if I didn't tell the truth—*the truth*—" It was a shriek. "—you were going to end up dead along with them. Did you see Amaran die? Do you know what they did to her? *Do you?*"

Bardo said nothing, his face carved against the window's light.

"I didn't know," Rye said. "I didn't know, I didn't know, I didn't know."

She *was* crying. She grappled with the front of the coat until the buttons tore, a whole long line of buttons that pattered like droplets of blood to the floor, and then stood shivering, too weak with fever to pull her arms out of the sleeves.

The ghosts were still there, trapped within the walls of Meheg-menoht by the seething lines, the biting torment, of the tahirr. The tahirr *was* Meheg-menoht, both of them a prison, a cage made of human souls, a palace built to house a door the owners kept locked shut. The ghost women pressed their bellies against the ice-gray walls while the stone-gray beasts stalked and turned, a restless Escheresque puzzle of sharp joints and angled limbs and claws. They swarmed the walls, billowed like angular fog within the floor until Rye felt the bed creep in an infinitesimal slip across corrupted reality.

The lights were out, the window a thin gray shape in the blackness, but Rye had stripped off her blood-streaked clothes and saw it all through her lesion scars. The movement within the walls was a subtle torment like the scouring of insect legs across her skin. She could feel the gray beasts. She could feel the women's infestations coiled within their bellies. She could feel the bite of the tahirr.

And outside, vast as the night she could not see, she felt the arcwright peering in.

Oh, it was there, the fever's twin, close as the other side of the mirror's glass. It had always been there on the edges of her delirium, a figment of her fever dreams until Mostahr assured her it was real. Real. Whatever that meant. Her fever incarnate. Or did real equal flesh? This great watchful presence—*here, lover, here*—had she been right all along? Was it only the fever, the shadow the fever cast across the world—

A black iron grid, and black iron chains, and the sting of sweat on chafed flesh. Someone's voice shouting in anger and fear. Mercury skin in a quick-silver slide over black-iron shadows, black-iron bones. The clasp of hands or are they claws, fever-hot. The touch of a smooth sex, hot as an oiled piston on her belly—

She turned away from the memory (hers? the ghosts'?) and saw Amaran's shade pressed into a corner of the lightless room, her face bent to the shape of the walls.

"I didn't know," Rye said or thought.

"You only told the truth," Amaran said.

"I had to save Dan," Rye said. "He was only ever here because of me."

"It's your fault," Amaran agreed. "This is your cure, not mine."

(The gray beasts prowl and prowl. Her fever is too big for her skin and reaches out, out, brushing the lightning-shot ghost-seething walls, pressing against the cold-as-ice glass. Hello? Let me in.)

"My cure?" Rye says.

"Help me," Amaran says.

"You're dead," Rye says. "There is no cure for that."

"You're the only one I can ask," Amaran says. "Please, I don't want to die like that."

"You already did," Rye says.

But Amaran is gone from her corner. The gray beasts are gone, locked angle to angle, frozen into invisibility within the stone. There are only the women hunkered in a line against the wall. Breath is spun into gossamer scarves by the cold. The air is delicately colored by the bread smell of fever and the sweetness of rot. The women have no choice but to be patient in their suffering.

There is nothing to do here but wait for death. They sit and breathe, spinning their sighs into gossamer scarves on the cold thin air, white in the alien sunshine.

"Rye."

Rye is startled. She had forgotten that Bardo is also here. Just for a moment! But her inattention is a sin, and amplifies her guilt. "Dan, this is all my fault!" she tells him, as if confession will help.

"Oh, God. Rye. No it isn't. I should have told you."

Told her what? "You're only here because of me."

Bardo is only a dark shape against the sunlight, but the lines of the tahirr reflect a little light across his features, flickering bites of light that bring an eye, the bridge of his nose, the corner of his mouth out of the dark. He moves and the sun behind him blinds her, making everything dark.

"None of this is your fault," Bardo says. "If you want to blame someone, blame Cleände. She's the one who got you into this mess to begin with. None of this has anything to do with either of us. Remember that."

"But what about Earth?" Rye says. "You said—"

"Forget what I said. I was pissed off at myself, not at you."

"And Cleände is here." Guilt kicks again. Is that her in the corner? Is that her, hunkered down within the wall? How would Rye know? She can't remember! "Dan, is she here? Can you see her? I'm so afraid I won't recognize her face, but she must be here!"

" . . . Rye . . . "

"Can you see her? Maybe if you just remind me what she looks like . . . "

A hand touches her face.

"Holy Mother of God. Rye, you're on fire."

Or is it a claw? A black and angular talon, soft as brushed steel, big enough to wrap around her throat, her ribcage, her skull.

"Please," she whispers as moisture drenches her loins, her mouth, her skin. "I'll make a deal. I'll make a deal!"

The gray beasts, tasting blood with their groping limbs, begin to peel themselves from the walls.

"Oh, Jesus! Rye, whatever you're doing, stop it. Rye! Wake up!"

She woke—if she had been dreaming, if she was not dreaming that she woke—woke and huddled with Bardo on her bloody sheets as the gray beasts folded themselves back behind the stone, as the outraged tahirr dimmed its seething lines, as the arcwright prowled outside like a cat in heat calling to its mate.

Hello!

Let me in?

come, lover, come

twenty

The guards roused them—roused Rye, who slept with an invalid's restless exhaustion. She suspected Bardo had not slept at all, but he was still there, unshaven, his black eyes ringed in sepia bruises. He was up and opening the door while she was still piecing together the bed, herself lying on the bed, the bed in the room, the room with the door, the banging at the door.

"Get some clothes on," Bardo said. "They're in a hurry."

Rye hadn't got as far as her nakedness. She groped for the sheet, found it was stiff with bramble-lines of dried blood. Her skin was dusty with it. She remembered Bardo had said something about clothes just as he tossed her a clean shirt from the cupboard. It unfolded against her shoulder before she could put a hand up to catch.

"Is it morning?"

"Almost."

Which would explain the gray light that showed Bardo's features while hiding his expression. He moved with a coiled silence that seemed appropriate to dawn. Rye figured out the front of the shirt, pulled it on. Got up to pull on the pants Bardo gave her and had to sit down again, legs going everywhere like a colt's. Skinny enough to be a colt's. Gray beasts' fluid angles in the walls. A start rapped her spine, like a sharp nod at the edge of sleep, but the walls were quiet. Probing a rotten tooth, she though, *are you there?*

The walls dissolved

"Are you ready?"

and came together with a thud. No. That was their escort banging on the door.

"Is this one of those things you can't be ready for?"

"Probably." Bardo put out a hand. Rye, her mouth watering at the bright-copper bitter-rose taste, let him pull her up.

There were six guards crowding the disordered common room. Two of them wore white.

Every door opened on the courtyard. Every other door opened on the pit. The courtyard. Or the pit. Or the corridors of Meheg-menoht, fragile with ghosts that no one but Rye seemed to see. She was so tired she could have lain down on the air and let Bardo tow her along. She felt almost peaceful with her terror taking up residence in the walls.

One of the white guards said something sharp. The tahirr woke, blink and sizzle, the bright bite of a lightning-bug spark. The light scraped like claws across the wall, but none of the guards seemed to notice that either.

The courtyard. The pit. The long gray halls. Then another door, and this one opened onto the smell of antiseptic and hot metal, stale food and decay, a smell that melted Rye's bones. The body's memory. She shrank into it, fitting into a prisoner's mold. The gray guards maneuvered them through one at a time, so Bardo had to drop her hand. She slid away from a guard's gesture, quick and anxious to comply. Her fear had come home.

Welcome, they had told her. Welcome home.

The heart of the heart of the world.

The only light came through the door they entered by. An enormous door, thick as Rye's body, matte black steel. A bank vault's door. They descended a flimsy aluminum flight of temporary stairs into a long room, so high that the ceiling was only a denser shadow in the poor light. The floor was hot and tacky beneath Rye's bare soles. Bardo had forgotten to give her shoes.

Mostahr was waiting, along with others of the tahinit, less like ghosts in their white cassocks than like chess pieces placed strategically about the board. Tehega was there, and a woman. Rye recognized her smock first, then noticed her face, and was touched by a glancing hint of recognition, here and gone. Bardo drew in his breath and stumbled on the last narrow stair behind her, so she guessed that the woman was Cleände. Rye might have wondered, stared, but Mostahr stepped before her, filling up Rye's view. She saw only in the corner of her eye how Bardo was herded with the other two down to the far end of the room, out of easy earshot, out of reach of the door.

"You have contacted your other," Mostahr said softly. "Meheg-menoht rang with it last night. You put us all in danger, and I am out of patience. You will call the arcwright back to us. Now."

Back to us? To this room, this lightless chamber in Meheg-menoht's stony heart. The tahirr swarmed the walls, the prison cage. The fever, the arcwright's attention, swarmed through Rye. She felt the thousand tahinit-sparks, the lightning bites that made up the tahirr, flicker to a thousand rhythms that, all together, were on the cusp of one rhythm, one pulse of the heart of the world. One beat of these stony walls that would crush them all.

Or choke, Rye thought, on her fever-clotted blood.

"Now," Mostahr said.

"Is this my cure?" Rye asked.

Mostahr, in no hurry to answer, glanced around, a player noting her pieces on their squares. Her face was wet with sweat. Dew beads traced the lines in her cheeks. Guards shifted at the head of the stairs, at the far end of the room where the prisoners stood. Violence, like silence, stroked through the heavy air. Mostahr looked at Rye: her last piece.

"You were shocked by Amaran's death," Mostahr said, her grandmotherly voice an offense. "You were meant to be. It was a useful example, and a lesson. How—what is the word?—how appropriate, that she should teach you something of the tahirr at last."

"Ironic," Rye whispered. "Are you going to kill me? Is that my cure?"

"No," Mostahr said. "Oh, no. But what of these others? What of this Daniel Bardo?"

"He never did anything to you."

Mostahr, shockingly, laughed. "My daughter, he has been an enemy of Nohai before he even knew the name of our world. Look at him. He is not surprised at where he is."

Rye did not have to look. She knew. "Let him go."

"And you will do as I say?"

Rye hesitated too long.

Mostahr spread her arms, stepping lightly back from Rye, inviting her to take in the room.

"How interesting it will be!" Mostahr said. Her warm voice grew to fill the space, but the heat, the tahirr, the arcwright's shadow, robbed it of resonance.

"How interesting," Mostahr's large, muffled voice said, "to learn where your loyalties lie. Who will you save? Which tie will you let me cut, and which will you let yourself be bound by?" Her voice fell again. "Or is the arcwright . . . is the arcwright . . . the only tie you will heed?"

"It's the only one I want you to cut!"

"And the only one I will not cut. Call it home."

Another no would mean someone began to die. "How . . . how will you . . . keep it here?"

"Do you need to ask?" Mostahr pointed, a finger-sketch of the prisoners, the invisible tahirr, the invisibly ghost-haunted walls. "As we keep and command you."

"It doesn't—Why should it—" Wrestling with both thought and language. "Why should it care what happens to me?"

Mostahr's eyes narrowed, contemplating something Rye could not see. Every pause was crowded with the tension of the heart's suspended beat. Mostahr's decision, whatever it was, took a lifetime.

"You are its other self. It has only you. It has no choice, and neither do you. Call it. Now."

"But I can't! It's free. I don't know how."

"You can." Mostahr's voice was unyielding. "It is no more free than you are. You bind it with the air in your lungs and the blood in your heart. Listen, my daughter. There is no 'freedom' for such a being. There is no 'choice.' It is nothing but the black shadow of God's will—"

"Then let God bring it home," Rye said.

"I bring it home," Mostahr said simply. "I am God's hand. I hold you. I hold them. I hold the arcwright like a shadow in my palm." She cupped her hand between them. Darkness pooled there, like blood.

"But it's real," Rye said, her own fever confusing her. "It's real, not a shadow. Isn't it?"

"It is, by some measure, a living creature. You showed us this most clearly when you killed its twin, its true other self. Oh, yes. Indeed you did."

"Liar." Rye could hardly hear her own voice over the roaring of blood in her ears. Or was that the tahirr singing? Did those invisible lightning bars thrum like struck iron? Did Mostahr's white-clad seconds stir and voice a warning? Rye thought they might have. She was distracted by the bloom of gray beasts within the walls.

Are you here?

Mostahr was saying, "Why it has not destroyed you before now I do not know, but consider. Consider how it must hate you for that killing, and for the power you stole. Consider how it torments you. Oh, we know how you bleed. Consider how much more you will suffer if it ever gets you within its reach."

"Liar." But this time Rye's voice was weak with uncertainty.

"We saved you once. Do you know how near it came to you when Amaran led you outside the tahirr's protection? Do you know how near it comes to you now, even within the sanctity of Meheg-menoht? Ryder-tahi. My daughter. Rye." Mostahr put out a beseeching hand. "Let us save you. Help us to bind it before it destroys you."

But Mostahr's hand was full of blood, and Rye silenced her with a scream.

"Liar!"

Shaking with the sudden heat of rage, Rye prowled towards Mostahr, forcing her back, step and step and step. "You lie and you lie and you lie."

"If you know what you did," Mostahr said coldly, stepping back again, "you know I tell the truth."

Black-silver eyes, twisted limbs, blood hot on her hands. Gray beasts blooming, like a photographic image rising from the red-lit darkness of a developer's bath, from the walls. Oh, no, no, she did not know what she had done. But:

"I know what you did. You're the one that did this to me. You're the one that stole. This—" She shoved her bleeding palms in Mostahr's face. "*This* is what you stole. Do you want it?" Self-control, such as she had, crumbling, gone. *"Do you want it?"*

Mostahr stepped back again, and Rye pounced. Cat-like,

tiger-like, she leaped forward and gripped Mostahr's face between her bloody talon-paws. Mostahr staggered, face blood-smeared and strange with horror, and fell back under Rye's weight. Rye, crouched astride the older woman, had a still, blind moment to wonder, what now? But Bardo was shouting her name, someone was keening with fear, someone else was chanting, all the voices muffled by the angular fog of gray beasts stepping out of the walls. Mold-gray images overlapped, double and triple exposures that stepped and stepped out of the walls, rose like mushrooms from the floor, dropped from the ceiling like rain, oozed from the walls like sweat from fever-torn skin—

Rye! Rye!

And Mostahr's ragged panting, her breath an intimate caress on Rye's face, and footsteps as someone ran for the stairs, and the strangely precise crunch and splatter as a flesh-and-bone body was opened like a door—

Rye!

And Rye's own voice, a child's voice, lost in the dark: "Are you there?"

come, lover, come

And she didn't know how, but she came.

Bardo

The gray beasts were gone between one step and the next. The floor was gone and here again, so he fell onto one knee. Bone struck wood. There was Rye, glistening scarlet crimson black. Sunlight from the window swirling with dust. Rye, leaning on the air. Cleände, in a coarse sacking smock. Rye, drifting through the sun-caught dust. Tehega, fist at his temple. The end-of-rainstorm patter of blood hitting the floor. Rye, noticed by gravity, falling.

Bone struck wood.

Cleände put out her hands as if to grapple with reality, mouth gaping to draw in one breath, another, beginning to pant. The sound was loud in the room. Tehega, much as usual in his neat frock-coat and polished boots, looked dopey with bewilderment. Bardo, nursing his bruised knee, went over to Rye, who lay unconscious in a patch of sunlight below the window. Her clothes were soaked with clotting blood, her face masked in it, scarlet drying to crimson, crimson to scabrous brown, black in her hair and along the lesion-scrawls. Bardo cupped his hand over her mouth, felt her breath like the caress of a stinging nettle across his palm.

"Daniel?" Cleände said. Even now, with her shock written across her elegant face, her voice held its unique music. "Daniel Bardo?"

He looked up from the ruin of Ryder Coleman. Cleände was still the most beautiful woman he had ever known, despite the marks of her captivity. She was thin, had sores around her mouth. She was also looking to him for an explanation as if she had never known what he was. God, to have her again, to have her ignorant and loving again …

"Daniel?"

He bent over the horror that was Rye and picked her up as gently as he could. Her clothes peeled away from the floor with a gruesome sound. He felt the scalding seep of fresh blood soaking the sleeve of his shirt, hot enough to raise blisters. His gorge rose at the smell. He shifted her weight higher on his shoulder and carried her out of the room—Cleände's living room—past the front door—Cleände's door—and up the stairs.

"Daniel!"

He laid Rye on the bathroom floor and ran cold water into the tub, rinsing out the spiders and letting the unused tap run clear. From below he heard the door open and close again. Tehega gone. Shivering with cold-hot fever-chill, thinking of Cleände alone downstairs, Bardo dropped the plug into the drain, peeled off Rye's sodden clothes, and lifted her, still wrapped in her cocoon of scabbing blood, into the bath.

Home.

God have mercy on his soul.

Rye

Blood like sweat, like the liquors of sex. She is lapped at, eaten, consumed. She surrenders, the surrender of orgasm, of death, but nothing ends. The monster nuzzles her, shadow against the stinging bars, the stubs of its severed limbs holding it above her. Lover, rapist, neither, it licks her like a hungry cat savoring a skinned mouse. Its tongue is hot, narrow, barbed like a bee's sting. It catches in her skin, thorny caress, again and again and again. The tongue is strong enough, the ruined creature, weeping out of one blind eye, is thirsty enough, that she is tugged across the floor. One tug, another, tiny increments of humiliation and pain. She puts her hands up, finds a bony head, a hot serpent's throat that ripples as it swallows. She squeezes, sick with horror at herself—herself, because this is her fault: the ultimate self-betrayal: she has agreed to this.

She squeezes and feels the breath broken and trapped between her thumbs, feels the desperate body kick and twist—knows it is not too late, she can stop, except she can't, having come so far.

She closes her eyes against the look on Marky's face, the unbearably innocent surprise, the blood hot on her hands.

The blood spilling from Amaran's blind eye as the breath is crushed out of her.

The teeth in her neck caressing her spine as they drag her along.

All her fault.

All.

The jaws are strong enough to bite through her spine. One clench, one meaty crunch. But the teeth only prick, the jaws only carry her, tiger kitten in its mother's hold. Tiger mother, tiger lover, hunched and snarling over its mate. The teeth hold her fast inside the pain of desire, the salty rush of love.

The size of him, and the weight. The strength of those muscles that seem too lean, stretched over those long, heavy bones. The fineness of his hidden skin, the curling hair that draws the line from his heart to his loins, the moist, lying softness of his mouth. He is so dark against her almond pallor, so cool against her fever, so smooth against her scars. He fills her and engulfs her, paradoxical as the fever that bears her and is borne by her. The tiger inside her

kisses her neck, and neon fish swim through her eyes, and she wants to laugh. Fireworks! But she is too full of him, her mouth is dark with him, her senses scored by rose thorns, their venom bright as copper and new wine as he moves above her, opening her skin

in the tiger's jaws

that bite her, wasp-sting tooth driving down her artery from her throat to her heart, sensation beyond definition as pleasure or pain. Burns her like a fire, eats her like a fire, swallowing her down to acid and ash, transformed

in the tiger's gut.

Transformed. The bed to an iron frame. The night to a shadowed pit. The tiger to

Bardo

There was still no electricity. He set candles around the room in preparation for the dark. Cleände's room. He could not have said whom he punished by laying Rye in Cleände's bed. All three of them, perhaps, or none of them. It was practical, the wide bed already made with dusty sheets. Rye stained the white cotton in a delicate pattern, pink over brown, that blurred like watercolors as he moved her, wiping her down. He took a saucepan and the rag made from his shirt into the bathroom, rinsed them, carried fresh water back to the room. Cleände was there by the bed. She had bathed, and now wore her own clothes, a wheat-colored shirt over cranberry leggings. She held herself as if she were ill or in pain, and looked from Rye to Bardo with her curiosity shadowed, now, by everything she knew.

"I would not have known her," she said. "Little Ryder."

Bardo came to himself, shirtless and burdened in the door. He stepped into the room and set the full pan on the table across the bed from Cleände.

"You care for her? I mean, you tend her. Of course you were always fond."

There was irony in the *of course*. Cleände knew as well as he how little time he had had for the kids.

He drew the sheet over Rye, hiding her nakedness. It would make no difference to the heat that radiated off her, stronger than the heat from the open window. The sound of traffic was almost musical after the silence of Meheg-menoht. Blood drew its subtle patterns, slow as the fading light, like frost or ferns. Bardo wrung out his rag, wiped Rye's face. Her eyelids quivered under his touch.

"Daniel," Cleände said. "This is my house. Do you have the right to silence here?"

He dropped the rag into the pan, folded his arms across his bare chest.

"My house," she insisted.

"My world. Even prisoners have the right to silence here."

She flinched, drew breath. "Here, perhaps. Not elsewhere."

"No?" He leaned a thigh against the table, heard the water slop against the pan's rim. "How much did you tell them?"

"You dare—!" Cleände was quivering with tension, fists clenched at her sides.

Bardo shrugged, tired of sparring, weary with self-disgust. "Do you blame me?"

"Of course I blame you! Who else should I blame?" With a wild gesture at the bed. "Who else does *she* blame? Look at what they have done to her!"

"'They'? You mean the tahinit lords? The ones who took you prisoner? Oddly enough, I gather they are the ones she blames."

"She will learn better!"

"Cleände—" Bardo's abrupt move spilled water from the pan. It dripped on the bare boards of the floor, a distressingly familiar sound. "You really think I betrayed you."

She laughed, raw and accusatory.

"If I had wanted to shut you up," he said softly, "do you think I couldn't have found a more efficient way?"

He heard her breathe. The room was almost dark.

"Do you threaten me now?"

He hated himself for how much that hurt. "No. But I'll make a deal with you."

Another laugh, shakier than the last. "A bargain. A bargain from Daniel Bardo. I wonder how many of those there have been?"

"Too many," he said.

"Ah. The ring of honesty."

"You've heard it before."

"Yes." She paused. "And how many of the too many bargains have you kept?"

"All of them."

"Poor Daniel Bardo."

It was her he hated then.

"Go on," she said, and in the dark he could almost believe her amused. "Tell me your terms."

"You keep your mouth shut around Rye," he needed an extra breath, "and I'll do my best to keep the two of you alive."

"I don't need you for that!"

"You let Tehega walk out the door. Did you even know who he was? Do you know what forces he can muster? I do. I know how to find them. I know what they want. I know what they need." A threat, he realized, after all. It gained no answer. "Do you know how much you need Rye?" Still no answer. "I know. I do know, Cleände, like I know you can't take care of her. Hell, you can barely stand. You damn sure need me for something." And please, God, don't let her hear that for the plea it was.

"But I don't understand you. You wish to protect her *innocence*?"

"Her life," he said harshly. "And yours."

She ignored this. "My God, Daniel, do you imagine they have left her any innocence to protect?"

"More," he said, "than you can imagine."

"My God. What is she to you now?"

He said nothing.

A third laugh, faint as a breath. "Poor little Ryder. Do you trust me to keep my part of the bargain?"

"No."

She hesitated, a long pause balanced over too many possibilities, and in the end did not speak. But it was there between them, Bardo's deal, weak as a straw bridge.

Cleände gave him a wide berth as she left the room.

Rye

Hands pull at her clothes, scrub her with harsh sponges, bind her arm to take a vial of her blood. She does not fight, made weak by the anticipation of a punishment she may—she is not certain—have earned. Walls, faces, medical equipment seem detached from her vision, far off and badly framed, as if her eyes have retreated into her skull. She catches a distant glimpse of a locked cupboard door, a burnt-out bulb behind a cage, a face stern and brown-eyed and old. Humiliation wars with dread.

Naked, she is led into a dark, reeking pit of a room. The hands bind her, ankle and wrist, to an iron frame like a tilted bed. She realizes too late that they are gentle because she does not struggle. Too late, but she fights anyway, sweating cold in the dry death-and-metal heat, rubbing the skin on her wrists and ankles raw. The door clunks shut, soft and heavy as a bank vault, and she is alone. Or not alone. The light is sifted by shadows like moonlight through leaves. They stand above her, foreshortened, their feet marked by the grill as her back is by the frame. She screams at them, stops herself, her very fear forcing her to think, or maybe it's only pride: don't give them the satisfaction.

Somewhere beyond the tunnel arch—she is tilted to face it squarely, but cannot penetrate the darkness beyond—another bank vault opens. A hot, sour wind blows around her, reminding her of her naked skin. She says, like an incantation to conjure courage, *oh God, death by cliché*. Thinking virgin sacrifices (not that she's a virgin); thinking princesses bound to the stake (not that she's a lady); thinking dragons.

Blackness coalesces in the tunnel mouth, dark movement running with a mercury gleam.

Gray beasts, she thinks, glimpsing that liquid glide, that shadow-puppet slide of long-jointed limbs, but no. It emerges, slipping around the corner to prowl the curve of the wall, and this—this quicksilver flesh, these iron-shadow bones—this is the living original that must spin off the gray beasts the way the dying spin off their ghosts. It glides, lazy-seeming and swift, behind her. It is silent, but she can feel the heat of it, a dusty scorch like overheated steel. She has forgotten the watchers. All her being is devoted to tracing its movement behind her . . . shadow-slipping the wall . . . around to her other side. She does not want to turn her head and see it again, but she must. Simply, must. And does.

It moans, or something does, deep as the axle that turns the world, and it parts itself from the wall. The quicksilver shadow swells into three dimensions: four long limbs; rib-sprung body; wedge-shaped head carved like an iron skull. Eyes, black as oil, as a star-shot night, look out on an infinity of pain. How does she—heart pounding so hard it surely must tear itself in two—how does she recognize that pain?

It moves in the dim light as if gravity were a sea for swimming in, as if its black-gleaming hide sheds distance the way Teflon sheds the rain. It is the most beautiful thing, and the most terrible thing, that she has ever seen. There is a part of her, compressed into diamond clarity by the weight of terror, that revels in that beauty. Even as it mounts the frame, even as she feels the hot, smooth weight of its sex on her belly, even as she whimpers, *oh God, oh God*, she clings to that beauty, and to the selfhood she still sees, even then, in its eyes. It is that that lets her whisper, breath timed to the agonizing rhythm of her heart, *Listen. I'll make a deal with you. Can you understand me? Listen. Oh God.* As it lowers itself against her, velvet hide and iron bone, hot enough to dry the sweat on her skin. *Please help me. Listen.*

I'll make a deal.

Bardo

Candlelight swims against the walls, stirred by the draft from the window. Bardo, half naked, aches for a wind to cool him, shivers at the lying premonition of autumn in the air. He sits on the floor with his arm propped on the mattress edge, listening to a candle gutter, listening to Rye breathe. He remembers her saying once that her fever inhabited her like a beast. He had not understood her then. Now, stunned by defeat, he can feel it, huge and hot as the night, stalking them both. Or perhaps that is only fate.

Or perhaps fate and the fever are one and the same. Did he ever in all his gambles, all the times he had wagered her, sold her—did he ever consider that he might someday need her help? Protect her innocence, Cleände says. Dear God. Rye's innocence is the only thing that might save him now.

Unless.

Candlelight and shadow chase each other across the walls until Bardo, dizzy with Rye's heat, wonders if he is right about them, darkness and light. Maybe they are not two sides of the same thing. Maybe they only come together out of choice, out of . . . call it . . . desire. Call it . . . love. A late night thought, fever borne, to be forgotten in the morning.

Also to be forgotten: Rye's mouth under his mouth, her sweet eyes, her breath, hot and soft on his throat. Her blood, that he had thought was only sweat as he moved on her, inside her, almost forgetting that last time with Cleände. Forgotten like Marducci, after the gray beast was finished with him. Like Marky, bent over a Nohan knife. Like Austad, his blood spreading while his eyes opened wide with surprise. All to be forgotten again in the morning.

As the marks on the hand that rinses Rye's face—the marks like wine-colored frost, or feathers, or scales, that spread up his arm until he takes his hand away—will no doubt also vanish, forgotten, in the morning.

twenty-one

There was yellow sunlight outside the open window. Traffic drove by, intermittent but never entirely still, drawing a thread of sound through the dusty silence of an old house on a hot day. For once Rye woke knowing where she was. Back in the real world. The sane world, even if she didn't know whose bed she was in.

yellow sunlight dancing yelling (dusky-sweet refraction) chemicals in the air

She sat up, pushing the brown-stained sheet aside. A little dried blood sifted out of her hair as she rubbed herself awake. Languorous with heat and the arcwright's pleasure, she recognized the room as a pleasant one—bare wood, bare plaster, red paper lantern on the ceiling's high slope—without taking much interest. She stretched, hissing a little as thin scabs plucked at her scars, and climbed naked out of bed. The floor boards were silky with dust underfoot as she went to the door.

She did not know whose house this was, either, but there was a bathroom across the hall.

Having washed, she went downstairs in a tank-top and skirt rummaged from someone's drawers and only began to recognize where she was when she was standing in the lower hall. Rain. She remembered the rain first, and then the house. Cleände's house hidden in the embrace of the dead factory's wall.

sour brick dust (reflected heat) tickle of broken glass (here)

Rye turned her face toward the back of the house and said, "Yes, all right." She felt calm, much too calm, until she heard movement, the scrape of furniture, and for a breath she thought—A backlit shape showed in the door at the end of the hall, shadowy and lean, and for a heartbeat she thought—

But it was a human shape, and it had a human voice.

A woman's voice. "I heard you moving upstairs. I am glad you found some clothes. Of course you are welcome to anything of mine. I hope you are recovered?"

A lick of recognition, gone as soon as it was felt. Rye had to guess: "Cleände?"

The woman hesitated. "Am I so changed?"

"No. I mean, I don't know." An uneasy laugh. "I am. Sorry. I don't remember very well."

The woman was faceless against the light. Rye had the uncomfortable sense of a whole complex weave of thoughts taking place out of her cognizance. Then Cleände said, "Forgive me. Daniel told me, of course, but it seems strange not to be known, when I know you so well."

"Is he here?"

"No." Cleände made a sound in her throat, the soft edge of a laugh. "Daniel has appointed himself our caretaker, and has gone for food, and to pay my electricity bill. I expect him to return soon, which is good, for I can only offer you water until he does." She moved, still in silhouette, so she was no longer blocking the door. "Do you mind sitting in the kitchen? I find I have a great hunger in me for sunlight after so long in a cell."

"You ..." Rye collected herself, walked down the hall. "You were a prisoner, then?"

Cleände looked at her, startled, speculative. "And would be still if you had not rescued me."

The kitchen had only one small window over the sink, but that window was full of sunlight and Rye could see the other woman's face in vivid detail now they were both inside the room. Another elusive burst of recognition lit inside her, bright and fleeting as a spark, leaving her more unsettled yet.

Or perhaps it was only that she recognized Cleände's beauty. The long bones of her face were arranged into a mysterious harmony of angle and arch, too unique to be a type, and stunning. She was also—and it did nothing to detract from her beauty, any more than did the lines of forty years of living—worn to the point of exhaustion. The dark blue of her eyes was made darker by the sepia bruising of the lids, the fine shape of her mouth scarred by half-healed sores.

"Oh, my little Ryder," she said, her voice rich with pity. "Do *you* grieve to see what they have done to *me*?"

Rye looked away, stepped away before Cleände's gesture could become an embrace. The room was long and narrow, stretching across the back of the house. A big farmhouse table was squeezed into one end, crowded with chairs, and there was a water jug on the table, a glass before the pulled-out chair. Another glass sat in the shallow enamel sink. Bardo. She wished intensely, urgently, that he would come.

(coming, lover, coming)

"No!"

"Ryder, forgive me, I presume as a friend, and should not. Forgive me."

stay! stay away! stay away from me!

Stark panic, bitter revulsion, that made a lie out of her waking peace. Her silent scream ripped through her, jagged as lightning, and created a silence so perfect she could hear the creak of her joints as they kept her balance.

Then: "My God."

Cleände. Avoiding her gaze, not wanting to know how much she had heard, or guessed, or knew, Rye went to the table and pulled out a chair. After a long, tense moment, Cleände moved to the cupboard by the sink, took out a glass, set it down at Rye's elbow.

"Thank you," Rye said.

"You are welcome." Cleände sat, poured water for Rye, set the jug down with concentrated, deliberate care.

The kitchen had glossy white walls and yellow cupboard doors. Bright in the sunshine, it tasted like salt. Rye washed the taste down with tepid water that tasted of chlorine and pipes. Bardo, she thought again, unable to stop herself, and was assailed by a tilting dizziness, by heat and smell and movement, by an anxiety so crushing it deserved a more powerful name. She blinked, and there was only the silent kitchen, the warm bitter water, the spark-limned presence of Cleände. Rye set her glass on the table, rested her elbows to either side of it, braced her head against her clasped hands. I'm sorry, she tried to think, not entirely sure why or to whom. A misery welled up inside her, so deep and confused it actually took comfort from the arcwright's delirious whisper.

here, lover, here

They heard him climb the steps to the front porch, open the door, close it, walk heavily down the hall. He stopped in the kitchen doorway, laden with grocery bags, and Rye suffered an instant of split perspective: looking at Bardo, big and hot and tired in a brick-colored T-shirt, standing in the doorway looking at: two women, a table between them, looking at: Bardo. Then she blinked, or Bardo did, and he came in and heaved the grocery bags onto the counter by the sink.

"When did you wake up?"

"Just now."

He brushed his hand across her hair. "All right?"

"Sure." She would have touched his hand, but he was moving again, crossing the long room to open the refrigerator door. No light shone, no motor hummed. "They said the power should be on this afternoon."

"You can still put stuff in the fridge," Rye said. "At least it's insulated."

Bardo looked at her as if this were a very strange thing for her to say.

She lifted her brows. "Well, it is."

He turned his back on her to rummage through the bags.

"Are *you* all right?"

He didn't answer. There was a sound of cardboard tearing, the clank of bottles, and then Bardo, beer bottle in hand, stalked out of the room. His shirt was dark with sweat along his spine, his black hair curling in wet spikes on his neck.

"Oh," Rye said at his retreating back. "Okay, *I* can put stuff in the fridge."

She watched his broad, bony shoulders tighten as Cleände began to laugh.

She found him, later, in a stuffy little room upstairs.

When she eased the door open a crack, she thought he was sleeping. He was stretched out on a too-short futon on the floor, the empty bottle standing by his hand. Sunlight slatted hot through a venetian blind to stripe the battered floor. Except for a fly that buzzed and rattled between the window and the blind, there was nothing else in the room. She was about to shut the door when he turned his head and opened his eyes.

"What?"

"Nothing," Rye answered, startled by his urgency. Realizing he was expecting some emergency, she showed him the plate she carried. "Lunch."

He let his head roll back until he was staring at the ceiling.

She stepped in, nudged the door shut with her foot, and crossed the room to kneel at his side, juggling plate and bottle and glass.

"I'm not hungry," he said.

"Here," she said. "This one's cold." She pressed a sweating beer bottle against his bare arm.

He winced. "Jesus, Rye! That's cold!"

She decided she had better not laugh. She put the bottle down, picked up her glass. "They turned the power on."

"Obviously."

"There's sandwiches."

Bardo groaned and dragged himself up to prop his shoulders against the wall. More or less upright, he looked more tired than ever, the lines around his mouth dug deep, his eyes ringed with bruises.

"Cleände said—"

"Spare me what Cleände said."

"—that you stayed up all night with me?" Rye's voice shrank in confusion. She took a swallow of milk. "Maybe you should eat something anyway."

"Rye's revenge."

It came out so bleak and hard she stared at him, her heart in her throat. She set her milk glass down on the floor. "It's just a sandwich."

Bardo pulled up his knees, braced his arms against them, braced his head against his arms. He took a deep breath, as if to answer her, and then didn't, and it dawned on Rye that he was suffering from more than fatigue. She touched her fingertips to the back of his hand, and he responded so suddenly, so ferociously, that she tried to duck. But he didn't hit her. He pulled her into a desperate embrace, indifferent to the awkward, bony knot her body made inside the hard circle of his arms.

Rye was shocked at first. The near violence spiked her body with adrenaline, the harsh handling of her tender skin set off synesthetic fireworks all down her nerves. But this was Bardo, her anchor *(other)*, her shelter *(lover)*, whose breath was ragged against her neck, whose hair was soft and damp against her face. She shifted to hug him back, awkward, for he would not relax his grip. When she bumped something with her knee, a bottle, and knocked it rolling across the floor, he flinched, and the flinch became a shiver. "Dan," she whispered, "Dan." She turned her face until her mouth touched his skin. "Shh," she said. Her breath against him, his breath against her, her heat working through him, his shiver working through her, resonating, circling, copper rose (quicksilver fire *(sun-hot tar (sex) reflected heat)* sun on glass shards) new bitter wine—

"Sorry," Bardo gasped. "Sorry, Rye." He put her from him, gentle but urgent, taking his hands from her bare arms as quickly as he could.

She fell back to sit on the floor, drenched with sensation, stupid with it, only now realizing that *that* had been *desire.*

Was desire.

"It's okay," she said, her breath coming all out of synch with the rest of her. "It's okay." And because she was suddenly, ferociously hot, and because she needed very badly just then to do something normal, she stretched out, leaning on one elbow, to retrieve the bottle of beer she had sent rolling, and twisted off the cap. Beer foamed up and over (bitter chocolate icy spangles) her hand.

"Here," she said, holding it out to Bardo. "It's still cold."

"So what happened to Tehega?"

The three of them were in the kitchen. It was evening. Bardo was cooking while the women sat and watched.

"He walked out while you were bleeding all over the bathroom floor."

"Just like that?" Rye said.

Bardo held a plate to the edge of the counter, shoveled sliced peppers onto it, set it aside, and reached for a stalk of broccoli. "What would you have suggested?"

"Keep him here," Cleände said, intense. "I would have if I had known."

Rye shrugged. She discovered that she had no particular grudge against Tehega. He seemed, after Bardo's dealings and Amaran's death, almost like one of them. More like one of them than Cleände, now that Rye thought about it. She was careful not to meet the other woman's gaze.

"What would you have done?" Bardo said to Cleände. "Fainted on him?"

"I have weapons here," Cleände said softly.

Bardo gave her a cold look over his shoulder, and Rye was reminded that he had once been a policeman.

"Dan," Rye started.

"What?"

"Nothing." She had too many questions, and didn't like any of them. She looked out the window at the velvety shadow of the factory wall. It was almost dark enough to turn on the light. The third week in August. When Bardo had told her the date, she had been tempted to ask him, *What year?* Because they had been on Nohai hardly any time at all, and far, far too long.

sun kissing the horizon (rich sky murmuring, murmuring) tar still soft with heat

Cleände was looking at her oddly. When she glanced at the other woman, the blue eyes turned deliberately to Bardo's back.

"I think," Cleände said, "that it is not too soon to discuss our situation."

Bardo checked the oil in the pan with a spitting droplet of water, then threw in a double handful of shrimp. "Discuss away," he said over the hissing burst of steam.

"But I do not know," Cleände said, silky with anger, "what our situation is."

Bardo shook the pan, throwing up further gouts of steam and noise.

"That smells good," Rye said, which was true: garlic and sesame oil, deliciously familiar.

"I hope you like it spicy." Bardo spooned the browned shrimp out into a bowl, added a little more oil to the pan.

Cleände slapped the table. "Are you both children?"

"No," Bardo said. "Hungry." He dumped the vegetables in the pan.

Rye tried to suppress a snicker.

Cleände slapped the table again in disgust.

Bardo gave the vegetables a toss, then turned around to say, gently for him, "Maybe it is too soon, lady. It was a fucking miraculous escape. Let's just be glad for a bit. All right?"

"Too soon for you," Cleände said. "But it will always be too soon for you!"

Bardo turned back to the stove, and Rye noticed that his shirt was dark with sweat. She was so used to her own internal furnace she had not recognized how hot the kitchen was. She got up to open the back door.

"Turn the light on," Bardo said.

Rye flipped the switch by the door, tasted/heard/felt the jump of electrons through the wires, watched the light spill her shadow across dry grass to the base of the brick wall. The evening grew darker by contrast. The arcwright could have been in any of a hundred shadows. Even hers. She turned her back on the night.

"Does someone want to tell me what's going on?"

Bardo: "There's plates to the right of the sink."

Cleände: "There is someone who does *not* want to tell you."

Rye: "This is already getting old."

She found plates, silverware, glasses. She had to brush past Bardo to fetch the water jug from the fridge; they were both, without looking at each other, careful not to touch. When Rye put the jug on the table and saw Cleände's face, she thought, well, maybe that was all it was. Jealousy, mundane and, in the circumstances, bizarre. But the look Cleände gave her while Bardo's back was still turned was not the glare of a rival.

It was the urgent, complicitous look of a woman who is trying to warn a friend.

twenty-two

Rye woke, confused by the creak of floorboards and the mutter of the approaching sun. Like an internal compass, the fever pointed *there*, to the arcwright, behind the house or maybe the factory wall, and only then could she orient herself in the living room, on the sheet-draped couch. She had refused to take Cleände's bed again, and Bardo had not offered to share. She tasted a dusty whisper *(brick tar shadows glass)* and made out the dim light sketching the curtain-edge, hardly brighter than the one weak streetlight outside. She had that much sorted out by the time the creak of floorboards gave way to the groan of stairs. Someone was coming down.

Bardo, she thought, and felt a hot twist of tension and relief in her gut. But it was Cleände who came to the living room door.

"Ryder?"

It was a whisper, and Rye might have pretended to be asleep. In a brief spasm of cowardice she considered it, but then sat up, rubbing her eyes, and Cleände came to perch on the arm of the couch at her feet.

"I am sorry to wake you. I cannot sleep, myself."

Rye murmured something meaningless.

The house had cooled overnight. Rye felt the chill as a pleasurable tightening of her skin. Cleände smoothed her long robe over her legs and breathed a laugh.

"I carried a hundred questions down with me, and only now it occurs to me that I may have lost the right to ask them of you. No, worse than that, I begin to ask myself if I ever had the right at all.

Daniel told me often enough . . . " Another laugh, crooked and faint. "It seems like years ago. A lifetime ago."

"What did he tell you?"

Both women spoke in near whispers, consonant with the tenuous light.

"That I had no right to draw the two of you, you and Mark, into my war. Of course he was justified. I had no right. But right was irrelevant to me then. It was necessary, that was all that mattered. Or rather, it seemed necessary. I have had cause to question my judgement in many things since then."

Rye ignored this last. "Necessary because we were within the tahirr."

Cleände lifted her head to give her an unreadable glance, then turned her face away. "If you were of my people, you would consider that a grotesque expression. But of course, you would have had no choice but to learn from the tahinit." Extraordinary, how much loathing a whisper could carry. "I thank God you are free of them. And yes, that was why I needed you. We came here and found an entire race ignorant of power, and yet with the seeds of power scattered within you as within us. It was a great mystery, but unlike the tahinit we do not have the luxury of time to spend in dissection and experimentation. We needed to know . . . "

Rye waited a beat before guessing: "If you could use us to fight them."

"Yes. To us, Earth is a reservoir of untapped power. As your own strength lay dormant until I found you, so, perhaps, does the strength of an entire world lie dormant until the gate is open to the source of power, the sea between worlds. It is the supreme arrogance of the tahinit that lets them imagine power is human, a matter of politics, of caste. We have learned otherwise, those few of us who dared, and who escaped torture and death. We have learned, at least, enough to grope blindly for the door to freedom. You, I suspect, have learned to see."

Rye was silent. The light pressing against the heavy curtains was bright enough to suggest Cleände's features, but not her expression. It was her voice, soft and sinuous as a forest stream, that bore the sting of her contempt, the heat of her need. Rye tried to coax some remnant of trust out of the story of their friendship, but the memory of Amaran's fear, of Mostahr's fanatical greed, was more immediate.

Cleände, still not looking at Rye, sighed. "And still I do presume. Forgive me."

Rye, stung at being so easily read, shook her head. "You might as well ask. But I don't think I know as much as you think I do."

"And so are safe from having to answer? No, I beg your pardon." Cleände lifted a hand as if Rye had protested her irony. "I know I have no claim. But . . . perhaps I may guess? As I say, it is a talent my people have."

"Guess away." This was a deliberate echo of Bardo, and it silenced Cleände for a moment. Or perhaps she was only mustering her thoughts.

"We were both captured the day Mark was killed. You, I think, were struck down, for you were unconscious when we were taken across. We were separated then, for I was senior, and from Scalléa, and so chosen for the interrogation. But I saw the women."

Her voice fell to no more than a breath. Her hands smoothed and smoothed the cloth of her robe, until Rye could feel the heat of it on her own palms.

"They showed me, of course, to frighten me, to infect me with despair. It was effective. I thought of you, my little Ryder, whom I had brought to this. But of course, mostly I thought of myself. I am no hero, God witness, and the tahinit know how to torture. I was half defeated before they struck a blow.

"But I also am what I am. A rebel witch, Daniel has named me, and in your language it is as good a name as any. We have stolen knowledge from the tahinit for generations. And though most of the tahinit are kept ignorant of the secrets hidden in Meheg-menoht, there are always rumors, so when I saw those women, Ryder, *I knew what I saw.* Terrible, yes, a nightmare. But still I guessed—you see, it is what I have been trained to do—I guessed what the tahinit were trying to accomplish.

"Because I know about the arcwrights."

Rye, within the heat of the fever, went cold. And within that cold *(sun near (glass and tar)* the arcwright came alert.

Cleände's eyes were almost blue now, her robe nearly red in the growing light.

"I guessed that the tahinit were attempting to breed an abomination: a human creature, born a slave, with the power of the arcwrights but free of their doubled nature, their doubled bond. It was madness, of course. I was long enough on Earth to learn how impossible such a thing would be, even with the foul manipulation of the tahirr. I tried to take comfort in that impossibility, for at least, whatever nightmare awaited me, I would not be freeing the Nohan lords to conquer other worlds. It was a thin comfort. I pray, Ryder, that if you also learned what it is to be crushed under the burning weight of the tahirr, you do not remember."

There were tears on Cleände's face, a hard tremble in her voice. She paused for a breath, two breaths.

"But then they stopped. I do not know," another breath, "how much I told them. Too much. But there was a long time when I was left alone to recover myself—another stage of the torture, I thought, I did not wish to know myself again—and then, when they came back, they asked only of you. I—" Another breath. "I do not ask you to forgive me. But what could I tell them? You were a girl, ignorant, good-hearted. What else could I say? But they asked me, over and over, who were you, what were you . . . And then they began to ask me about Daniel Bardo. Daniel Bardo, who was not even captured with us two."

Bardo cooked breakfast, pancakes and bacon, too heavy for the quick heat of the August morning. None of them ate much. Rye, who had looked for signs of jealousy from Cleände, felt the bite of it herself as she watched Bardo pass between table and stove. He knew the kitchen too well. But then, maybe Rye had known it, too. Maybe if she got up without thinking, she would be able to find the spatula, the coffee filters, the napkins soft from many washings. Maybe. She didn't try it. She looked at Cleände's profile, fine-drawn as an ivory cameo against the yellow wall, and thought, *I know her, I have sat here with her before, in this room, with Bardo there at the counter and the water running* . . . But trying to remember only raised a ghost of recollection, a tissue of images that could have been scavenged from the memory of a second, a minute, an hour ago.

Bardo put a glass of water down by Rye's plate and she, her mouth sweet with syrup, smelled his clean scent, felt his warm shadow blocking the window light.

"Eat something," he said. "You get skinnier every time I look at you."

Rye glanced up, but he was already back at the stove, and she did not know which of them he had been speaking to. It wasn't until she was washing the dishes that she realized that there were only two sticky plates. Bardo had not eaten at all.

Bardo left the kitchen. Cleände did. Rye strained to hear, not only with her ears, but with the skin on her arms and the nape of her neck and the backs of her knees, footsteps, voices, the meeting of two bodies. Stop it, she told herself. The house was silent, until the silence was broken by a knock at the front door.

It was Tehega.

Bardo, having opened the door, crowded the Nohan lordling back onto the porch, keeping him out of the house. The look Bardo gave Rye suggested he would have kept her inside by the same tactic.

"Leave it to you?" she said. Seeing Tehega woke a shadow of Meheg-menoht in her mind: the trial, the army, Amaran's death. Her look at Bardo was cold. He failed to meet it as he let her by.

He shut the door and propped himself against it, arms folded across his chest. Tehega pointedly stepped to the far side of the porch and leaned on the porch railing, where his white golf shirt glowed in the sun. He looked Rye over in her borrowed tank-top and skirt, and gave her a little bow.

"I owe you," he said, "a very much. You have my thank-you."

Bardo said, "Just stopped by to say thanks, huh?"

Tehega laughed. He seemed pretty cheerful about being an exile again. But then, he had been in Meheg-menoht. "Not only that."

"No," Bardo said.

Tehega tipped his head to indicate the house. "The pretty rebel has no interest in who comes to her door?"

"She's asleep."

"And trusts you to keep her door."

"For the time being."

Bardo's voice was as loaded with meaning as Tehega's had been. There was a whole layer of masculine negotiations taking place at a level Rye could not access. Posturing, but with serious intent.

"I also owe you a thank-you," Tehega said to Bardo. "You did what you could at the court. It was no mistake by you that it was not enough. And I will thank even you," he made Rye another little bow, "that you put the weight on Amaran, and not so much on me."

"Don't bother," she said, freshly wounded by guilt.

"But it saved my life," he said smiling.

"You're welcome," Bardo said. "Anything else?"

Tehega's smile died. "So. I am alone, and you are back home." His eyes touched the house at Bardo's back: Cleände's house, the "pretty rebel's" house. "Is it that?"

"Back on Earth," Bardo said like a correction. "All the rest of it was another time, another planet. You know?"

"And the tahinit are not here," Tehega said, understanding.

"And neither are your friends," Bardo said.

"Yet."

Bardo gave that the small silence it deserved. "You know something I don't?"

Tehega laughed. "A thousand somethings, friend Bardo. But you know the try I make to find a way free of the tahinit, the way Amaran closed—the coward. I am not alone in this try, and other tahinit who are loyal to my friends may be more brave now that we cannot give Rye-tahi into their hands. Or they may want her all the more." He bowed a third time at Rye. "Rye-tahi, you prove to my friends, my people who desire freedom, that the tahirr can be escaped, even from Meheg-menoht itself. They will pay you anything, everything, for this. They will give you worlds."

"You mean, she could give *them* worlds," Bardo said.

"Wait," Rye said.

"She can give them doors for the passage," Tehega said. "They can give her every other thing."

"Armies," Bardo said. "Enemies."

"Allies," Tehega said, and his eyes shifted again to Cleände's house.

"Wait," Rye said.

"Allies in what conflict?" Bardo said. "Earth isn't at war with anyone, unless you people find a way to invade. As far as I can tell, Tehega, right now you're nothing but a lonely exile with all your friends on the wrong side of the universe. You have nothing to offer us, and they have nothing to offer us but a fight."

"Fucking wait!" Rye cried. "Just wait a minute! What are you doing? Are you negotiating a world war?" She was breathless, incredulous. "Who the hell do you people think you are?"

"But they are not always—" Tehega began. He broke off when Bardo jerked himself hastily away from the opening door.

"They are not negotiating over a war," Cleände said to Rye, a shotgun in her hand. "They are negotiating over you."

Tehega licked his lips, his eyes on the gun. "If I have Rye-tahi in my hand, then there is no war."

"Perhaps not on Earth," Cleände said. "What of all the other worlds? What of Scalléa? No," she added when Tehega would have responded. "You have said enough. You." She looked at Bardo, the shotgun not quite aimed. "What do you have to say to Ryder?"

Bardo also eyed the gun. "I was just hearing what the man had to say, Cleände. What are you going to do? Blow us into the street?"

Bardo's gesture drew their attention to the world beyond the porch. Rye was startled, as she thought they all were, at the background brought suddenly, noisily—for there was traffic—into the foreground.

"Now," Bardo said, "it seems to me that with Rye here and with the wasp-nest stirred up on Nohai, we should maybe hear the man out."

"Oh, is that what it seems to you, Daniel? Because I have heard enough, and more than enough." Cleände hid the shotgun behind her skirt, but no one was likely to forget it was there. "And you, Ryder? What have you heard?"

Even then Rye was stung by Cleände's keen understanding, and keener manipulation. But she was too focused on Bardo to give it much consideration.

"You," she said to Bardo.

"Rye," he said.

"You said," Rye said. "You said, let them have some reason to hope for real power. You meant, let them have some reason to hope they'd get *me*."

"Rye."

"Just like the tahinit had me."

"Rye."

"Will you stop saying my name?" she screamed.

And he yelled back at her, *"Will you listen to me?"*

"No," she said, her voice gone very small, and she blundered past Cleände, past the gun, past the door, and into the darkness of the house.

Where she heard Cleände—Cleände with the gun—say, "No. Leave her be. You have done your part. It is my turn now."

twenty-three

But Rye wanted nothing to do with Cleände. She wanted nothing to do with any of them. She took refuge in the only room with a key to the door, the old fashioned bathroom with the rusty claw-footed bathtub and the fly-speckled mirror on the back of the door. She had not realized until now how terrible betrayal could be, not only for the blow it struck at her faith in Bardo, at her belief—her hope—in his affection for her, but also for the cut it took at her own self-worth. Who was she, what was she, that he could bargain over her like a . . . her imagination failed her . . . like a used car? Or is that really what had happened? Words tangled in her memory, muddled by unhappiness, adrenaline, fever. The arcwright scrabbled in a dusty corner, chasing a rat for amusement, aware of Rye—*lover*—indifferent to her state.

Until she started, her taut nerves plucked by the sound of the door opening, closing, footsteps in the downstairs hall. The fever inside her shifted as if it turned its head in mimicry of the arcwright, who listened along with Rye.

Bardo: "Is that how long our deal is good for?"

Cleände: "You wished to protect us. Do we need protecting from your friends?"

"You know damn well he is no friend to me."

"And how do I know that, Daniel? I am well acquainted with the doings of the tahinit's torturers, but as to what you have been engaged with while Ryder and I were captive in Meheg-menoht—"

"Give it a rest, Cleände."

"Do you tell Ryder that as well? Give it a rest, little one, your suffering is none of Daniel Bardo's concern."

"And you know damn well that is a load of bullshit!"

"But Daniel, how am I to know that? How am I to know anything about you now?"

"You know one thing, and you think you know everything."

"I know almost nothing. But it is clear to me that you have your own side to play. I will be kind and not require you to play more than one."

"And that's how much our deal is worth. Kindness at gunpoint."

"It was always only your deal, Daniel. It was never mine. And we are well enough, Ryder and I. I thank you for your concern, but I think we can fend for ourselves from now on."

"So you're speaking for Rye now, are you?"

"By all means, ask her yourself. I confess, I am also curious to know what she would say."

Bardo said nothing. The stairs complained as Cleände climbed to the second floor. Rye clenched around herself as she perched on the edge of the tub, but Cleände did not knock. She went into her bedroom across the hall and closed the door. Rye, knowing Cleände had intended her to overhear, stayed where she was, locked in suspense while the silence hardened, dense as stone. Finally the arcwright lost interest, turned back to its rat-play, and as if its movement released her, she got stiffly to her feet and unlocked the door.

Bardo was standing where he must have been all along, at the foot of the stairs. He was leaning on the banister, head hanging, eyes closed.

"Is she kicking you out?" Rye said from the top of the stairs. He started when he heard her voice.

"It's her house," he said, eyes still closed.

"Don't go." She said it without thinking—thinking, in fact, that she would not say anything at all. Something hot knotted itself in her throat once the words were out, too late.

He tipped his head back as if looking up at her took more energy than he had to spare. "Why in God's name would you want me to stay?"

But her throat was locked now, and in any case, she had no answer. She could not reconcile her anger with her sense of loss, as if the desolation of his betrayal and the desolation of his departure were blood from the same wound. She could do nothing but shake her head. He rubbed his eyes with the heel of his palm.

"Adventure's over, kid. Time to go home."

"But I don't have a home," she whispered. "And it isn't over for me."

Bardo sighed, "I know," and started up the stairs. His step was heavy, his shoulders bowed with fatigue. He stopped at her side and passed his hand over her hair. Even that minimal touch struck hot reverberations between them. "Listen, kid, we've been living in each other's pockets, and—"

"You'd stay," she said abruptly, bitterly, "you'd stay if *she* asked you to."

He started one response, another, before he said, his dark eyes avoiding hers, "It's her house."

"Dan—"

He stopped her with a touch on her cheek, a caress of his thumb across her mouth. She was drenched with heat, with roses, with sparks like electric fishes, like the bite of copper thorns. Sensation so complete that by the time she registered that he was no longer touching her, he had walked back down the stairs.

And by the time she registered that, he was out the door and gone.

In the heat of the afternoon, Cleände stood at the kitchen door with a glass of water in her hand. She made no sign that she heard Rye come in behind her, and Rye saw a faint vibration running through the other woman's form. Rye's mouth filled with a sour prickling, and for an instant, a skipped heartbeat, she was locked in a dim world where Cleände was a star hanging within a skeletal shadow black against the darkened sunlight—and then, for another instant, a heartbeat like the clench of a fist, she saw that caged spark from the other side, as the arcwright peered at her through the bars of Cleände's bones.

Unless it was only that she saw herself in the mirror of Cleände's suffering.

"No," she said, denying that empathy, not knowing to whom.

Cleände dropped her glass, and a vague moment later glanced down as if she wondered how there came to be water staining her skirt and broken glass around her feet. The world was bright again. The wet shards glittered with dewy prisms in the sun.

"Don't move," Rye said harshly as she fetched a towel from beside the sink.

"Your feet are also bare," Cleände said.

Rye said nothing, anger sullen as an ember in her chest.

The glass had broken into a few big pieces, easy to handle, and a wet scatter of splinters that Rye mopped up with the towel. Cleände's narrow, high-arched feet were freckled with water. When the towel brushed her toes, she flinched.

Rye carried the glass to the garbage and, towel and all, dropped it in without meeting Cleände's gaze.

"Thank you." Cleände did not move from the door. With her face to the sunlight, she said, "I am glad we did not come back to winter."

Rye poured herself a glass of water from the jug in the fridge and leant against the counter to drink it. She saw through the window what Cleände saw: dead lawn, weeds, the factory wall. It was a Nohan view, the wall, the strip of sky. The arcwright was hidden behind the bricks and padlocked door, but Rye was sure that Cleände knew it was there. Cleände was a witch, just like Mostahr and Amaran. Rye swallowed the threat of tears along with the cold water that etched blue frost down the back of her throat.

When the silence was too heavy to bear, she said, "Why did you get rid of Dan?"

"'Get rid of'?" Cleände mused. "I gave him leave to go."

"That's not what it sounded like to me."

"Ah, but perhaps you were hoping that he wished to stay. Or perhaps you were hoping he would take you with him. Did he ask you to go?"

Which hurt, precisely as it was intended to. Yet Cleände's voice was gentle, her regret on Rye's behalf palpable. Cold-heartedness had never come naturally to Rye, but she tried.

"You always wanted him to go, didn't you, since we first got here?"

Cleände cast a sun-blind gaze along the length of the counter. "True."

"Why? He was one of . . . He used to fight for you."

"He was one of us." Cleände's voice was soft. "Shall I burden you with my truth? Ryder, he might be still. But it was Daniel Bardo who led us into the trap that killed young Mark and made the two of us prisoners, yet left Daniel Bardo free and unharmed. It was Daniel

Bardo who led you, by your own telling, into the Nohan lordling's hands. And although I have heard no account of your second sojourn on Nohai, I know that Daniel Bardo, who was one of their enemies, and who has no such intrinsic value to the tahinit as you do, suffered the least of us who were in the tahinit's hands. With all of that, and that pretty bargaining session we heard today . . . "

Rye could feel the cool of the glass in her hands, the warmth of the sun on her face. The tangle Cleände made of her certainties, her anger. "Dan took care of me."

"And why should he not? You were what the tahinit wanted. What use would they have for a Daniel Bardo if he could not keep you well?" And she said the *well* so weakly that the emphasis was all on the *keep.*

Rye turned to the window, filling her sight with refracted sunlight. After a moment she set her glass gently down and pressed her damp fingers to her eyes. "He kept us both safe until I could get us out, that much I know. Do you want me to question his methods?" She dropped her hands, braced them on the edge of the sink. "Or do you only want me to *not* question your motives?"

"But my motives are easy to read!" Cleände said with an expansive gesture of both hands. "I lay them out before you: I am a citizen of Scalléa. I want my people freed, and I want the tahinit and their slave-takers thrown down. Hold this fast in your mind, judge everything I say and do against it, and you will see whether I am true or false. I am a much simpler being than Daniel Bardo. And I can, therefore, be a much truer friend."

"So long as you think I can help." The brick wall was dark in its own shade, almost black against the blue sky. "Or so long as you aren't being tortured."

Cleände took a breath, another. "Now that," she said, "now that was worthy of the man himself."

Rye dropped her head and stretched out her neck. In a way, she believed Cleände. Everything the woman said and did probably was aimed against her enemies. But believing was not the same thing as trusting. What Cleände had just said, in essence, was that she would sell Rye down the river in an instant if she thought it would further her cause. Rye was still framing this accusation when Cleände, having collected herself, spoke.

"And it is true that I need your help."

"What for?" Rye might have been asking the faucet, or the window above.

"You need to ask?" Cleände's voice was wounded. "To free my world!"

"But it is free." Rye pushed off from the counter and turned to face the other woman. "Scalléa is safe. Earth is safe. Everybody is fucking safe," bitterness welling up from the depths. "The tahinit aren't going anywhere. This is the happy ending!"

"Don't be a fool," Cleände said, cold, sharp, and deflating as an arrow fired at a balloon. "Would the Nohan lordling have risked coming here if that were true?"

Rye tucked her hands in her armpits and scowled. "What do you know about it?"

"Oh, my girl!" Cleände laughed, though not happily. "More than you, and my God, isn't that a frightening thought." She shook her head, crossed the room to sit at the table. "I am always so tired now."

She looked it, pale beneath the flush the sun had brought to her cheeks. More disturbing to Rye was the sudden vagueness in her voice, the daze in her eyes. Rye filled a clean water glass and set it by Cleände's elbow, and Cleände picked it up with a sweet, surprised smile.

"Thank you."

Rye shrugged, uncomfortable, and pulled out a chair. "So why isn't it over?"

Cleände took a drop of water off her lip with the touch of a prim knuckle and set her glass down. "In all the universe of universes, what can be said to end? Even if the worlds are severed, with no gate left for any traveler to pass through, still, there is Scalléa with its slave-takers and armies and their overlords, and the tahinit who lord over them, if they but knew it. And there is Nohai, with too few workers and too many idle rich, and lordlings who depend upon the tahinit lords' power for their status and wealth, and tahinit underlings who depend upon the lordlings. And here is Earth. Do you say your world is 'over'? I say, here it is, and there they are, and separation—mark this—separation is not the same as freedom."

Cleände picked up her glass. "But that is only if the worlds are severed." She drank, set the glass down beside the damp ring it had made on the table's scarred wood.

"But the arcwright is here," Rye said without thinking, forgetting how much Cleände knew, or guessed. She added, her voice tight with the painful truth of it: "I am here."

Cleände's eyes were bright again, full of awareness as she studied Rye's face, void of surprise. She addressed, as if out of kindness, only the first half of Rye's statement.

"The arcwright, you say. Singular, as if there could be a reflection without an object to reflect. Must I guess what became of the other?"

Rye dropped her gaze. It was the same as with Amaran, the same as with Mostahr: one did not have to trust in order to learn. But it did not feel the same. Cleände already knew so much, and her eyes were so kind.

"The tahinit had . . . had crippled it, I think." Rye could feel the fever swell at her unease, or perhaps that was only the arcwright listening. "They crippled it to keep it bound, and . . . to keep the other one. One to be the anchor, Mostahr said, the other to be the bridge. I think the crippled one was tortured to make the other one do what they wanted."

It moans, or something does, deep as the axle that turns the world. Rye clasped her hands before her mouth, but she could not stop the shudder that worked its way outward from her bones.

"Ryder." Cleände stretched her hand across the table.

Rye caught a breath. "It died." Another breath. "The other one killed it to escape." Another breath.

"How?" Cleände whispered.

"It used me!" It was a cry of anguish, the voice of instinct, the certainty of her fever dreams solidifying only as she spoke, leaving her shaken and appalled. "How do you think? Why do you think I'm here? Like this?" She was asking herself as much as Cleände. "What else did you think I was for?"

Cleände, as if physically impelled, jumped up and started around the table, her face taut with reflected pain.

And although the issue of trust loomed so large between them, and although Cleände's embrace was physically trying, Rye could not help the deep childish softening in her core at the sympathy of someone, perhaps the one person in three worlds, who could understand.

twenty-four

Rye spent that night in Bardo's bed.

It was Cleände's spare bed, of course, the futon on the floor of the empty room upstairs, but it was Bardo's to Rye. His bitter, musk-rose smell permeated the sheets, a scent shaped to the hollow of his absence, his self. With her head on his pillow and her skin blinded by his sheets Rye could almost imagine he was there with her. In the deep shadow by the window, say, sitting with his long legs drawn up and his shoulders braced against the wall. His eyes would be black and opaque, deep water on a moonless night, hiding his thoughts. His large hand, graceful with bone, would chase a trickle of sweat through the scant hair around his nipple and down his naked ribs. (She could almost taste the saltiness, daisies ripening in the heat of a copper sun.) He would shift to stretch one leg out straight and lean an elbow against the other knee, draw his thumb across an eyebrow, unknotting some idea. (She could almost feel the heat of him, a bass growl colored by the perfume of soap and shampoo, sweat and the oil of his skin.) He would be blind in the dark, his face open, hidden even from himself. Phosphorescent patterns would chase themselves across his vision, the shining net of his firing nerves cast across the sea of night. She could almost touch the strands, could almost feel him stir, as if those nerves were hers, as if she could shiver for him, restless and aroused by the hot breath of darkness across his skin. As if she could swallow for him, her throat gone dry, his heart's rhythm heavy with desire and fear. As if her blood burned through his veins, a tidal bore racing through narrow channels until it reached the vast chamber of her heart and crested, and broke, thunder of a heartbeat, echo of a wave: *alone.*

(alone)

((alone))

(((alone)))

The fever inside her, flowing to this shadow tide, crested and broke, crested and broke, resonance building on resonance until she rang like a midnight bell. She cried out, though she only knew it later by a shiver in the air. She was deaf in that moment, deaf and blind and numb, so that all she could feel was Bardo's orgasm, and behind that, one bell's note throbbing against another's, the arcwright stretched across the city's night, ecstatic as a bridge of stars.

(alone (alone (alone)

As a broken wave retreats mild with foam across the sand, the fever ebbed into the recesses of her flesh. The dusty darkness of the spare room crept up to her bed, the sheet touched its thousand threads against her skin. She could feel the air in her throat, the quiver of her eardrums, the salt tears pooling in the corners of her eyes. She could smell the ghost of Bardo's scent, the living musk of her own body. She put her fingers to her mouth, summoning silence, and listened to the quiet of the house.

If Cleände had heard her, she made no sound.

Cleände insisted on cooking breakfast, as if having ousted Bardo she needed to fill his role. She, like Rye, was too thin, and had the sores around her mouth to prove her captivity had not been an easy one. But she was not obviously injured or ill, so it was disconcerting, those few times when she froze, her eyes gone blind, her hand, once, suspended in a stream of tap water, as if her nerves had literally, physically, failed her. She stood locked in precarious balance until life returned and she looked around, her gaze touching the reality of the room while shards of water fell from her trembling fingers. One moment, measurable in seconds, but Rye, with her own cross-wired brain, felt her throat tighten with sympathy.

While Cleände prosaically dried her hands on the dish towel and went back to slicing peaches against her thumb.

"Tell me something," Rye said when they had eaten, putting off the moment when she had to wash the dishes.

Cleände smiled. "Tell you what?"

Rye gathered her courage. "Tell me what the arcwright is."

"If only I could. But let me think." Cleände frowned out the window. "Can you be a little patient? I will begin with what I do know, so you can follow me to what I guess. If I may?"

Rye opened her hands in silent permission, and wondered if Cleände were only being tactful in the face of her tense ambivalence.

"So, then." Cleände sat straighter in her chair, almost visibly assuming the teacher's role. "I begin with the thadís. As the blood in our veins is a current borrowed from the oceans of our worlds, so the thadís is a current borrowed from the ocean between the worlds. This is the source of power, the source of the life in our souls. On Scalléa we teach that every human born has the thadís, though the tide runs more strongly in some than in others. The tahinit claim otherwise, and say the thadís, the 'mark' of tahid, is the mark of a caste, a confraternity born into brotherhood regardless of each person's mother's womb. They divide themselves from their own world and all the humans on Scalléa and Earth, claiming they are chosen by God.

"But on Scalléa we believe all souls are alive by God's grace, and the only difference between those with a strong and a weak thadís is that those with the weak thadís can only swim in the divine waters in their dreams."

"Amaran said . . . " But wasn't it Tehega who had said? Rye hesitated over saying his name. He was too close to Bardo in her mind, and, she feared, in Cleände's.

But Cleände prompted, "She said?"

"The tahinit used to reach out to God and share with their people. But you know, I don't really believe in God."

"God is a word to swear by in English, yes? Perhaps a risky word to use in translation. 'The divine' might be a better term. Sodué, the ocean between the worlds, source of power, enlightenment, life. But I could spend a lifetime discussing our beliefs, and I am no scholar of the divine. I am merely a rebel witch in exile." Cleände seemed to enjoy labeling herself with Bardo's term.

"But the thadís's has something to do with the arcwright?"

"The arcwright." Cleände's mouth quirked. "Another clumsy translation, though a pretty one. But it might be more accurate to say that the arcwright has everything to do with the sodué, and the sodué has everything to do with thadís. But here is my difficulty: everything we know about the arcwrights is culled from the rumors of rumors smuggled out of Meheg-menoht. Do you know that even among the tahinit there are many, very many in the lower ranks, who do not know of the arcwrights' existence?"

"I guessed."

"The tahirr binds them and hides them, both. Or I should say, bound. But where does this get us?" Cleände gave a sighing laugh. "Oh for the leisure only to talk and talk! Listen then. Our guess is that the arcwrights are creatures born to the sodué, born to swim the oceans between the worlds. They are born *of* the sodué, and partake of that substance. They are thadís incarnate, power given flesh. Or so we say, because having to invent, we prefer poetry, mystery, to crude ignorance."

God's black left hand. Rye twitched at the memory of Mostahr's voice.

"And I must guess again to say what all this means for you. You are infected by the arcwright's substance, by thadís, by the sodué itself. Your blood runs so hot with it, it bursts the boundaries of your skin. Yes? No? All I know is that living between you and the arcwright is like living between a planet and her moon, the tides of power are so strong between you."

Rye stepped out onto the front porch. Why? To test her freedom to come and go, to test herself against her loss of Bardo and the anger she still felt towards him, to test her return to the world and the city she called home. To test Cleände's assertion, that she was the arcwright's moon. Sunlight, refracted through dust and clouds and city fumes, sang like a hysterical choir against her bare arms. She could hear the darker reflection of it swimming off the pavement, the parked cars, the graffitoed workshop across the street.

She could hear it, too, on the quicksilver hide of the arcwright, who lay, somnolent as a crocodile on a sandy bank, amongst the broken glass and bird shit and trash that littered the factory's upper floor. She felt the *tilted square* of the sun through a high window, she felt the *lofty height* of the factory ceiling, she felt the *shadows* limned with *sunlit dust* in the corners of the room, and she felt the *hot-blooded quick-hearted life* of rats paralyzed with fascination for the alien being.

There were *pigeons stirring the dust* among the beams overhead. There were *slumberous flies* cruising their pointless patterns in the sun. There were *ants* scurrying through the disturbed trash at the arcwright's taloned feet. There was the *alert stillness* of a watchful hunter, the *slow deep sorrowful patience* of a being wise with experience and age, if not with thought, and the *unaroused threat* of a dangerous creature a long way from *home*

cars become glimmering fish sliding on currents, buildings become electric tracery hollow shells, people become smoke and ember ghosts, shadow-light, mist on the surface of the quicksilver star-shot midnight sea—

"Ryder?"

She blinked at the glare off a windscreen, the ashy residue of a touch on her arm. She looked around, trying to regain her bearings, and for a panicky moment could not make sense of where she was or what was around her. Huge blank mirrors in a vast row, enormous metallic fireworks shooting one after another into the distance, tall fleshy angular puppets—

Store windows. Cars. People.

Jesus, Rye. People.

"Ryder?"

She stepped away from Cleände, into the dense heat of noon sunlight, and stammered, "Mostahr said, Mostahr said I could be cured. She said I could be cured."

"Come," Cleände said gently. "Come inside."

They sat in the dim living room, the pale curtains drawn against the heat. The room still had an uninhabited feel, barren and thick with dust. Rye remembered it in the rain, an abandoned house and weedy lawn in the shelter of the factory wall, and wondered if it had ever felt like anyone's home. Not Cleände's, she thought. Cleände was an exile, indifferent to any place that was so far from her home.

"Tell me," Cleände said, "how they did what they did to you."

Rye told her, haltingly, some of the things she had not been able to tell Bardo. Some things, though not all, about the courtyard, the cold white sunlight, the women. Some things about the pit.

(I'll make a deal.)

(No, not that.)

"I think it—I think the arcwright knew what they were doing. What they were trying to do. And I think it figured out a way to turn it back against them. I think it knew that if I changed, if it changed me, then I could, then it could send me where they didn't know I could go."

"To its other self."

Rye nodded, fighting against her own tension to breathe.

"But why? How, if it could not go itself?"

"I don't know that it couldn't," Rye said tersely. "It poisoned me and sent me like a box of fucking chocolates."

Cleände frowned, a gentle expression that hid her thoughts. "Poisoned you how?"

"It bit me. Stung me, I guess." Rye touched the puncture scar above her collarbone, felt the painful/delicious synesthetic rush like a shower of warm rain/mown grass/peach satin down her nerves. "When it . . . when it made them think it was doing what it . . . what it did to the other women."

"And poisoned your blood so you could poison its other? The other that the tahinit had crippled and held captive, and so harnessed them both, and all their power . . . Yes, I begin to see: like and not-like. It made you like enough to itself to be deadly, like enough that its other would be affected by your alienness, to which it might otherwise be indifferent or immune. And therefore—Could it have been deliberate? I wonder. But therefore, you were also then like enough to take the other's place. Yes! And like and not-like to the tahirr as well, which would recognize human or arcwright, the elements from which it is built, but not the third thing, the new thing—ha! And there is the measure of their success. For you see, Ryder, you are the very thing they were trying to create, yet rather than make you a slave, they made you to break out of their cage and lock them inside!" Cleände laughed, her blue eyes shining, her thin face flushed. Her beauty shone out through the mask of her suffering.

Rye was offended by the laughter. "Nobody made me. The arcwright changed me, but it didn't *make* me anything."

"Forgive me. I see how terribly you were used. But I cannot help but wonder at the triumph that arose out of your suffering. Out of all our suffering. Such a terrible, and such a wonderful, thing. Freedom!"

"I am not free." Rye jumped off the couch and paced across the room. "I am not free, and neither is the arcwright. We're still stuck with each other, and I can't stand it, Cleände, I don't know how much longer I can stand it, it's driving me crazy—" A word she bit off, appalled at its truth. She pressed her hands against her eyes, because the fever was up again, its electric fur spitting sparks beneath her skin, and because she did not want to see the expression, whatever it might be, on Cleände's face.

"Forgive me, Ryder. I would share your pain if I could."

"But can you cure me?" Rye was so tense the words sounded angry, gritted out through her teeth.

"Can you be cured of the sodué?" Cleände lifted her hands, a graceful, helpless gesture. "I do not know what the tahinit know, but to me, it is like saying, can you be cured of thadís? Can you be cured of your soul? Not even death can effect that miracle."

"I don't want to be cured of my soul! I want to be cured of the arcwright!"

Cleände lowered her hands to the arms of her chair. "Yes. That is the question. It would be messy indeed to divide you from your blood. But to divide you from the arcwright, to untangle thadís from thadís . . . This, perhaps, is something we might dare to try. But there is a risk, perhaps a great risk, and I want you to be certain. I will not interfere unless you ask."

"So I ask," Rye said, and held her hands out, the palms damp with tears.

While the arcwright scratched its black-silver hide, sensuous and leisurely, on the factory's splintered floor.

twenty-five

Sitting cross-legged on the living room floor, almost knee-to-knee with Cleände in the drawn-curtain gloom, Rye was reminded of childhood seances, complete with Ouija board and candles. The memory and the state of her nerves made her fight down giggle after giggle, until she had to put her hands up to hide the twitching of her mouth.

"Be calm," Cleände said. "I want only to trace the ties between you, if I can, nothing more. Not today."

How interesting! Mostahr said. *Which tie will you let me cut?*

Rye sobered. "What do I do?"

"Can you feel my thadís?"

Rye, blessedly free of hallucination, said, "No."

"But sometimes you can?"

"I guess." Why should she feel embarrassed? "Sometimes I see . . . sparks. Like lightning in people's heartbeats. But I'm never sure what's real and what's just the fever."

"The fever is your thadís," Cleände said patiently. "Trust what it sees. It shows you only the truth."

Rye thought of Meheg-menoht's ghosts, the melting walls, the burning-coal flicker of Bardo's bones. She shook her head, but did not argue.

Cleände sighed. "You have seen the thadís of others, yes? You have seen the lines of the tahirr?"

"Yes."

"That is truth. That is real. Trust to that. Trust in me. I will show you how to open that inner eye. I will show you how to wake your soul. Listen. Only listen to my voice. It is as simple as opening your hand. As simple as opening your fist, as turning your palm to the sky to feel for rain. Think of the rain. Think of that one cool touch, the drop of rain in your palm. Think of that drop of rain . . . "

She's hypnotizing me, Rye thought wisely. She did not feel hypnotized. Her thoughts skittered about, not so much like a drop of rain as like a drop of mercury chasing itself across a pane of glass. The rain the day Bardo brought her to this house. The arcwright's dusty pleasure. Kissing Bardo. The arcwright in her soul.

The fever was the arcwright's shadow. She knew that, if Cleände didn't. *Hello?* she thought. Not a word: an impulse, an internal motion as physical as opening her hand. *Hello? Are you there?*

here, lover, here.

The fever bloomed. The thadís-spark inside Cleände bumped and flickered, a firefly's bite sharp as a static charge. A hint of light in a shadow of bones, a sour metal sting on the tongue, a flutter of moths against Rye's skin.

Cleände, pupils huge in her blue eyes, looked beautiful enough to pain the heart. "There," she murmured, "there."

"I see it," Rye said.

"Yes. Now. You must trust me. Just trust me a little. Only a little, just a small trust. Just this one moment. Just this one thing. This one small thing. Give me your hands."

Rye put out her hands. Cleände covered them with her own. Sparks leapt against Rye's palms, chalk dust/green limes/red silk, a sweet-sour dusty scarlet taste in her mouth, a dusty sting along her nerves. *Silver-black in sunlight slips to black in the late hot shadow of afternoon.* The queasiness of another heart beating out of synch with her own, bumping in her chest, a fist demanding entry, wings beating against the bars of her ribcage. *Pigeons flutter sifting dust down, chalk dust on burning black hide, silver-starred eyes brilliant with heat, long limbs prowling in a predator's glide.* Red silk wings, chalk dust everywhere, sour dust muting, numbing, blinding even the eyes in her skin. *Talons bite old wood, sharp black tongue washes sharper teeth, flies butt ferocious black hide.* Spark of light sharp as the wink of a knife blade licks the fever's fur, stabs the fever's eye. *Star-shot eye blinks, slow shutter on yellow sun.* Honey-brown eye blinks, stabbed by a tear.

"There," Cleände whispered. "There."

Red silk threads, red as the blood in their veins, a silken tangle of firing nerves. Red threads spun by a red silk moth *blue flies butting, biting the alien hide* red heart beating the alien rhythm.

"There."

Chalk dust like ground glass sifting down all her nerves *fireflies biting, sparking, lightning-threads spinning, biting, binding—*

"No!"

NO

One of them screamed.

The fever turned and turned in the cage of her bones. The arcwright prowled *dust-bright sun-squares* the confines of its factory lair *rat-fleeting wall-shadows,* huge in its ferocious vexation. Rye's senses seethed with wet clay, the taste of rose-scented soap, a blinding shade of electric blue that melted into burnt orange, rose soap curdling into sour milk, wet clay transmuting into wet wool. Not synesthesia, just a human nervous system unable to cope with the alien outrage. Even gravity had gone sideways with the arcwright's fury. Rye found herself whimpering, "It's okay, I'm still here, I'm still here, it's okay . . . it's okay . . . please stop . . . "

HERE, LOVER. MINE.

"Okay," she whispered. "Okay."

Slowly the arcwright settled. Slowly the assault on her senses ebbed. (Green limes, styrofoam between the teeth.) Down became down, the floor reasserted itself under her buttocks, ankles, thighs, and Cleände was sprawled across it, her hair come loose, her hands showing their pale palms against the dusty floor. Unconscious or dead, Rye could not at first tell.

Was afraid to tell.

Dizzy and loose-jointed with fever, she maneuvered herself to her hands and knees, and crawled the short, the very long distance to Cleände's side. With the curtains between the room and the sun, it was hard to tell if Cleände was breathing. Rye put out a hand, watched it hover, trembling, over the pulse-point in Cleände's neck. Someone else's hand, bony, ragged-nailed, and scarred. It hovered, trembling, then lowered its palm to touch the air before Cleände's mouth.

Warm breath lapped her skin, gossamer silk the color of sunlight on blood. Rye snatched her hand back, pressed it against her shirt. Her own heart knocked away, a strange, slow, surging rhythm. She knelt there a while, half-hypnotized by the rise and fall of tides in her own chest, until Cleände stirred, expressions chasing across her face too quickly to name. Rye scrambled back and up. Weaving slightly, her feet a long way down, she fled the house, a criminal impelled by the horror of her own unknown crime.

But the arcwright was still with her. It was with her, even though it was also on the factory roof like a hot-blooded gargoyle in the blazing sun. Its shadow spilled like black water down the wall and crept toward the house, so that Rye was afraid, in small, momentary flickers, for Cleände, alone.

Guilt blasted her, breaking up the fear.

So the arcwright was there, crouched so still in the sunlight that the earth seemed to revolve around its unmoving point, and it was with her here, in the shadow her body made on the sidewalk, in the black crescents of her scars. And sometimes Rye was with it there, motionless in the sun, so that the awning shade that crossed the sidewalk, the flash of sun-glare off passing cars, flitted over her like the shadows of pigeons on the wing. Birds wheel through three dimensions of air while their shadows slip two-dimensioned across the curve of her skin. Was she moving or still? Did the world turn beneath her feet or did she walk upon the unmoving world?

The sunlight interpenetrates them, ringing through them, wave after wave, a feast of frequencies and refraction, a chorus of bells.

"Stop," she said to the arcwright, to herself. "Just stop."

She stopped, and found herself in the middle of a block of apartment buildings, storefronts, restaurants, bars. A tavern's air-conditioner rumbled warm, smoky air and an anemic trickle of condensation out of a vent above her head. A postage-stamp park across the way, dusty grass and a chestnut tree limp with heat, displayed a microcosm of family life: an elderly couple on a shady bench, a young woman with two children on the tiny jungle gym, a very young couple solemnly necking under the tree. Someone walked by Rye, jostling her arm, and she shrank back against the wall, suddenly self-aware: young woman, scarred and barefoot, shaggy hair going every which way, talking to herself.

Crazy girl, she thought, and was desolate.

Here, lover, here.

"I know."

The street was swimming with tears. She went on, *shadows black as doors across the street,* so she was blinded again and again, *sunlight like doors across the street,* and could only trust to her naked feet, to the skin bared by Cleände's short skirt and sleeveless top, to the arcwright's *subtle tilt and gravitic sway, this way, this way,* to keep her from walking headlong into traffic. Sometimes the sidewalk came clear, a block, two blocks of normality. Sometimes it went as slippery as ice, sea ice murky with layers, with electric wires and radio waves and human lives. Once she would have sworn she saw Tehega's face, clear as it had ever been on Nohai, his smooth fair hair bright in the sun, but a shadow swept her up just then, the arcwright leaned her *this way,* and when she could see again he was gone, the block was gone, the whole riverside district was gone.

Crazy girl. Dangerous girl. Run and hide yourself away.

She washed up onto the sidewalk in front of the boarding house like a jellyfish washed up by the tide.

Where else did she have to go?

twenty-six

She collected herself as best she could, combing her hair with her fingers and straightening the borrowed skirt, as if tidying her clothes could tidy her mind, and then pressed the button by the door, awakening the buzzing racket of the doorbell. After a moment she opened the screen door and stepped inside.

A figure appeared at the end of the hall and said in a gravelly tenor: "Who are you looking for?"

"Glenn? It's Rye Coleman. I used to, um, live here?"

"Rye Coleman. Jesus Christ. We thought you'd wandered off and got yourself killed." Glenn came down the hall, skinny hard-living androgyne with a peroxide-orange brush cut and permanent smoker's squint. "I'll be goddamn, it really is you."

"More or less."

"In one piece?"

Rye felt a treacherous impulse to laughter. "More or less."

Glenn scrutinized her in the shaded light of the screen door, blue eyes more interested than sympathetic. "Uhuh. You come by to pick up your stuff?"

"Yes. I guess there's no chance you—"

"Kept your room? Yep."

"You did?" This seemed so unlikely that Rye, flat-footed, stared.

Glenn chuckled, a laugh like pebbles rattled in a pop can. "Been a slow summer for rentals. Besides, that social worker of yours and—uh—you know, the one at the hospital who was leaving you all those messages? I called him up after you hadn't showed your face for a few days. He seemed to think you'd lost your memory and were wandering around the city looking for home. So he asked me to keep it for you as long as I could."

Rye felt spat out by one world, swallowed up by another. She said inadequately, "Well, thanks."

Glenn shrugged skinny shoulders. "So did you?"

"Did I?"

"Lose your memory."

Those faded eyes were hard to meet, curious and keen. Rye felt her eyes flicker to the side, felt her face start to flush. Shifty girl, she thought, and then remembered: crazy girl.

Great. She had a cover story.

She said, "Not exactly."

Glenn grunted, and then said, still without noticeable sympathy, "Got your keys?"

"No."

"I hope I don't have to worry about who does have them. Or you'll be paying for a new front lock."

God, where were they? Cleände's? Meheg-menoht?

"I don't know . . ." They could well be in Tehega's pocket, now that she thought about it. "Maybe I should . . . " What? She foundered.

But Glenn waved her off. "Talk to your social worker first, he'll probably be good for some of it. Just give me a minute to find the spare and I'll let you in."

A fan in the communal living room to the right of the door buzzed and whirred, a repetitious cycle of sound that weighed, somehow, more heavily than silence. Someone in the house was talking, a mumble without tone or words. Rye had to question what she was doing here, and she felt that sway towards unreality that might have been fever, or uncertainty, or the arcwright's seduction. Glenn finally returned with a shiny key, its wards rough from the locksmith's grinder, and a handful of pages from a message pad.

"I'd appreciate it if you called him soon and got him off my back."

Social worker, Rye guessed, and looked at the top page. A date in August, the name, Hardesty, and a phone number.

"Okay," she said. "I really appreciate . . . "

But Glenn was already halfway down the hall, and only responded with another shrug and a wave of the hand.

Rye went up the stairs with a knot in her throat and the messages crumpled in her fist.

Home.

The window had been closed and the room was hot and smelled vaguely of feet. Rye stood with her back to the door and looked around, more desolate than before. Circling back, she thought, but not back to anywhere she wanted to be. The curtain drooped at one end of its rod, exposing the dusty window and its view of the houses across the street. The Indian throw on the narrow bed was rumpled, the mattress askew from its frame, as if someone had pulled the bed out from the wall and shoved it hastily back in again. Maybe she had. She couldn't remember.

It was all so long ago.

"Rob Hardesty."

"This is Rye Coleman. Mr. Hardesty?"

"Coleman . . . "

"There were a bunch of messages here for me to call you."

"Ms. Coleman! I'll say there were. Where are you calling from?"

"Glenn Roeder's boarding house?"

"Well, sure, if you got my messages. Sorry, I'm just a little bit thrown. I'd started to wonder—Where have you been?"

"I'm . . . not really sure."

Pause. "That's what I was afraid of. Ms. Coleman, have you called the out-patient clinic for an appointment? That was a big part of why I was trying to get ahold of you. Dr. Sandstrom said she was having a hell of a time getting you to come in for your follow-up."

"Not yet."

"I hate to sound unsympathetic, but if you're still having symptoms, it's pretty important that you go in for your appointments. There's a public health issue, don't forget."

"Right."

"I hope you didn't, ah, come to any harm?"

"So is that the only reason you called?"

"Uh, no." Pause. "Ms. Coleman, have the police been in touch with you yet?"

There were two detectives, middle-aged men, one skinny, one bulky, both looking hot and tired in their over-worked suits. The skinny one, Ohannes, had a thick black mustache and graying hair. The big one, Sidney, was balding, and his face was a dangerous red in the afternoon heat. Rye met them in the hall. Sidney asked her if they could talk somewhere more private.

"I don't even know what this is about," Rye said.

"Neither does anyone else in the house, and we'd like to keep it that way. How about your room?"

Rye led the detectives reluctantly up the stairs. While Ohannes was shutting her bedroom door, she started for the bed to sit down, then veered away to stand by the window. There was a moment of silence while both men studied her scars. Rye dropped her head and waited for the questions to start. She couldn't think why they were there. It only added to the dislocated sense of one reality imperfectly joined to another.

Sidney, the big one, said, "Did you know your social worker filed a missing-persons report on you?"

"No."

"You mind telling us where you've been?"

Rye hesitated. She knew there had been deaths and disappearances, conspiracy and violence—she remembered Bardo's story, at least in outline—but why exactly were these men here?

"Are you from Missing Persons?" she said, temporizing. "I didn't even know they had real detectives."

"Sure they have real detectives," Ohannes said. He was propped in a corner like a beanpole sagging under its own weight. He sounded like he was pretending to be amused.

"I mean, I thought you only actually looked for kids."

"Your social worker seemed pretty concerned," Sidney said.

Rye just looked at him. He looked back. His eyes seemed small in his fleshy face, dark and cold as gun ports in a wall. Rye's fever swelled, coming alert to an imminent threat, tracing a shadowy echo across her vision with every heartbeat. She could actually feel the arcwright watching through her eyes. Distracting.

"You got some reason why you don't want to talk to us?" Ohannes said, still with that sour pretence of good-humor.

Rye, as she had once done with Mostahr, took refuge in sullenness. "You got some reason why you want me to talk to you? Or did you just want to make sure I'm back? Because, hey, I'm back."

"Why are you being so cagey?" Sidney said. "What's the big deal about telling us where you were? Do you have something to hide?"

Rye thought, for an awful moment, that she was going to laugh. The fever turned over inside her, and she had to lean against the window frame.

"If you talked to Mr. Hardesty, then you know I had a fever that burned out part of my brain. I hallucinate, I have black-outs. I've forgotten whole fucking years of my life. I don't know where I was, I don't know where I'll be next week, and I don't know what business it is of yours. Are we done?"

Sidney looked at Ohannes. Ohannes shrugged.

"So your memory's messed up, huh?" Sidney was skeptical.

"Yes." She felt more and more tired as it began to seem they didn't want anything at all.

"Because the thing is," Sidney said, "we're not the first cops to come looking for you."

"So I was missing a while?" Rye guessed.

"No, I mean before your social worker called us. Actually, before you got out of the hospital, as far as we can tell. The name Dan Bardo mean anything to you?"

twenty-seven

Sidney slipped it in so deftly, without pausing for breath and in the same bored, hectoring tone, that Rye had the sensation of skidding on a patch of black ice.

"He . . . he was looking for me?"

"Oh, so you remember him. Detective Bardo."

"No, I . . . I don't know. The name's familiar. That really shakes me up," she added confidingly: "I go someplace or I hear someone's name and it's like I know it, but I can't remember. You know?"

Sidney wasn't buying it. Ohannes wasn't buying it either. But what could they do? Rye quit trying not to look rattled.

"God," she said, the jump of her pulse in her voice. "Was I in trouble or something? Did they know that, at the hospital? Nobody even said anything! Oh my God."

The detectives exchanged another glance. This time Ohannes spoke. No more fake amusement.

"Detective Bardo was looking into several incidents of gang violence that took place during the winter. You have any recollection of being involved in anything like that?"

"That was when I got sick," she said sadly.

"But how about before that?"

"You have to understand," Sidney interjected, "we're not looking to get you into trouble. We can see you've had a rough time of it. We're just looking for some information. Several people were killed, including three policemen. You know anything about that?"

"Oh my God. No. Honestly, no."

"The name Mark Sejwa mean anything to you?"

"No." This time it came out mostly as air, but Sidney nodded like he believed her.

"Well, we had to ask. Sorry to have to bother you. You know how it is, we have to keep going over the same ground until we turn up something new. I guess you must be sick of us, first Detective Bardo, now us."

Hey, copper. I'm crazy, not stupid. Rye frowned. "But I don't . . . Sorry. You mean I already talked to the other detective? I don't . . . Oh, you mean before the hospital? Before I got sick?"

"Since the hospital," Sidney said. "We have it on record that he was trying to track you down just a few weeks ago. He was heavily involved in the investigation into the gang situation. In fact, his partner was one of the policemen who were killed. You sure he hasn't talked to you?"

"No."

"No, he hasn't talked to you? Or no, you aren't sure?"

"I don't know. I haven't been in such good shape lately. I don't remember him."

"Maybe he left a message?"

"No."

"With a friend, maybe. Your friends must be worried about you. You keep in touch with them? Maybe Detective Bardo could have left a message with one of them. Can you think who that might be?"

"I don't remember anyone."

"Oh, come on!" Ohannes again. "You seen a few too many movies, maybe? Amnesia doesn't work that way in real life, kid. Quit jerking us around."

"What the hell do you know?" Real anger, now, swelling the fever again. "Talk to my doctors! You want the neurologist, the immunologist, the epidemiologist, the fever specialist, or what?"

"Okay, okay," Sidney said.

"I don't remember anything since I was sixteen years old. I barely remember yesterday. Is that *okay*?"

"Take it easy. Nobody's accusing you of anything."

"Well, what then? What do you want from me?"

"Nothing," Sidney said soothingly. "Listen, we didn't mean to upset you. We're just looking into a dangerous situation, trying figure out what's going on. Come on, you can sympathize, right? We've got to follow up every lead we have, even the weak ones. We'll get out of your hair."

He nudged his partner's arm, got him moving toward the door, then turned back as if on a sudden thought.

"Look, here's my card. If you hear anything . . . And I'll tell you what. While we're asking around, if we run into any of your old friends, maybe we can do you a favor, drop you a line. Okay? That sound fair?"

"Okay," Rye said, off balance again.

"Okay then. Thanks for your time."

They were on their way. It was only belatedly, when they were out in the hall, that it occurred to Rye that it might seem more natural to ask, "Hey. If Detective Bardo is investigating this gang stuff, why don't you just ask him?"

"Thanks for your time," Ohannes said, and shut the door.

The arcwright had not moved.

Rye could feel, in a seductive multiplicity of sensations, the sexy bitter-sweet of roof tar under taloned feet, the watery jangle of sunlight through thickening clouds, the dusty shadows of pigeons. There was no cry of *alone*, no insinuating promise of *coming, lover*, no jealous denial, no *mine*. The creature was simply there, like the touch of skin against her skin, a shadow the fever cast along her nerves. Rye's thoughts skated the edges of that shadow, avoiding her growing awareness of the complexity that lay beneath. Alien emotions summoned a confusion of response: grief and desire, a melancholy exultation, an elusive sneeze, the prickle of wool, the taste of spearmint gum. None of them was more appropriate than the next, they were only ghosts summoned by the firing of synapses aroused by an inhuman stimulus.

Ghosts like the taste of limes and the image of Cleände lying in the bruise-colored dimness of her living room.

Ghosts like the elusive lightning-fish echo of Daniel Bardo.

(roof tar (sex (sweat-damp sheets)

Rye could almost imagine herself in the rough wooden cavern of Bardo's loft, could almost hear the rattle of his old refrigerator, the softer hum of the fan stirring dust and the machine-oil smell. She could feel her own fever, and she could feel a loneliness, a reaching out that could have been her, the arcwright, Bardo across the city somewhere. Or did she only wish it was Bardo? Maybe it was all three of them, maybe it was only the arcwright. Maybe it had always only been the arcwright, filling the gaps in Rye's memory. The gaps in Rye's personality. How would she know? It had been there, whether she knew it or not, since she had woken in the hospital. There in the fever dreams, there in the weeks of trying to make a life in the city, there that hot, muggy day Bardo had followed her, warned her, led her—led the arcwright—halfway across the city.

There in the instant that Cleände had, at Rye's urging, tried to pry them apart. What if it had not been the arcwright that had reacted so violently? What if it had been the fever in Rye? Or rather, the spaces in her that the fever filled, the lost spaces that might swallow her whole if the fever, and the arcwright, were taken away.

But that was a thin place in the ice, with cracks showing the deep, cold sea waiting below. Rye-the-skater veered aside. The point was not her sanity. The point was that she needed to get to Bardo, who was in some depth of trouble she could not plumb, and who was, will he, nil he, threatening to drag her down as well.

Oh, hell. She could lie to the police, but can she lie to herself? The arcwright knows better. Her throat is full of a musk-rose perfume, her mouth full of it as if it were petals or smoke, she has no choice but to breathe it in, breathe it out again, the longing that the sound of his name has evoked. Dan, oh Dan. Dan Bardo. Dan.

(breath caught, fire ants biting, twisted sheets (gravel and tar (sex (come, lover, come)

Dan Bardo stands behind a bar of sunlight, shouting, blind to ghosts. He sits beside her, tucks her against his side, indifferent to her scars. He leans toward her in the dimness of his loft and asks her if he had been right to save her, right not to shoot her when she came to his door. When the arcwright led her to his door. The door above the alley

that twists and turns, gray and tenuous with fog, dream alley carved from the melting ice that holds back, that does not hold back, that leaks through a thousand cracks the lightning-shot midnight sea. The alley becomes a maze she walks, following the shadow cast by the light of the stars. This way, this way. She walks, slips on ice, swims. Swims through the fog, the flooded alley, the underwater hall, until she comes to a door. A door of three dimensions, four dimensions whose substance is

the dusk of blinds, the purr of the fan, the mild, warm, dusty smell of wood and machine oil and sweat.

And the sound of Bardo's voice saying, "Rye, I know you're not there. I know you're not there. Rye. Are you there?"

Bardo had Rye's fever.

Of course he did. Not that Rye had anticipated it, but that she recognized it instantly, as surely as she recognized his face.

He sat naked on the edge of his bed, shivering. His sweat-slick skin shimmered with ruddy patterns like a live ember touched by a vagrant breeze. When Rye knelt before him on the tangle of a discarded sheet, he put out a clumsy hand to touch her and nearly jammed his thumb in her eye. She caught his hand, pressed it to her cheek.

"I'm here," she said. "I'm real."

A sound shuddered out of him, dry and light. It might have passed for a laugh. He put his other hand to her face and drew her up to press his forehead against hers. His breath was arid, bitter-sweet with burnt metal, a furnace's exhalation. She could feel his fever swarm through him, hot as molten copper, seeking an alignment with her own.

"I," he said, "I had a gun here somewhere."

His hold was not tender. Though he shivered, his fingers bit into the muscle at the base of her skull. Rye knew the threat was real, whether it was Bardo's or the delirium's, but she wasn't afraid of him. Careful, perhaps. She clasped his wrists and felt the tidal ebb and race of his pulse. Her heart tried to match his rhythm. Her mouth filled with the black, dusty heat of fur.

"Let me go, Dan." She tugged at his wrists, not a struggle, a communication. "I'm going to bleed in a minute. You have to let me go. Daniel." Another tug.

"I," he said. "I." He released her face, but only to gather her up, still clumsy, shivering badly, into a hard, hot, hateful embrace. "When do *I* start to bleed? God damn you to hell, Rye, *when do I start*?"

He had no balance, and she, her feet sliding on the loose sheet, nearly pulled him off the bed. She braced one knee on the mattress between his legs, and fought, not him, but herself. Instinct said that to struggle would precipitate violence Bardo could not, and perhaps would not want to, control. But he was raging with heat, and her fever swelled, fighting to encompass him as he, the hard bony sweating strength of him, encompassed her. It wasn't blood she feared, or Bardo, it was . . . she didn't know. The arcwright hummed in the fan's breeze, stank in Bardo's sweat, prickled in Rye's scars. Bardo grappled with her, his hands digging into her flesh as if he could haul her in beneath his skin. Her sheet-tangled foot lost its traction on the floor. She put her arms around his neck, and held on.

"You have me," she whispered. He left her no breath to speak. "I'm here. You have me. Dan. Dan." She was weeping, tasting her tears with his sweat, through the lesion scars. She hardly knew what she said. The black heat of his fever drowned her. "I'm here. I'm here."

Drowning, she felt a shift in the tide. He turned his face into the angle of her neck. She felt the shape of a word against her throat. And then he let her go.

She dropped to the floor with a thump that spat sparks across her eyes. She hardly felt the strike of his heel against her thigh as he toppled in a half-controlled fall across the bed. She sat, while the fever, still bristling from the contact with Bardo, settled back into her core.

"I don't want you," Bardo said. "Go away."

twenty-eight

Rye gathered herself up off the floor. Something cold and hard under the sheet had bruised her ankle. Bardo's gun. She gathered it up with the sheet, and carried them to the kitchen corner where she dumped them on the counter by the sink. All the windows were covered by blinds, and the slats of gray light were growing dim. It was either evening, or the clouds had thickened enough to rain. She suffered through a moment's disorientation, while she stood in the kitchen and lay on Bardo's bed and slipped, like a fish through eel grass, through the first lines of rain. A dusty misery sifted through her at the thought of spending a whole lifetime split into three perspectives—never mind sanity, how would she, practically, *cope*?—but after a breath or two she was herself, Bardo was himself, the arcwright was *(coming, lover, coming)*. Rye sighed, tilted the faucet lever to cold, and rinsed Bardo's sweat off her face and arms. She found a glass, drank cool tapwater, and filled it again before carrying it to Bardo. The patterns under his skin had faded, but they roused again, a scale pattern like her scars, at her approach.

"Here," she said. "You need to drink something."

"Sure," he said. His deep voice was a hoarse whisper. "Drink lots of fluids, get lots of bed rest."

He made no move to reach for the glass. Rye touched the damp bottom against his bare chest. He opened red-rimmed eyes to glare at her. Beneath the testiness lay a deep black well of confusion.

"Sit up and drink."

"Hell did you get so bossy?" But he hauled himself up on his elbow, took the glass, and drank. His shaking hand spilled water down his chin. He pushed the empty glass at her and lay back down, his arm crooked against his eyes. "How'd you get in?"

"How do you think?" Rye tugged one corner of the fitted sheet back over the mattress.

"It's a bird, it's a plane, it's . . . Super-Rye."

"Fuck off." Close to tears, she stomped back into the kitchen and slammed the glass down on the counter.

Bardo said something. His voice was too raw to carry that far. Rye stomped back around the corner.

"What?"

"I said," Bardo said wearily, "that you're lucky I didn't shoot you. But you would probably have caught the bullet in your teeth."

She breathed. "Do you want more water?"

"Yes."

She brought him some, took the glass away when he was done. In the kitchen, she eased the gun out from the bundled sheet. It was big and heavy and oily and black. Memories of long-past TV shows suggested it was an automatic rather than a revolver. Beyond that, Rye did not want to know. She could imagine what Bardo would say if she asked him how to unload it. She opened a cupboard, put the gun in a saucepan, and closed the door. Bardo said something else inaudible.

She yelled, "*Will* you just go to *sleep*!?"

Silence from around the corner. Rye twisted the rod that opened the blinds over the kitchen window and looked at the rain streaking the dusty glass. She remembered another rainy day: Bardo leading her to Cleände's house; Tehega, with his man's knife at her throat, ordering Bardo to put down his gun. How many did Bardo have? Her shoulders twitched. There was far more to that memory than the gun. She went back around the corner.

"What?"

But Bardo was asleep, or unconscious, one foot still resting on the floor.

It was strange, how the fever marked him without breaking his skin. Strange how beautiful the patterns were, a fluid shimmer under the sweat-bright olive skin, when her own scars were so ugly. Rye was fascinated by the way her proximity roused that flickering tracery, and afraid that her presence might be all it took to start the bleeding.

Afraid, but not only afraid. Had she looked like that in Meheg-menoht, before the arcwright had shown her the way to its crippled twin? Was Bardo's blood as poisonous as hers? Was she the cripple he was meant to bleed for, and kill? Her thoughts twisted around each other, black snakes of fear and guilt and pity, yes, but of fascination, anticipation, hunger, too. She wasn't alone. She wasn't alone.

She tended him, and watched the crimson patterns chase the wet cloth she drew across his skin. She took her time, learning his skin, the muscles and veins beneath it, the sparse hair on his chest and the soft black line that grew down into his loins. Learning his shape, his density, his feel. Learning the shiver that trembled in his limbs as she wet the cloth again, drew it again, slow wet caress, across his throat, his chest, his belly, his sex, his thighs. And wet the cloth again, and drew it down him again, and again. The rain gathered the evening close and dark around them. She did not bother to turn on a light. In the wet summer heat, his heat, hers, she pulled off her clothes and felt the feathers of his fever rouse, tremble, lie flat again against her skin. She saw the thorns of the arcwright's poison etch their crimson mark against the shell of his inner darkness. She breathed across him, like a woman who rouses an ember into flame, and it was only his voice, inarticulate and pleading, that made her realize that she was not offering comfort but taking some measure of revenge.

She dropped the cloth and backed away from the bed through the cluster of furniture in the middle of the loft to the windows in the far wall. Appalled at herself, she slid down to crouch on the floor. An open window dribbled rain down the inner face of its blind to drip on her bare shoulders. She bowed her head under the cold touch, feeling the trickle down her back like the trickle of blood. She supposed she had known she loved Daniel Bardo.

She would never have guessed she might come to hate him as well.

"Why did you come?"

It was morning. Rye had made Bardo a cup of chicken bouillon from a packet in his cupboard, dropped an ice cube in the mug to cool it, watched him drink it from where she sat on the floor several feet from the bed.

Bardo's tone denied any welcome, and Rye was briefly, pointlessly, tempted to lie. But she didn't know what she would say besides the truth, and the truth was spiteful enough.

"The police are looking for you."

Bardo, sitting with his shoulders against the headboard, looked at the empty mug in his hand. "How do you know?"

Somehow, Rye wasn't surprised that he wasn't surprised. She told him about the detectives and the questions that seemed oddly vague now that she repeated them to Bardo. Where was the threat? She knew it was there, but where? Bardo wasn't saying. They sat in mutual silence, Bardo staring into space, Rye with her head leaning against her knee, until Bardo said, "So they found you. Who was it? What did you say?"

"A couple of detectives. Sidney and . . . I forget. Something weird."

"Ohannes."

"I guess you know them."

"What did you tell them?"

"The truth." She lifted her head and gave him a thin smile. "My memory was scrambled by a fever. Talk to my doctors. What do I know?"

Bardo rubbed his wrist across his forehead. His hand was shaking again, still, but he was lucid. Rye was beginning to think the fever was not taking him as hard as it had her, the arcwright's poison weakened, perhaps, in its transmission from Rye to Bardo. She wondered if Bardo guessed as much. Wondered if he feared the loss of his memory, the eruption of lesions, the scars. She did not ask.

He said, "Did they believe you?"

"Do cops ever believe anybody? No, they didn't believe me, but what can they do? Half the staff of the university hospital can swear to the fever and the amnesia, not to mention the social worker who put them on to me to begin with."

"'Put them on to you'?"

"Filed a missing persons report."

Bardo gave her a bleak look. "Sidney and Ohannes aren't Missing Persons. They're Major Crimes."

His old colleagues. Maybe even his friends. Rye shook her head in confusion. "I thought they were looking for you."

"Police are always looking for someone." Bardo rolled his head against the headboard, a kind of shrug.

"But they're looking for you." Rye swallowed, but she had to ask. "Why?"

Bardo must have been waiting for it. His expression did not change.

"I told you. When Marducci—When my partner and I went looking for feuding illegal aliens—" The twist of his mouth gave it a sarcastic cast. "—he was killed. So was another policeman, a patrolman we called on for backup. By the fucking gray beasts, okay? So what are we—What am I supposed to tell them? It's not like they don't want to know what tore two armed men to pieces, and I was there. I was right there."

Bardo's voice cracked, and he rubbed his forehead again. Not quite as in command of himself as Rye had thought. Her breath quickened and slowed in sync with his.

"So they have a few questions, maybe. Okay?" As if he had said all he needed to, Bardo slid down until he was lying flat, pillows pushed aside. The mug in his hand bumped against the floor. He let it go. It tipped over and rolled to a stop against its handle.

"But that was a long time ago," Rye said. She was angry at him, and afraid for him. She held herself so tightly her voice came out thin, uninflected. "That was before you ever met Cleände, before . . ." *. . . you ever met me.* "Two cops are killed, you quit, and they're only asking questions now?"

"Nobody ever called Dave Sidney the fastest horse in the stable."

"Bullshit."

"No, really." Bardo sounded almost whimsical. "They never did."

Rye bit off her first response. She crawled over to the bed, picked up the mug, and knelt there with it in her hands. The thorn-scratch patterns traced themselves across Bardo's arm, shoulder, chest, so faintly she would not have seen them if she had not been watching for them. He kept his face turned toward the wall.

"Dan. You don't want to know how they found me?" He did not respond, but he lay too still, listening. "I went back to the boarding house—you never knew it, I moved in when I left the hospital. They kept my room for me, and all my stuff. Glenn said—Glenn runs the place—Glenn said my social worker asked that my room was kept. Glenn said, 'That social worker of yours and—' *And*. You want to know who else wanted me to have a place to come back to? You want to know who told Glenn to call them as soon as I showed up again? 'Cause it wasn't the social worker, and it wasn't the hospital, and it sure as hell wasn't Missing Persons. You want to guess?"

Bardo rubbed his forearm over his face, a rough, clumsy gesture. His hair was black and oily with sweat. With his arm across his forehead and his eyes still closed he said, "The hell do you want me to say?"

Rye's hands clenched around the mug. "Why are they looking for you?"

"When cops die, somebody has to take the blame, that's all." His voice dragged out into a mumble. "That's all. Somebody has to take the blame."

He was not going to tell her any more, she knew that, but she still had to ask the real question, the question she had been silently asking him all along: "Dan. Why were you looking for me?"

But he was asleep, or wanted her to think he was, and had nothing to say.

twenty-nine

Afternoon again. Not so hot since the rain, but muggy. The fan stirred the air like a spoon.

Bardo had gotten up earlier to shower and pull on a pair of shorts. Rye had retreated into the kitchen, but not before she had seen the way he flinched and stared at nothing, the way he nearly fell before he gave in and sat on the bed to dress. Her retreat was not tact, it was avoidance. Sympathy was as painful as her anger. (Yes, she knew that what she felt was guilt, but shame would have sent her running, as it had from Cleände. Anger let her stay, even if it made her cruel.)

He was sleeping now. If she listened, Rye could feel the lightning-fish flicker of dreams around the edges of his fever, a slippery whisper like the whisper of daylight through the blinds. If she listened, she could feel the arcwright as well, luxuriant with tar, worrying at a bit of gravel caught between its toes. It was as absorbed in its grooming as a cat, but it weighed overhead like a boulder poised to fall, a thunderstorm poised to break. Rye knew it was there, as close as wood and insulation and gravel and tar would let it come. The air below the ceiling shimmered with its presence, a pool's surface rippled by a cat's paw. Bardo's dreams touched it and danced aside, touched it and danced aside, until Rye was ready to scream, to shake him awake, to drag him away. But there was no away.

She paced the loft, thinking about guns, thinking about a lot of things, but with Bardo right there, even sleeping, she couldn't bring herself to snoop. And thinking didn't help. Thinking was what kept her moving, shedding thoughts behind her, shaking off memories—Bardo washing her blood away with his hands; Bardo kissing her, wet and electric as wine—until they crowded the big room. Until *she* crowded it, bits of her peeling off like ghosts. The image of the crippled arcwright's cell came to her, the nightmare blooming of gray beasts, echoes, memories, ghosts, from the lightless walls. She whispered to herself to stop it, *stop it*, jammed her fingers through her hair. It was stiff and greasy with sweat, still too short to curl, but long enough to have sprung into cowlicks after a restless night on the couch. All her self-disgust was focused in an instant on her dirty hair, the smell of Cleände's over-worn clothes. She rummaged ruthlessly in Bardo's drawers for a shirt and a pair of boxers and carried them into the bathroom.

With the door closed, the only light filtered in over the top of the unfinished partition wall. The air was still damp from Bardo's shower, a fresher humidity than the city air seeping in from outside. She turned the shower tap until tepid water hissed over her arm—she had another flash of memory, the first showers after the hospital, the water like razorblades stroking her skin. It still felt that way. She had only gotten used to it—and it wasn't until she had pulled off her clothes that she spotted the electric clippers sitting on an open shelf.

They buzzed like a handful of bees.

When she came out, shorn and clean, Bardo was lying prone on the floor by his bed. Rye thought he had fallen, but when she started for him, he scrambled up, dusty, weaving, and mad.

"Where the hell is my gun?"

Rye pointed a thumb toward the kitchen. He scowled and started toward her. Toward the kitchen, but he looked as if, if she didn't get out of his way, he'd just knock her down and walk over her. She skipped aside, trailed around the corner in his wake. He banged a couple of cupboards open without looking inside, then spun around and caught his balance on the stove.

"You think this is some kind of game? Where is it?"

Rye did not really think he would shoot her, but the arcwright's weight bore down on them, a pressure that threatened to crystallize her distress, and his. Again, she thought of the cell at the heart of

Meheg-menoht, the gray beasts spinning themselves out of the walls. The arcwright was listening from its perch in the sun.

"What . . . " She tried to sound like she was just asking a question. "What do you want it for?"

"It's my damn gun. You don't just leave it lying around. Where is it?"

"It's not just lying around. It's safe."

"Rye. I'm not going to ask you again."

"God damn it! What is it with guys and guns?"

"Rye." He stepped toward her, then stopped, the menace in his stance softening to confusion. "For God's sake. Do you think I'm going to shoot you?"

"You see anyone else around here?"

He looked so strange for an instant, his shoulders hunched, his eyes slipping sideways, that her heart quailed. And then she thought, with a rare flood of cold under her skin, I do that. *I do that.*

It only lasted a second. Bardo collected himself, and said, "Not yet."

His dry, ironic tone reassured her, before his words sank home.

"Dan! For—God—What are you going to do? Get in a gun battle with the police? Are you insane?"

The word hung between them. Then Bardo sighed and dropped his head to rub at his eyes.

"You're forgetting about Cleände's folks. And Tehega's. None of them have any reason to like me, and now you're here . . . "

Rye was taken aback. "Nobody knows I'm here. That was the whole point—!" She caught her breath at the memory, hers or the arcwright's, of that ghostly journey, that foggy swim between the boarding house and here. The world throbbed around her, a sudden pulse of quicksilver lightning inside the walls. Inside Bardo. He ran his hands over his face, his hair, to clasp them at the back of his neck.

"You think you can use your superpowers without any of them noticing?"

"Don't call it that! It's not—"

"I know. It's not power. It's a fucking disease."

And he stared at her, black eyed, while the realization unfolded inside her. Bardo had the fever. Bardo had—

"Where's the gun?"

"In the corner cupboard," she told him, subdued. "It's in a pot."

"A pot." It came out on a sigh. He found the gun, pulled the slide and let it snap home. Rye jumped. She didn't like the way his hand shook under the weapon's weight. She didn't like the way he looked, dark-eyed and hot and off balance.

"Dan," she said carefully. "You can't get in a gun battle with them either. Tehega and them. You know that, right? I mean, you can't just fight a war with them. Not with . . . "

"Not with Major Crimes already breathing down my neck?" He looked her over, the gun hanging at his side. "You're really scared of these things, aren't you?"

Rye shrugged, unable to say, No, just you. He sighed.

"It's just a tool. If we had time, I'd teach you how to use one." He gave her a crooked smile: an offering. "I bet you don't know how to use a screwdriver either."

"Screwdrivers don't kill people."

He laughed. "Sweetheart, I could tell you stories . . . "

"Well, don't."

"I forgot. You could tell me some stories, couldn't you?"

The cold came over her again. She shivered, and saw the shiver pass through him a moment later. He walked by her, carefully steady, heading back to his bed.

"I'm not planning on using it," he said. "I just needed to know where it was. You never . . . " He passed the bathroom corner, but she could still hear him, just. "You never lose track of your weapon. It's one of the rules."

But she had seen him hesitate. She had seen him tilt his head, and stop himself, and walk on. The arcwright rolled over to stretch, gravel pebbling its tarry hide, sunlight singing and yelling all around it, a chaotic chorus Rye took for granted now, except when she heard it through Bardo's skin. She felt him sit on the bed and hold the gun between his trembling hands, felt him breathe, felt him struggle to separate the strands of his fear. He set the gun on the top of the headboard, and lay down, and Rye knew the way his blood surged through him, fighting to break free from the rhythm of his heart, and she knew the way the fever sprawled inside him, gathering itself into the arcwright's shadow, and she knew the way his skin burned and sparkled and sang with color, but she didn't know what he was thinking. She didn't know what he knew. She didn't know why he was so afraid.

She didn't know why she was.

A red sunset bled through the blinds.

Rye had lost track of when she had last slept. She lay on Bardo's rough blue couch, her knees up, her midriff bared to the fan's breeze. The color of the dying sunlight had reminded her that she had not bled, which reminded her she had not eaten, which reminded her she had not slept. Food held no appeal, and lying here, she could not tell if she was tired. Tracing her fingers over her bare middle, she felt the sharp lines of her ribs, the sudden taut hollow of her belly, the peaks of her hipbones. She could not deny a certain satisfaction in being so skinny, but the associations that slipped through her mind had nothing to do with fashion models or her own plump adolescence. Or, worse, those *were* the associations, but they lay alongside the memory of women's bellies swollen with false and deadly pregnancy, alongside the beauty of mercury hide stretched over black-iron bones. Those images that had haunted her for so many months had settled into the depths of her mind. They had become a part of her: a realization that twisted a new strand of sorrow through her core. She remembered something Bardo had once said. *This is what I am.*

Except he had been talking about guilt.

The arcwright watched the red sun go down, mouth open to feel the last light sing across its tongue. Roof tar clung to its skin, hot with its own bass hum, the burnt-oil reek of love. The arcwright bore it, sphinx-like, but the sexiness made Rye restless. More than restless. Worse than restless. Associations tangled again, an ugly mix of Bardo's mouth tracing half a circle from her belly to her thigh—the crippled arcwright clasping her with the talonless stumps of limbs—Bardo washing her bloody skin with his hands—the crippled arcwright's lapping tongue—and blood—and the arcwright lowers itself against her, velvet hide and iron bone, hot enough to dry the sweat on her skin, and she feels the smooth weight of its sex on her belly *(and bodies black as gold running with tar wet with lightning twine, talons like slick spurs star-bright, the bite of love)* and he eases himself inside her, careful with his weight, and turns his head so she will not hear the whispered, shuddering groan he cannot silence—

"Jesus Christ."

Sunlight was gone. The arcwright had closed its eyes. The loft was dark.

Rye pressed her fingers against her tender mouth, swallowing a protest. It was like one of those dreams where nightmare images refuse to bear the burden of horror they should carry. She hung in the chains of the arcwright's desire, and knew how twisted they were, knew how twisted they threatened to make her, and still could not fight free. She ached with the throbbing heat of the fever. The shadow-tiger yearned for its mate, and there was Bardo, his curse, his plea, still hanging on the air. Rye slipped off the couch and walked toward him through the dense, charged, dust-and-lightning gloom.

He saw her coming, or felt her in the reverberation of heat striking heat. He rolled onto his side, his back toward her, and whispered, "Go away." But she had no pity. Her bones were leaden with cruelty and need. She trailed one finger down his arm, feeling the fever-thorns rouse to score his flesh, feeling his flinch turn to a shudder that matched the deep tremble in her belly's pit.

"It's too late," she murmured, her voice twined with the fan's purr. "You know it's too late."

He tried to move away from her touch. "Rye. Please. Leave me alone."

Rye knelt on the bed where her heat and her smell engulfed him like a silken shroud. She felt it, tasted it, her peppery glass-and-iron scent a cage for his copper-musk roses, and knew a dissonance, a grief. *(no burnt-oil smell. not the same.)* But that was all she was, dissonance and grief, the fractured edges of her rubbing one on the other with an unbearable friction. This was only one more edge, only one more lick of wrongness, only one more step before the fall.

"Who else will you ever have?" She leant over him, not touching him now with anything but her breath, her words. "Who else will either of us ever have?" And then, with a black triumph that was not hers, and was: "You're mine now, and I'm all you'll ever have."

Bardo turned on her. Struck at her, thrust her away with a wide, desperate sweep of his arm. But when she had fallen in a hard sprawl across the dusty floor, he tumbled after her, as if her fall was his, as if they had to fall together. He came down on her with all his long hot bony weight, driving the breath out of her—she struggled beneath him, not to get free but to have all of him against her, to capture his skin against hers—her shirt torn, his nails catching the scars on her hip as he hauled at her shorts—her teeth, sudden as her pain, in his neck—the taste of him, the taste—

—and the arcwright tore its attention, and its desire, away.

Rye was fractured yet again. Hollow where the arcwright had been, her body still engrossed by Bardo. Bardo on her, Bardo inside her, Bardo holding her with his hands, his heat, his sweating weight against the hard wood floor. Bardo frozen in that moment, shaking with the violence of his heartbeat, his breath harsh against her face. Shocked, and distracted, as she was, by the arcwright's sudden attention on *something coming.* He made a noise in his throat, a small pained groan of confusion, of distress, and Rye put her arms around his neck.

"Don't stop." Her body ached, liquid with unsatisfied need, but it wasn't only that. It wasn't that at all. The absence of the arcwright's desire left room for something else to swell and spill through her. Something tender, something vulnerable, something she could never, in Bardo's hearing, name aloud. So she turned her face against his, a small, gentle movement after the violence, and she whispered, her mouth soft against his sandpaper cheek, "Don't stop."

"Ah, Rye," he said, a moan of grief. His heart still pounding through them both. His sex still hard inside her. "Not like this. God. I can't. I never wanted—"

"Shh." She kissed his cheek. She buried her hands in his thick, soft hair, pulled his head back so she could kiss his mouth. "Shh."

He said her name, a whole lifetime in his voice, a whole dark history in a single syllable.

"I know," she said, though she didn't. She did. She kissed him. "Don't stop."

"I can't," he said against her mouth. "I can't do this, Rye."

"Please," she whispered. Her body's need, her heart's. Salt in both their mouths. "Please, Dan. Please don't stop."

"Don't beg," he said, wounded. "Not here, not like this."

"Yes like this," she said, and kissed him. Kissed him, and rocked her hips against him, and finally he was kissing her, soft, despairing kisses, and his hands were gentle on her body, clasping her naked scalp. And he was moving inside her, softly, softly. And she said his name, and melting ripe as peaches, streaming sweet as summer honey, pouring electric as wine, she came.

Knowing, as the arcwright knew, that someone *firefly (seeking shadow) cage of bones* was on the way.

thirty

It was Cleände who came. Rye knew her through the arcwright's eyes.

The arcwright's antipathy was distinct from Rye's own, although she dreaded the other woman's approach. What lay between her and Bardo was so delicate, so fragile. They moved around each other, dressing, gathering up their torn and damp-stained clothes, as though the air itself might shatter if it were touched by too vigorous a movement, too loud a sound. For this brief moment, they were the only inhabitants of a tiny, vulnerable world no larger than the arcwright's shadow. Rye was afraid, strangely, viscerally afraid, of what would happen when those other, larger worlds—Nohai, Scalléa, Earth—intruded again. The arcwright slipped an offer through her mind, a temptation that sent quicksilver running inside the walls and scattered stars across her tongue, and although she was helpless to ignore it—if there had ever been barriers between them, they were gone now—she refused it. The walls became solid again, but the offer still lay on the floor of her mind. *(away, lover: home)*

Rye found another T-shirt for herself and pulled on Cleände's wrinkled linen skirt. Hot with shame, she tidied the bed, as if Cleände could read the recent past in an untucked sheet, and when she returned Bardo's pillow to its place she saw the gun on the headboard. Take it? Hide it? The sight of it made her cold. But she had pushed Bardo too far, she could not bring herself to interfere with him, with his weapons or his decisions, any further. When he emerged from the bathroom, she was on the far side of the loft, watching the dark alley through the blinds. He padded barefoot across the dark room to stand at the other window. She knew what he saw: Dumpsters, a stack of wooden pallets, the wall of the neighboring building.

"She's almost here," she said quietly.

"Who?"

"Cleände."

"How do you know?"

Rye had never heard him speak so gently. His voice was low and dark, scoured by fever and emotion to a rich bass purr. Reassuring, until this question tripped her up.

"I—Don't you—" Didn't he, even now, know about the arcwright? Suddenly short of breath, she retreated in a panic she could not analyze: "I see her. On the street. Here she is."

And here she was.

Bardo turned on a lamp on his way to the door, and Rye could see that he had tucked his gun into the waistband at the back of his jeans. Disaster knocked with Cleände.

Who asked, with nerve-scraping politeness, "May I come in?"

Standing before Rye, Cleände clasped her hands beneath her chin and let go a breath she might have been holding for days. "Ryder. Thank God. Are you safe?"

"Safe?" Rye could hardly encompass the thought, safety was so far beside the point.

Cleände let her hands fall and turned to look at Bardo. It was a meaningful look, from a face sharp and drawn with the memory of pain.

"Are you—" Rye began. Bardo did not let her finish.

"Why are you here, Cleände?" He stood near the door on the edge of the lamplight, his hands at his sides.

Cleände, facing him, reached out a hand that did not, quite, touch Rye. "She left me so suddenly that I was afraid. I have been searching for her." She turned back to Rye and smiled. "You can blaze like the sun when you choose."

The dim yellow radiance of the single lamp suited Cleände, reminding Rye of her beauty, and so of her relationship with Bardo, that Rye had never yet understood. Beside Cleände, beside Cleände and Bardo's commingled past, she felt young, ignorant, inferior, scarred. And afraid. Afraid of losing Bardo again, and afraid for Bardo, which she could not understand. Under the deep-sea pressure of the arcwright's regard, that tension became nearly unbearable. Rye thought that even Cleände was aware of it. Her elegant face shone with sweat, but still she smiled.

"And you did choose, did you not? Little Ryder. You are braver than you know."

Rye looked past her to Bardo. He met her eyes.

"You have no idea," he said, still gentle, looking only at Rye.

"No." Cleände glanced again at Bardo. She could not see both Bardo and Rye at the same time. "No, there is a great deal I do not know. But Ryder, do you know—"

Bardo, like a spring uncoiling, pulled his gun.

Rye's whole body jolted with surprise. Cleände, looking at Rye, did not see.

"—do you know what you flee from, and what kind of man offers you refuge? I—"

The air was so dense. Rye moved like a diver maneuvering through deep water to place herself between Cleände and the gun. And she did it without knowing—even now—without knowing that she could make Bardo hesitate, without even knowing that she was not his target. His eyes were so black, devoid of light. She wanted to weep for him.

Cleände broke off, but then said, "Is this how you preserve her innocence?"

Bardo said Rye's name. She could see the lamplight tremble on the oiled gun barrel. She could taste his desperation. She could feel it burning through her flesh. She still did not know why.

"Dan," she said. "You didn't have to let her in. Why did you let her in, if this was going to happen?"

He shook his head, his mouth twisted with a painful irony. The lines on his face looked like scars.

Cleände said, "He let me in so he could kill me quietly."

"Lie," Bardo said, his voice a husk.

"Truth," Cleände retorted.

"Then why did you come?" Rye cried at Cleände. She could not take her eyes from Bardo's.

"In the hope," Cleände said gently in her beautiful voice, "that you would not allow it."

The room began to buckle under the arcwright's weight. Rye could feel it, as if the air in her lungs were compressed, mercury running to a tilt in gravity only she could feel. The walls dripped with shallow light, the floor slipped like a raft across a wave.

"Stop," Rye said, to the arcwright, to herself. To fate. "Stop."

"Cleände." Bardo caught his balance with a sudden step. "Why do you have to do this? Why do you always have to use everyone, everything you can get your hands on? You could just let it lie, Cleände. *You could just let it lie.*"

"But Ryder will not let you lie, and she must. Ryder, I beg you, listen to me. You must let him go before he destroys you."

"Before *he* destroys *me*?"

That silenced even Cleände. Bardo closed his eyes, and had to open them again before he fell. Cleände caught her breath.

"Listen."

"No," Rye said. "No. Dan, let her go."

"But I do not wish to go," Cleände said, silencing them both.

Eventually Bardo caught his breath. "Cleände." It was a whisper, a plea.

"You will have to kill me to stop me," Cleände softly replied. "And if you kill me, you will have to kill her as well."

Bardo's hand was shaking, not badly enough to disrupt his aim. "You're willing to make that gamble?"

"Yes."

"Don't," he said in anguish. "Don't do this to her. What did she ever do to deserve this?"

"Nothing," Cleände replied. "It is what you have done that I am here to discuss. As you know."

Rye covered her eyes so she did not have to see Bardo's face.

And so she only knew from the small sounds he made, from the shift of his balance and the sudden lightening of his hand, when he set the safety switch on the gun and dropped it onto the seat of the nearest chair. Cleände put a hand on Rye's shoulder and she flinched.

"Go away."

Echo of Bardo. Go away.

Cleände removed her hand, but she did not leave. She said to Bardo, "Shall I tell her, or will you?"

What she wants me to tell you, Bardo said to Rye, what she never bothered to tell you before, is that I'm a killer. A cop-killer, which is a bad thing for a cop to be.

Should I tell her about the night I told you, Cleände? Is that part of the story you want me to tell?

I told her—God knows why. Maybe I thought she'd understand. Maybe I thought she'd blame the gray beasts, like I did, or the tahinit. Maybe I thought her hatred would make her safe. It doesn't. You should remember that.

The gray beasts. God, I loathe them, even now.

One of the Nohan foot soldiers took a local lover, and learned English off her, and talked just a little too much before he was recalled. Not the truth. The fact that he was an alien would be hard to let slip in casual conversation. But we were looking for foreigners, and found his girlfriend, and she gave us a couple of leads, a couple of places she thought his friends might be. It's not that big a city.

So we went to a beat-up old triplex at the foot of the Glens. We checked it out, quietly, not wanting to spook them. Marducci was good at that. He was a canny old bastard. But we don't—The department doesn't have the resources for long-term surveillance, so we just waited until we were sure there were only three people inside, and we called a couple of patrolmen in for backup. Austad and De Luca, precinct men, we hardly knew them.

So I go with Marducci to the front; the patrolmen are posted at the back. We're talking to some shy young fellow, doesn't speak any English, so sorry, he says, maybe we can come back when the grown-ups are home. And we hear a shot fired behind the triplex. The kid runs for the street, we run for the back . . .

It's fall. Did I tell you that? One of those gray days where the clouds sit on top of the buildings like a roof, but it's not too dark to see. To see it. You know.

(*I know,* Rye whispered.)

So De Luca was down, and this *thing*—I didn't know how to think of it, I hardly knew how to *see* it—this thing has a claw in De Luca's armpit. De Luca's screaming. The blood jumps out the way it does from an artery, bright red, it's the brightest thing in the yard. It's all weeds back there, busted cement and pissy dirt, and this thing trying to rip De Luca open like a can of sardines. Austad opens fire. He's out in the yard, so Marducci and I have to take cover to keep from getting shot. I'm inside the doorway, Marducci ducks down by the back steps, two measly busted concrete steps.

The thing gets De Luca open. I've seen a lot of carnage, but I've never seen it like that. Colorful. Fresh. The brightest thing in the yard.

Austad is screaming. His gun is empty. Marducci's is empty. I'm still firing, trying to pick my shots, but I'm a little crazy by then. Probably we all were. The thing starts toward us, and Marducci's shouting we have to get the fuck out of there, get the fuck out of there. I've got a couple of rounds left. I'm telling him—I'm right in the middle of telling him—*Get inside, I'll cover you*—and he's shouting at Austad, *Get the fuck out of here*—and the gray beast is there, it's just there, and it's putting its claw through John's face, and I run. Austad runs. There's no reason the gray beast didn't kill us as well.

But what do we say? What the hell can we say?

What Austad says is that it was a bunch of gang-bangers out of their heads on crack or dust. Pick-axes, he says. The son of a bitch is crying, he's pissed his pants, and he looks at me and says, Bardo, was it five guys or six? I couldn't keep track of them, they moved so fast. Was it five guys or six?

And I say, Six.

But that kind of lie . . . Any interrogation takes you over it a hundred times, from a hundred different angles, until the suspect confesses just to shut you up and get some peace. A debriefing for an incident that sees cops killed-in-the-line is just the same, except your interrogators know how much you're supposed to have noticed, and they think you're supposed to cooperate. You're supposed to be eager to cooperate, unless you've done something wrong. Unless it's your fault. Which it might be, they never forget that, and they don't let you forget. So you can't tell just one lie. And I still don't know . . .

I still don't know what I saw. I don't know what it was, and *I don't know if it was real*. Here's Austad, picking faces out of photo line-ups, naming names, and here's me thinking I've got to be out of my fucking mind. What did I see? What did he see? What if the gang-bangers are real?

They are real. They're being arrested, interrogated, charged. Austad's giving statements, I'm giving statements, the press won't let it go, and I'm going crazy. My boss says, take some stress leave, so I do that. But what did I see? What did Austad see? I go over it and over it, and it just gets crazier. And then it turns out one of the gang-bangers, the one guy Austad named by name, has an alibi. A perfect alibi. He was visiting his brother in jail. Signed in, signed out, security cameras on him the entire time. Gorgeous. Perfect. And he and Austad have a history. So Austad was lying, and the department knows he was lying . . .

And I know he was lying. So I went . . . I went to tell him . . .

I went to tell him that he had to tell the truth. That we had to, however insane it seemed. God! I can almost laugh. I wasn't the best cop, I wasn't even the most honest cop, but it wasn't my job, it was my life, and his lies were taking it away. And we were going to end up in jail. I'd rather everyone thought I was crazy—I'd rather *be* crazy—than that.

But I forgot something. No. I never thought of it. It never occurred to me.

Austad thought he was going crazy too.

So there we are. Two crazy men with guns.

He drew his first. That was how badly he didn't want to hear what I had to say. He drew his piece, and I drew mine, and I shot him. Once, in the chest. He went down. The shock will do that at close range. He went down with a bullet in his lung, and that was the end of my career, the end of my fucking life, and it was his fault, so I stood over him and I looked him in the eyes and I shot him again. Through the heart. Dead.

And that's murder, Rye, in case you didn't know.

Bardo's voice, rough with fever, was a whisper after his long speech.

"I was on leave, so I wasn't carrying my service weapon. It wasn't even registered, the gun I shot him with. Should I tell her why I had that piece, Cleände? Should I tell her where I got it from?"

Cleände's gaze was on her clasped hands. She could have been a Madonna, serene and still.

"I guess not," Bardo said. "It doesn't matter. The department figured it had to be a gang-banger killing the cop that put too many members inside. They told me to keep my head down, get out of town in case I was next. And I should have. I should have gone and kept on going. Do you have any idea what happens to cops who go to prison? And a cop who killed a cop—solitary confinement for the rest of my life, and even then, my life would be short. But I didn't run. Too fucking crazy, still, and I was a murderer, and I needed someone to blame. You won't know what that's like, Rye, you don't have it in you. But I did. I do. So I went hunting gray beasts, and I found . . . "

"Us."

Bardo met Rye's eyes and said, "You."

Cleände, at the end of the couch she shared with Rye, drew an audible breath. Perhaps she did not even mean to speak, but Rye did not give her the chance.

"Don't," she said. "Just don't."

"Doesn't matter," Bardo said. He looked sick, sprawled in his chair, the single lamp throwing shadows across his face. He was thin, Rye realized. Even in a few days the fever had eaten away at his flesh. She looked away.

"It doesn't matter, Rye." She had never heard him so gentle. "I had you for a little while, but I was never going to be able to keep you."

She flinched. He had told her to go away. She should have gone when she had the chance. She got up and went to the kitchen. It was dark in the corner. She found a glass by the shape of the air against her palms, filled it with tapwater, carried it back and gave it to Bardo. He threw it across the room.

"Don't you fucking pity me."

"What do you want me to do? Hate you?"

"What do I want you to do?" he mocked her. "Love me?"

It would have hurt less if he had hit her. It would have been easier to forgive.

She walked away, across water and broken glass to the door. Did she bother to open it before she stepped through? The night was almost cool, her blood a familiar slippery warmth under her feet as she descended the steel-grid stairs. Feet sounded behind her. She refused to look back. She stepped into the street, into the garbage smell and the hateful illumination of sodium lights and the flowering song of the city. Cleände was behind her, uneasy with triumph, hunting her down. Rye turned and screamed, "Leave me alone!", meaning Cleände, the arcwright, Bardo. The world.

But someone was running, several someones, their footsteps striking sharp echoes off the deserted buildings, and Cleände, slick as a movie heroine, pulled a handgun from her clothes, a sleek little gun that snagged light from the streetlamps. And there was Tehega's voice shouting commands from the near corner, and an answering shout from the farther end of the block, and Cleände was grabbing Rye's arm. "Now," she said. "Now! I will show you the way!"

It was panic, sheer panic and a desolate loneliness, that reached for the arcwright. If she had had a moment to think, one clear moment to realize that Tehega was no threat to her, to consider whether Cleände had engineered this whole situation—

But shots were fired, and Cleände was an electric force beside her, and she wanted—oh, she needed—

She reached out to the arcwright, and it took her away.

Bardo

Like a lovesick boy, like a man half-crazed by a dark and lonely life, he leaned his face against the door and heard or felt through the bones of his skull the women descending his stairs. He could feel under his bare sole the tacky imprint of Rye's cut feet. He could feel the pain of glass biting into muscle, and did not know if it was her muscle or his own. He had driven her away, wanting, needing her gone—and he still wanted it, still needed it—and she was still here. He felt her pain in a way that had nothing to do with empathy. Her movement was a sympathetic vibration inside his own body, a twitching of nerves that felt her bare feet in the alley three storeys below. Damn her, could she not leave him alone?

The word twisted through him like an eel to show him its other face: not peace, not freedom from responsibility and resentment and guilt, but a stark mask of solitude. *Alone.*

When he had confessed to Cleände the first time, he had felt the almost orgasmic release he had seen on suspects' faces. A careening, emptying rush, a welcome loss of control that put his fate, his soul, in another's hands. Not that Cleände had wanted to take on such a burden. At the time he had taken that, her refusal to react, to judge, to take some action in response to his confession, as a measure of grace. Even then he had been so naïve.

There was no such relief this time. All the weight he had shed onto Cleände had been returned, doubled and redoubled, until his own past threatened to drive him to his knees. His past, and the look in Rye's eyes. His past, and his future as Rye walked away. He wanted her gone. Look what she had done to him. Look what she had done. When all he had wanted was for her to save him. When all he had wanted was freedom. When all he had wanted was to be left alone.

Alone.

He did not know anymore what his truths were, and what were his lies. He had wanted her gone as if she could take back the fever she had given him, make it so it had never happened. As if she could take back her trust, relieve him of his betrayals, excise the knowledge that he had deliberately tempted fate from the first time he saw her bleed. As if her absence could burn out of his mind the tangled motives he had had when he fucked her the first time, the tenderness she had shown him the last time, the tenderness that felt so dangerously, so fatally, like forgiveness.

And still, the Dan Bardo he loathed wanted to blame Mostahr, and Tehega for giving them up to Mostahr, and Cleände for telling her torturers everything, and Rye for being worth all the scheming, all the betrayals, all the lies. All the truth. Damn her. He wanted her gone. He wanted that whole ugly chapter of his ugly life amputated like a rotting limb, to hell with the consequences, to hell with the rest of his life on Earth, he wanted her *gone.*

So why, when he heard through the steel fire door three storeys up and the length of the alley away—

Why, when he heard Rye scream at him, at the world, *Leave me alone!*—

Why was he struck by such a great sense of loss that he really did fall to his knees on the blood-printed floor?

"Rye," he said, mourning, begging, apologizing.

And then he heard, with his face still pressed, slick with sweat, to the rough-painted door, the snap of a gun being fired a block away.

Rye

Riding the tiger between the fog smoke alley walls.

She has felt this before, the velvety suede of its black-silver hide, the oiled glide of fluid muscles between her thighs. She has felt her own muscles coil and release in response to that long, easy, shambling stride. Round, heavy paw *black-steel talon* turns like a dancer's hand as the powerful limb *sharp-jointed, insect-angled* reaches ahead, skimming the pavement *ice rotten with stars* to step, heavy and silent *flowing weightless*, and step again.

She has been the rider before, but she has never been the tiger. She has never been as hot as this, ashy black like iron heated in a forge. She has never been as heavy as this, like an iron rack of bones slung in a web of muscles and arteries and veins, nerves and lymphatic vessels and skin. She has never walked fluid and weightless as the tiger's shadow that slips and flickers, two dimensions over many, across the quicksilver alley walls, the midnight-shining currents of the star-shot, ice-dammed sea.

Sodué, whispers Cleände in awe.

She has never been ridden before. The tiger shrugs. She shrugs, tiger's shadow, and her whispering burden clutches at her with a cub's tiny claws, sharp as needles, static-charged.

This way, this way!

Fear has a salty taste, chewy and running with juice, like a mouthful of steak. The tiger shrugs. She shrugs, and her burden starts to fall.

Ryder!

Named, she grabs by reflex, snatches, digs deep with her claws.

This way! This way! And then, the dying whisper she cannot ignore, though the tiger broods like a summer night, waiting: . . . *home* . . .

This way. The alley turns, the ice breaks, the starry waves pull her down into

a cold white winter courtyard, bright and dry in the colorless sunlight. *This way.* A hot hand pulls her past the waiting line of women. *Please, I don't want to die like that.* A woman like all the rest in her stiff white robe and hygienic headcloth, terrifying only to the initiated. *Please.* Rye pushes her off, but every time she detaches one hand from her arm, the other takes hold, a cold fist of extraordinary strength, the knuckles sharp under the skin, the tight webs between the fingers soft as silk. She pulls free, and pulls free, and finally strikes out, beating with her fists like a child in a tantrum, and then clutches, her own blood constricted in her neck as she wraps Amaran's headcloth around her throat and sees her face swell, her eye bulge and begin to bleed—

Amaran! She lets go, too late, and then grabs, clumsy with haste as Amaran starts to fall. No, not Amaran. Cleände? Limp and broken, the sores of long suffering bleeding around her mouth. Suddenly so much blood. She struggles to raise the other woman against her shoulder, tries to wipe her face, make it clean, see if she is still alive. But she has killed her, she has killed her —wiping with her hand, her sleeve pulled down over her palm —trying to see the face of the girl she knows, the girl from Earth, herself, blood mask running red as a warm, bright rain begins to fall.

Bardo

The stairs spilled away from his feet like water from a broken glass, fell away like the trap door of a gallows, dropped him to hang . . . to fall . . .

. . . rusty steel *wet stone* under his bare feet, dirty brick *soft air* under his hand, shadowed streetlight *rainy sunlight* in his eyes . . .

He caught his balance against the wall, heart lurching from the fall that never happened, eyes burning with a sudden sweat. The same sweat made his grasp on his gun dangerously uncertain. He took it in his left hand, wiped his right on his shirt, resettled the grip in his fever-trembled fist.

And only then noticed that the gunfire had stopped.

The city teemed with sound, traffic, music and voices, the throb of a million air conditioners and fans. But the local air shivered with silence, a dark well rippled by pebbles still sinking down. Bardo, confused by delirium, certain that Rye was lying dead in the street, sat on the steel grill of the first-floor landing and pressed his hands, and his gun, between his knees. It's over, he thought, and when he heard the first siren a heartbeat later, he thought he had conjured it out of his despair. Rye was gone, and his destiny was arriving at last.

Movement in the street caught his eye. There was the sound of scuffling footsteps and panting breath from the alley, and then a shadow groped for the railing at the bottom of Bardo's stairs. He sat and watched with a kind of affectless curiosity as the figure began to climb, and noticed Bardo sitting on the landing, and lurched to a halt a few steps down.

"Bardo." It was Tehega, sounding not particularly surprised.

Bardo could not summon much surprise himself. "Is she dead?"

"Who?" A word between gasps.

The siren was nearer, another singing farther behind.

"Rye."

"Gone."

"Gone?"

"The rebel." Tehega coughed and spat. He cocked his head, a silhouette against the mouth of the alley, listening, and added, "She got Rye before we could take a good position. The rebel took her, or she took the rebel . . . "

The sirens howled in the street now. Red and blue lights danced across the alley walls, colored Tehega's face. Bardo felt like he had been split by a maul. Gone, not gone. Dead, not dead. Gone. His mind doggedly went on working.

"So who's dead?"

"No one." Tehega spoke with unmistakable disgust. "The rebel was right beside her. We fired over their heads, hoping they would break up and look for cover, but she took them—" He coughed.

"Where?"

A patrol car, roof-lights swirling and spotlight glaring from the hood, idled up to the alley. Tehega ran past Bardo, up the stairs to Bardo's door. The patrol was checking the alley where it continued across the street, but in a moment the light would turn their way. Tehega said in a carrying whisper, "Bardo."

"Took them where?"

"Bardo!"

"It's unlocked," Bardo said. "Make yourself at home."

Tehega, who had left Cleände's with Bardo, who had followed Bardo home—who knew about Bardo's fever—said, "Bardo! We can still get her back!"

The spotlight turned like a glaring eyeball toward their side of the street. Bardo lowered his head. The gun was still between his knees. That was, as it had always been, an option.

So was hell.

He got to his feet and climbed to his door just as the searchlight began to tilt toward the stairs.

Rye

Rain fell.

Rain fell through a strong slant of sunlight, and individual raindrops flashed in the sun, heavy raindrops flashing through the air in glints and streaks, so the air shimmered like a sequined gown, a shimmer of rain.

Rain fell on the leaves of small delicate trees, umbrella trees with one layer of pale waxy leaves held aloft by branches clad in nothing but peeling gray bark that was dark on the upper sides. Slender crooked branches reached out from leaning trunks, shading bare ground with an umbrella of leaves that pattered and rustled and dripped with a whispery sliding sound in the rain.

Rain fell on white cement paving stones, big and square, that gathered glass-shallow puddles and danced the raindrops that fell like shining sequins back into the air. The rain was so hard that the drops that fell in glints and streaks leapt up again in a low white spray, water the color of white cement, making a hissing sound and a musical mutter like a stream that lowers its voice to whisper in someone's ear.

Rain fell on people, a warm, heavy, shining, driving rain that fell through a strong slant of sunlight to strike the scalps and faces and shoulders of two women who stood on the wet white cement at the edge of the umbrella trees. Two women stood while rainwater weighted down their hair and trickled their faces like tears, a storm of sunlit weeping that soaked their shirts and ran down their arms and dripped off the weapon one of them held. The gun hanging by her side dripped rainwater onto the wet white cement paving stones, another sound, small and almost lost in the sound of the rain.

Rain fell on the arcwright, a shining heavy rain that lifted a faint mist off the black and silver gleaming hide, a soft silent blur of white above the narrow bone-ridged back and the shadow-sprung ribs and the head with the skull-like muzzle and the gun-slit eyes. Rain fell on the arcwright and ran like rain down a windowpane, raindrops chasing each other into streaks, that streamed like tears across the open black gun-slit star-shot eyes. Rain fell, a shimmer of rain, through a strong slant of sunlight to dance and hiss into spray in the arcwright's shadow, a dark angular shadow like a crooked stain on the white cement paving stones.

Rain fell.

Rye blinked. A raindrop struck her lashes and she blinked, and she breathed warm wet air that smelled of lightning and junipers, and she shifted her weight to take the pressure off the cut foot that bled a pink stain into a warm white puddle, and as if that were a signal, Cleände blinked and breathed and moved, coming alive in the sunlit rain. She took in a second, larger breath and raised the handgun and pointed it at the arcwright. Rye said, "No," and the arcwright lifted itself on its odd-jointed legs and swam through the sequin-shining rain. It brushed past Cleände, who flinched and threw herself aside, and ran until it reached the shadowy shelter of the umbrella trees where it disappeared. Cleände picked herself off the paving stones, scraping the wet white cement with the barrel of her gun, a sound exactly like the sound the arcwright's talons made as it ran. She looked at Rye. Rye wiped at the rain that ran unimpeded down her scalp and across her face, and said, "Oh yeah. Here we go again."

Bardo

The loft felt empty without Rye. That came as something of a relief.

Tehega looked around him in the light of the single lamp, as if he were trying to guess the value of Bardo's possessions. Bardo turned on more lamps, as if to make it easier. *See what I have to offer? Nothing. Nothing at all.* He tucked his handgun in the waist of his jeans and fetched out the broom to sweep up the glass on the floor.

Tehega said, "I would ask, what leaves you here when your Rye has gone away?"

"Cleände is the jealous type," Bardo said, sweeping.

Tehega grunted, a small *huh* of comprehension that did not imply belief. He tucked his hands in his pockets—he was utterly Earth-like in dark jeans and shirt, a dark blue ball cap pulled over his fair hair—and strolled around the loft. He looked like a bargain hunter.

"See anything you like?" Bardo said dryly, leaning on his broom.

"The rebel should take you as well. Yes?"

"She probably thinks Rye will be easier to manage."

"Will she be?"

Bardo shrugged and began to maneuver his pile of glass shards into the dust pan. If Cleände had succeeded in detaching Rye's stubborn affection from Bardo, it was a prize up for grabs, the handle that would give Cleände—or whoever won it—everything else. Everything worth having. Bardo did not share this painful thought with Tehega. He carried broom and dust pan into the kitchen, where he dumped the trash.

"You think you know where they've gone," he said, not a question.

Tehega gave him a brooding look from under his heavy brow. "Where do you think? Do you think the rebel is still a rebel after so long in Meheg-menoht? She took Rye, or had Rye take them both, straight back to Nohai."

An ugly thought. Bardo, disturbed, realized he could not judge from what he had seen of Cleände how likely this was. But he shook his head at Tehega. "You don't know how much she hates the tahinit."

"Slaves always hate their masters." Tehega spoke with the certainty of experience. "You don't know how the tahirr can twist a witch's tahid. Tahid is not mind. Tahid is soul, and the tahirr is built of souls. A cage of souls."

Bardo's skin prickled. Rye had used exactly those words in one of her deliriums. He said harshly, denying the chill, "What do you know? You're no witch."

"No. But I know my people's past. I know the stones the tahinit builds their prison on." Tehega stopped prowling and turned to face Bardo. "I know as much as Amaran did about the old ways, the ways of the tahid before the tahirr was dreamed of, for I taught her what I learned of the past. And she taught what she learned to Rye. Where do you think Rye learned what she knows of power?"

Bardo considered the Nohan lordling. Tehega stood with his chin up and his shoulders square, which might have been arrogance, but which looked like defiance, as if he expected Bardo to challenge him. Bardo turned it over in his mind.

"I do know," Tehega said. "I know more than the tahinit think I know, which I am lucky for, or I am dead now. I was dead when I came into their hands."

"Would have been dead," Bardo said slowly. He was acceding to an old relationship when he said it, and knew it, and saw Tehega realize it as well.

"We can get her back," the lordling said again.

"We?"

Tehega just looked at him. Bardo could feel the fever, quiescent since Rye had gone, but there, breathing quietly beneath his skin. Power, he thought. He understood what Rye meant when she insisted it was just a disease, but he also remembered the way she had pulled the gray beasts out of Meheg-menoht's walls, the way she had dragged them all back to Earth.

"You really think I have that kind of power?"

"You have her fever. You are the second success to slip from the tahinit's hands. Yes, I think you can learn to do what she does."

Bleed, hallucinate, lie unconscious for days. Bardo's mouth twisted in a kind of smile. "Then why, if you don't mind me asking, do you want to get her back out of Meheg-menoht, if that's really where she is?"

"If she is in the tahinit's hands, then they win everything. Even if you are not, for you do not have their armies." Tehega frowned, studying Bardo's face. "But do you leave her there? Do you not want her free?"

"*If* she is there," Bardo said. But although he could perhaps have played this game, he suddenly, finally, did not have the heart for it. His shoulders slumped and he said, defeat like the black fever in his mouth, "Yes, I want her," he hesitated over that truth, and finished it: "I want her free."

But even then, honest as that was, he was also reaching for one more chance at escape from his past, from his life, and from Earth. One more attempt, weary as a drowning man snatching for the life ring as the waves carry it out of reach.

thirty-one

The umbrella trees grew up from roots that snaked through the quarried stones of a broken-down wall. The stones were a dusky gray-gold, more gold than gray against the white cement, the prying black roots, the herbage that outlined the masonry with green. The low wall formed one side of a terrace. Over it, through the bare trunks of the trees, Rye could see buildings. White cement, gray-gold stone, something dark gray that might have been granite, and green everywhere, shades of green like new paint gleaming in the wet sunshine.

here, lover. The arcwright's murmur brushed sulkily along Rye's nerves. She wiped rain out of her eyes, off her face—pointlessly, it was like standing in a tepid shower. Swallowing the water that trickled across her lips, she turned and looked at Cleände.

Who turned and looked at Rye. "In God's name, why did you bring us here?"

"Me?" Rye was still stunned from the crossing. "Isn't this where we're supposed to be?"

Cleände let out a humorless gasp of laughter and looked away. Her elegant profile, rain-streaked and pale, showed against the backdrop of a hollow-eyed stone building. They were oddly alike in that moment, the beautiful woman with her sodden, unraveling hair, and the abandoned building, Spartan and severe even under its cladding of moss.

"You said 'home,'" Rye persisted. Even riding the fever's swell she felt the rock-hard lump of an impending fuck-up growing under her ribs. "Isn't this Scalléa? It isn't Earth . . . "

She thought it wasn't—the colors were all a little strange under the saturated gold of the sunlight—but how much of Earth had she seen in her short, muddled, impossible life? If this wasn't Earth, and it wasn't Scalléa, and it wasn't any part of Nohai she had seen—

But before panic could set in, Cleände said, her voice thick with emotion, "Oh, it is Scalléa. It surely is Scalléa. But of all the places you might have asked me to call home . . . "

Rain pressed in to fill the silence, and a distant heart-thump of thunder.

here, lover, here

The clouds were luminous with sunlight, gray-white-gold mountains of vapor edged in brilliant silver. The sun was a huge yellow orb hanging between the clouds and the wall that footed the terrace. Raindrops swam like lavender fish across Rye's scars. Sunlight rolled like musical waves against her skin. The lesions opened their mouths to drink it in. The scars darkened as they opened, and in the instant the blood welled up, each one was limned in scarlet. They looked like the markings on Bardo's skin.

"Excuse me," Rye said as the rain ran the blood into streaks and the dripping added itself to the pattering music of the storm. "I'd like to be alone for a little while. Is there somewhere I can be alone?"

Cleände looked at her. Perhaps she would have shared Bardo's horror if she had not been insulated by her own shock. Perhaps not.

"What?" Cleände said.

"I'd like some privacy for this."

Cleände blinked rain out of her eyes and pointed away from the sun. The greenery was thick there, bushes over-spilling the wall. Rye started walking as the hot blood come all in a rush, making the warm rain seem cool.

Cleände said behind her, "There is—there was—there should be a pavilion in the garden if you want shelter from the rain."

Rye raised a hand in acknowledgement, spattering pink and red drops across the paving stones. She glanced back when she had achieved the gap in the hedge. The watery trail of blood she had left across the white cement was a red carpet laid out and ruined by rain. Cleände stood at its other end.

Rye, dizzy and tired and sick to death of the taste of blood, pushed painfully through the leafy gap in the bushes and entered the garden. It was a jungle of greens gilded by sun and rain, surely decades past its last encounter with a gardener. Rye could see the pavilion roof, a pale stone pagoda tilting above the rain-ruffled leaves of a white-flowered shrub, but she could not bear the thought of wading through all the foliage with her open skin. She peeled off her shirt—Bardo's shirt—whimpering a little as the soaked cotton pulled away and exposed her to the heavy rain. She took off her skirt—Cleände's skirt—as well, and dropped them on the, well, it wasn't grass, but it might as well have been, and stood on them to spare her feet, and shivered under the assault of rain.

here, lover, here

The clouds pulled away. The bleeding stopped. The sunlight soaked the liquid air with gold.

Cleände found Rye naked in the garden wringing bloody water out of her clothes. Cleände looked more dismayed at that than she had at the sight of Rye's blood.

"Ryder, forgive me." She hunkered down within arm's reach, her head tipped to peer earnestly into Rye's face. "Oh, my dear. I am so sorry. To have left you—"

"I wanted to be left. Do you think I want an audience?"

Cleände jerked her gaze away. Rye, weak and dizzy still, and stubborn, made a long slow business of wringing out Bardo's shirt, heavy as it was with blood and rain. She made a skinny twist out of it and pink water ran down her arms to drip off her elbows. The rich air was full of insects, they flitted around Cleände's head like a halo, but they wisely let Rye alone. She untwisted the T-shirt and shook it out. It was still wet, and heavy, and she was suddenly too tired to care. The air was soft, and she had little modesty left after the hospital. After Bardo. Bardo, Bardo. He was a thought lodged in her like a bullet too close to the heart to remove. Rye let his shirt hang between her bare knees and looked where Cleände was staring, at the pagoda roof and the white-flowered shrub that rustled to the movement of some creature hidden within. There were no swallows in the air, no robins singing at the passing of the rain. Just the many-layered dripping of garden plants and the regular thump thump thump of the distant thunder.

Regular thunder?

Rye glanced at Cleände, and realized she was listening too.

"What is that?"

"Artillery," Cleände answered. Then she blinked and looked at Rye. "Do you mean the noise?"

"Artillery! You mean *guns*?"

"Field guns. Cannon. Artillery." Cleände looked back into the distance, listened to another barrage. "It—my people are at war."

"'It seems'?"

Cleände shrugged with a tilt of her head. "I have not been home for several years. Home. This—" She waved her hand at the garden, and by implication the ruins beyond. "You were not so wrong to bring us here. This place . . . I was brought here as a child. My family lived not far away, in the city below on the plain. This place and others like it are our history, the reminder of what we were before the Nohan came. Perhaps it is a home of a kind . . . "

But for once Cleände sounded as if even she found her rhetoric unconvincing.

Rye plucked a willowy leaf from the groundcover and studied the droplets clinging to the fine hairs along its edge. Definitely not grass. And artillery was a whole other thing from lovely Cleände with a handgun tucked between her waistband and her blouse.

Thump-thump. Thump, thump, thump.

Someone somewhere was taking a beating.

"So," Rye said finally. *What are my chances of getting some dry clothes?* But before she could ask, she was interrupted by a wet thrashing in the bushes behind them and, very soon after, the appearance of a soldier—two, three, several soldiers—damp and insect-plagued and pointing their rifles at Cleände and Rye.

Who, even though she knew it was absurd, lifted Bardo's damp shirt to cover her naked breasts.

Cleände slid a hand toward her gun, and stopped even before protest jumped in Rye's throat: a tiny grasshopper of a wordless *don't* that sounded loud in the dripping silence. Cleände lifted her hands and spoke in a lilting, sliding language that sounded exactly as her accent led one to expect. Rye admired her calm. She herself felt stupidly naked, and plucked at the wet shirt, trying to find the bottom hem without taking her eyes from the guns.

One of the soldiers spoke. Cleände raised herself to her feet and said her own name, and a great deal else. Rye could not get the twisted mess of the T-shirt sorted, and one of the guns she was eyeing began to twitch nervously in her direction, so she stopped. The setting sun tolled against her back and stretched Cleände's shadow across the foliage to the foot of the white-flowered bush. Creatures still stirred there, cautious movement betrayed by the pattering of leaf-caught rain. When Rye could bring herself to look beyond the gun barrels, she saw the mismatched semi-camouflage of guerilla soldiers, and the wide eyes of men and women who were staring at Cleände in awe.

After another brief exchange, Cleände turned to Rye and said, "These are my people. They have a shelter nearby. We are not so far off our course as I feared."

Good. But Rye, relieved of immediate danger, only felt more naked, more humiliated, and more angry as she crouched on her blood- and grass-stained skirt.

"Great. I'll be with you in a minute."

Cleände hesitated, looking down in puzzlement.

"If," Rye said through her teeth, "I could have a little privacy to get dressed?"

"Of course." Cleände turned to relay the request to their escort.

Rye doubted she would ever forgive the older woman for the amusement that quivered at the corner of her mouth.

The ruins were disappointing to Rye, lacking the grandeur of Mayan ziggurats or Egyptian temples. The buildings, even the stone ones, all had a utilitarian look about them. But they were crumbling, especially the white cement ones, and abandonment made them melancholy. The silence of this human place was profound. Rye could imagine her own city like this. Not so clean, perhaps, more cluttered with rusting cars and broken glass, but not so very different. Not nearly different enough. The lowering sunlight was merciless on the tilting walls that were streaked with rainwater and patched by the living green that took hold in every niche and crevice, even on the tilted roofs and in the fissured pavement where they walked.

Where Rye limped. Her bare feet were tender, especially the one cut by Bardo's broken glass. She imagined a line of bloody footprints that led back through the overgrown streets to the white terrace with its shallow puddles and broken wall, and even beyond, to Bardo's alley, Bardo's stairs, Bardo's door. The gap between them was immense, a black abyss, blacker than the shadows cast by the setting sun, that crept behind her, sly stalking beast sniffing down the trail of blood.

"Ryder." Cleände gave her look that was half warning and half concern.

It was only the arcwright.

Only the arcwright.

The fat yellow sun rolled itself into an orange blur on the horizon. The last of the rain dripped thick light through the leaves, dribbles of sunset that ran over them as they passed beneath the umbrella trees. The air was warm and wet, dense with earthy and growing smells, and electric with insects. Their escort led them around the corner of a large building and down a sloping alley that became, with startling abruptness, a forest path. The sun was behind the building and the slope. The path was deep in shade, a liquid purple twilight that rose up over Rye's head like the water of a lake. On the surface, leaves still caught fragments of sunlight and cast it down in burning droplets that died into cool water by the time they reached her face. Down below, the dusk was deep enough to hide the footing, and the slender trunks and airy bushes were heavy with darkness. Was she afraid of the dark now? No, but there really were monsters out of the reach of the light, and the artificial calm imposed by the shock of the crossing, the bleeding, the sudden appearance of the soldiers, cracked, giving her glimpses of terrifying things. The arcwright, black and solid in the rain-spangled sunlight. *(coming, lover, coming)* Bardo, just as black and as solid, in the darkness of his loft. *(which is murder, Rye, in case you didn't know)* No wonder she felt as if all the shadows and all the ghosts of three worlds had coagulated into a night that was about to swallow her whole.

thirty-two

"How does Cleände find us here?"

"She—"—*didn't.* Rye swallowed that and substituted: "I don't know."

When her questioner, Tesuth, frowned, his black brows bunched like provoked caterpillars to either side of his fleshy nose. He had introduced himself to her in careful English, along with the dozen others who crowded Rye with their elbows and their stares. They hunched like conspirators around a mess hall table, straining to make sense of the foreign words through the noise of the communal meal.

"She was away many years," Tesuth said.

"I guess."

They had given her food in a high-sided tin tray: something green, something yellow, something brown. The arcwright had found a last moment of sunlight, and the clean light pummeled its skin like the shimmering music of a gong. Rye envied the creature. The smell of food was nearly buried under the redoubt's stink of dirt and mold, chemical toilets, sweat, and other, harsher things Rye could not identify. Redoubt was Cleände's word for this place. Rye would have chosen something more basic to describe the cramped tunnels dug below the ruined city's foundations. Walls were lined with rotten-looking stones and seeping sandbags, the only lighting was blue-white tubes dangling from wires looped across the rough plank ceilings, everything was dim and dank with a permanent subterranean night. Bardo would have hated the low ceilings, the lower door lintels he would have had to duck.

The wary, inquisitive "hosts."

"You were a part of her work on . . . hmm . . . ."

"Earth."

"Earth."

"Sort of." Rye prodded the something yellow with her spoon, then pushed the tray away.

"Eat," said the young man on her right. "It is not to waste."

"Thanks." Rye picked up her tin mug and sipped water, tepid and tinny, but clean. "So I guess you know all about Cleände's work."

Tesuth scraped his spoon around his tray and licked it. Everyone at the table had eaten the dubious food as if they wished there was more.

"Cleände," the older man said, putting down his spoon with regret, "Cleände is outside of us. What she knows, what we know . . . " He rocked both his hands, an ambiguous separation.

We, Rye thought. "We" the inhabitants of the redoubt? "We" the people at this table? Cleände had been led off by the people with guns, while Rye had been politely handed over to these folks. She could almost feel Bardo, anxious and paranoid, hovering at her shoulder. "But you speak English."

"Ah." Glances were exchanged around the table. "Some. We, some of us, we look at Earth. You understand? We go when the tahinit go, we stay to see what the tahinit see, we come to Scalléa again."

"Some of us," said the woman beside Tesuth, the one with the long beautiful eyes.

"Most of us," Tesuth corrected. "Cleände is there, we are here when the . . . hmm . . . when it is closed . . . "

"Door?" Rye suggested. "Passage?"

"Door?" Tesuth pursed his mouth, but accepted the translation. "We are here when the door is closed and the fighting begins. Cleände is there. So we know Earth a little, but not all that Cleände does there."

"Me neither." The young man beside Rye was eyeing her tray. She pushed it towards him. He pushed it back, offended. She picked up the spoon. "Is that what you meant when you said Cleände is 'outside' you? Just that she was on Earth?"

Tesuth picked up his own spoon, set it down again. "You are very careful with us."

"I was brought here by armed soldiers."

"But you are welcome!" Tesuth exclaimed, as if he were astonished to discover the source of Rye's wariness. "Do you think Cleände is enemy to us? No, no, no!"

He laughed. Other people laughed. The woman with the beautiful eyes began stacking trays.

"No, no," Tesuth said. "It is that we, you see, we here are with the fighting. We are with the 'armed soldiers.'" He seemed to like the phrase. "We make the war with the Nohan here on Scalléa. You understand? We fight them here. Cleände is outside, beyond, on Earth. This is other learning, other fighting. Ah!" He threw up his hands. "My English is too small."

"No," Rye said slowly. "I get you." Here were the real rebels, the ones taking the rebellion to the conquerors at home. But all the same, she realized, that was not what the "we" meant. "We" really did mean the people at this table, because, under the many strangenesses and discomforts of the redoubt, Rye was beginning to distinguish a delicate prickling, a sweet electric flicker, the familiar multiple firefly pulse of thadís. She was talking with the Scallese witches.

And Cleände was, and was not, one of them?

"Cleände is always thinking outside: Nohai, Earth. Outside." Tesuth's hands built a wall. "We are thinking inside: Scalléa. We study the tahinit on Scalléa, and when the door closes and they are trapped, we fight ... on Scalléa. Cleände is outside ... learning what? She comes back, with you, with ... ouf!" Tesuth's hands described something fiery and vast. Several people chuckled, reflecting his excitement. "So much thadís we say to the oriense, the 'armed soldiers', something very great is come here. The tahinit, the Nohan army, God!" More laughter. "So the soldiers say, yes, we will go and see, and everyone looks for disaster, the end of the world, but they find Cleände, like a hero!"

"And you," added the woman with the beautiful eyes, kindly.

Rye hardly heard her. Of course the Scallese witches had felt their arrival, the same way Cleände, looking for Rye, had felt her slip between the boarding house and Bardo's loft. *You can blaze like the sun when you choose*, Cleände had said. So ...

So what had Amaran been thinking when she used Rye to return to Nohai? Had she known they would blaze like a sun to the trained senses of the tahinit in Meheg-menoht? Had Amaran, like Tehega, believed they would be invisible, just a few more fireflies in the swarm? Had she ever betrayed Tehega, or had it all been a ghastly mistake capitalized upon by the tahinit, who were searching for their stolen prize?

Sickened by the thought, by the memory of Amaran's death, by the guilt and shame it aroused—deserved, undeserved, she hardly knew anymore—Rye dropped her spoon and shoved the tray aside. An uncomfortable silence fell. The dinner hour was over and the mess hall was empty save for their one table, crowded as a life raft at sea.

"Perhaps," the woman with the beautiful eyes said, "you eat different food at home?"

Rye shook her head, unable to speak. Linking her hands before her trembling mouth, she wondered when they would start asking the hard questions. Questions like *who are you? What are you? Why are you here?*

But to Tesuth, Rye had been an afterthought. It was Cleände who had returned in a blaze of glory. Instead of an interrogation, Rye suffered an offer of more food, better food, different food. Tea, water, a bath, a change of clothes? An elderly woman with a broom was called over, and a peppery exchange took place, including many gestures towards the uneaten food and skeptical looks at Rye's scarred and weary face. Rye propped her forehead against her hands, wondering if this was all a ploy to put her off her guard. But what did these people know? Nothing about the arcwright, nothing about Meheg-menoht, nothing about Rye. Even if they felt, as Cleände claimed to, a great reserve of power in Rye's blood, all they knew was that Rye was Cleände's companion. Cleände's sidekick, Rye thought with self-directed irony.

But maybe it was just that the people who had clearance to know what Cleände had been up to on Earth were the ones who were already talking to Cleände.

A fresh cup of water, the only concession the broom lady was willing to make, was set before Rye. Thirsty after the bleeding, she drank.

Cleände came in not long after.

She refused a seat on one of the crowded benches and propped herself against an adjacent table. The other witches redistributed themselves, spreading out to other tables, pulling benches around, as if Cleände's presence gave them permission to reorganize things to their liking. The broom lady unplugged an electrical cord, halving the illumination in the long, low room. No one seemed to notice. Cleände answered a lot of rapid questions in Scalléan, but she looked often at Rye, and when the witches gave her a chance, she asked how Rye was.

"Fine."

"We have try to make her comforted," said the woman with beautiful eyes, adding something in Scalléan.

"Sharienne is worried because you would not eat."

"I'll eat when I'm hungry. I'd rather know what's going on."

Tesuth said hastily, "We do not have time to tell her much."

"Time," Rye muttered, and Cleände gave her narrow glance, understanding and amused.

"Let me tell you what I can," she said, and the witches settled like children waiting for a tale.

"We have always known this war would come," Cleände began, "and if it were only a matter of soldiers and guns, we would win. Not easily, perhaps. There are many slaves who will fight for their masters, preferring the security of slavery to the risks of freedom. But even so . . .

"The Nohan lords take their power from the tahinit—the tahinit have ensured that this is so, whether or not the lordlings are aware of it—and have been led to rely too heavily upon the tahirr. In their arrogance, they have armed us, and trained us, and we are not all willing slaves. We have not all forgotten what we were.

"However." Cleände's scanned the arc of listeners, fire in her eyes. "However. It is *not* only a matter of soldiers and guns, and the lordlings' arrogance is not unfounded. The tahinit hold more than just the keys to the gate between the worlds. We know—*we* know—how much of their power they have held in reserve."

"But the gates are closed," said Sharienne, the woman with the beautiful eyes. "And the tahinit lords are on the wrong side."

Cleände looked at Rye. "Yes. The gates are closed." She turned to Sharienne and the rest. "And that is the very argument Commander

Vaidunne used with me. The gates are closed. We are armed. Pediyoht is in disarray with the colonial government cut off from Nohai. Indeed, General Marhoud is *on* Nohai, recalled for consultation before the gate was closed."

The rebels stirred: this was clearly news to them. Maybe even good news, though not if Rye judged by Cleände's expression. One of the young men said something in a tone of barely restrained excitement.

"So *Desouth Prediré* sent out the call," Cleände said sharply, apparently correcting him. She paused to let comprehension pass through the group—a comprehension Rye could not share, not that Cleände seemed to care, for all she still spoke in English. She went on:

"Prediré and the Scall-hite Maïjou sent out the call, and it was the panic-stricken response out of Pediyoht as much as anything that roused the rebellion to full revolt. Vaidunne assures me that the fighting is going well, that Prediré's lines of communication have held up well, that Pediyoht is all but paralyzed by the mutiny of the Home Regiments. Vaidunne is convinced the war will be won by the end of the dry season. Vaidunne," Cleände's mouth curled in scornful emphasis, "has been convinced by Prediré that the tahinit are no longer a concern. Perhaps even that they never have been a concern. Prediré, God as my witness, has become a hero, shining with the apparent justification of the nonsense that he has been spouting for the last twenty years."

"The tahinit are liars, their power lies and smoke." This from the Tesuth, a thoughtful murmur.

Cleände pounced on it, her hand slapping the table by her knee. "Nonsense! Deadly nonsense that has corrupted the Maijou into a crowd of ineffectual—"

"I speak words of Prediré," Tesuth said mildly, "not me."

"And he takes the closing of the gate as proof that he is right," Cleände said scathingly, "as if the gate's closure undoes all the implications of the gate's existence. As if it proves that the tahinit, having lost control, never had it to begin with. And this is the man, the hero, who has led the world into war!"

After an uncomfortable silence, Tesuth said, still mildly, but not weakly, "But the gate is closed. Cleände, you know I know the tahinit power, and the power and the soldiers they save on Nohai.

But the gate is closed. Predíré is not all a fool. The tahinit are on Nohai, and *the gate is closed*."

"Yes," Cleände said, her expression as sharp and as hostile as a knife. "Yes, Tesuth, the gate is closed. Now assure me that it will remain so."

Tesuth's startlement rippled through the group, a stone dropped in a pond. As if she felt the reins slipping through her fingers, Cleände drew a breath and physically reached out to her group, spreading her fingers wide.

"Listen. Only listen. We have lived under the tahinit's power and secrecy for so long, we forget there was a time before."

"Forget?" The young man beside Rye reached out his arms as if he could embrace the ruin above them, the redoubt all around. "Forget? What do we fight for?"

"Thank you, Adoin. You make my argument for me." Cleände smiled faintly at his confusion. "We, here, on Scalléa, had a life before the gate, before the tahinit, before the conquest. Yes . . . and so did they. So did they. *Think*. It was such a triumph in my grandmother's day when we discovered the secret of the arcwrights, the foundation of the tahinit's power, the keys to the gate between the worlds. But have we ever discovered where the arcwrights came from? Have we ever discovered how the tahinit found them, bound them, used them? Have we even thought to wonder? Am I truly the only one to ask myself, what if there are other arcwrights in the sodué? To ask myself, what if the tahinit can conjure up another pair?"

thirty-three

Cleände's diatribe had shifted its focus from Rye to the Scallese witches. Rye felt, she was sure, the same chill the others felt. But as the shocked silence gave way to questions Rye began to realize that whatever purpose Cleände had intended her rant to serve, informing Rye had been the least of it. Rye felt herself slipping further and further from Cleände's attention, and her own ironic *sidekick* came back to sting her pride. So when her bladder prodded her, she got up and began to ease herself towards the mess hall door.

Cleände glanced up from a three-way argument, eyebrows raised.

I have to pee, Rye mouthed.

Cleände nodded, waved a vague direction, went back to her conversation.

And that, unnervingly, was that.

Rye found the latrine by the smell, used it, and escaped back into the redoubt's less potent fug. According to the arcwright, the night outside was *warm (insect shrilling) soft pale mud (stars whispering through the clouds)*, and Rye was tempted, she could not deny it, to go out as the creature suggested. *(come, lover, come)* But that insinuating caress along her nerves, that wordless murmur as intimate and sensual as the fever's inner rise, was tainted by the memory of that last afternoon with Bardo, that hateful desire that had been partly hers, partly his, partly the arcwright's. That tenderness that had been all Bardo's, and a lie.

come, lover, come

A wistful plea that faded as if the arcwright were aware of Rye's unhappiness. *I doubt they'd let me go,* Rye thought to herself, or to the creature. But she was too haunted to do nothing, and she knew that if Bardo were here—she winced at the thought, but completed it—he would insist she discover the limits of her freedom.

Besides, what else could she do, go back and listen to Cleände politicking in a language Rye could not even understand?

The bluish lights dangling on their wires had been dimmed to a violet glow. A pretty light, except for what it did to faces, turning them into masks with purple lips and bruised eyes. Ghost faces, Rye thought, and felt that subtle internal slip that was the fever waking up inside her. Just as well there were few people about.

The tunnel turned a corner and on the left hand wall the rude sandbags gave way to masonry. The quarried stones looked weathered as if one of the ruined buildings overhead had sunk into the earth. Perhaps it had. Rye touched it and thought she tasted, powdery-sour, lichen as old as dust. Rye felt an unanticipated touch of awe, something she had never felt on Nohai, to realize again that she was on an alien world with its own histories, its own lost civilizations, its own nations and cultures and cities and towns. An ordinary wall, dirt-stained, scarred, unadorned, but it opened a door in Rye's mind, opened her imagination just enough to let her glimpse the dizzying wealth of another world. Another universe. Plants and animals, oceans and stars, and all the human things: friendships and enmities, self-sacrifice and hatred and the vast, unguessable number of ordinary kind and selfish lives. Think of the families and the lovers. Think of the homes and jobs and gardens. Think of the parks and beaches, the polluted rivers and vacation islands, the shops and the crafts and the heirlooms, if people here even thought in those ways. Was it only the armies, only the enormities of power and greed that made all humans everywhere seem the same to Rye?

"You is lose?"

Rye realized she was propped half asleep against rough, damp stone. Too fever-tranced to be startled, she blinked at the man who had stopped beside her. He was in his thirties, maybe, with thick, dark hair, wearing a camouflage jacket over a brown shirt, all the colors made dismal by the violet light. His face was grim for the same reason, but also familiar.

"Lost?" he tried.

"Do I know you?"

"I find you." He pointed at the ceiling. "You, Cleände. We give you here."

"Brought us," Rye corrected automatically. He was the man in charge of their escort, the soldiers who had investigated their arrival.

"Brought," he echoed, rolling the "r." "I have small words. Small." And, charmingly, he pinched the air.

"I'm amazed you have any," Rye said. He was, by the indifference of her fever, a soldier, not a witch. "Have you been to Earth?"

"No. My . . . ah . . . " He clasped his hands together and raised them to his mouth. "My she, she goes, and is give to me small words. Is brought to me small words."

"Teach." Rye was more interested in *my she*. "She's a witch? She has the thadís?"

"Thadís," he said in relief. "Yes. Sharienne?"

The woman with the beautiful eyes. "I met her. We had dinner together. She's talking to Cleände now, or she was when I left."

"Yes, Cleände."

Language was no barrier to his tone, which was complicated with reserve. Rye's interest was piqued, especially since he seemed to have stopped just to talk, not to take her officially in hand.

"You know Cleände?"

"Know?" he said, doubtful of the word.

"I know Cleände. You know Sharienne. I know Sharienne a little. You know Cleände?"

The conversation, or English lesson, limped along. He did not know Cleände himself, and Sharienne knew her only slightly, but more by reputation, or rumor, or some such thing. But what that reputation or those rumors might be was hard to say. Rye suspected the soldier, not nearly as simple as his "small words" made him sound, took refuge behind the language barrier whenever she tempted him to be indiscrete. Finally, frustrated, she began to yawn. The soldier caught a yawn from her, and laughed.

"You have . . ." He groped, shrugged, took refuge in sign language: a curled hand under his chin, closed eyes, a gesture at the corridor and the redoubt all around them.

"Somewhere to sleep?" Rye guessed, and shook her head.

"Sleep," he said. "I brought . . . ?"

"Bring?"

"I bring you to sleep."

"I take you to sleep."

"Take?"

"I bring you here. I take you there—" Rye heard how absurd she sounded and broke off into laughter.

The soldier laughed as well, and bowed, and said something fluent in Scalléan. How long had it been since Rye had laughed with anyone? On impulse she put out her hand and said her name. He looked at her hand, gingerly sandwiched it between his own large and callused palms, and said, "Meduine."

So there, Rye thought with a childish lick of triumph: her first night on Scalléa, and already she knew someone Cleände did not know.

Meduine played the host well, showing her to a bathroom (only slightly more salubrious than the latrines, being gritty and slick with mud) and rustling up some clothes before finding her a bunk in a room. There were other bunks and a human smell, but Meduine said, or she thought he did, that the inhabitants were on patrol and she would have the place to herself, at least for tonight. He said a (she assumed) Scallese goodnight, and twitched the blanket-curtain across the doorway, and left, and it wasn't until then that she realized, with a small bump of dismay—scarcely that, more a tiny burst of illumination, almost of amusement—that in fact "they" had not let her get very far at all.

Rye, divided into actor and observer, almost knew she was dreaming. She knew, some fragment of her knew, that it was impossible she should be in Bardo's apartment, but she lost track of why. They had been arguing. He was furious. She was huddled on his couch in a welter of sweat, as ashamed of the bloodstains on her clothes as if they were menstrual stains. He paced large and restless around the edges of the room. It was dark. Sunshine oozed like honey through the slatted blinds, too thick to shed any light. It was hot.

What do you know? Bardo was saying.

I know everything, Tehega said. She knows more.

She knows what I am. She knows who I am. She knows what I have done.

And she told you none of those things?

No, Rye said.

No, Bardo said.

Why not? Tehega said. I thought she trusted you.

Too much. Not enough. I don't know.

Too much, Rye said. She was ignored as if she was not there.

She told me nothing, Bardo said. But I saw her bleed.

The arcwright, Rye realized. I never told him about the arcwright. That's what they mean. That's why Dan is so angry. I never told.

Why should you? he said to her, a brusque aside. I'm a murderer.

I don't believe you.

Then you're a fool.

I'm not. I'm old and aching with how wise I am.

Then you know it's true.

I know what else is true. Listen, I have to tell you about the arcwright.

But Bardo was pacing again, arguing with Tehega. The arcwright oozed up to her through the lines of sunlight, a black insectile weight that made the couch dip and tilt alarmingly.

Hush, no, go away, Rye whispered. He doesn't know about you. You can't be here.

He knows what we know, the arcwright said. It spread itself across the couch, beside her, behind her, an iron statue blazing with heat.

But he's here and we're there, Rye said. How could he know?

What do here and there have to do with us? the arcwright said. I bring you here, I take you there . . .

They laughed.

The arcwright's heat was a comfort in the cold thin night of Meheg-menoht. She nestled against its velvet-and-iron side. Though she was slick and sticky, foul with blood, it did not care, and she was grateful for its embrace. It hid her in its blackness, buried her in shadow in the corner of their cage where even the searching lights of the tahinit could not find them. The tahinit were, in any case, distracted by the constant shuddering grind of the moving army. Safe then, together then, Rye and the arcwright slept.

"Wake up," Cleände said. "We are wanted."

"I'm awake," Rye said, but she did not sit up right away. The arcwright was lying head down on a steep hillside, and its cavalier attitude towards gravity tilted the bunk precariously, so that Rye wondered how Cleände kept herself from tumbling off the edge and down the slope of the floor. She had to wrench up and down into their proper relationship before she sat up and propped her arms on her knees.

"I am glad I found you." Cleände put her hand on Rye's blanketed foot. "You were so tired last night I was afraid you might have lost yourself in the maze."

"Um," Rye said, rubbing the sleep from her eyes.

"You are still asleep."

"No. Who wants us?"

"The commanders." Cleände rubbed Rye's foot through the blankets, an abstracted warmth. "I am told they have been conferring all night. I suppose they have been conferring about you and me."

"Your bosses."

Cleände's hand stilled. "Not precisely. Yes, I suppose you could say as much. They lead the rebellion now."

Rye would have been subtle if she knew how, but even when Rye was wide awake Cleände was out of her league. She said, "So who are your bosses?"

"Hmm." Cleände, her face a shadow against the lighted doorway, watched her fingers tap Rye's ankle. "There are a scattered few, I suppose, who have found themselves distributed amongst the ranks."

"Meaning you don't have any."

"Matters changed while I was away. I cannot say the order of things has changed, because the order I knew was never more than theoretical. We, each of us, did what we saw needed to be done. This military order, these commanders and ranks . . . " Cleände lifted her hand to gesture, in helplessness or dismissal, Rye wasn't sure which.

"And they want to fit you in," Rye guessed.

"Yes."

Rye did not have to see Cleände's face to know how she felt about that.

"And," Cleände added, "they will want to fit you in as well."

"Me?" Rye said, though without much surprise.

"Are you not my talented young recruit?" Cleände sounded amused, though irony dried her voice.

"Am I?" Rye said slowly. "Then what's the arcwright?"

"Our little secret." Cleände gave Rye's ankle a complicitous squeeze.

thirty-four

"So what did you tell them about how we got out of Meheg-menoht?"

Rye asked her questions in an undertone as she hurried after Cleände. The tunnels were brightly lit again and full of people, but without the arcwright *(sun bells, leaf-tremolo shade)* she would never have known it was day.

"I told them," Cleände murmured, her eyes on the passing faces, "that the tahirr was constructed to imprison witches from Scalléa, not witches from Earth."

"Why? Why lie?"

"But it is quite true. The tahirr was never made to imprison one such as you."

"You know what I mean."

"Yes, I know what you mean." Cleände's voice was a warm buzz in her ear. "If you were alone here, would you trust them with that secret?"

"But I'm not alone," Rye said, "and they're your people."

"Are they? I have been on Earth for years. Grant me a little time to be sure."

"Fair enough," Rye said, because it was.

But she was trying to remember how much Cleände had told the other witches about the arcwrights. Something, she was sure. Not everything. But that was before they had started speaking in Scalléan, and before Rye had left the room.

They came to a cross-tunnel and stopped, and Rye lost track of what she had been thinking. There had been fighting somewhere, this morning, the night before, and the tunnel was full of wounded soldiers.

The electric lights were pitiless to the wounded, the stretcher-bearers, the soldiers who helped their injured comrades limp, stumble, lean against the seeping sandbag walls. There were not many of them, too few to be a faceless crowd. Each face had a person behind it, a person who suffered. They were quiet, but they stank of sweat and piss and bile and blood, of smoke and charred cloth, of charred flesh, a smell Rye unwillingly recognized from backyard barbecues, and of the summer-firework smell of guns. Rye hated to watch, but could not in all conscience turn away. She wondered helplessly if some of these were her absent roommates, the men and women Meduine had said were out on patrol. While she had been sleeping, they had been . . . But she found she could not picture the fighting, only the rough blood-soaked bandages and burned fatigues and the shocking exposure of flesh and bone.

And the eyes, patient only because there was nothing else to be except unconscious or dead, that Rye went on seeing long after the small group made its way out of sight, because they were eyes she knew, the eyes of the women in the courtyard, the eyes of the victims of Meheg-menoht.

Cleände was silent, leading her to the command center. It was near the redoubt's entrance, where there was a smell of green warmth and a dampness that had more to do with yesterday's rain than with mold and over-worn socks. Even without the arcwright's *sunshine insects itchy mud (here, lover, here)* she would have yearned for outside. But either the artillery had moved closer, or the wounded soldiers had reminded her, for she could feel the startling red thud-thud-thud of the guns in the arcwright's hearing. Outside was not a safe place to be. She hovered unhappily at Cleände's side just inside the command center's door, still haunted by those eyes.

A large, low, busy room, it was lined partly in sandbags and partly in cut stone. A vast table had been set up at one end, stacks of electrical equipment at the other, and there were people bustling between the two. No one took much notice of Cleände and Rye. Cleände made several small shifts of position, visibly impatient, but she did not try to gain anyone's attention. Rye could not guess whether this was protocol or pride.

Finally, someone separated herself from the group around the table and came to talk to Cleände. It was Sharienne, the witch with the beautiful eyes, the wife/sister/friend of the soldier, Meduine. She gave Rye an absent-minded, though not unfriendly, look, but it was Cleände she spoke to. Cleände responded in a tone that was not intended to disguise her impatience, and turned to Rye.

"She says they have had to wait too long for us, and have received important information in the meantime. We will have to wait for their kind attention."

"It is a small time," Sharienne said, not quite apologetic. Whatever her personal respect for Cleände, the witch was confident in her position here. "We ask for you to come long before."

"It took some time to find you," Cleände said to Rye. "No one could tell me where you were."

Rye shrugged, not feeling she had anything to apologize for. She was puzzled that Cleände, who had spoken about the brilliance of Rye's thadís, had not been able to follow it straight to her door. Maybe she had misunderstood something Cleände had said. A tall, balding man looked up from the table and gestured to Sharienne, who ushered them across the room.

The man spoke at length to Cleände. The others at the table (it was a map table, although Rye could make little sense of the geography, the maps were so cluttered with symbols) made an interested audience, but Cleände listened impassively and, Rye suspected, consciously beautiful. She looked like a soon-to-be-martyred saint. The balding man's voice rose; he gestured at the table, the doorway, the world outside with a wide sweep of his hand. His voice rose again to shout what could only be a question, and folded his arms impressively to glare at Cleände.

Who spoke a terse phrase that did not seem to make much impact.

"What," Rye said, testy with nerves, "is going on?"

The group's attention shifted to her with palpable force. Rye's mouth went dry. She locked her gaze on Cleände's profile, and so saw the faint twitch at the corner of the other woman's mouth.

"The injured soldiers we saw were surprised by an enemy reconnaissance unit early this morning. The fighting was fierce and the enemy unit withdrew, but this, apparently, is the closest the enemy has come to the redoubt, and Commander Vaidunne believes —Sharienne and others have so advised him —that the tahinit on Scalléa perceived our arrival just as our witches did. He says that our arrival has betrayed the redoubt's position, which will very shortly be under attack by a large enemy force —an attack which will be difficult to defend against given our own troops' current deployment —and he wishes to know whether this was in fact our intention when we arrived here in so spectacular a manner."

"Again," Rye whispered.

"What 'again'?"

But if Cleände did not share Rye's guilt, Rye doubted she could explain it to her. Rye was silent a moment, then said, feeling Bardo-ish, "It didn't feel very spectacular at the time."

Cleände's mouth twitched again. "No?"

"So what did you say?"

"That we certainly did not intend this result when we left Earth to come home."

"He doesn't seem very impressed."

"No, he does not."

The "he" in question, Commander Vaidunne, had followed this exchange with a kind of savage patience, waiting to see what would be revealed by it. Rye might have been able to guess with some of the other faces who understood, or almost understood, or did not understand English at all—Meduine was there, frowning in concentration—but Vaidunne was impossible to read. He had a bony, ascetic's face and deep-set eyes: a good Inquisitor to play opposite Cleände's martyr. He said something sarcastic into the silence. Cleände answered with a tilt of her head, an offhand Scallese shrug.

"What—"

"He wonders," Cleände said before Rye could finish, "how we found the redoubt. I told him, as I have told him several times already, that as we had no way of knowing the situation on Scalléa, nor any way of guessing who might hold Scallese authority, we simply sought out our fellows by the signature of their thadís."

"Oh." Rye risked a glance at the commander, and found him staring at her. He said something in a new tone, thoughtful and slow, which Cleände answered after a noticeable hesitation.

"What—"

"He asks whether I think it was the, ah, brilliance of our arrival, or the simple fact of our arrival, which gained the tahinit's attention. I said I do not know."

Vaidunne spoke again; again, Cleände was careful with her response.

"What—"

"He now wonders whether the Nohan forces are staging an attack on a revealed position, or staging an attack, or an attempt at acquisition, on us."

"Us," Rye said faintly.

"The source of the thadísé."

"Ah."

"I have told him that I do not know."

The commander waited for Cleände to complete her translation, and his patience made Rye realize that he was deliberately including her in the discussion. This time, after he had spoken, Cleände was silent.

"What did he say?"

"He said," Cleände said grimly, "that he is now in the uncomfortable position of harboring what is either a very dangerous enemy or a very useful ally, and he would be very happy if we could prove, you and I, which we are. Preferably the latter, because the former would be messy and time-consuming and he has a great deal of work to do."

"He really said that?"

"Yes."

"How?"

"I beg your pardon?" Cleände turned on her as if she were at the end of her patience.

"How are we supposed to prove—"

"Ask him!"

"Well." Rye gave Commander Vaidunne a sidelong glance. She would not like to be dealing with him without Cleände to hide behind, but she said, because she thought she had to, "How—"

Cleände rapped out the question. Vaidunne smiled, not pleasantly, and said something pithy. Their audience, which had been quiet and almost faceless with concentration, reacted with a few faint laughs.

Cleände translated in the tone of a woman whose good-humor is being tried by a tedious joke. "The commander suggests that we send the Nohan occupiers back where they came from."

"Oh."

"Just so."

Rye did not want to ask. She did not know if she were really responsible for putting all these people in danger or for the wounded soldiers in the corridor, but her very ignorance made her feel she *had* to ask, so she said, "I guess we can't?"

And had her proof that Vaidunne did not know English, because it was not until he had demanded a translation from Cleände, and Cleände, with a long, cold look at Rye, had responded, that he reacted. He spat out a short, quick sentence that required no translation.

Can you?

Cleände said, in English, without compromise, "No," and said it again in Scalléan.

Vaidunne snapped something back at her, and Rye guessed at that one, too: *Then what the hell* can *you do?*

"Cleände," Rye said softly, "are you sure?"

Cleände, a martyr much put upon by fools, drew in a calming breath. "Do you," she said just as softly, "believe for one moment you have that degree of control?" Her voice rose. "And even if we could, does it strike you as a wise strategy to allow—no—to *help* our enemy's divided army to join into one force, under one high command, with the full power of Meheg-menoht behind it? Do you have so low an estimation of the tahinit lords' knowledge and abilities as to assume they will never, whatever is stopping them now, open that door again? The enemy here on Scalléa has proven itself to be ill-managed and ill-prepared. Very well. Let us defeat them here and now, as quickly and as thoroughly as we can, before—"

"Cleände."

"—we find ourselves facing—"

"Cleände."

"Ryder!" Cleände turned on her, furious. "Can you not hold your tongue!"

"They can't understand you," Rye said tightly. "You're speaking in English."

Cleände glared at her, then threw her head back to glare at the ceiling, her throat working as she struggled for calm. Finally she gave a faint, dry laugh, and began again in her native tongue. It was probably a good speech. People listened, and there were nods and glances exchanged around the table. Even Vaidunne listened, skeptical to begin with, thoughtful by the end. But he had a question when Cleände was done, and again, she was slow to respond.

Rye was hesitant to prompt her, not wanting to make herself a target, but finally she had to say, as the silence stretched out, "What did he say?"

Cleände threw up her hands. "'Help us defeat the enemy. Prove your loyalty. What can you do?'"

"Well, what *can* we do?"

thirty-five

"This is a simpler matter than moving between the worlds. The world itself makes its own boundaries, its own reality. You need not breach the walls, only slip for a moment within the fabric of the boundary itself."

"Meaning how exactly?" Rye was cold with tension, her teeth threatening to chatter when she spoke.

"But you have done this once before. At least once, on Earth, when you found—In the days before we came home."

"When I found . . . You mean when the arcwright took me to Dan."

"Yes, that day."

"But I didn't do anything. I just asked the arcwright."

"Then it will be as simple now."

"I don't know where we're supposed to go, and I don't know how to take anyone along."

"One does not precisely 'take' anyone. One provides a passageway. Or becomes it."

"That's not what it felt like coming here."

Cleände blinked, the merest quiver of an eyelash, the tiniest fragment of a pause. "As I said, the passage between worlds is a somewhat different matter."

"I still don't know what I'm doing."

"That is what you must trust me to show you. That is why we are here."

Here was an alcove, a sandbagged niche at the edge of a vast indoor staging area floored in mud and shored up by columns of cement and stone pilfered from the ruins. The cavern was warm from the evening air that slipped through the camouflage curtains that hid the entrance, and the three hundred soldiers who were scrambling to find their equipment, their units, a place to sit down, added to the stink of the trampled mud. Cleände had tucked herself and Rye out of the way, and was close enough in the cramped space to feel Rye shiver. She put her arm around Rye's shoulders and gave her a hug.

"I can help."

"That sounds kind of ominous after the last time." Rye tried to sound more rueful than scared, but the humor was weak.

"The last time?"

"At your house. When you tried to separate us."

Cleände frowned. "Do you judge my abilities from one mistake?"

"I only meant . . . " Rye gave up. *. . . that you wound up unconscious on the floor,* did not seem like a politic way to end that sentence.

"Ryder. You have said you will help us, but it is only your offer that binds you to do anything. You may always withdraw."

"I said I would help! I just don't know how."

"And you do not trust me to show you the way."

"That is not what I said." It was hard to glare at Cleände when her face was only a foot away. A lover's distance. Rye glared out at the soldiers she was supposed to be transporting instead.

Cleände sighed, a soft breeze in Rye's ear. "Dear Ryder. I know how brutally Daniel Bardo used and abused your trust. I do not blame you in the least—"

"Who said anything about Dan Bardo? He doesn't have anything to do with this. He doesn't have anything to do with anything. I don't know why you brought him up."

"I do not blame you if you are wary now. Let be. I will tell the captain you must withdraw."

"Will you cut that out?" Rye was angry now, and felt both the fever and the arcwright come alert.

"But you owe us—you owe me—nothing."

"Bullshit. You know damn well I do. There's a whole fucking army coming down on these people. You think I don't know that's my fault? I *said* I'll help and I *will* help. All I'm saying is I don't know how!"

"And do not trust me to show you."

"I do!" Rye did glare at Cleände then, but the older woman's features were almost lost in the quicksilver shadow of the sodué. In Rye's semi-blindness, the heart-flicker of Cleände's thadís burned brighter than the electric cable-garlands flowering on the walls.

"Thank you," the Cleände-shadow said mildly. "And now that you have roused your thadís, I can."

Rye breathed, just breathed for a moment, but it had to be said: "Bitch."

Cleände laughed. "Yes. I do thank you for your trust, nonetheless. Shall we begin?"

love! love!

If the arcwright has been waiting for anything, it has been waiting for this. A black and terrifying tenderness sinks its teeth into Rye and swallows her down. As simple as an open scar, the alley opens itself before her—a glassy hollow through the quicksilver fog, but that is how she sees it, a gray winter alley silver with ice and shadowed by night. Sparks leap against the mirror-walls, strike back in reflection from the other side. Bardo is there behind the glass, a jealous reflection, a ghost raised by Cleände, reaching, his face blinded by blood. Mostahr is there, teacher and prison guard, furious and ignorant in the pain of her own confinement, reaching. Cleände is there, pointing, *there, this way, here!* as if she does not know there is no difference. No *here*, no *there*, only the arc, the ecstatic line drawn like a scar through the seething fog. The scar is the crack, the movement that defines the passage and the walls. But Rye's thadís-sparks strike too hard against the delicate mercury mirror-ice. Too many sparks hammer at the other side—the tahirr like a rain of furious fireflies, Bardo like one aching, raw-knuckled fist—hammering, hammering, *let us in!* The perfect arc, the crack in the ice, threatens to grow, to spin out new arcs, to rip itself into an ugly yawn of need—

Here, insists Cleände. Is she blind? Doesn't she know? *Here*—

For an instant, Bardo is so close Rye can almost touch him, can almost—

(What? What happens? What do you see?)

(Nothing. (Rye? (Rye!)

Here!

The split threatens, begins—

—a wound that cannot heal—

"Here!"

And they were there.

A last purple stain of dusk, red-limned clouds, the chime of a single star. A rustle of leaves, a murmur of voices, the click and rattle of equipment and weapons in careful hands. Tough weeds and lumpy dirt.

Weedy dirt under her, cloudy sky over her, if she could only figure out which was up and which was down. *Let go,* she thought at the arcwright, and for a wonder it let her go. She took a step and nearly fell, back in gravity's domain. Cleände's hand tightened on her arm.

"Well done," she whispered.

Rye started to shiver. The images of the sodué slipped sideways, nightmares like all the rest. She clung for a moment to the dream-taste of Dan Bardo, a dream-Bardo who wanted her, and then remembered—murderer, betrayer—and spat it out again. Dreams, she always dreamed in the arcwright's realm.

"Did you notice—"

"Shh."

She leaned her head against Cleände's. "Did you notice anything strange just then? Did you hear . . . someone . . . say my name?"

"When? Now?"

"No, then, during the passage."

"What is to notice? We are there, we are here—"

Someone said, "Shh!"

There was a drone in the distance, so deep and constant it was hardly audible, and a smudge of light against the clouds. The enemy encampment, one of the moving pincers that threatened the rebel redoubt. Their strike team was close—not as close as the commanders had wanted, but still close enough for surprise. The order was passed in a whisper to advance. The plan had been for Rye and Cleände to hold their arrival position and not to get caught up in the fighting.

But Cleände was moving with the rest, no one suggested to Rye she stay behind, she was still too dazed to be certain that if she stayed she would ever be found again. She walked with the rest, stumbling over the rough ground in her heavy boots, and when she had caught up with Cleände again, Cleände grasped her wrist and pushed something cold and hard into her hand.

"Promise me you will only use this on the enemy."

Cleände's whisper was not really amused, but an immense excitement trembled underneath, making her sound on the verge of laughter. *This*, Rye realized, was a gun, maybe even the handgun Cleände had brought from Earth. She tried to give it back, but Cleände was jogging ahead. Everyone was running as quietly as hundreds of boots can move across uneven ground. More quietly than Rye would have expected. They sounded more like a football team than an army. She stumbled again, felt a gliding lift as the arcwright lent her some of its grace. It ran with her, somewhere near, in her shadow maybe, the shadow cast by the encampment's lights. They were nearer than she had realized, the lights few and dim for security's sake. No one shouted an alarm. They had arrived close enough to be within the enemy's patrols.

The rebel force was dividing, units splitting off to circle the camp. Speed counted now, the soldiers ran at full tilt. Rye had lost track of Cleände. Several of the soldiers glimmered faintly with thadís, she could not distinguish between them. She hesitated and someone grabbed her arm and pulled her along with a sharp whisper in Scalléan. In the dark, no one could distinguish her, either, as the foreign witch. She did not fight the Scalléan's pulling hand, but ran, afraid of being left behind. *(here, lover, here)* The arcwright was amused by all this scampering about. Amused, or attracted, or piqued the way a cat is piqued by mouse-like scurryings. It flowed in the soldiers' shadows like a predator at the edge of a herd, and Rye was confused all over again between its gliding tiger-prowl and the soldiers' half-panicked flight. Which was she?

The hand pulled her into the camp, then released her to follow as best she could. They slipped between two tracked vehicles—tanks, Rye supposed, though she hardly saw them, only felt/tasted the warm metallic bulk of them, the sexy/oily reek of cooling engines. Her fever set her on the trail of the rebel in front of her, she hunted him through an angular maze of machines, back-lit by rust-colored lights that painted everything black and red like a fever dream. The arcwright teased her with slips through gravity and time, so that she slid in one step up to the rebel's heels, and in another was before him, hunting down the next soldier ahead.

The night was hot and smelled of exhaust fumes, cooking, people, mud.

Someone far away was shouting. They were through the line of tanks. Hunter-Rye glided into the shadow of tents, a field of bivouacs that were only blankets strung up against the expectation of rain. More people were shouting. Small arms popped in the distance, cracked and banged near at hand. Human ember-shadows scrambled from under blankets, stared into the darkness, cried out. Some of them groped for weapons, many stood or knelt empty-handed, mouths open with surprise, as the rebel soldiers opened fire.

Muzzle flashes took snapshots of the carnage. People dying everywhere. People waking up to die. Blood flashed red then black then red again in the weapons' fire. Rye still ran, she did not know where, the gun in her hand long forgotten. The arcwright set her on some path, tucked her into its shadow as it glided, insect-tiger, glimpsed at the corner of her eye. Something was burning. Munitions trucks. Great wheeling spires of exploding ammunition fountained into the sky. A truck's gas tank exploded, a deep, solid boom beneath the firecracker crackling of the guns. Another one went, or something did. Boom like the artillery guns. Boom!

The arcwright reared up against the fires. It was huge, ten feet tall, a burnt iron monstrosity that gleamed black-silver-orange. It had started to rain. Someone was screaming. Guns went off, very close. Rye felt the whip-crack of bullets snapping through the place she and the arcwright stood. Neither of them was touched. The arcwright slid them aside, gone and there again, the fires burning behind them instead of to their right. There were dead people on the ground here. The heavy automatic rifles that stuttered kuh-kuh-kuh-kuh-kuh! could tear a body in half at close range. Rye had seen someone's guts before. She could not, just at this moment, remember when, but she recognized them, even covered in dirt. The arcwright stepped through them with its precise long-legged insect glide, its taloned feet stamping body parts into the mud. Firelit rain streaked its back, stealing a shape for it out of the dark. Rye-shadow followed, no shape at all.

There was a shelter in the center of camp, a tent made of canvas stretched between transport vehicles. The gunfire was heavy here, there were defenders sheltered behind the armored trucks. Bullets spanged and whined off the steel, striking sparks even in the rain. Tracer bullets stitched blazing lines through the canvas. Smoke spiraled up and died before it could turn into flame. Within the tent, Rye could see/feel/taste the poisonous sting of the tahirr. A nascent structure that fought to grow, expand, impose its order on the world. It was under assault, darts of thadís needling through the canvas to no greater effect than the bullets. Compared to the burning-lead ferocity of the mundane battle, this was a petty squabble, a war of static charges and paper darts. Not for long. The arcwright poured through the night, tiger-striped in black and orange by the burning rain, and soon after that the defenders' tahirr-wall collapsed, thadís fireflies snapped up, very quickly, one by one.

They tasted like blood going down.

thirty-six

They had guns, Dan. But so did the man you killed.

Which is murder, Rye, in case you didn't know.

Rye did not join the breakfast line. She sat alone at the witches' table with her tin mug pressed against her mouth. The rim bit into her lip, making the lesion scar quiver like popcorn in hot oil, a small distraction from the hard knot in her gut. The arcwright lay sphinx-like along a fallen tree somewhere in the ruined city, neither brooding nor smug. Last night's rampage had less impact on the creature than the *drip of rain*, the *fall of wet leaves*, the *tickle of bugs* attracted by the hot black alien hide. Rye shivered her own skin. Cleände put a hand on her shoulder to balance herself as she swung a leg over the bench, and Rye jumped.

The other witches settled in around them, too many for one table, so they had to sit squeezed hip to hip. Rye found herself trapped between Cleände and Sharienne, who both smelled of cordite, sweat, and sleeplessness. Sharienne was talking to Cleände in Scallese. Cleände interrupted her to say to Rye, "We are discussing our next step. In English, I think, for Ryder's sake?" She glanced around the table.

"Ryder must learn," someone said.

"But not all in one day," Cleände said with a smile at Rye. "Certainly not in this day, or the next. Commander Vaidunne intends to keep us occupied with winning his war."

"His war?" Tesuth said from across the table. He sounded exasperated, as if he had said this before. "Our war!"

"Our world. Our freedom. His war." Cleände pointed out the distinction with her spoon.

Tesuth frowned at her. "We must fight. Pediyoht does not give Scalléa away, even when the gate is closed. Very much not when the gate is closed. They are locked in a room with no door."

"Of course we must fight," Cleände said. "But the war the Maijou fights—Vaidunne's war, which is really Prediré's war—is not the war we must win. No, let me say it like this: the order the Maijou intends to establish with their victory is not necessarily the best order we could establish for a free Scalléa."

"What say?" a young man down the table said. Sharienne leaned over her tray and gave him a translation. The young man frowned and glanced over his shoulder. The mess hall was dense with noise, voices and the clatter of spoons and trays. No one was listening, even if anyone could have understood the English words.

"Win the war," Tesuth said, oblivious. "Then make your order."

"I disagree," Cleände said. "The means by which we win this war will determine the shape of a free Scalléa."

"Who leads," Sharienne said. "*Who* wins."

"No one wins," Tesuth said, "when you break us from one to many." He added something in Scallese, emphasizing his point with a firm tap of his spoon on the table between him and Cleände.

Who smiled at him and said, "I agree." He blinked, and she went on, "Truly, Tesuth, I do not think we should be challenging Vaidunne for command. Even Prediré is useful enough in his place. They have unified the resistance, and the military operation is undeniably effective. Better than effective, now that we have proved how useful we can be. But while Vaidunne spent half the night drawing up missions for his new tactical tool, Prediré's lapdogs have been muttering vague warnings about the dangers of using the enemy's tactics. Vaidunne finally wants to use us, and he will, but the more useful—which is to say, the more powerful—we become, the more Prediré will insist that we be hedged around by checks and barriers. In other words, Prediré will invent a hundred rules and regulations intended to keep himself safe from us, but because it is the thadís he is afraid of—the thadís which he does not remotely understand—he will never feel safe, and those hundred rules will become a thousand. I do believe this, Tesuth. It is how his mind has always worked, and because of his role in the Pediyoht uprising—the uprising that was only possible because Ryder closed the gate from Nohai!—he has the authority and the popularity to turn his fears into policy."

"Say the truth," Sharienne said. "These are not only Predire's fears. Who does not look at us and see tahinit?"

Their crowded table was an island of silence in the clamor of the mess hall. Then the same young man leaned forward and said, his forehead wrinkled like an anxious puppy's, "What say?" and his neighbor murmured a translation.

"Therein lies Predire's power," Cleände said. "And I wish I could believe we will be able to start afresh once we have won this war, but how can we when the legacy of Nohan oppression lives in people's minds? We cannot wish it away. And it is not only a legacy of fear. It is a legacy of government, of legalities, taxes, property, privilege, power. Even if we could wish away that whole history, what would we replace it with?"

"We do replace it!" Tesuth said. "This rebellion is not unordered. We give power to the good and useful, we . . . " He groped, then went on in a spate of Scallese.

"He says the hierarchies of the rebellion are based on merit, on knowledge and skill rather than inheritance or corruption," Cleände said to Rye, who was startled at being included in the conversation. The language might have been English, but the subject was Scallese, and she had other things to worry about, things much closer to home. Like murder. Like guilt.

Like Bardo saying while Rye bled, *This is what I am.*

Cleände was going on, "Tesuth, do you say then that you believe the order we establish within this army will survive the war? That what we do here and now will effect, or even determine, the order a free society will take once we have won our peace?"

Tesuth's triumphant "Yes!" was barely spoken before he recognized the trap Cleände had led him into. His look changed, anger tempered by rue. Cleände gave him a wry smile of acknowledgement.

"What I say is that if we let Vaidunne determine our role in this war, and even more so, if we allow Predíré's faction to dictate rules to limit our power, and Vaidunne codifies and records those rules, then they will become law once the war is over."

"No thing is certain." Tesuth sounded fierce, but looked as if he were loosing a battle against conviction.

Cleände spread her hands. "Convince me I am wrong, Tesuth. I am always willing to be convinced."

Tesuth looked down at his half-eaten meal, and after a moment pushed the tray away.

"But you do not say we do not fight," Sharienne said. Rye thought she was voicing the earnest worry she saw on several faces. "Cleände, you do not say . . ."

"No. Of course we fight. But we must fight our war, not theirs."

"But what is our war?" someone asked.

"But Vaidunne," Sharienne said, "Vaidunne has make his plans. This day, the next day. Do we say no? Does Ryder say no? What do we say we do instead?"

Rye put her mug down, the knot in her gut twisting tighter. "What do you mean?" she said, interrupting Cleände's response. "Do I say no to what?"

Cleände seemed as taken aback by Rye's speaking as Rye had been earlier at being spoken to. She hesitated before she said, "Forgive me, Ryder, we have not had an opportunity to discuss the details. Vaidunne needs another passage for a company that has been cut off from joining the redoubt's defense. And Sharienne, as I was about to say, no, I do not believe we should refuse to help. These tactical maneuvers are not at issue. But I do believe—"

"Wait," Rye said. She had that heart-thumping sense of having missed a stair. "Wait, wait, wait. You don't think *we* should say no?"

"Ryder," Cleände said carefully, "perhaps this is a private discussion we should have another time."

"Private? You mean this *we* we're talking about here is really you?"

"You will not refuse my advice?" It was obvious Cleände was speaking to the witches as much as to Rye. "Our advice, I should say, for while I have experience in the thadís and understanding of the arcwright—and, I do hope, some reason to expect your trust?—it is these people here at this table who understand the rebellion, and the situation on Scalléa."

"And it's your advice that *we* make another passage for Vaidunne." Rye was breathless with anger, giddy with it, as if anger were the safest emotion that could break the shell of shock last night's violence had wrapped her in. "It's your considered opinion that these 'tactical maneuvers' are no big deal?"

"Ryder . . . " Cleände seemed at a loss. "I know this is all very new to you, but—"

"God! Are you blind? Sharienne, you were there! How could you not have seen it?"

"You are distressed by the deaths, of course, but—"

"Death! I've seen *death* before. Good God, you really didn't see it, did you?"

"See what, Ryder?" Cleände's voice was patient, soothing, cloying as cream.

Rye was outraged at being humored, but shaken by it, too. Did she really know what she knew? Had she sensed what she thought she had sensed? Bardo's memory said, *I still don't know what I saw, and I don't know if it's real.* But it had been. It had been.

She said, her voice trembling slightly with restraint, "Mostahr and the tahirr are trying to open the gate between Nohai and Earth, and Dan Bardo is trying to do the same."

"Daniel Bardo!" Cleände was almost laughing with surprise and disbelief. "What makes Daniel think he can open a gate that resists the entire strength of the tahirr?"

"He has my fever," Rye said tersely. "And it *isn't* resisting them. That's what I'm telling you! There's cracks . . . there's cracks all through the walls . . . "

The witches were looking at her as if she were crazy. At least Cleände had sobered. Her face had taken on a tense, speculative cast.

"So. Daniel Bardo has your fever, and he is trying to open a passage. A passage to Nohai?"

"Yes! I don't know. I think so . . . " Why did she think so? Rye's anger slipped towards panic. She could not remember why she thought—

"And the tahinit are reaching for Earth? Looking, no doubt, for you?"

"I . . . I guess. I think so."

A small silence fell.

Then Sharienne exclaimed, "But this is good news! They will not come for us if they go to Earth!"

"What?" Rye stammered it. *W-whuh-what?*

"Do we think it is truth?" Tesuth said earnestly.

Faces all around the table had lightened with interest and hope.

"She is untutored, as you know," Cleände said to Tesuth, though she did not quite look away from Rye. "But she may have access to the arcwright's—"

"Just you fucking *wait*."

"Ryder." Cleände was being patient again. "Scalléa is the world we can save now. You would not do Earth any good by going home when the tahinit are ready to take the planet apart stone by stone to find you, and we—you—can surely do them harm—"

"Shut up." Rye shoved at Sharienne, fighting to drag herself off of the crowded bench. "You meant this to happen, didn't you? Didn't you?"

Cleände's face went blank. "No, of course I did not. What do you mean?"

"You fucking liar. You fucking lying bitch!" Rye won free from the bench, staggered, stood panting over Cleände, who had to twist around to meet her eyes. "You never were recruiting witches, were you? You *have* witches. You just wanted to set us at the tahinit, to attract their attention, get them to turn the tahirr on Earth instead of here. God! That's why you had us hunting gray beasts, isn't it? The only clue the tahinit ever let out about the arcwrights, and you set us straight on them. No wonder they started kidnapping Earth women, doing their fucking experiments on us! They wanted to know how strong we were, how we knew how to fight the gray beasts. How much of a fight we could put up against an invasion. God, and you did it, didn't you? You guaranteed they'd be so worried they'd *have* to invade. No wonder you're such a fucking hero! You did it all!"

"Not alone," Cleände said, cold and precise as a scalpel. "You helped a great deal."

Breath locked in Rye's chest. She had to force it out on a kind of sob before she could say, "I didn't know. You know I didn't know!"

"Are you sure?" Cleände's neck must have been hurting. She turned her back on Rye and added, "I do what I must for Scalléa. I always have, and I always will. I make no apologies for that. Nor will I accept responsibility for what you did in Meheg-menoht. You killed one arcwright and stole the other. If the tahinit are invading Earth, you have only yourself to blame."

thirty-seven

Liar, Rye thought. She timed the word to her steps. Liar, liar, liar.

Where she was going, she could not have said. If she stopped to think about it—If she stopped to think—

Liar, liar, liar. Except she did not know where Cleände's lies actually lay.

here, lover, here.

Yes, Rye thought, *yes, you, at least you—!* She hardly knew what she meant.

mist rising (flavor of earth) rotten wood splintered under claws (tickle of bugs) silver sun behind clouds (muffled singing) come, lover, come

Yes! she thought, and *No!*

come the ruins spilled heat like a broken cup, a hill gullied by erosion, a building with every window shattered *lover* heat that spilled through Rye, a fever, a drug, a poison *come* that burned in her flesh, her bones, her every cell—

Revulsion, desire, revulsion at the desire: *No!*

But oh, God, if only she could get away.

The arcwright or her fever, Rye no longer knew which, offered to hide her in a soldier's shadow as he walked down the tunnel. Even that light touch cast quicksilver snail-tracks across the walls. Heat washed through her again, and for an instant she tasted the stroking copper warmth of Bardo's big hand, the electric-sweet anger of Mostahr and the tahirr. As with the arcwright, the ghosts of Meheg-menoht, it seemed that all Rye had to do was put out her hand and touch them, put out her hand and crack that too-delicate scrim of ice between the sodué and the world.

How could they not feel this? How could they not—But she hadn't told them. She had not had a chance to tell them how thin that wall had become.

come, lover (he moves above her, inside her (swallows peel away from the bank to chase insects above the sun-scaled river's surface) his sweat in her scars, bloody roses with copper thorns) lover, come

Rye stopped, shocked, wanting *here* so ferociously that her senses tangled. The blue-white light from the electric tubes sheeted like sweat down her face, the stony walls crunched like brown sugar between her teeth, the many stinks of the over-populated tunnels braided themselves, wires of a thousand colors, down her nerves, and a voice brought fluid springing into her mouth like a sweet berry or a lover's kiss.

"What?" she said. Blinking, twitching, she must have looked insane. "What?"

"You are lost two-ise," the soldier said.

Meduine. Rye recognized him while he was still developing from a smoky shadow with ember bones into a human being.

"Twice," she said feebly. Her mouth was still full of Bardo's taste, the arcwright's promise. Or did it, also, lie?

"I," Meduine said, "am practice with Sharienne to talk to you."

At which, she could not help herself, she burst into tears.

"Fear comes," he said, gentle and unperturbed. "Sometimes in front, sometimes behind. It comes. It goes. It does go."

Rye said past her hands. "It isn't fear."

"You are good," he said, making her stare at him. He had got her walking. She stumbled on the rough floor, blind in her clothes.

"In the fight," Meduine explained. "Sharienne tells me, you are good."

"I did what they wanted me to," Rye said stupidly.

"I mean, you have no fear. You do much good. You are . . . Sharienne says . . . brave?"

"Thanks," Rye whispered. She was going to cry again.

Perhaps Meduine sensed this. He walked in silence for the length of a corridor. Perhaps he was only summoning words.

"You do what Cleände want you to do."

"I did," Rye said bitterly. *I refuse to take responsibility.* Who was the liar, her or Cleände?

"Always this? Cleände want you to do, you do?"

Rye stopped so she could see his face. "Would you, if you were me?"

"Do I do what Cleände want me to do?" Meduine made a rueful grimace, a smart man with too few words. "Do we? Do we today, do we tomorrow . . . "

We. A different "we" from the witches'. This was the other side of Cleände's politicking. "Do you trust her? Did Sharienne teach you that word?"

"Trust." He shrugged in the Scallese way, with a tilt of the head.

"If Cleände stood behind you with a gun, would you let her? Would you want her there? Would you turn around, or run away, or what?"

"Why is Cleände shoot me with gun?" Meduine said. But he was not that ingenuous. He gave Rye a narrow smile. "If she is behind me with no thing in her hand, I look behind. Yes?"

"Oh, yeah," Rye breathed. "How about Commander Vaidunne? Would he let her stand behind him?"

"Vaidunne . . . " Meduine touched a finger to the corner of his eye, then pointed it at an invisible Cleände. "Vaidunne always look Cleände." He curled his finger back into his fist, and started walking again.

A moment later, they were at the command center door, and Rye realized he had been taking her there all along. Suckered by kindness. Again.

"I don't—" she said. "This isn't where—" She stopped.

Commander Vaidunne was there.

So was Cleände.

"Ryder. Forgive me. I spoke—"

"I don't care."

Vaidunne, who was reading one report while listening to another one from Meduine, glanced at them from across the table. Cleände lowered her voice even further.

"Do you blame me for the truth, or only for speaking it?"

"What truth?" Rye whispered coldly. "You mean the truth about Earth?"

"The tahinit found Earth long before we ever did. Even without the tahirr, do you imagine ambitious lordlings like the Tehega would make kind masters?"

Rye turned on her and hissed, "There are street gangs who cause more trouble than Tehega ever did!"

"So far. He was only scouting, he had not begun to act. You do not know what would have happened once he and his kind began their assault on Earth."

"*Whose* assault? You're the one who caught the tahinit's attention!"

"I was fighting a war!"

"Not my war." Rye echoed Cleände's own words with an ugly smile. "Not Earth's war."

Cleände's blue eyes narrowed. Her whole face was honed by fury. "Oh, yes. Earth's war, too. Do you imagine Meheg-menoht would allow the Tehegas of Nohai to hold such a powerful position as Earth? The tahinit would have watched until the lordlings had broken your resistance and then stepped in—"

"Oh, because we're such a bunch of pushovers! Do you really think we'd just lie down and let them—"

"I think you are so badly divided you would be more likely to shoot at each other than—"

"Cleände."

Vaidunne's voice made them both jump. He was watching them, as was Meduine and a dozen other men in soldier's gear. Sharienne was there, a few of the younger witches, Tesuth. Rye had forgotten them, forgotten where she was.

here, lover, here.

Cleände drew in a careful breath. Reacting to Vaidunne's stare, or to the arcwright's reminder? She nodded her head at the commander, almost a bow, and said something conciliatory. Vaidunne looked from Cleände to Rye, and Rye saw a gleam deep within his shadowed sockets.

The other side of politics, she recalled, and said recklessly, "We were just talking about how the tahinit are invading Earth."

And then quailed when Vaidunne looked to Cleände for a translation.

Cleände took a quick breath, and then a careful one, and then turned a long, cold look on Rye. There was speculation in her eyes, but no forgiveness.

"Listen," Rye said to Vaidunne, and then had to lean on the table as the fever swelled in a sudden black wave behind her eyes. "They aren't telling you . . . they aren't . . . " The fever rose and turned, sudden as a storm-cloud bitten by lightning, a tiger shocked awake by electric prods. The air was singing with unseen bees. Thadísé.

Cleände.

Cleände gripped her elbow, and a red silk knife sliced down her nerves. A thousand red knives that cut along the lines Cleände had laid down that day on Earth, the day Rye asked her to separate her from the arcwright. Remember the queasiness of someone else's heart bumping in her chest, a fist demanding entry. Remember the red silk wings, the lime-flavored dust blinding even the eyes in her skin. Remember the silk threads spun out, remember the lines as red as blood laid down, remember the ties that bind.

Cleände's ties. Not the arcwright's. Cleände's.

Rye tried to pull free. Cleände was saying something, her voice as cloying as artificial limes. Rye had to swallow and swallow at the sour-wet drench of the arcwright's warning. Sun (white (wall) green) leaves flashed across her eyes. The arcwright was rousing. The fever threw off sparks like charged steel. She no longer knew if she were falling. Gravity had side-slipped. The table or ceiling or wall was a hard smooth surface against her palms. Paper clung to sweat or blood. Sparks swirled around her, tornado-lightning, whirlpool-fish. Rye vomited, bringing up nothing but watery bile.

I help, someone said from outside the red-weaving lightning storm.

help, Rye agreed. *help*.

The arcwright reached out, a black night between her and the pain, between her and Cleände. (Cleände, something inside her mourned, even now. How could you, Cleände?) Rye was blind, numb to everything but the fever's deadly swell and the sting of electric bees. Somewhere out there, people were arguing. Somewhere out there, Cleände argued . . . argued under the threat of the arcwright's growing fury . . . and lost. Or perhaps, wisely, let herself be talked down before the arcwright could strike —before Vaidunne and the rest realized the source of Rye's distress. Somewhere out there, Cleände (dry scarlet (sweet limes) ground glass) let Rye go.

And reached—was that what that flurry of scattered sparks was?—Cleände reaching for the other witches?

Come, someone said. I help. Come.

lover, come.

The storm receded a little. She felt the ground under her feet, felt the cool, smoky grasp of a human hand around her arm. Known and unknown. She looked up and made out, like a translucent mask over hazy flesh and ember bones, Meduine's face. She took a breath. Cleände's thadís still burned, sizzling with rage, somewhere a few walls away. The fever still burned. The arcwright was still poised to strike. And somewhere else, drawn to the cracks laid down by the red silk threads, the cracks Cleände tried to score between the arcwright and Rye, other sparks bit and clawed, attempting entry. Not the Scallese witches, not yet. This had the flavor of the tahinit, and Bardo. If Cleände had not stopped when she did, afraid of exposing her attack to the rebel command . . .

Of all of them, Cleände was the one Rye feared the least.

"Here," Meduine said. "You good now?"

Meduine had taken her out of the command center, further than she had realized. They were near the heart of the redoubt, somewhere in the thick of the maze. *Wrong way,* Rye thought, incipient panic swelling in her throat.

this way.

The arcwright leaned her, gravitic slide, toward the silver-licked walls. But Meduine's hand still anchored her here, where Cleände could find her. Cleände, who wanted Rye silent. Cleände, who wanted Rye obedient. Cleände, who wanted Rye tied to her will. *What else did you learn from your torturers, Cleände?* Rye asked her in her mind. She wondered if some echo of that would brush across Cleände's thadís, and sting a little. Maybe just a little. But God knows, Cleände was not likely to give up now.

"You good now?" Meduine asked again.

Rye caught her breath, her mouth bitter with sickness, and tried to get her feet sorted out. "Better," she managed.

come, lover.

I'm coming.

Meduine loosened his grip, but did not let her go. He frowned down at her, deceptively earnest. And when, Rye wondered, would she stop falling for the appearance of caring? She detached his grip with a shaking hand.

"Thanks," she said hoarsely. "I'll be all right now."

He patted her shoulder, doubtful. "This is Earth bad? This bad come from Earth?"

Rye stared at him, and then said, "This bad comes from Scalléa, and its name is Cleände."

come, lover, come.

The fever turned over inside her, turned her away from Meduine's worried face. *Don't trust her,* Rye meant to say. *Don't ever let her stand behind you, with or without a gun.* Maybe she did say it. She would never know. The fever stood up and reached for its other half.

Tunnels coiled and uncoiled around her, passing her through like an earthen gut. Sparks nipped at her heels, stung in the walls, shone in the cracks in the melt-glossy ice. Seeking, herding, trying to hem her in. Cleände? The other witches? Skeleton cages with firefly hearts, she slipped through their bars, hidden in the arcwright's shadow, and away. But how far, and for how long?

here, lover, come.

Her feet, step by step, pressed on packed dirt. The walls, step by step, contained her in sandbags and buried stone. She swam, step by step, between frozen gray waves ribboned with electric sweetness and peopled by bloodless shells. She slipped through the ghost alley, yes, quiet as a pigeon's shadow hidden in a tiger's shade. Whose thought was that? Reality escaped her like a stream of mercury, elusive as light, heavy as sin. Was this what it was to be insane?

No. Cleände attacked her to shut her up, to put her in her place, and the arcwright was helping her get away. She stepped and stepped again, her balance too uncertain to run, and slipped into the redoubt's entrance where there were enough people that one ghost more or less would not be seen. She drifted toward the curtained exit.

But it was getting harder. There was resistance, as if her smoke-body was having to swim through denser and denser air, and the floor was beginning to slide with that uneasy loose-ice feel of the sodué. The stacked columns holding up the ceiling began to melt into quicksilver streams, the floor heaved like water at slack tide, and Rye, like a bad swimmer, began to panic. *Too deep,* she thought at the arcwright, but it only responded with that mournful, sensual *come, lover, come,* and her next step took her through the camouflage curtains, each thread trailing through her like a strand of molten silver. Then she was outside among the trees and broken sunlight speared through her, making her vibrate as if she were a bell and the sun were a clapper

hammering, hammering (leaf-broken sunlight like cracks in the sky) thadís-sparks like claws in the ice (rotten with pressure, the fever-heat of spring) broken mirror bowing to the weight of mercury (glass shards reflecting

ripe peaches, new copper, neon lights, slow cars, rain-streaked window etched by streetlights, musk roses, gas fumes, rainy dawn, dusty boards caressing bare feet, china bowl, falling leaves, sour wine, the slow fever-borne movements of prayer, river mud, beer, freshly fired gun, God, please let me out

mirror shards reflecting

desert sand, cloth-bound book, cracked tiles cold underfoot, fish pond, fast train, armed soldiers, white sunlight like warm bars across the floor, crackling radios, heart bump, electric shock, the slow forbidden movements of prayer, winter cold, rumbling tanks, drought-shrunken brook, the passage exists, we only have to open the door

reflecting world beside world) sun beside sun (hammering, hammering)

let us in!

thirty-eight

White cement, shallow puddles like sheets of glass, a scattering of tough green leaves. Lesioned skin that felt scored by broken glass, a trip-hammer heart, a fever like suffocating black fur. Slender-trunked trees, dusky stones bound by black roots, insects whizzing through the damp-hazy sunlight. Gravity last of all.

Rye staggered, fell with a painful thud on her ass, caught herself with one hand in a puddle and the other on a stone. That was down. Up was the sky, where clouds hung so close to the ground that they looked like mountains, like vast deflating moons about to fall to earth. She closed her eyes, dizzy, and said, to herself, to the universe, "Just give me a minute." Just one minute to get herself sorted, while the rainwater soaked through the seat of her borrowed fatigues.

She was afraid she did not have a minute.

She could not sort out her impressions from her sensory confusion. Very well. She was in the ruins above the redoubt. Cleände was looking for her. Bardo, fevered with the arcwright's taint, was trying to open a passage away from Earth. Mostahr and the tahinit were trying to open a passage away from Nohai. To where? Did Mostahr want to go to Earth to find Rye? That made more sense than Bardo trying to get to Nohai, but Rye could not shake the conviction that that was what he was reaching for. Maybe not. Maybe it didn't matter where Bardo wanted to go, if he even had a destination in mind. It also felt like he was reaching for her.

It didn't matter. The point was, the tahinit wanted to go to Earth, and Bardo was about to open a door to let them in.

Oh, fuck, Rye! she told herself. What if you're wrong? What if it's just fever dreams, arcwright dreams, your own wishes and fears? You were always terrified of Mostahr, you were always desperate for Bardo to want you, to be your friend. How do you know?

But the arcwright's dreams had always been proven true. Even the worst of them. Especially the worst of them.

So maybe the question had to be, what if she was right? Think of the tanks rolling in from nowhere, people rousted from their beds to die, cities left empty for the trees and the rain. Think of the café waitresses and the ex-cops who had no notion of the thadís in their blood, and no way of understanding why they were to be crushed by the tahirr. Think of the soldiers of only a night ago, dying with their guts ripped open by bullets and their mouths still gaping with surprise. Think of Earth.

What a towering contempt Cleände must feel, if she could believe that Rye would stand by and let Earth fall to the tahinit's army purely for the pleasure of serving Cleände's cause—or serving Cleände. Rye hated her for that, even as she understood her better than she ever had. Earth was her home, as Scalléa was home to Cleände. But then, with the same furious, predatory jealousy that the arcwright had felt when Cleände had tried to separate them, she thought, *Earth is MINE*. Her whole world was about to be dragged into the conflict between Nohai and Scalléa, exactly as she and Bardo had been.

Only this time it would be her fault.

She held on to that knowledge with everything that was in her. She filled herself with guilt until she was as filled by it as she was filled by the fever, because she was about to do something terrible. She knew it was terrible. Worse, she knew it might be wrong. What if it was? It was the only solution she could think of. She would do it anyway, and be damned. Her innocence was dead. One more sin was nothing to her. Just try to paint the devil black.

Oh, God, is that what Bardo thought? Is that how he had been thinking about himself all this time?

Come, lover, come.

This time it was Rye who called.

Sunlight poured itself through a gap in the clouds and the arcwright, blackest shadow, poured itself over the root-bound wall. Even in full daylight it was hard to see. Sharp-jointed limbs, rib-sprung body, prow-nosed head—the details did not blur, but caught the eye in fragmentary instants. A stilting leg and taloned foot, the ripple of light off a black-silver hide. Step and step, glimpse and glimpse, and the creature itself poured, smooth as spilled mercury, up to where Rye sat on the wet white cement. She held herself still, her weight propped on her stiff arms. *Not afraid*, she thought. *Not afraid of you.*

For the first time since Meheg-menoht, she looked the creature in the eye.

A long, narrow eye, shallow-set in the sharp bones of its head. A black eye, reflective as polished obsidian, that mirrored the trees, the ruins, the billowing clouds, Rye, before the angle changed and all she saw was the perfect black of night, shot with stars.

Lover, it thought at her. Not a word, just a claim, a sensual insistence, a denial of loneliness that expected and required an equal response. Reflect me, it said. Be me.

Lover, she agreed.

It circled her, prowling tiger, stalking insect, spiraling pool of silver-black ink. Rye was so hot herself she could hardly feel its heat, though its taloned feet dried narrow prints across the wet cement, dusty bone-white against damp white-gray. *I was here.* Rye pulled off her camouflaged overshirt and felt the sun and the arcwright blaze in weird dissonance against her arms and neck. She fought with the boot buckles, pulled them off, her socks, the heavy trousers. She crouched in undershirt and pants, bare toes and fingers flexed for balance on the ground. Her scars breathed like silvery scales in the hot moist air. The touch of her skin dried prints on the pavement. *We were here.*

Lover.

The arcwright pooled itself around her. It covered her, embraced her, its immense weight balanced against the turning of the world. Her heart stuttered and surged, trying to match the pulseless ebb and flow of its blood. Her skin loosened, blurring the boundaries, trying to make two into one. Her courage failed her, just for an instant, less than an uncertain heartbeat, at the clasp of those taloned forefeet, those claws that were too much and not enough like hands. But the arcwright's touch, the arcwright's heat, woke the fever as if it had only ever slept, restless and dreaming, until now. The arcwright's touch roused it and aroused it—love me—be me—*be me*—

(Rye twisted, arched, cried out, stretched on this rack, trapped within this cage of quicksilver shadows and black-iron bones.)

Lover, the arcwright insisted, and: *lover,* Rye agreed. She would have agreed to anything. The fever was awake now, complete now, and Rye would never know which of them—which of them, both of them, all three of them—said/thought/did, *Lover, let us open this door.*

Meaning, the door between Scalléa and Nohai.

They did that, because they were alive, and that was what there was to do.

No crossing. They went nowhere. The worlds came to them.

They felt it all happen with exquisite clarity. The arc spun away from them, a crack opened by their weight on the ice, a seam parting as sweetly as it had been made to do. They might have dived like polar bear and seal into the star-shot ocean beneath, but they did not. They stayed, anchored to this reality, pinning one end of the arc as it spun itself out and out, perfect as a beam of light, perfect—

—until its perfection frayed, spinning thread after thread, arc after arc, crack after crack across/into/through the boundaries of the real. Nohai, yes, Nohai was there, white sunlight casting the shadows of Meheg-menoht across the gold-lit ruins of Scalléa. But even those shadows wavered and spun out echoes. Not two shadows, but three. Not two suns, but three.

Stop, they thought. *Wrong! No, there is no wrong. All is real, all is here. Yes, and there! And the other . . . there . . . ? No here, no there. Movement, unity, completion. Two and three make*

the ground was torn as stone and cement and dirt and tile all tried to occupy the same space at the same time, the world/s bedrock heaved and groaned

two (perfect anchors, they did not stir) and three make

the world/s screamed, humans screamed, engines screamed as vehicles skidded across pavement/dirt/stone, buildings collapsed without all their walls, leant and trembled against new neighbors, humans shouting and the absurdly irascible honking of horns

two and three (Rye!) copper roses) electric wine) make
"Oh, Christ! Rye! *Get away from her! RYE!*"
two and three make one.

"Stop," she whispered, she did not know to which. Too late. The arc had shattered itself into a thousand splinters, she had no idea which splinter belonged where, she could not free herself and the arcwright from each other, she could not—if she only had more time, but time was broken too—she could not free them from Bardo, she could not—she was in as many pieces as the worlds—she could not make Bardo put down his gun. The arcwright was anchored. It was with Rye. It was here. It had nowhere to go.

The bullet ripped through its ribs and out the other side.

thirty-nine

rye

Rye.

"Ryder Coleman, goddamn you, don't you do this to me. Rye, come on, baby, *please*."

The body knew it was alive first. It hurt. It needed to breathe.

"Rye?"

She breathed.

"Rye?"

Sunlight brushed her eyes.

"Rye?"

She took another breath.

"Will you quit," another breath, "saying my name." Another breath. She opened her eyes and added plaintively, "What did you do?"

Bardo gathered her up and held her, hard.

He was sitting on the ground, holding Rye across his legs, her head on his shoulder. He felt strange, his hands too soft, his arms too short, his smell all wrong. She struggled, weak as a child and then, suddenly, not. She shoved, hard.

"Let me go!"

He let her go. She sprawled painfully on her elbow and hip.

"I thought you were dead," Bardo said in a thin, breathy voice. Not his voice at all. "I thought it killed you."

Or maybe he said, "I thought I killed you." Rye wasn't tracking too well.

It was there, the arcwright, almost near enough to touch. Limbs sprawled all ungainly, hide dimming to black. The heavy orange light of Scalléa's setting sun spilled a single low shadow away from the corpse, trying and failing to hide the black mess of the arcwright's blood. She touched it, blind to her own blood, and *pain* shocked through her, and the creature's *lover* cry. She lost the air in her lungs, the ground under her knees *splinters flying out into the night—*

Lover! "Rye!"

"Is that you?" she said. It/he was holding her again . . . he was . . . broken mirrors only hold one reflection.

Like a single frame on a scroll of film, she saw Tehega over Bardo's shoulder, eyes wide, mouth open to say something urgent. Tehega, bright and solid in the slanting Scallese sunlight. Tehega, there and gone again like a ghost.

"What's going on?"

Bardo gave her a little shake. "That's what I'm asking you!"

The ground was shaking. She was. She pushed him away, hovered over the dying arcwright, not quite daring to touch. Its eye was already dull, reflecting nothing, a night without stars. "What did you do?"

"I thought it was killing you!"

"So you killed it instead," she whispered. "Fucking typical."

"I'm sorry. Am I sorry? What the hell is going on?"

"What the hell is going on?" Rye scrambled around to face him on hands and knees. "What is going on is you trying to open a fucking door to Nohai! What is going on is you and the tahinit banging on the door until the whole fucking wall breaks down! What is going on is you—"

Yes, how fortunate, said a ghost, *someone else to blame.* Cleände's ghost. Was she there too? One single flicker of thadís, a spark of miniature lightning, seeking, searing, there and gone. Rye caught her breath.

Bardo said, "Tehega said you were there. He wanted me . . . Oh, Christ. I don't fucking know."

"What is going on," Rye whispered, "is me trying to save Earth from the Nohan army. But I just made things worse, didn't I? Oh God, oh God, I knew I was wrong." She folded herself down until her face was against the cement, the arcwright's blood tacky under her blood. "I knew I was wrong."

Was this the real world? It scattered in a thousand directions, splitting off as the arc had frayed, and then snapped back again: the pain in her knees, the sun on her back, Bardo's voice, everything so normal it made her feel crazier than before. But Tehega *was* there, somewhere. She could hear him shouting, hear the whine of over-worked engines, the pop and crackle of guns. The slip-crack-slide of falling stones. The searching electric fury of Cleände's thadís.

"I didn't know where you were," Bardo was saying. "I didn't know."

Rye sat up. They stared at each other, their guilt between them like a third party. He looked bad, Rye thought. Too thin, bruised-looking eyes, his white shirt smeared with her blood. His expression one of final, broken-hearted defeat.

"You were looking for me?" she said in a small voice.

He looked away. "I just wanted," he said, "to get away."

He was in shock. They both were, to be so calm.

The ground heaved them up like a massive ocean swell, then dropped them with a violent series of jerks. Rye thought with horror of the redoubt full of rebels below the ruin, one flashing shard of rational dread before Bardo fell into her, and she fell over the arcwright *splinters like sparks in the night, like rain, like tears, like cracks in the ice, spinning out, spinning out, spinning—*

"Jesus," Bardo prayed, hauling her back from the dying creature. She clung to him, mistaking him for the arcwright, and for an instant they spanned the shortest arc of all, Rye to Bardo, Bardo to—"No!" He pushed her away.

"God damn it!" she yelled. "What the hell did you think—"

But the splinters were still flying, the mirror still breaking apart, *running cat*, falling trees, *grinding tanks*, setting sun, *wailing sirens*, popping guns, *crying child*, dying arcwright etched like night's first shadow across the bloodied white cement, *come, lover, come.*

This time Rye cried, "No!" But the ground heaved again—a round stone fell into the river—black roots lost their grip on dusky stone—books tumbled off the cupboard shelves—splinters flashed through the air like knives, spun like threads, sang like cracks that heal themselves as they chase across the ice. Like the last crack that leaps like a bridge from here to nowhere.

Come, lover. Come.

"Where?" Bardo said, sounding mortally confused.

Home.

"Home."

"No," said Bardo.

The stubborn bastard. Rye refused to leave him within Cleände's reach, refused to leave without him. She grabbed him, hugged her arms in a strangle hold around his neck, and wished them

but Earth was not the arcwright's home. The arcwright's home was a bridge with no ending, an ocean without a farther shore. Dying, it spun out and out . . . *come, lover, come* . . . and she might have gone, but she wanted . . . *(yes, Bardo thought, I'll go)* . . . no, she wanted . . . *come (come, Rye) lover, come* . . . no, she wanted

love! love! love!

(is that what death is like?)

lover, I'm sorry you're dead, I'm so sorry, I'm so glad, thank you, goodbye

she wanted to go

home. Sirens screamed far away, broken pavement was hard and cold beneath her, the chilly air smelled of smoke and sewage and freshly fallen trees. The ground quivered once, as if in protest of a slammed door, and went still. As still and solid and cold and hard as the earth ever was. Bardo, in the circle of her arms, was as breathing and solid and warm and alive as he ever was.

"I would have gone," Bardo whispered.

"I know."

He pulled a little away from her to look around. "Where are we?"

A fragment of gold-gray wall leaned across the street, crowding the buildings to either side. They had glass shards in their windows and steel rebar showing where the granite facing had fallen away. A dangling sign that read *Mayfield Apartments 1218* skidded to the ground as Rye watched, reproachful commentary on their arrival.

"Riverside, I think," Rye said. She felt perfectly numb, as if the arcwright's death had pithed her like a frog. Gone, lover, gone.

Bardo pushed away from her, floundered back until he found an unbroken piece of curb, and started to laugh. Such a painful laugh that he might have been crying. He bent over and hid his face in his arms. Sirens still sang. Car alarms chirped out of sync. A strange kind of silence in the broken street.

"I killed someone," Rye said, on what impulse she never knew. "One of the pregnant women in Meheg-menoht. Someone from Earth."

Bardo looked up slowly, wiping his face on his blood-streaked sleeve.

"I strangled her," Rye told him. "I think she asked me to, because of what they'd done, because of how she was going to die, but I'm not sure. I'll probably never be sure."

He stared. She shrugged.

"I just thought you should know."

Another long, noisy silence.

"I just wanted," Bardo said eventually, "to get away."

He was repeating himself. In shock, Rye thought, then remembered she had thought this before. He looked around as if he were just noticing the street for the first time.

"What happened?"

"The worlds were too close together. The tahinit were trying to open a passage without the arcwrights. A passage to Earth. I thought they were going to bring the army through looking for me, and it didn't seem fair . . . " An inadequate word, but she could think of nothing better. "It didn't seem fair to land Earth with the Nohan army when Nohai's fight was really with Scalléa. I thought, the Scallese were winning the rebellion there, so why not let them fight it out with the Nohan. So I tried to open the door to Nohai and make them come here instead of Earth—I mean, to Scalléa instead of here—but—"

His laugh silenced her, harsh and appalled. "Little Rye. Didn't you just grow up into something big, bad, and ugly."

"How's the view from that mountaintop of virtue you're on, Detective Bardo?" she said bitterly. "Fuck you *and* your horse."

"Why the hell did you tell me, then?" he demanded.

"You asked!"

"Not that, I meant—" He broke off, wiped his hand over his face. A siren whooped into silence a block or so away. Bardo said, "What happened after that?"

Rye said nothing.

"Sulking, bad girl?"

She looked at him, looked into his eyes, until he dropped his gaze. Eventually she spoke.

"The worlds were too close, or there had been too many passages between them. The boundaries gave way. You must have felt it."

"I can see it," Bardo said with a ghost of his usual sardonic tone. "And that thing is why it broke?"

"'That thing.'"

"The thing I shot. Killed."

"'That thing'?"

But it was too deep a wound. The anger that had kept her bickering was too trivial a response. And then, Rye remembered, Bardo really did not know. A slip of reality no less strange than all the rest. She studied him.

"That thing," she said after a long silence, "was our fever. It got us out of Meheg-menoht, it helped me open the door, it brought us home. And you killed it."

His eyes flinched away from her, searching for something he had lost on this ordinary street, on this cool, gray, disastrous day. One more murder. One more sin. She could see he did not want to hear.

"I killed it," Bardo said, his voice as flat as hers, "before you brought us home."

"You wanted to stay on Scalléa with Tehega and Cleände? I'm sure they would have welcomed you with—"

But suddenly Bardo was on his feet and shouting, "Why the fuck did you bring me here?"

"You wanted to die?" she asked him. She was still much too calm.

Bardo wasn't. "Everything I ever did—*everything* I ever did—was to get away from this place! *You have no fucking right*—"

Glass fell from a window behind him with a lovely shimmering crash. Bardo leapt back and nearly fell over the broken curb. Rye stood up, but did not move from her spot in the street.

"I have no right?" she said, cool as the pavement beneath her feet. "It was *our* fever, Bardo. If you hadn't killed it, you would have had the same power I did. You could have gone anywhere you damn well pleased."

He stared at her, black-eyed and wild-haired, and she saw the violence that inhabited him like a fever rouse and stir. *Your fault, my fault*, she thought with sudden disgust. Neither of them was innocent.

A head appeared in a third storey window across the street. An elderly woman shrieked out, "What are you doing down there? We need help!"

Rye and Bardo stared up at her. Don't ask the crazy man, Rye thought. Don't ask the naked girl covered in blood.

"Is the gas line broken?" the woman yelled. "Our stairs are blocked. We need some help up here!"

Don't ask me, Rye thought again. More sirens swelled among the buildings. She looked at Bardo, an automatic glance, and saw nothing but his back as he walked away.

"Are you going for help?" the old woman cried. "Come back! We need your help!"

Rye said nothing, feeling the arcwright die all over again.

Gone, lover, gone.